DUKE
by
Scot

AMY
JARECKI

OLIVER
HEBER
BOOKS

Book Cover Design by: T.A. Straley

Published by Oliver-Heber Books

0 9 8 7 6 5 4 3 2 1

1

"Jules Smallwood here," announced Lady Julia St.
Vincent in her deepest, most masculine voice.
The effort grated her throat, though she had no
choice but to grow accustomed to it.

She blew on her gloved hands while a puff of grey
mist billowed about the interior of the carriage. After
an unbearably long journey via the mail coach from
London to Edinburgh, she'd hired a hackney to ferry
her to Newhailes, one her new employer's many residences.

With a shiver, she tugged her great coat about her
shoulders. And though she'd been wearing it for the
better part of a week, the coat still felt too large, swal-
lowing her petite frame in the folds of the thick
woolen weave.

Having no other option in the matter, Julia had altered a number of her father's castaways. The suits of
clothes were a tad dated but, as a working man, she
doubted anyone would scoff overmuch. Still freezing,
she also tightened the wool scarf around her neck. But
nothing helped. Scotland was bitterly frigid, every bit
as unpleasant as her father's butler, Willaby, had said
it would be.

"Jules Smallwood," she repeated, her mind recounting the details of her fabricated past as she had done every five minutes since the entire solution had been concocted with dear old Willaby. Indeed, the Brixham butler was the only other person privy to the truth.

And it must remain as such.

Her hands shook, and not from the cold. Her journey was near its end and Julia was actually going through with this. Again, she'd had no choice. Well, in truth there were two options—go hungry while her father's health continued to deteriorate or take a position that would pay enough money for her to eventually settle her father's gambling debts and provide for his care. With luck and the right physicians, the Earl of Brixham's health would recover soon as well.

And then what? Papa will change his ways?

"Pshaw!" Julia loved her father, but in two and twenty years of trying, she'd never been able to change him. Moreover, he had not only borrowed money from the despicable Silas Skinner, as collateral her father had given the scoundrel the deed to Huntly Manor which had been the home to the Earls of Brixham for generations. With the Papa's collapse from biliousness and their lack of funds, the estate had begun to crumble, leaving her no other option but to personally take matters in hand lest Mr. Skinner make good on his threats and cast them out.

As the hack rolled to a stop, Julia's stomach lurched. For a moment she sat immobile, unable to breathe. This was the hour of truth. Once she stepped out of this carriage there'd be no turning back.

"We've arrived sir," said the driver, to the sound of the man hopping down and pulling out the steps. Of course, he didn't open the door or offer a hand, yet another thing to which she must grow accustomed.

Julia wiggled her toes, burrowing them into the lambswool used to fill out her father's shoes. They were positively enormous on her slender feet. But there had been no time and no money to have a proper pair made.

With a trembling hand, she pulled on the latch, gaining her first peek at her new place of employment.

This is his "wee cottage"? At least that's how Mr. MacCutcheon, the barrister who'd hired her, had phrased it. During her interview in London, Julia had also learned that the Duke of Dunscaby, her employer, owned an enormous castle on a seaside estate on the northern tip of mainland Scotland. In addition, His Grace enjoyed a hunting lodge in the Highlands, owned numerous smaller properties throughout Great Britain, and kept a sizeable town house in London. But despite his vast estates, Newhailes was the duke's favorite...although he'd had little time to arrive at such a decision.

Still leaning forward and gaping, Julia instantly gained an affinity for the house. Though not a castle, any English manor would pale in comparison—a Roman façade, dual and opposing staircases curving upward to the front door, three stories, and more windows than she cared to count. Before she did something entirely inappropriate like swooning, she drew in a reviving breath and climbed out of the carriage. The tip of her shoe caught on the lower rung, making her stumble forward, her too-large beaver hat slipping over an eye.

Quickly recovering, Julia straightened her brim, gripped her lapels, and cleared her throat, glancing to the porch to ensure the entire MacGalloway family hadn't filed outside to witness her inelegance. "It seems four days of travel has made me a tad clumsy," she said in her practiced masculine voice. "Ah...would you mind fetching my valise, if you please?"

For a five-mile trip out of the city, the driver had insisted on payment up front, but still held out his palm when he handed Julia her case, chock full of altered clothing and a few necessities.

She dug in the pocket of her greatcoat, forced to bend down to reach her small stash of coins. Pulling out two pence, she deposited them in the man's hand. "Thank you."

With a smug grin, the driver tipped his hat and the coin disappeared. "Good day, sir."

As the hackney drove off, Julia turned to the house, her eyes taking in the iron grillwork, the foreboding black door, the enormity of the estate. In an instant, rather than the vast, welcoming home she'd first envisaged, the manor seemed to lean forward and snarl as if it were a monster with fangs.

So many windows.

Clutching her valise to her chest, Julia whipped around. "Driver!" she called, cringing at the high pitch of her voice. Moreover, the man and his coach were already headed out the gates and down the long, sycamore-lined drive.

Still alone, she watched as the hackney grew smaller, turned right, and eventually rolled out of sight.

"For what I am about to undertake, may God have mercy on my soul," she mumbled under her breath as she shifted her valise to one hand and tightened her grip, for a self-respecting man would never clutch his valise in front of his chest, no matter how heavy it may be.

At the top of the stairs, a brass knocker in the shape a lion's head greeted her. Or at least it warned her. Looking over her shoulder once again, contrary to her wishes, the hack had not returned. Before she lost her nerve, she inhaled deeply and gave the lion's mouth a good, solid rap.

The door eventually opened to a tall, gaunt butler peering above her head. After she cleared her throat, the man's beetle brows knit while he dropped his gaze and examined her from head to toe as if she'd just flown down from the moon. "May I help you, sir?" he asked, his brogue unmistakably Scottish.

"Indeed, you may." Julia reached inside her breast pocket and produced a calling card—one flawlessly crafted in her own hand. "Jules Smallwood, Esquire, recently appointed steward and secretary to the Duke of Dunscaby."

The man took the card, gave it a look, and deposited it on a silver plate. "Ah, yes. His Grace mentioned you'd be arriving soon."

"Excellent."

"I'm Giles, I'm certain our paths will cross often enough." The butler showed her to a parlor. "May I take your coat and hat, sir?"

"Thank you."

"Very good. I'll have your things sent to your rooms."

"Rooms?" Julia asked, allowing him to take the valise as well. At Huntly Manor, no one had *rooms* unless they were family. Though her father was an earl, she had acted as his steward and secretary for the past five years. Before that, Papa had employed solicitors to take on such responsibilities.

"Aye," Giles explained. "A gentleman of your station is allotted a sitting room and bedchamber—adjoining His Grace's library."

Of course, the steward to a duke, a member of the gentry, would have rooms. "Ah, yes." She could have kicked herself if it weren't for her oversized shoes. "Thank you."

Once alone, she paced. The walls were adorned with family portraits and on one side of the parlor stood a marble hearth with a gilt mirror above the mantel. Even higher was a portrait of a dour man wearing a gauche periwig, his cheeks flushed, his brow stern, and his mouth brooding as if his frown had been painted for the sole purpose of accusing her of impersonating a man.

Julia held up a finger and looked the painting in the eye. "You may know my secret," she whispered. "But I'll tell you here and now, I can perform my duties as well as any m—"

"Mr. Smallwood," interrupted the butler. "His Grace will see you now."

Good heavens that was fast. She gave the painting a fierce glare before turning to the man. "Excellent."

After leading her along a corridor festooned with more frowning portraits, Giles opened the door to an enormous library with volumes of books on shelves wrapping around the entire chamber from floor to ceiling—aside from the windows, of course. Great streams of light beamed through the glass panes while dozens of candles flickered above, supported by two opulent crystal chandeliers.

"Smallwood," said a kilted man climbing down from a ladder with a book in his grasp. "I didna expect you before the morrow."

The man skipped the last rung and hopped to the Oriental carpet. Dropping the book onto a table, he grinned, his teeth white and healthy, one incisor slightly crossing over the other. Before she was properly announced, the man marched across the floor and thrust out his palm. "Welcome to Newhailes."

This is His Grace?

Good Lord, the duke wasn't only enormous, his blue eyes sparkled like seafoam. Julia's knees wobbled as if they'd suddenly become boneless mollusks while she stifled a gasp. Had she ever seen eyes so light and intense? Realizing she was staring, she gave herself shake, squared her shoulders, and took the offered hand. "Thank you...*ah*...you're His Grace, the Duke of Dunscaby?" she managed in her manly voice.

He splayed his fingers and pushed up the black mourning band around the arm of his doublet. "Och, do you find it all that hard to believe? I may have recently taken on my father's mantle, but I assure you I've been groomed for this role my entire life."

Julia dipped into a hasty bow. "Forgive any impertinence, sir, I entertained no such assumptions."

"Good." The duke turned to the butler. "Thank you, Giles."

When Dunscaby's disarming gaze again met hers, he stroked his fingers along his jaw as if not quite certain what to do with her. "Do you fancy a refreshment? A glass of wine? A wee tot of whisky?"

Good heavens, whisky? Because too much drink was the cause of her father's ill health, she cared never to allow a drop of liquor pass her lips. "Perhaps a spot of wine for warmth. 'Tis quite cold here."

Rather than ringing for a footman, the duke moved to a table, pulled the stopper from a decanter, and poured two glasses with his own hand. "Aye, February is rather bleak. 'Tis even colder in the Highlands."

"My thanks," Julia took the offered glass. "Mr. MacCutcheon said your books of accounts are in quite a state."

"Unfortunately, aye." He gestured to a chair by the fire and took the opposite, crossing his legs, making his kilt ride up his well-muscled, hairy thigh. "My father wasna one for change."

"Oh?" she asked, forcing her gaze to shift away from his legs. For the love of God, he was only a man. Very un-duke-like, though. Were all Scottish nobles so...*casual*? "Mr. MacCutcheon also said the estate has been without a steward for two years."

His Grace swilled his wine, gazing at her from above his glass. "Closer to three, is more apt."

"But why did the former duke not appoint another?"

"As I said, Da didna care for change. Also, I believe he was ill for far longer than he let on."

"Forgive me, I didn't mean to pry. Please accept my condolences for your loss."

Dunscaby sighed and stared at the coal smoldering in the hearth for a moment. "My father was a good man. Far better than me, I'm afraid." He glanced up, his expression forlorn. "Aside from the records being a shambles, the estate is sound with the backing of one of the oldest, most established families in Scotland, but I'll be counting on you to sift through and set the books to rights as well as ensuring rents have been collected and the delegation of the servants' duties are equitable. Of course, Giles oversees the male servants and the housekeeper oversees the female. They will both report to you now."

"As I would expect." Julia moved to the edge of her chair. "And I assure you I have ample experience, Your

Grace. I've brought letters of reference from the Earl of Brixham."

"Aye, MacCutcheon advised that your references are impeccable." Dunscaby narrowed his gaze and drummed his fingers on the stem of his glass. "But tell me, why the devil did Brixham let you go?"

Julia bit her lip. It wasn't proper to speak poorly about one's betters. But then again, the duke deserved to know the truth. At least as much of the truth she was able to tell. "I'm sorry to say the earl fell upon difficult circumstances." The words tasted like bile on her tongue. Though her father had well and truly lost his fortune, she preferred not to discuss his failure with anyone aside from Willaby.

"I see. Too much drink and gambling."

Julia's gaze dropped to her folded hands. "'Tis not for me to say."

"Indeed. You may be aware that, I've just spent the past few years enjoying bachelorhood in London." A faraway look filled His Grace's eyes as he sipped his wine. "Needless to say, Brixham's name was mentioned a wee time or two."

"Mm-hmm." Of course, Julia was woefully aware of the rumors. The gossip papers enjoyed blackening her father's name. Not that Papa hadn't done plenty to bring on the besmirching. "To explain in a few words, I found myself in need of employment just about the time Mr. MacCutcheon's advertisement appeared in the *Gazette*."

"Fortunate for me, then." Dunscaby stood. "Well, Smallwood, you must be weary from your travels. I'll have Giles give you a tour of Newhailes. He'll acquaint you with the servants as well. After you've had a wee bit of time to familiarize yourself with the ledgers, we'll chat."

MARTIN WAITED until the butler led the new steward out the door then strode straight to his father's writing table, opened the bottom drawer, and poured himself a healthy tot of whisky. By the gods, he felt like a fledgling flapping its wings and going nowhere.

What he wouldn't do for a high-stakes game of Whist or going a few rounds in the ring at Jackson's Saloon. Only five months ago he'd been content with his marquess courtesy title, enjoying a bachelor's freedom in London. Now he had a yoke around his neck the weight of a frigate's anchor. His eldest sister, Charity, had only begun her first Season when she'd been forced into mourning and now she was back in Scotland without a single prospect. Moreover, Martin had four brothers who would soon be looking to him for help landing on their feet.

Why the devil hadn't Da been forthright about his illness? Why hadn't he called Martin back to Scotland when he'd fallen ill? There he'd been, a complete fop, sipping port at Whites, spending his nights in London's exclusive gambling hells, the theater, the opera, flirting at balls, boxing, riding, and driving a shiny black phaeton through Hyde Park while attempting to act like a bloody Englishman.

Speaking of Englishmen, Smallwood certainly mirrored his namesake. The man wasn't only the size of a jockey, he had to be the bonniest fellow Martin had ever seen. Even his hands seemed inordinately small, well-manicured, and feminine.

Though I suppose an educated steward isn't going to develop callouses from driving a team.

But it was rather odd to see a man who was distractingly handsome. Unsettlingly so. If it weren't for

Smallwood's enormous feet, he might have seemed more woman than man. What fellow in his prime had a face as smooth as silk? Aye, the chap seemed a bit fresh, aside from his unfashionably clubbed hair and outdated clothing which smelled of camphor—that part was definitely not feminine.

Staring at the portrait of his father, Martin took a long, thoughtful sip of whisky. "It wasn't your time, old man. Not by half."

"I'll second that," said Mama from the doorway, moving toward the settee with the black skirts of her mourning gown whisking the floor. "How are you settling in, dearest?"

"Would you like the truth or should I respond as Da would have done?" As his mother sat, Martin took the chair where he'd been sitting across from Smallwood—the wingback once exclusively used by his father. "I'm a duke. I am impervious to trifling matters that trouble everyone else."

Mama almost snorted, though the duchess would never snort. "The truth if you please. It would be very nice for a change."

Martin nodded. No, he couldn't say how unbearably awkward it was occupying his father's library. He couldn't say how strange it was to be called Dunscaby. His father was Dunscaby, Your Grace, and Duke.

"Son?" Mama persisted.

"Och..." Rubbing the back of his neck, Martin met his mother's gaze. The sadness reflected in her eyes expressed the torturous twisting of his own heart. "The new steward arrived."

"Giles told me. So..." Mama leaned forward. "What is your impression?"

"I think he'll do nicely. He seems a reserved, unpretentious sort." Martin tapped his fingers on the leather armrest. "I'll give him a wee bit of time to settle in and set the books to rights before I discuss my ideas for establishing a dynastic new venture for the lads."

"You mustn't wait too long. The twins are set to graduate in the spring. And worrying about Gibb on a warship whilst Napoleon ravages the continent makes for very little sleep at night especially after my son's ship took such heavy losses. Your brother may have been decorated for his valor, but the mere idea of losing him is too much to bear."

"I ken. I want him safe as well. And you have my word I'll make a sound decision—one to benefit all." Martin again glanced to his father's portrait while his throat tightened. "It is just—"

"Just what, my dear?"

"Da's shoes are awfully big to fill."

"Yes." Mama sighed. "Not to worry. You'll come into your own. Just give it time."

The problem? With his father gone, Martin had no more time.

2

Finally alone in her small suite of rooms, Julia buried her face in her palms. Yes, she'd imagined this day would be difficult, but she'd never dreamed it would verge on catastrophic. Her nerves were frayed. Her hands shook.

She already hated pretending to be a man. Her throat ached. And though she was fully capable of performing the work she'd been employed to do, she felt like an imposter. If only a woman could hold the position of steward to a duke, she could have interviewed as herself rather than Jules Smallwood.

Staring at her reflection in the mirror, she took a reviving breath that stretched the bindings around her breasts. "This situation is not forever."

Dunscaby was paying her three hundred pounds per year which would cover her father's medical bills as well as the wages of the two servants who remained at Huntly Manor. Of most import, she must immediately start making payments on her father's gambling debt. Eventually, Julia hoped to pay off Mr. Skinner, the vile moneylender from whom Papa had borrowed. Unfortunately, that creature was the absolute last person with whom she cared to associate.

Her employment with Dunscaby mightn't be for-ever, but she desperately needed the salary. And that meant she must never.

Ever.

Not once.

Allow herself to gaze into Dunscaby's eyes. Good heavens, she'd had a Season—not much of one since there were no funds for gowns, but she'd met several gentlemen when she was *out* and nary a one had made her knees grow weak, or made her lose her train of thought, or made her blush.

Well, admittedly she'd blushed a time or two. But blushing certainly would not do in the presence of His Grace.

Julia dropped her head back and groaned. "Why could he not be an old man with a wart on his nose? Or a young man who looked like a troll? Anything aside from...from..." She refused to utter the words on the tip of her tongue—splendid, sumptuous, magnifi-cent. Even his well-muscled, hairy legs were impos-sible to ignore.

But he was a duke and as far as he was concerned, she was a lesser man, the son of a knight, a fellow of the middleclass who must work to earn his keep.

She straightened. Things could be far worse. Her sitting room was lovely with a writing table and book-case at one end, though the table was overflowing with bills of lading, unopened letters, and Lord knew what else. At least there was plenty with which to keep her occupied.

There was a round table with a wooden chair where Giles said she would take her meals—appro-priate since she wasn't a servant. And before the hearth was an overstuffed chair and a candelabra for reading. Judging by the volumes of novels on the top shelf of the bookcase, Julia imagined the last steward enjoyed reading a great deal.

Beyond the sitting room was a neatly appointed bedchamber and against one wall stood a narrow military couch-bed both useful and ornamental with a practical tent-like drapery suspended from a scepter rod. The curtains presently were tied open, but when released from their tiebacks, they completely closed off the sleeping space. A sideboard sported a decanter containing something amber that she mustn't ever allow to touch her lips. Through an archway was a small garderobe for her personal effects and toileting needs. In truth, if Julia must pose as a man, this was the ideal setting where she'd have plenty of privacy to conceal her sex.

After adding another block of peat to the fire, she set to unpacking her belongings and recited the servant's names in her head.

Mrs. Lamont the housekeeper. Of course, Giles the butler. The three footmen I met were Tommy, Fergus, and... what was the other's name? It sounded Gaelic to me.

She folded her nightshirt. "Tearlach!"

"I beg your pardon?" said a youthful voice from the sitting room.

Practically jumping out of her skin, Julia clutched the nightshirt to her chest, tiptoed to the doorway, and found a freckle-faced, redheaded girl grinning as if she always barged into the steward's chambers. "Are you lost?" Julia asked.

"Och, nay. I ken every wee inch of Newhailes. Could wander about in the dark all night and never bump into a thing." She beamed as if very proud of herself. The child leaned in and cupped a hand to the side of her mouth as if she had a secret. "I've a pot of chocolate waiting in the embrasure. Cook thinks 'tis for me and Lady Grace, but my sister wouldna care if Mama sold me to a band of traveling tinkers."

Julia couldn't help but smile at the child's antics. "Your sister doesn't care for chocolate?"

She swayed in place, making her grey skirts swish across her calves. "Nay. She loves chocolate. 'Tis me of whom she's not fond."

"And you are?" Julia asked.

The girl curtsied, presenting a full head of fiery red hair tied up in ringlets. "Lady Modesty MacGalloway, the youngest and the most exasperating, according to my mother."

Ah, no wonder the lass appeared to be clad in half-mourning. Julia clicked her heels and gave a respectful bow, one she'd been practicing. "Pleased to meet you, my lady. I am Mr.—"

"Smallwood. Everyone's talking about you."

Cringing, Julia straightened. "I hope the gossip isn't too disparaging."

"Not at all." Lady Modesty beckoned. "Except I overheard Tearlach say he wondered if you were an elf."

"Preposterous," Julia scoffed as she followed the girl across the corridor to a lovely window alcove with opposing cushioned seats. Upon a low table between the benches was a chocolate pot and two dishes.

Modesty sat and wriggled in place. "Aye. I rather like your stature. You're not towering over me like most adults."

"I daresay, I don't do much towering. Pray, what is your age?"

"Eleven." The girl poured, the chocolaty aroma wafting with the steam. "Can you believe it? I'm a wee lass of eleven and nearly as tall as you."

"Hardly." Julia pretended to frown. She was almost five feet tall, and Modesty had to be at least three inches shorter. She sipped the chocolate and licked her lips. At Huntly Manor, the delicacy had certainly been too expensive of late. "Mm, this is delicious."

"Cook makes the best." Unable to touch the ground, the child swung her feet. "He has a secret recipe."

"I'll wager 'tis not kept a secret from you."

Modesty drew a finger across her mouth. "My lips are sealed."

"Very good. Confidences are meant to be kept, not revealed."

"You sound like Miss Hay."

Noticing the child's dish was already empty, Julia poured. "Is she your governess?"

"Mm-hmm."

"I'll wager she's a good teacher."

"I suppose. Lessons are oft tedious, though."

"Oh?" After setting the chocolate pot on the silver tray, Julia lifted the lid of a sugar bowl, scooped a spoon and held it up. When Modesty nodded, she sprinkled it into the child's drink. "What do you find most interesting?"

"Dancing."

"A worthy pastime. I'm sure you will need to be a proficient dancer when the time comes for your introduction to society."

"Aye, 'tis why I must have plenty of practice."

Julia took another sip. She'd best change the subject before she was wrangled into attending dancing lessons. One thing she definitely had not attempted during her short transformation in gender was dancing a man's part. Doubtless, she'd present with two left feet. "Tell me about your family. I haven't had the pleasure of meeting them all." In fact, the only MacGalloway she'd met thus far was the duke.

"Well, of course Mama is now the dowager duchess, but she is staying with convention and has decided not to take the dowager title until Martin marries. Her name is Patience, though I'd only ever heard Papa refer to her thus."

Julia's gaze shifted to the window. She knew all too well what it was like to lose a parent at such a tender age. Her own mother had passed away when she was only a year older than Modesty. "The change must be difficult for you all."

"I do miss him. Though Da was more like a portrait to me than a father."

"Oh?"

"Well, when Martin was home he told me stories and sometimes played with me. Da never did that. My eldest brother is more like a father, I suppose. He's fourteen years older, mind you."

Julia almost sighed, how wonderful to have a handsome, blue-eyed brother who took the time to read stories to his sister. "Fourteen?" she asked, trying to sound surprised and definitely not sighing. "That's quite a difference."

She squeezed her fist, making her fingernails gouge into her palms. *His Grace is my employer. He is not handsome. He is an ogre with no redeeming qualities.*

"Aye. What with eight children, I suppose fourteen years is to be expected between the eldest and the youngest. At least that's what Mama says."

"Eight children? So, you mentioned your sister Grace," Julia said, moving the conversation along and away from the duke. "Is she second to the youngest?"

"Unfortunately." Modesty raised her dish. "Because she's fourteen she thinks I'm a bairn and doesna want a thing to do with me."

"I'm sorry. If I had a sister, I'd be grateful."

"Why?"

"I don't have any siblings. I'd be happy with a brother or a sister."

"You can have some of mine." Modesty counted on her fingers. "As I said, Martin's the eldest. Gibb is three and twenty and serving as an officer in the Royal Navy. Andrew and Philip are twins and they're away at university. A fortnight ago Charity celebrated her nineteenth birthday. Before that, she was supposed to have her first London season, but it was cut short..."

Julia knew why. "Oh, I am sorry."

"Charity isna. Aside from mourning Papa, of course." Modesty sipped her chocolate and smacked her lips. "I canna forget Fredrick. He's seventeen and almost as nice as Martin, except Freddy's away. 'Tis his last year at Eton and then he'll be attending Saint Andrews University come autumn."

"Why Saint Andrews and not Oxford or Cambridge?" Julia asked.

"Are you jesting? The MacGalloways of Dunscaby have always attended Saint Andrews. Mama..." Modesty leaned forward as if she had an important tidbit of information. "She's English, and she wanted Martin to go to Oxford so he wouldna '*sound like a Scottish heathen*' but Papa would have none of it."

Julia laughed as she set down her cup. "Bless him."

"There you are," said a woman looking rather harried as she entered the corridor.

Immediately hopping to her feet, Julia bowed. "Good evening, madam."

"Och..." Modesty stood, though hesitantly. "This is Miss Hay."

"The governess?" Julia asked.

Miss Hay didn't look happy. In fact, if she were to admit she'd just been sucking on lemons, Julia wouldn't have been surprised. "Aye, and I've spent the past half-hour searching for this wayward imp."

Modesty clasped her hands behind her back, feigning complete innocence. "I thought I'd introduce myself to Mr. Smallwood. He's awfully affable. The pair of you ought to be friends."

A splay of heat burned Julia's cheeks as the taller woman eyed her. "I'm certain we'll see each other now and again. Come along, m'lady, and the next time you ask Cook to make you chocolate, you must tell him who it is really for."

As the pair walked away, Miss Hay's voice grew more distant, but there was no mistaking the irritation in her tone. "You mustn't ever visit a man's chamber."

"But—" the child tried to interject.

"I'll hear no excuses. You are a young lady of exceptional breeding and—"

A door closed cutting off the governess' chiding.

Julia sat back and poured herself another cup. "This secret recipe is too good to have it go to waste."

In truth, the governess was correct, though Julia recalled being Modesty's age and frequently paying Willaby a visit. However, even when Julia was a child, Papa's butler had been with the family for years.

As SNOW FELL outside bringing an eerie silence, Martin paced the library. He was restless and weary of winter with its short and dreary days. In truth, he never remembered being this agitated before. Why must taking on his father's mantle be so bloody tiresome? Life was far more enjoyable when he didn't have to worry about his estates, or his mother's welfare, or his sisters' prospects. Hell, if the lassies would just stop growing up, he'd be a happy man.

Stopping beside the enormous globe, he stared at the door to his steward's quarters. They hadn't spoken since morning when Smallwood came in to say there had been some unrest with crofters up north—a report that had arrived when Da was pretending he wasn't ill. Doubtless, however, the Stack Castle caretaker had taken matters in hand.

Mr. MacCutcheon had been right to hire Smallwood. The man worked from sunup and well past sundown. Martin had never seen a person apply themselves with such vigor. Surely the fellow needed a respite. After all, he'd been at it for a fortnight.

Martin gave the door a knock before he pushed inside.

Looking up from his work, the steward jolted and stood. "Your Grace," he squeaked, offering a curt bow. "I...ah...would have thought you'd be preparing for the evening meal by now."

"I decided to go without the pomp for a night." Martin pulled a chair across from the writing table and sat. "There's no need to stand every time I pop my head in."

Smallwood dubiously slid back into his seat. "As you wish."

"What do you do when you havena your nose in a ledger?"

"Do, sir?"

"Aye? Certainly, a man such as yourself would enjoy a great many pursuits—shooting, a turn at cards, billiards, reading the—"

"I quite enjoy reading," Smallwood said, tapping

his fingers together. "I also write in my journal on a regular basis and, for exercise, walking is most invigorating."

"Walking?"

"Yes. I fancy long strolls and fresh air."

"What about riding?"

The steward's brows arched above a pair of expressive brown eyes. "Ah yes, I do enjoy a ride in the countryside. Managing a sturdy horse is every bit as invigorating as walking."

Martin rubbed a sore spot at the back of his neck and looked from one wall to the other. Not spotting what he was looking for, he asked, "Did I not instruct Giles to fill your decanter with whisky?"

"Are you referring to the contents in the decanter on the sideboard in my bedchamber?"

"Dunna tell me you havena had a wee dram."

"I'm afraid to admit, I've been spending so much time reading correspondence, replying to them, and combing through ledgers. After hours I've found myself too tired for much of anything aside from sleep."

"Well, that is a dilemma which must be remedied." Martin stood, dipped into the next chamber, and poured two drams. "Here we are. My, you do keep your rooms tidy."

Smallwood looked at the glass as if he'd never seen a tot of whisky before. "I like things orderly."

Martin sipped and savored the aged, oaken flavor. "As your employer I bid you set your quill in its holder and join me." He raised his glass. "No man cares to drink alone."

The fellow grasped the tot and raised his pinky finger as if he were about to take a sip of tea. "Is that so?"

"I dunna ken for certain." In truth, though Martin

enjoyed time with his friends, this setting suited him just fine—an intimate little chamber enjoying fine drink without a boisterous crowd. Though the dandies in London would never believe it.

The steward touched the glass to his lips and took a wee sip, then blinked and held in a cough while his eyes watered and his face grew red. "My, that is potent."

"The finest. From the Dunscaby stills in Caithness."

"Ah, yes. 'Tis a quite profitable business venture from what I've seen thus far."

"Indeed." Martin leaned across the table and studied the odd little chap. "You've never tasted whisky before, have you?"

The steward shrank. "Is it that obvious?"

"Och aye."

"Forgive me. My father imbibed in enough spirits for the both of us."

"Unfortunate. And then your former employer did the same."

The red in Smallwood's complexion transformed into a pallid green. "Yes."

"Well, whisky is to be enjoyed. Sipped, not swilled, mind you. Anyone who guzzles it ought to be on the streets of London's East End, swigging gin." Martin held up his glass and nodded for Smallwood to do the same. "But a chap who kens how to enjoy a finely dis-tilled spot of whisky is a man of the world."

He watched as the steward took a second sip. His enormous brown eyes still watered a bit, but Jules licked his lips and smiled. "My, it does warm one's in-sides, does it not?"

Martin smiled, giving Smallwood a good once-over. His eyes weren't only brown, they were luminous like a well-oiled sable. "Nothing better on a cold evening than a glass of whisky by the fire and a volume of *Colonel Jack* in your hands."

"You enjoy Daniel Defoe?" the steward asked.

"You sound surprised."

"No, 'tis just I do as well. I enjoy reading if you recall, sir?"

"Aye, that's right." Martin sat back, crossed his ankles, and changed the subject, "I've been thinking 'tis time to pay a visit to my hunting lodge."

"Hunting lodge, sir?" Smallwood stood and pulled aside the lace curtains, revealing a cedar its limbs heavy with snow. "Is it not snowing?"

"I dunna plan to leave today. Soon, though. There's no better time to track a buck than toward the end of winter."

"Is that so?"

"My word, Smallwood, you need to crawl out from under your ledgers and live a wee bit. Besides, you are steward over all my estates. We will need to visit each one in time." And to tell the truth, Martin enjoyed the little man's company. After three years in London, it was refreshing to fraternize with a gentleman who wasn't absorbed in the pursuit of women of easy virtue or a needling desire to impress polite society.

"We, sir?" the man asked.

"Of course, *we*. There's no chance I'll allow you to have all the merriment."

"But just yesterday did I not overhear Her Grace mention the need to return to London?" A bit of mischief flashed in Smallwood's eyes as he pressed his fingertips together. "Finding a suitable spouse and providing an heir to the dukedom, and whatnot?"

"Wheesht. Perhaps I ought to reinforce the door between the library and your rooms. And remember who pays your wages, laddie. Keep in mind my mother is nay the Duke of Dunscaby. I will decide when it is time to return to London and make no bones about it, I am in no way ready to marry, nor will I be. There's something to be said for enjoying one's bachelorhood, and I fully intend to be free of the proverbial ball-and-chain for years. In fact, with four younger brothers, I may not marry at all regardless of Her Grace's wishes."

The fellow set his three-quarters full glass aside. "I would think no less, Your Grace."

Martin tsked his tongue, and sat for a moment, perhaps Smallwood was familiar enough with the estate's affairs to discuss creating a lasting dynasty for not only the benefit of the dukedom but for his brothers and their heirs. "There is one thing I'd like you to put some thought into, however."

The man's eyes widened with intelligence and intrigue. "Yes?"

"My mother worries about Gibb being in danger, what with the wars and all. On top of that, the twins will be graduating university in the spring. I'd like to help them land on their feet—but not in the usual way with allowances and whatnot. I intend to embark upon a venture that has the potential to make them all wealthy men—a lasting legacy so to speak. I'm just not certain what enterprise would provide the least risk with the greatest potential for growth."

"Very forward-thinking of you, sir." Smallwood held up his glass and examined the amber liquid. "What about your whisky operation? It is very solid indeed."

"Aye, but my uncle has the business in hand, though I'll admit I've considered there might be an opportunity for expansion." Martin shook his head. "I just dunna see it as solution for all four lads—ye ken Fredrick is seventeen. He'll be looking to find his place soon as well."

"I understand." Smallwood stood and stirred the fire. "Let me ponder it for a time and see what I might come up with."

"Verra well. I think if we put our heads together, the Dunscaby...or should I say *MacGalloway* dynasty will be as solid as a mountain, enduring for generations, which would make me a happy man." Martin finished his whisky and stood. "Enough about business ventures. I have realized of late that there are things a duke must do to clear his head—at least this duke. The weather ought to turn for the better in a matter of weeks and once it does, you and I shall ride for the Highlands and enjoy a wee hunt."

3

Dunscaby hadn't paid Julia a visit all day, though she'd heard him milling about in the library. In her short tenure at Newhailes, she'd grown accustomed to his mid-morning visits. And of course today, when she had something of import to discuss, he hadn't called in.

She drummed her fingers on the wages ledger. No voices had sounded through the walls, so the duke most likely was alone, and this discrepancy shouldn't wait. Gathering the volume into her arms, she lightly knocked before popping her head through the doorway. "Have you a moment, Your Grace?"

Martin's eyes appeared over the top of his newspaper. "What tells me your query will take more than a wee moment?"

Ignoring his question, she walked across the floor and pointed to the list of wages for the female servants. "See here, Georgette was promoted to lady's maid this past summer when Lady Charity was preparing for her debut."

"Aye."

"Not only is the maid tending to Lady Charity's toilette, she is also attending to Lady Grace's needs."

Knitting his eyebrows, Dunscaby folded the Gazette. "Is she?"

"Indeed she is. Lady Grace has decided that her hair must be done both in the mornings and when she dresses for the evening meal."

"I suppose that makes sense. Mama has started having her take her meals in the dining hall rather than the nursery. Honestly, Modesty ought to join us as well. It must be awfully lonely up there now everyone is grown aside from the youngest."

Julia recalled Lady Modesty had mentioned that Lady Grace wouldn't care if the child were sold to a band of traveling tinkers. "Possibly, though your youngest sister might enjoy the solace."

The duke coughed out a laugh. "You are speaking of Modesty, are you not? She's chattiest social butterfly in the family."

He was right, of course, and Julia's duty wasn't to involve herself in the family's dining arrangements, but it was to ensure equitable pay for the servants. Shifting the ledger under Dunscaby's nose, she pointed to the lady's maid's wages. "That may well be, but before we stray too far from the matter at hand, have a look at this. Sara is an upper housemaid making fifteen guineas a year. Your mother's lady's maid is more senior, of course, and she's paid twenty. But Georgette's wages are only fourteen guineas—the same as the laundress and the lower housemaid."

Martin frowned. "Well, that doesna seem fair."

"Absolutely not, especially since I've also discovered that her wages weren't adjusted a penny upon her promotion."

"Well, then, 'tis up to you to make it right." The duke tapped his finger atop the page. "That is why I hired you."

Julia closed the volume and tucked it under her arm. "Do you not wish for me to discuss the wages with you before I make a change? If you ask me, Georgette ought to be paid at least eighteen guineas per year."

"Then I leave it to you to inform her. And to your first question, for the time being, do discuss such changes with me."

"Thank you, sir." Julia bowed and started toward the door.

"One moment, Smallwood." Dunscaby set the newspaper aside and moved to his writing table. "Are all the servants' wages listed in that book?"

"Only those who are employed at Newhailes."

"Bring it here, I'd like to have a look."

Julia returned and placed the ledger on the table where together they leaned over to examine the volume. Except the duke's arm brushed hers, making tingles course all the way up the back of her neck. She clapped a hand over her mouth to muffle her gasp. Holy macaroons, gasping in His Grace's presence was utterly untoward!

Clearing her throat, she tilted away from the ever so masculine, yet entirely offending shoulder and started at the top of the page. Though the dukedom employed hundreds of servants there were only thirty-six at Newhailes. "There are sixteen male servants including the coachman's son. And twenty female servants, the two scullery maids and the dairy maids being paid the least at seven guineas each per year."

Dunscaby turned his face toward her, his breath skimming her cheek while a riot of gooseflesh spread down her arms. "That seems fair, is it not?" he asked. Goodness, today he smelled like freshly milled soap with a hint of pine in the mix.

Straightening, Julia patted her chest in an attempt to still her thundering heart. Bless it, she'd been at Newhailes for three weeks now. It was time she grew accustomed to the duke's looks, his casual and overly familiar manner as well as his entirely intoxicating scent, no matter how disarming. "Yes, quite fair. I'd say on a par with wages paid by the English nobility."

"Hmm. I would assume no less." Oblivious to her adoration, Dunscaby ran his pointer finger down the list of names and opposing wages. "What do you think—"

"Martin!" Modesty hollered, bursting into the library in a whirlwind of skirts and petticoats. "You absolutely must come to the drawing room and be my dancing partner."

He arched an eyebrow at Julia. "Chatty butterfly, aye?"

She gave him a knowing grin, then bowed to the lass. "My lady."

"Isna there footman up to the task?" asked Dunscaby.

"Nay. Tearlach is out with the carriage, assisting Mama. Tommy is partnering with Grace and Fergus is with Charity."

"Such a dilemma." Martin again turned to Julia, though this time her heart didn't palpitate. Instead, her stomach dropped to her toes. "I reckon Mr. Smallwood might make a better partner for you than I."

Modesty beamed. "What an excellent idea. It will be like attending a real ball, except in miniature."

Julia picked up the ledger and tucked it under her arm. "I assure you there is nothing miniature about me. And I hate to disappoint, but I must return to my—"

"Nonsense," said Dunscaby. "You could do to

stretch your legs a wee bit. You've hardly been out of your chambers since you arrived."

Drat, and double drat. Dancing was exactly the type of thing she'd wanted to avoid. She gave the child a pointed frown. "Surely you would prefer to partner with your brother. I am ashamedly out of practice and cannot promise I won't step on your toes."

The lass grasped her hands behind her back and swayed. "Och, you wouldna do that."

"Come, Smallwood," urged the duke, pulling the ledger away. "If you're as clumsy as you claim, you ought to benefit from a lesson or two."

"I—" From His Grace's stringent mien, she'd best concede defeat. "Oh, very well. But I'll not be held accountable for any missteps. It has been quite some time since I last graced a ballroom."

Modesty latched onto Julia's hand and practically dragged her through the house to the drawing room where the carpet had been rolled back and Giles, of all people, sat at the pianoforte. The butler regarded her over a pair of glasses and smirked.

"Ah, Mr. Smallwood, how nice to see you're able to join us," said Miss Hay.

Julia bowed to the MacGalloway sisters to whom she had been introduced shortly after her arrival. "I'm surprised a house this size doesn't have a ballroom."

"We usually host balls at Stack Castle," said Lady Grace.

Lady Charity ran the ribbons cinching her gown's empire waist through her fingers. "But we've hosted them here as well. We take up the carpets in the library. 'Tis such a large space and the chandeliers are so beautiful, they deserve to be seen."

Julia had taken an instant liking to the eldest MacGalloway daughter. If she weren't posing as Jules

Smallwood, she would have enjoyed striking up a friendship with Her Ladyship. Instead, she just smiled pleasantly. "They are quite remarkable."

"Enough idle chatter." Miss Hay clapped her hands. "Shall we continue with the lesson?"

Modesty grabbed Julia's wrist and forcefully pulled her to the center of the floor while the other two ladies faced their respective footmen.

"For Mr. Smallwood's edification, I was explaining the waltzes that have recently taken over ballrooms across Europe. There are four main variations, the German, the slow French, the Sauteuese, and the Jeté."

With a sharp intake of air, Julia stifled a groan while she fixated her eyes upon the ornate plaster on the ceiling, which sported a circle of filagree surrounding what appeared to be a depiction of Neptune commanding the seas with his trident. *Please, not a waltz.*

"Today we shall practice my favorite." Miss Hay whacked Julia's shoulder with her baton. "Are you familiar with the slow French waltz, sir?"

"Vaguely," she fibbed. She was proficient at the lady's part but had never attempted stepping in as a man.

"Not to worry, this is why we must practice." The governess drummed the pianoforte with her baton, proving quite thorny with her little stick. "We shall start with a facing posture and move around the hall in a counter-clockwise line of direction. And mind you, everyone must keep their place in formation."

Julia held out her right hand and put her left on Modesty's waist.

"Silly," the girl giggled, taking Julia's right hand and moving it to her waist.

"I warned you, did I not?"

"No talking," clipped Miss Hay, swinging her stick at Giles who started playing.

Julia began on the correct foot but both of them stepped backward. She immediately corrected. "Sorry."

The governess rapped a cadence to the beat of the bass notes. "One, two, three. Smallwood, keep moving to your left, sir!"

By the time they'd made a complete turn around the chamber, Julia had stumbled over the toes of her enormous shoes no fewer than three times.

"You do need a great deal of practice," Modesty whispered after Miss Hay's attention had shifted to Lady Grace.

Julia eyed the little redheaded imp. "That's exactly why I'm a steward and not a dance master."

"Oh? You canna always hide in your rooms."

How the devil did an eleven-year-old come to be so perceptive? "I rather like the solace."

Miss Hay clapped her hands and Giles abruptly stopped playing. "Lady Modesty, I shift my attention away for the briefest of moments and you turn into a chatterbox."

Growing as red as her hair, the lass looked to her toes. "I'm just trying to help Mr. Smallwood."

By her leery-eyed glare, Miss Hay did not appear to be impressed. "Again!"

Resigning herself to her fate, Julia concentrated, and the next time around the room resulted in only one misstep, definitely attributable to her miserable shoes. However, the experience cemented her decision. She'd had enough of clomping about like some pigeon-toed clod. On her next outing she would purchase a pair that fit.

MARTIN STOOD in the shadows of the corridor and watched through the half-opened drawing room door while smothering his nose and mouth in his hand to keep from laughing aloud.

Perhaps he should not have encouraged Smallwood. The poor man danced like an alehouse drunkard. And by the furrow in his brow, the chap was concentrating harder than he did when he had his nose in a pile of ledgers.

The man's feet absolutely did nothing for his stature. Comically, what Jules lacked in height, he made up for with the length of his insoles. However, by the third time around the chamber, his clumsiness had waned.

Modesty might have hit the nail on the head. The steward needed more dancing lessons and, in Martin's opinion, Smallwood could benefit from boxing lessons as well. But presently there were too many other things to contend with aside from his new steward's masculinity.

The eldest MacGalloway sister waltzed past, reminding Martin that she was old enough to marry. Unfortunately, Charity didn't seem eager to leave the nest. Had Da not passed away, the lass would have been overjoyed when they left London. Nonetheless, Martin didn't understand her aversion to the *ton* and polite society. She certainly looked as polished as a swan, twirling about the floor in the drawing room.

Grace was coming along as well, dancing with flair and finesse. Of all his sisters, Grace was the most likely to marry a prince, or a king. She was a tad snobbish and took to being the daughter of a duke with utmost vigor. Mama loved the middle lassie's fervor, of course, and if the Duchess had her druthers, all three MacGalloway daughters would behave exactly like Grace.

Unfortunately, his parents should have thought twice before they named the middle girl. If she were to marry a duke, she would not only be Grace, she would be *Her Grace.*

Martin snorted loudly.

"Duke!" exclaimed Miss Hay, beckoning him from the corridor. "How long have you been watching, Your Grace?"

His gaze slid to Smallwood who'd turned as red as the scarlet gown in Great-grandmama's portrait just behind the fellow. "Long enough to ken our steward ought to practice dancing with you ladies a wee bit more often."

"Oh, no." Jules released Modesty's hand and took a step back. "I have far too much work with which to occupy myself."

Giles cleared his throat from his place at the pianoforte. "Aye, and the silver isna being polished any faster either."

Martin ignored them both. "What say you, Miss Hay? Perhaps you and the lassies ought to take these working men away from their duties one afternoon per week?"

"No. Please," Smallwood objected.

The governess smacked the little man's arm with her twiggy baton. "This one certainly needs the practice, I'll say."

"Then 'tis settled." Grinning like a sated cat, Martin turned to the steward. "I've returned your ledger to your writing table. Please do speak to the lass about the adjustment we discussed this afternoon."

Martin started off but stopped and spoke over his shoulder, "Oh, and Smallwood?"

"Yes, Your Grace."

"Keep in mind dancing lessons will not be expected on hunting expeditions. We shall depart for the lodge on the morrow."

4

EN ROUTE TO THE DUNSCABY HUNTING LODGE.

For the second day, Julia sat astride a horse, trying to move her icy toes in her new, better-fitting and more fashionable boots while her gloved fingers gripped the reins, her breath billowing from her nose as if a dragon's fire smoldered in her lungs. "I see why Highlanders are renowned for being hearty characters."

Over his shoulder, Dunscaby gave her a quizzical look, his eyes even more stunning in the sunlight. "Why is that?"

"It takes a bit of grit to ride into the mountains in winter. Wasn't it during the Jacobite risings when the English had difficulty pursing the rebels?"

"Aye, and not long after the crown built roads and bridges. You may think this is rough going, but the journey has markedly improved in the past hundred years."

"Well then, I'm glad to be living in the nineteenth century."

"Come, Smallwood. Dunna tell me ye have no adventurous spirit."

"'Tis not the adventure I mind. But I was raised in

the South of England. Flat country mind you—rolling hills and whatnot."

"Well, then, I reckon you're in for an adventure you'll never forget."

Julia couldn't agree more—though her agreement had nothing to do with the man's remarks. During this jaunt, she'd already realized how ill thought-out her ruse had been. She hadn't considered the complexities of traveling with the duke, nor had she ever envisaged His Grace would bother traveling with her. Things as simple as relieving oneself had grown entirely complicated.

And Dunscaby seemed not to have inherited the tiniest bit of bashfulness, opening the falls of his buckskins right on the trail and...

Lord have mercy.

She'd tried not to look, she truly had.

Well, Julia thanked the stars he didn't wear a kilt when riding. Heaven only knew how mortifying that would have been to her sensibilities. Dukes were supposed to be aloof and pompous and absorbed in their pursuits, which didn't include taking an active role in managing their estates. Which is precisely why they needed stewards and dozens of servants to cater to their every whim. For heaven's sake, Dunscaby hadn't even brought his valet along on this outing. What the devil was he thinking?

Julia grumbled under her breath. Blast her St. Vincent luck, she'd earned a position with a positively, overly independent duke. Goodness, her father was an earl, and Papa had never taken more than a cursory interest in running Huntly Manor. Though after Julia's mother died, her father had preferred to stay in London where he gambled away his fortune until he succumbed to biliousness. Now the estate was in ruins. Papa had become an invalid, leaving Julia with no choice but to gallivant about the High-lands of Scotland, doing her best to hold things together.

Slowing the horses, Dunscaby pointed up the hill. "You can see her turrets from here."

Julia craned her neck. Sure enough, two conical towers peeked above the trees just as they might have done in the Middle Ages. "Who knew one would find a castle all the way up here?"

"Och, we've hardly climbed into the mountains. Beyond the lodge's gates is where the real hunting lies."

"Fascinating," she said, genuinely amazed, but barely able to believe they would be venturing farther into the wild the following day.

It took another quarter of an hour to ride up the steep slope. "The two towers of the castle were built by my ancestor during the Scottish Wars of Independence—Robert the Bruce's era, ye ken. Up here my kin were safe from the English. Moreover, it was an ideal location from which to stage many a raid."

Now that the ground had evened out, Julia had a much better view as they rode toward the lodge. The turrets flanked a keep with three stories. The entry was hidden by a recessed archway with a lamp swinging from medieval iron grillwork which appeared to be original.

"I loved this place when I was a lad," Dunscaby continued. "Played King Arthur with my brothers—especially Gibb. He and I dreamed of becoming knights whilst we learned to spar with wooden wasters."

"Lord Gibb," Julia recalled. "You mentioned he's an officer in the Royal Navy."

"Aye, a commander, champing at the bit for his first captain's commission."

"Oh my, a captain? Wouldn't he be rather young for such a post?"

His Grace grinned, his crossed incisors making him appear a tad devilish. "You forget, he's the son of a duke."

"Ah, yes. Such a lofty birthright does open doors."

"That sounds rather cynical, but you, sir, are a gentleman. Surely you've enjoyed privileges of the gentry."

"I suppose." Oh, the arguments rifling through Julia's mind. It was wonderful to be well-bred and wealthy. It was also quite the boon to be well-bred and male. However, being well-bred, penniless, and female had its extreme disadvantages.

After they dismounted, Dunscaby pounded on the enormous oaken doors, studded with blackened iron nails.

Julia looked upward, expecting to see the teeth of a portcullis staring down at her. Though the tracks for such a gate were in place, the sharp iron spikes were gone. Her gaze trailed to a foot-wide circle a different color than the other masonry. "I see you've filled in the kill hole."

"Aye, my grandfather decided it was no longer hospitable to pour boiling oil on the heads of marauding guests."

Julia chuckled as the door opened. The stunned face of an older gentleman gaped at them. "M'lord... er...beg your pardon, *Your Grace*? This is quite a surprise."

"Is it?" asked Dunscaby. "I sent word."

The man scratched his bald head as he stepped

aside. "We havena had a missive delivered since re-ceiving the news of your father's passing."

"Unfortunate. Nonetheless, I suppose it seems we've arrived." The duke gestured toward Julia. "This is my steward, Mr. Smallwood." His hand swung to-ward the caretaker. "Mr. MacIain."

She exchanged a cordial nod with the chap before turning her attention to the array of deer heads on the wall, flanked by medieval pikes, axes, several pieces of armor, and blackened iron wall sconces. The previous dukes may have filled in kill holes and removed a rusted portcullis, but Julia imagined there hadn't been a great many changes made to the hunting lodge over the years. Despite the cold, she already loved it here. No wonder His Grace had such fond childhood mem-ories of it.

"Show him to the summer bedchamber," said Dunscaby. "And there's no need to fret. We willna eat much and, with luck, on the morrow there'll be venison hanging in the cold room."

Mr. MacIain bowed. "Verra well, Your Grace."

Dunscaby headed toward a wheeled stairwell. "We've both been freezing our ballocks, riding through snow for the past two days. Each of us will need hot baths and something warm for the evening meal including soup if you have it." He disappeared, his voice echoing. "And fresh bread. I'm certain Mrs. MacIain has a loaf or two to spare."

"Bloody hell," the man mumbled under his voice.

"I'm so sorry for the inconvenience," Julia whis-pered still trying to recover from the duke's comment about her *absent* testicles. "His Grace did write ahead."

"'Tis the master's lodge. Should he arrive in the dead of night, we've naught but to smile and bring out the silver." The caretaker beckoned her toward the same stairwell where Dunscaby had disappeared. "Follow me."

Julia gripped the handle of her valise and climbed the winding stairs, her footsteps echoing loudly as if announcing she was going back in time and soon would be joining the Scottish army as they raided an English garrison at Stirling Castle. No wonder the duke and his brother imagined they were knights when they visited this place. Even the air felt so very archaic.

After leading her through a stone corridor lined with faded tapestries, Mr. MacIain opened a door, the hinges screeching. "Per His Grace's request, this will be your bedchamber. There ought to be some flax tow and wood by the hearth. If you'll excuse me, there is much to be done."

"Thank you." Julia expected the room to be yellow, or perhaps green, but the walls were lined with tapestries and the plaster ceiling striped with wooden rafters. "Can you tell me why they call this the summer bedchamber?"

"It faces west. When the sun's shining in summer, 'tis overwarm in here."

As the door closed, Julia set down her bag and rubbed her arms. If only the chamber had a modicum of warmth now, but presently she could see her breath. She hastened to the hearth and set to lighting the fire, elated when the flax tow ignited. With ever so much care, she blew on the little bundle and watched the flame build as she added twigs. Once it had grown strong enough, she put on a sizeable piece of wood. Rocking back onto her haunches, she removed her fur-lined gloves and stretched her hands toward the fire.

If only she could continue to warm herself beside

this hearth and read or embroider while the duke was out finding his stag come morning. Although stewards read, they most certainly did not embroider. No matter what Julia might want to do, on the morrow, she would be off on a shooting expedition.

The problem? Her father had never bothered to take her hunting or shown her how to shoot a musket for that matter. In truth, her nurturing had ended at the age of twelve when her mother succumbed to consumption.

Bless her soul.

STANDING BEFORE A RAGING FIRE, Martin stretched and ruffled his fingers through his wet hair. It felt reviving to be clean and warm. There was nothing as soothing as a steamy bath to thaw one's bones after a long winter's ride.

Even still, his melancholy had shed from his shoulders as soon as they'd set out from Newhailes. So many things had weighed heavily on his spirits, beginning with his father's fatal bout of dropsy, followed by the rush home, the funeral, the seemingly endless days of mourning. On top of that, being informed by Mr. MacCutcheon that the business dealings of estate had been neglected for the better part of three years hadn't helped matters.

No wonder Martin had suffered a spell of self-doubt.

Well, no more. Of all his estates, the lodge provided a capital escape and it was exactly what he needed to reestablish his priorities. Da wouldn't want him to drop into melancholy, nor his mother and siblings for that matter. It was time to start anew. Besides, it was almost spring. A season of fresh beginnings.

And now that Smallwood had been hired, the business side of his inheritance was in good hands. In fact, when Martin returned to Newhailes, he'd tell his mother to begin her plans for his sister Charity to embark upon a fabulous London Season—one that would make up for this year. Andrew and Philip would be home from university soon, and Martin needed to put his head together with Smallwood about coming up with a plan to see them well-placed. Of course, Martin missed Gibb the most, and the commander presently posed the greatest worry. His closest brother had chosen a life at sea at a time when Britain seemed to be at war on all sides. However, barring his ship sinking, Gibb was man enough to handle himself.

Martin checked his pocket watch. Nearly time for the evening meal, he ran a comb through his hair and headed for the summer bedchamber.

Not bothering to knock, he pushed open the door, finding Smallwood sitting in a tub of water up to his neck.

"Aaaaaaah!" the man squawked like a hen, sat forward, and wrapped his arms around his knees. "Do you not know how to knock...ah...Your Grace?"

"Bloody hell," Martin said, sauntering inside. "'Tis nearly time to eat. And here you are languishing in a bloody bath."

Smallwood's gaze shifted to the top of Martin's head, his hair still damp. "Did you not linger in your tub? Did you not enjoy the warm water helping you feel your toes once again? Besides, I'll wager Mr. Mac-Iain brought your water first."

Martin slid into the chair by the hearth, his mouth suddenly dry. Good God, Smallwood had slender shoulders as well as an inordinately long neck. The man's skin was lily white, oddly making Martin think of tracing finger along the arc where the fellow's neck met his shoulder to see if it was actually as soft as it appeared. Instead, he clenched his fist and growled. "I shall grant you quarter on that count, but it doesna allay the fact that 'tis time to go below stairs and eat. I'm bloody starved. And by the looks of your bones, you could do with a month of hearty meals."

The steward leaned his chin atop his knees. "Come to think of it, I am rather famished."

"Och, is the water too hot?" Martin dunked his fingers. "The back of your neck has turned scarlet."

"No—ah—I'm fine—I mean, I am well." Smallwood peered out the corner of his eye like a nervous finch. "'Tis just I'm not accustomed to having my *employer* pay a visit whilst I'm bathing."

"Come now, we're both men."

"That may very well be but—"

"Never ye mind." Martin sat back, spread his knees, and adjusted his loins, the touch causing a zing of arousal. He quickly moved his hand to the armrest. Devil take it, there wasn't an unmarried female within a day's riding.

"I've never met a man as bashful as you," Martin grumbled. *Nor as delicate.* Hell, the wee man either had a bladder the size of a gallon cask or he was the most bashful fellow in all of Britain. *Mayhap he's embarrassed about the size of his wares.* "'Tis obvious you had no brothers to contend with when growing up. I suppose there'll be no changing you now."

"I-I suppose not."

Stretching out his legs, Martin crossed his ankles. "Have you given any thought to establishing a business venture on behalf of my brothers?"

"Um...I have..." Smallwood curled deeper into the tub. "Cotton."

"Just cotton?" Martin asked, his gaze again slipping to the man's shoulder—gently curved, oddly fascinating.

"Not *just* cotton, but the industry has grown, increasing shipments from the Americas by twelve hundred percent. Why not ship MacGalloway whisky to America and return with cotton?"

Standing, Martin swiped a hand across his eyes, his mind cogitating on what he'd just heard. "Good Lord, I kent the industry had grown, but I didna realize it has exploded." Still, there were many reasons to be skeptical. "I'm not convinced. Ye ken as the Duke of Dunscaby, I must remind you that only four years past King George signed the Slave Trade Act. Not only as a high-ranking member of the House of Lords, I personally canna support an industry and profit either directly or indirectly off the backs of the enslaved."

"Though I'd much prefer to have this conversation after my bath, I must advise that we are of like minds, sir. Before I presented you with the idea, I wanted confirmation from a Mr. O'Brian, who recently wrote a letter to the Gazette about Irish sharecroppers in America joining together to produce cotton by the fruits of their own labor."

Suddenly, Smallwood's shoulders didn't look so bloody weak. "Irishmen, you say? But can they compete with the yields from large plantations?"

"That is exactly why I wrote to Mr. O'Brian first. However, since you brought it up, I must say his letter to the editor states that the coalition *can* compete, though evidently the plantation owners are trying to shoulder them out. Which is why—"

"They need a sole customer who can quietly acquire the entirety of their harvests."

"Exactly."

Martin kicked his heels and danced a jig. "Bloody brilliant! Gibb could sail to and fro, expanding my whisky venture whilst we're establishing ourselves in cotton. The twins could take orders, outfit a mill with looms and the like, and with the dukedom behind it, the lads would soon gain a reputation of making the finest muslin cloth in Europe."

"Look there, Duke, a kernel of an idea and you already have a mind to build an empire." The water trickled. "Perhaps we can discuss it more after I dress. Then I'll join you in the dining hall."

"Verra well. Ten minutes." Martin headed for the door. "I'll meet you anon."

5

After dinner, Julia glared at herself in the mirror, furiously bushing out her shoulder-length locks. Though it was still unfashionably long, she'd had Willaby cut her hair to her shoulders to masquerade as a man. Of course, with this venture she'd given up her chances of ever finding a husband. She'd left her home and everything familiar.

But her woeful state of affairs wasn't why she was taking out her ire on her tresses. Because of her situation, she was in a very precarious position and at all times she needed to exercise the utmost care to hide her gender. How could she have allowed herself to luxuriate in the bath when she knew dinner would soon be served?

For the love of God, Martin had walked in on her when she was submerged in a tub of water.

Not Martin! Never, ever think of the man's given name again, blast you!

The *accursed duke* had walked into her chamber when she wore not a stitch of clothing. Moreover, he'd tried to make idle conversation while she was naked, obviously uncomfortable, and curled into a tight ball.

It was a miracle he hadn't realized she was a woman right then and there.

She stood back and tugged on her nightshirt, then slipped into her father's old silk banyan and tied the sash. She must find a way to go about performing her duties without spending half her waking hours in His Grace's presence. Perhaps when they returned to Newhailes she ought to suggest he take the family to Stack Castle.

Most likely, they did head north for the summer. From what Julia understood, the castle was on the shore overlooking the famous Stacks of Dunscaby. The only problem was she needed to visit the old fortress as soon as possible as well. There had been some accounting questions she had with the distillery, and the crofter's rents needed to be reviewed not to mention she truly ought to make an effort to meet them all.

Perhaps she ought to arrange a journey up there by herself while the family was still at Newhailes. She could inform Dunscaby hours before her departure, too late for him to change his schedule and accompany her. Yes, her plan would work. She'd spend a month at Stack, then return to Newhailes after the family moved north. Doubtless, the MacGalloways would go to London for the Season come autumn, especially since Lady Charity was on the marriage mart.

And if the Duchess had her way, her eldest son would take marriage seriously as well. Though Julia's heart twisted at the thought of Martin courting a potential wife.

I cannot possibly care. He's the dratted Duke of Dunscaby!

Regardless, if she played her cards right, Julia

would be able to communicate with His Grace through correspondence for ages. Her responsibilities would be efficiently dispatched, and her secret kept under wraps.

Sighing loudly, she flopped onto the bed. Now all she needed was to undertake a bit of manly hunting in the morning, let the duke shoot to his delight, and they'd swiftly return to Newhailes where she'd immediately leave for John o'Groats the tiny northern village near Stack Castle.

And not a moment too soon.

When Dunscaby had caught her in the bath, Julia hadn't merely been mortified. She smoothed her hand along her throat. Something in his gaze had made her insides stir like warm cream.

Mortified or not, she'd thought he might touch her when he dipped his fingers into the water. Worse, she'd wanted him to do so. Her entire body ached for his touch. Even a slight brush of his fingertip would have done.

Julia moaned at the thought, closing her eyes, and imagining Martin smoothing his big hands across her shoulders. Martin sliding his fingers into her hair. Martin's lips caressing hers.

Gasping, she bolted upright.

No. No. No!

AWAKENED FROM A DEAD SLEEP, Martin's eyes flashed open. "What the blazes?" He could have sworn he heard a woman scream. Stumbling out of bed, he wiped the sleep from his eyes.

The sound couldn't have come from Mrs. MacIain. The couple slept in the chamber two floors below just off the kitchens. There was at least a hundred tons of stone between the upper rooms and the servant's quarters.

I ken what I heard.

As the cobwebs of sleep cleared from his mind, there was naught to do but investigate. He pattered across the floor, took a twig from the wood pile, and lit it in the smoldering coals, then put the flame to a candle.

How the bloody hell had a woman managed to slip into the castle? No matter how much he tried to rationalize it, nothing made sense.

He'd left Smallwood to his own devices shortly after the evening meal, but even if the steward were a womanizer, they were twenty miles from the nearest village where one might find a willing female.

And Smallwood most definitely didn't seem the type.

Unless some unsuspecting, terribly lost woman stumbled upon the lodge, which was more unlikely than the prospect of a pint-sized steward riding forty miles to fetch a damsel, bring her back to his bed-chamber, and ravish her.

Martin grabbed the brass candlestick and marched along the corridor, this time knocking rather than pushing through the door. "Smallwood?"

"A moment," the man said to the tune of rustling and what sounded like a chair scraping the floorboards.

Well, if the steward was indeed buggaring a woman, Martin would catch him in the bloody act. "What the blazes are you on about?" he bellowed, barging inside.

Standing beside the hearth with a burning twig in

his hand, Jules gaped, his eyes round as shillings and filled with terror. "I-I b-beg your pardon?"

"I heard a woman scream." Martin marched across the floor and threw back the bedclothes. "I swear I did."

"I heard the scream as well, Your Grace." The man's voice warbled as if he were terrified out of his wits. "But it came from no woman."

"Come again?"

"I admit, my voice tends to be a bit high-pitched when I'm frightened."

"Wait a moment." The coverlet slid from Martin's grasp. "*You* made that hideous noise?"

Smallwood raked a hand through his hair—hair that had no right to be shimmering in the goddamn firelight and then falling across a chocolatey brown eye. Damnation, the fellow was effeminate. "I haven't suffered a night terror in some time," he explained. "But one came on so violently, I'm afraid to admit that I'm still shaking."

He was. The twig in his hand flickered through the air like a firefly. Well, Martin certainly was not going to give the namby-pamby a pat on the head and a comforting word. He thrust a fist onto his hip. "Good God, man, get ahold of yourself."

"Forgive me. As I said, this sort of thing hasn't happened since I was a g—*uh*—much younger. Not to worry." Smallwood managed to steady his hand enough to light a candle. "I doubt it will happen again for years."

Martin spied a flagon on the sideboard, then gestured to a chair. "Sit. I'll pour you a drink to calm your nerves."

"Allow me, I'm coming good. You mustn't serve me with your own hand, sir."

Martin pulled the stopper out of the flagon and waved it at the wee man. "Ballocks to that. Sit your arse in the chair whilst I pour."

"Yes, sir."

"Ye ken what you need, Smallwood?"

"Aside from a good night's sleep?" asked the wee steward, crossing his arms and ankles and looking quite out of sorts.

"A bloody woman." Martin couldn't believe those words just spewed from his mouth given he'd suspected the fellow of inappropriate ravaging. But damn it all, what Smallwood needed was *appropriate* swiving with a *willing* partner.

The man sputtered. "I beg your pardon, but I disagree. A woman would provide too much of a distraction."

"Perhaps you're right." Martin poured two glasses and handed one to Smallwood. "But I sense you're bloody tense. I tend to relax when I visit the Lodge, but you, on the other hand, seem to be strung tighter than a harp string."

"Forgive me. I suppose I'm worried."

"About?"

"Well, I would have liked to have had a few more weeks to work through the ledgers at Newhailes. And I do need to pay a visit to the distillery and the crofters up north sooner than later. Perhaps accompanying you on this *diversion* has made me feel as if I'm shirking my duties."

"First of all, you're not shirking." Martin slid into the chair opposite. "I required your companionship. Most of my friends are still in London for the Season. My brothers are off at school or sailing the high seas. Quite frankly, you were the most accessible traveling companion."

The steward sipped his whisky, not blinking or coughing this time. "Well, then, I must say it is an honor to be included in your company."

"That's better." Martin took a long drink, savoring the fire as it seared his throat. "I find I quite enjoy your company as well."

Smallwood's eyebrows arched—they, too, were delicate, just like the man. "Why is that, sir?"

"Och, you're not full of bravado for one thing. You also dunna seem to be afraid to tell me your mind." Martin pondered as he fetched the flagon to pour another round. "Interestingly, there are certain circumstances when you come off as a bit unschooled and timid, and other times when you are more straightforward than any man I ken."

Jules tugged the sash of his banyan. "When it comes to matters regarding the estate, I feel I am qualified to advise you. Otherwise, it is best for me to practice restraint with my opinions."

"Hmm. But when it comes to matters of the world I suspect you are duly inexperienced. Pray, how long were you in Brixham's employ?"

"Five years, sir."

"And during that time did you travel with him? Visit his rooms in London, perchance?"

"Brixham treated me more like a servant than a gentleman of the working class as you do. He preferred me to remain out of sight and rarely ever took my advice, thus he spent and spent..." Smallwood let out a breath. "Forgive me, it seems whisky makes me wag my tongue overmuch."

"Aye, I suppose it does affect many men that way." After depositing his glass on the table, Martin stood. "I'll leave you now. We both need a good night's rest and neither of us will receive it if we continue to talk about irresponsible fops like the Earl of Brixham."

Before he left, Martin could have sworn Smallwood cringed. Poor fellow. Working for the earl must have been nothing short of miserable.

6

W hen Mrs. MacIain came into the summer
bedchamber carrying a porcelain ewer, Julia
opened her eyes. "Good morning, madam."

"Good morn." After setting the pitcher on the
washstand, the caretaker's wife stirred the fire. "His
Grace suggested ye break your fast with him in the
dining hall below stairs at half-past seven."

"Thank you." Julia said, retrieving her pocket
watch from the bedside table and checking the time.
Wonderful. She had been cowering in the dark since
the duke left her chamber last eve and hadn't slept.
Now she needed to ready herself for today's hunt
within a half hour. Rolling to her back, she stared at
the bed curtains until Mrs. MacIain took her leave.

Bless it, the last thing she wanted to do was traipse
around the Highlands with a musket. If hell actually
existed this must be what it felt like to be there...a
very cold hell, that is. She was so entirely daft. Why
had her dreams chosen last night to terrorize her to
the point of screaming? Even now, every time she
closed her eyes she saw Mr. Skinner's ghoulish face as
he'd threatened Papa with eviction. Why her father
had stooped so low as to borrow funds from an insect

like that moneylender was beyond Julia's comprehension.

She'd only met the chap once and he'd acted as acerbic and unpleasant as he looked, as if he'd been born with a cruel frown fixed upon his face. Julia shuddered. The venom in his threats still haunted her.

Yes, she'd told Dunscaby that she hadn't had a nightmare in years, but that wasn't exactly the truth. Of late, Julia nearly always awakened to a cold sweat in the dead of night because of Mr. Skinner. Because of his demands she had been forced to don men's clothing and cast away her dreams of one day falling in love and having a happy family of her own.

But never before had she come awake screaming. She'd been sound asleep and unable to deepen her voice. Worse, Dunscaby had heard her.

I must never, ever cry out in my sleep again!

Realizing her list of *never agains* was growing rather large, Julia lumbered out of bed, shrugged into her banyan, and hastened to the washstand. After splashing her face, she still felt as if Satan had taken a hammer to the inside of her head. But there was naught to be done but to quickly dress and ready herself for a day of shooting.

Breakfast was enormous—similar to the fare Julia remembered being served at Huntly Manor before her mother had passed away. Mrs. MacIain must have been awake half the night preparing eggs, ham, bannocks, blood pudding, sausages, and more. Over half the food still remained when they headed outside where Mr. MacIain already had the horses waiting.

The caretaker handed Julia a musket, a powder horn, and a pouch heavy with musket balls. "This wee beasty has a bit of a kick, but she shoots straight."

"Kick?" Julia asked, balancing the weapon in the

crooks of her elbows while juggling the shot and power.

"'Tis already charged. Just point and shoot, ye ken?"

She glanced at the trigger. Though she hadn't fired a musket before, she'd seen it done. Her father even owned a pair of dueling pistols, not that he'd ever used them. "Jolly good," she said, trying to sound like Papa.

"We'll ride through the glen," said Dunscaby, mounting his horse. "MacIain says the deer have been grazing in the moors near the shore of Loch Tulla."

Julia slid her musket into a sheath affixed to the saddle, shoved her boot into the stirrup and swung onto the horse. Smiling to herself, she'd grown rather adept at mounting and riding astride. It was actually far easier than negotiating a sidesaddle, which was one activity in which she professed to be rather proficient.

Clad in a beaver hat with a woolen scarf wrapped around her ears and tucked into her great coat, she took the reins into her fur-lined gloved hands and looked to the skies. "I say, we may have a spot of fine weather for this outing."

"For the hunt, Mr. Smallwood," Dunscaby corrected as he headed into a grove of trees, parted by a narrow path. "Och aye, with luck, we'll have a fine day of shooting as well."

Julia said a silent prayer and crossed herself. With luck, she'd survive this excursion without showing her hand.

AFTER AN HOUR of following the trail to the loch, Martin spotted deer droppings. He hopped down from his horse and crouched, stirring the spoor with a stick. "This is fresh." A low chuckle rumbled in his throat as he cast aside the stick and pulled his musket out of its scabbard. "We'll walk from here."

"As you wish." Smallwood dismounted, retrieved his weapon, and stood holding the barrel with the butt on the ground. He posed an amusing sight—the musket was as long as the man was tall. But he didn't seem to notice anything amiss. "The lake is beautiful."

"'Tis a Highland loch," Martin corrected, giving the water a cursory glance. "Aye, the morning's ice is still rimming the shore."

"Swimming is out of the question, then?" the steward jested with a shudder.

"Not unless you want your cods floating in your throat."

Smallwood snorted. "You do have a way with words, Your Grace."

"What four years at university will do for a man."

After they hobbled their horses, Martin led the way along the shore. He knew exactly where they'd find a good hide. "No talking from here on out," he whispered looking to the steward's boots. "And watch where you plant your feet. A snapped twig will echo across the water like a cannon blast."

Martin paused. "You've a pair of new Hessians."

"Yes, sir."

"But they're distinctly smaller than those enormous shoes you have been wearing."

"Ah..." Shifting the musket to his shoulder, the wee man shrugged. "The others were borrowed from Brixham's butler."

Martin looked to the heavens with a soft chuckle. "Mayhap your dancing will improve."

Smallwood smirked.

Holding his finger to his lips, the duke led the way, not surprised that the wee man had suddenly become much lighter on his feet. Once they reached the outcropping, he pointed up the crag and turned his lips toward the steward's ear. "If I'm right, there'll be a buck or a herd just over those rocks."

The man tilted his bright red nose upward. "Lead on."

"I like your spirit." Martin slung his musket over his shoulder and started the climb. He'd scaled these rocks more times than he could remember and in all seasons. After he reached the top, he crouched behind the craggy rock and peered across the swath of moorland sloping toward the water.

Without a deer in sight, he shifted his gaze beyond the shores of the loch and up the four peaks of Black Mount where their white peaks dominated the crystal-blue sky. By God, no matter how many times he visited this spot, its raw beauty always took his breath away.

Behind him, Smallwood grunted to the tune of a boot slipping on stone. Aye, the man needed a good turn in the wilderness to toughen up. It was eminently clear the steward had spent far too much time with a quill in his hand. True, he'd lost his father when he was but a lad, which was yet another reason why Martin felt the need to take the steward under his wing.

He pulled the spyglass out of his coat as the chap joined him. He waggled his eyebrows before he raised the glass to his eye and panned it from the first peak down to the grasslands, and along the shore of the loch. Detecting a bit of movement, he drew in a sharp breath and held very still. Ever so slowly, he turned the barrel to sharpen the image. "Och, he's a beauty."

"You have a deer in your sights already?" Small-wood whispered.

"Eight points, mark me." Martin snapped the spy-glass closed. "And if he's lived that long, he'll be skittish. We'll have to be stealthy for certain."

Smallwood rubbed his palms together. "And I'll wager you have a plan."

"I take hunting verra seriously, sir." Martin pointed away from the buck. "We'll climb up the slope, creep around, and come down along that far ridge where we'll have cover. The beasty will never see us coming."

"What will we do once we shoot him? Will he not be too heavy to carry?"

"That's what the horses are for—but only after the hunt."

Martin took the lead, picking his way up the slope. About a half-mile up, he found a game trail. "I'll wager the beast uses this path himself."

The foliage grew thicker and the trail waxed and waned, sometimes appearing to have vanished. When finally Martin was certain they had circumnavigated the buck, he readied his musket and slowed the pace, hunching over as he crept, carefully placing every footfall. Smallwood's footsteps had grown fainter as well. The man possessed natural hunting instincts for certain. If nothing else, he was a quick learner and what he lacked in skill, he made up for in intelligence.

Ahead, a tree rustled. Raising his palm, Martin immediately stopped.

A low grunt came with the snap of a twig beneath the beast's hoof.

After raising his musket firmly against his shoulder, Martin caressed the icy trigger with his finger. He inched forward, peering through the foliage, his heart beating a thunderous rhythm in his ears, his senses honed, keen to detect the tiniest sound or movement.

And then his quarry moved, the soft blur of the stag's tan coat barely discernable from the barren branches surrounding him. Holding his breath, Martin dared to take another step. The snow beneath his feet crackled like fireworks at a fête.

The deer's head snapped up, his ears shifting forward.

As their gazes met, the buck froze.

With the next explosive beat of his heart, Martin closed his finger on the trigger.

Boom!

Smallwood stepped beside him as the smoke cleared. "Excellent shooting, Your Grace."

"Bloody beautiful shooting. Right between the eyes. The beast didna ken what hit him." Together they marched ahead and stood over the stag. "He'll feed the MacIain's for months to come."

"Shall we fetch the horses?"

"Och, nay. You havena taken a shot." Martin nudged the fellow with his elbow. "Do you not want to find a beast of your own?"

Smallwood glanced to the horizon. A swell of black clouds had risen above the peaks, the grey blur warning that show was already falling on the hills. "It appears as if we're in for a squall. Perhaps I'll have better luck another time."

"Verra well," Martin agreed. "We'll walk along the shore. The going will be easier."

By God, it felt good to be away from his responsibilities. A day in the Highlands and all the duties of dukedom diminished as if nothing mattered except, perhaps, the next meal.

But they hadn't walked but a dozen yards when gusts of wind swept down from the mountains, turning the loch from glassy and peaceful to tempestuous, tipped with caps of white. Martin stepped up the pace, hopping across the same rocks where he'd played as a lad. A snowflake landed on his nose as he leaped onto an enormous crag with a sheer drop to the water. "My siblings and I played king of the mountain on this stone."

"I'll wager you claimed the royal throne more often than not."

"Och, Smallwood, you wouldna be insinuating that I might have had an unfair advantage would you now?"

"That's exactly what I'm saying." Smallwood looked up from the boulder below. "You're the eldest and the largest, I presume."

"Such is the way of things." Martin toed the groove in the stone where he protected his youngest sister. "Though after Modesty came along, I always allowed her to be my chief minister."

"I can picture it now." Smallwood fisted his hips, assuming a commanding pose. "'I'm holding the rock and you'd best not challenge me, else you'll dunk the wee bairn, and then there'll be hell to pay!'"

"Your Scottish accent is abominable." Martin guffawed. "If you believe I'm such an ogre, then you dunna ken how underhanded Gibb, Andrew, and Phillip can be. And Frederick is the most devious of the lot aside from Grace, of course."

Smallwood climbed up beside him and peered over the edge. "Good heavens, 'tis farther down than I realized."

Martin eyed him. The poor fellow had never been privy to a bit of brotherly love. Perhaps now was the time to give him a taste of what it was like. Bellowing with a devious laugh, he grabbed the man's arm as if he were going to toss him into the loch. "Ye'd best watch yourself, else ye'll be plunging to the icy depths!"

"Not me!" Smallwood squealed as he yanked his arm away, the jolt making him totter toward the water.

As Martin lunged forward to steady the steward, the heel of his boot skidded across the slippery rock. "Whoa!" he bellowed, completely losing his footing, suddenly plunging toward the white-capped swells. With a smack, his toes pierced the surface while the back of his head hit something hard. His ears rang with the same shrill scream from the night before.

Every sinew in Martin's body tensed with the attack of frigid water enveloping him. The air whooshed from his lungs. And as his head went under, the sky faded into blackness.

7

Julia clapped her hands over her mouth, watching the duke plunge into the ice-encrusted lake. "No!" she shrieked, not caring a fig about how she sounded.

With a dunking thud, an enormous splash splattered across the boulder. "Your Grace!" she yelled, peering over the edge, clutching her fists atop her hammering heart.

His body floated in the white-crested waves, face down and unmoving.

God, no!

In two leaps, Julia landed on the shore and plunged into the frigid swells. "Martin!" she cried as she trudged forward until she was hip-deep and grabbing him by the shoulders. Using the water's buoyancy, she bore down, struggling to flip him onto his back. Good Lord, he was already blue. With all her strength, she dragged him onto the shore. "Your Grace!"

When he didn't respond, she patted his face. Hard. "Please!"

With a sputtering cough, the duke's head lolled to the side.

Thank God he's alive!

But if she didn't act quickly, he'd succumb to the cold, no question. She unbuttoned her great coat, shrugged it off, and covered his legs with the dry half. Next, she removed her woolen topcoat and draped it over His Grace's torso. Dropping to her knees, she clasped his face between her palms. "I'll fetch a horse. I can see them from here. I'll only be a moment, you hear? Stay alive, blast you!"

Tears streamed down her face as she sprinted toward the horses slowed by wet trousers and water squishing from her boots.

This is all my fault!

Julia had feared the danger straight away. She never should have climbed up beside him. The rock was slick with a dusting of snow. But did she offer one single word of caution?

No.

She'd been too afraid of sounding like a ninny. Instead, she'd joined the duke and played along with his antics.

And now look at what has happened.

Her teeth chattered and her hand shook terribly as she unbuckled her horse's hobble, mounted, then galloped back to where Martin lay motionless on the ground.

"Your Grace," she called loudly, hoping to rouse him. "I need you to help me."

Dunscaby opened his eyes but budged not an inch.

Hopping down, Julia steeled her mind against the cold as she straddled him, grasped his collar, and shook. "You need to mount the horse this instant!"

She shoved her hands under his arms, dug her heels into the snow, and tugged him to a sitting position. "Come, you must do better than that. You're twice my size. I cannot lift you on my own."

Grunting with the strain of his weight, she shouted. "Help me, dash you!"

When his head dropped forward. She looked toward the trees. They'd ridden nearly an hour before they reached the loch. He'd die if she left him and ran for help. Making her decision, she moved one hand to his nape and slapped the duke across the face as hard as she could. "Wake up!"

He grunted and jerked away.

"Martin," she said in a most forceful masculine voice. "If you want to survive, you will mount the horse this minute."

As he started to move, Julia pulled him by the hands. "That's it. All you must to do is stand."

Once he was on his feet, she kept one arm around his waist, reached for the reins, drew the horse beside them, and urged His Grace to place his hands on the saddle. Tightening the grasp around his waist, she helped him raise his foot and guided it into the stirrup.

"Excellent," she said, breathless, crouching low, she moved behind him and placed both hands on his buttocks. "Pull yourself up whilst I push."

Using both her legs and her arms, she shoved his bottom with every ounce of strength she possessed, but it wasn't enough. Julia clenched her teeth and strained. "You will *die* if you do not mount this horse!"

Threatening Dunscaby with certain death seemed to do the trick as with a guttural groan, he somehow managed to add enough effort to drag his leg over the saddle.

Muttering a swift prayer of thanks, Julia grabbed her coats then quickly mounted behind him. Leaning

forward to gather the reins, she spotted a slick swath
of blood on her glove.

Oh, no.

The duke hunched over the horse's withers, blood
oozing from his head, staining his collar and
neckcloth.

"Hold firm, Your Grace." She kicked her heels and
slapped the reins. "There's no time to spare!"

"Mr. MacIain," Julia roared as she pulled hard on the
reins, stopping the horse outside the lodge's entry.
"MacIain!" she yelled louder.

The door swung open to the wide-eyed caretaker.
"What the devil?"

"His Grace fell in the lake and struck his head.
Quickly, I need your help taking him to his chamber."
Julia rapidly patted Dunscaby's back. "Are you awake,
sir?"

Not moving, the duke still hung precariously over
the horse's withers and neck.

"Martha!" MacIain called over his shoulder. "We
need your help out here."

Julia said nothing, but the man was right. She was
too small to carry even half of Martin MacGalloway all
the way above stairs. For heaven's sake, she never
would have been able to lever him onto the horse if he
hadn't the wits to add some effort himself.

Together the three of them struggled to some-
what-carry, somewhat-drag an unconscious Dunscaby up the narrow, winding staircase. Julia's
affinity for medieval architecture waned. The ma-
sons of eras past put no thought whatsoever into the
fact that human beings were not curved and would

not easily be carried through tight-walled, circular stairwells.

By the time they managed to roll the duke atop his mattress, Julia was ready to collapse. But time was still of the essence. She shook her arms and stretched to her full height. "We must remove his damp clothes and stoke the fire. We need hot water and clean cloths. He suffered a blow to his head when he fell. Moreover, his horse is still hobbled by Loch Tulla and there's a horrible squall brewing."

"His musket?" asked MacIain as if the gun were almost as important as His Grace.

Julia shrugged. "Most likely doused in the lake. I must have left mine nearby as well, and I'll doubt you'll be able to find the deer he felled."

"If you can remove his clothing, Mr. Smallwood, I'll fetch the horse and see what I can do about finding those muskets—especially Dunscaby's. 'Twas His Grace's great-grandfather's, used in the '45," MacIain said, turning toward his wife. "Boil water and bring up some cloths."

"Do you have a salve to ward off infection?" Julia asked.

The woman started away. "Aye. With eight Mac-Galloway children, there's always a need for a medicine bundle. I'll bring it as well."

Though the chamber seemed warm compared to the air outdoors, Julia added two sticks of wood to the fire. After brushing off her hands, the realization dawned...the MacIain's were gone and left her alone to remove His Grace's wet garments. Her gaze darted to the bed while awareness swirled in the pit of her stomach—awareness and trepidation.

She must undress Dunscaby quickly. The problem was she'd never actually disrobed a man before. Certainly, she was supposed to be a man and had removed her clothing, but if the duke ever discovered her ruse he'd be mortified.

Or she'd be mortified.

Regardless, he'd never forgive her. Of that there was absolutely no question.

Mortification aside, she mustn't waste one more minute. What had to be done, must be done. The duke's lips were blue and if he remained in those damp clothes, he'd catch his death.

Julia started with his boots and hose. "We'll have you warm in no time, Your Grace," she said, tugging his boot with all her might while Dunscaby offered no reply.

"Bless it, are these monstrosities fused to your feet?" Julia widened her stance as she twisted and heaved until the blasted boot finally dislodged. She did the same with the other and removed his hose, finding his feet stark white, wrinkled, and icy cold.

Rather than attack his buckskins next, she moved to his collar and untied his neckcloth. Then made quick work of unbuttoning his greatcoat, coat, waistcoat, and shirt. It took no effort at all to spread them open.

And then she staggered backward.

Lord have mercy.

Julia tried not to look, she truly did, but what young woman could avert her eyes from such a display of masculinity? She'd never seen such a chest—square and powerful, peppered with blond ringlets and tipped with succulent nipples. Unable to resist, she tiptoed forward and lightly brushed her fingertip over a tiny peak.

Snapping her hand away, she gasped.

'Tis as taut as mine when I'm cold.

Something warm fluttered low in her belly, something very low, indeed. So strong the pull, it made her breathing more labored, made her want to kiss him as well. She shifted her gaze to his mouth—pink, slightly parted in repose. Before she thought, her tongue grew a mind of its own and ran across her bottom lip.

No!

No matter how much she wanted to kiss this man, he wasn't hers. He could never be hers regardless of the fact that she was the daughter of an earl. She'd donned her father's clothing and thus had ended her days as a marriageable woman.

Shaking her head, she set to the arduous task of rolling him from side to side and fully removing his coats and shirt. When at last his upper half was bare, she covered his chest with a blanket and unbuttoned his falls.

"Do you need some help?" asked Mrs. MacIain, entering with a kettle in one hand and a basket in the other. "I've brought everything you asked for."

Julia straightened. "If we can pull off his buckskins, we'll be able to move him beneath the bedclothes and he'll be all the warmer."

Together they managed to inch the trousers away, revealing only a paper-thin pair of damp smalls which left nothing to the imagination and Julia unable to breathe.

Mrs. MacIain smiled as if she'd just won a prize. "Och, MacGalloway men make fine specimens, they do."

Julia's face burned and she quickly grabbed the bedclothes and covered him. "I beg your pardon, madam."

"Nothing I havena seen afore." Mrs. MacIain

stepped away, sighing. "He'll make some woman happy. That's for certain."

Julia didn't want to think about Martin—*er*—the Duke of Dunscaby making any person of the female persuasion happy. Especially since he would never be able to make *her* happy. The idea positively made her shoulders tenser than they already were. She must put the idea out of her mind until the day came when she had to face the inevitable reality. Besides, her plans were to avoid His Grace's presence as much as possible, leaving him to be a wife-seeking duke and her to be a content and efficient steward, not some simpering, swooning waif.

She reached for a clean cloth and doused it in the water. "Did you say you brought a salve?"

Mrs. MacIain pulled a pot out of the basket and set it on the bedside table. "This is my own recipe. Nothing better."

"Excellent." Julia gently turned the duke's head to the side and dabbed the wound with gentle brushes. "Thank you."

"Would you like me to tend him?" asked the matron.

As she shook her head, Julia's stomach clenched. There was no chance she would step aside and leave Martin's care in the hands of a woman she hardly knew. "I ought to do it. After all, I feel responsible."

"Verra well, then. I'll bring you a bite to eat and—"

"I'd love a pot of tea if it is not too much trouble."

"'Tis no trouble at all. But once you have His Grace set to rights, you'd best don some warm clothes of your own, else there'll be two of you abed."

8

Sitting on a chair at Dunscaby's bedside, Julia ran her hand across the duke's forehead for the umpteenth time. He hadn't developed a fever, thank the stars, but he was still unconscious.

"I would give my life to see you open your eyes," she whispered, her face hovering above his. Up close, his features were more prominent. Etchings of crinkles at the corners of his eyes, the shadow of the evening's beard along his jaw. How interesting that his whiskers were so much darker than the hair on his head. "I might even deign to share with you all of my secrets, which are more shocking that you'll ever guess."

The truth danced on the tip of her tongue as if it were a bird trying to escape its cage. But even though she had a captive audience who was oblivious to everything Julia said, she mustn't utter a word to reveal her true identity.

Instead, she combed her fingers through the sunkissed hair on his crown. "I cannot believe a man as robust as you possesses locks this soft."

But she wasn't stoking his forehead for her own

enjoyment. With luck, Dunscaby would find it soothing somewhere in the depths of his mind.

"My mother died of consumption when I was on the verge of adolescence." Continuing to swirl her fingers, Julia figured revealing tidbits of her past wouldn't be too telling. "I was devastated. Of course, that's where my nurturing stopped. My father took to the bottle and never returned. He passed away not long after, leaving me not only to fend for myself, but to manage the estate as best I could."

The story she'd relayed about her fictional father was that he'd succumbed to jaundice, which she and Willaby had decided was similar enough to her father's disease of biliousness—though Julia prayed Papa would fully recuperate.

"Truly, he wasn't a bad man," she continued. "Mama's passing left him with a broken heart from which he never recovered. Except it wasn't only drinking that led to his ruin. He developed an insatiable appetite for the card tables in some of the East End's most unsavory gambling hells. I received and paid invoices for his innumerous losses, even some from ladies of the night. I even knew about a mistress he kept in a town house in Chelsea."

Julia swirled her fingers over Dunscaby's crown. "With the help of father's solicitor, I dutifully took care of everything. But don't think I didn't try to pull him out of the mire. Several times I pleaded with him to return to his country estate and take his respite. As time passed, he grew more and more belligerent and more careless with his money, until there was nothing left aside from the furniture and household effects. By that time, most of the servants had been dismissed, the solicitor was long gone, and I was trying to make ends meet in a decaying manor staffed only with a butler and a cook who also served as a housekeeper."

She stilled her hand and sighed. To her chagrin, everything she'd just uttered aside from the tidbit about her father dying was true to this day. Willaby and Mrs. May were the only two remaining servants at Huntly Manor.

"What did you do with the manor once your father died?" Dunscaby asked.

Startled, Julia yanked her hand away. Goodness, had she said too much? "Y-you're awake?"

"Aye." One corner of his mouth turned up. "I was dreaming a bonny woman was caressing my head. Imagine my dismay when I discovered it was my steward."

"Forgive me, Your Grace." She clapped a hand to her chest. "I-I thought rubbing your temples would bring you comfort."

"Och, you'd best not tell a soul you comforted me thus, else there will be hell to pay. Especially if Gibb hears of it."

"Of course not. I would never share any of our confidences."

"That's what I like about you, Smallwood. You are a good man." The duke licked his lips. "Now answer my question. Do you still have the manor?"

"I do. And the coin I earn is put to use keeping it from complete ruin."

"But what of your rents?"

"Unfortunately, my father saw fit to sell off most of his land." Julia stopped herself from saying more. There were still some rents coming in, but Papa had used the estate as collateral to borrow money and, until his debts were repaid, there would be no rest.

She offered him a cup of water. "How are you feeling?"

"Aside from a torturous hammering in my skull, I'm ready to find another stag." He pulled himself up, but not without a grunt of pain. "That fella was a beauty, was he not?"

"Yes, sir." Julia urged the cup into his hand. "But I daresay you'll need to stay abed for at least a day."

"Good God, if I wanted to be mothered, I would have brought the Duchess along." Dunscaby sipped, then spewed the drink across the bedclothes. "What the devil is this?"

"Water."

He shoved the cup into her face. "How is a man supposed to recover from a blow to the head with water? Fill it with whisky."

Julia took the cup, on one hand relieved to see His Grace sitting up and ornery, on the other, wishing he'd fall back to sleep and forgo cantankerousness. Instead, she chuckled and headed for the sideboard. "I have the feeling you're a difficult patient."

"Difficult? Me?" He slapped the pillow beside him. "Balderdash. And I'm not a patient."

Removing the stopper from the decanter, she poured a dram and carried it across the floor. "Of course not, sir."

Dunscaby took his drink and held it aloft. "I should thank you."

"No need." Julia sat. "It was an accident."

"Aye and if you hadn't been with me, I would be dead for certain." His brow furrowed as he shook his head. "How the blazes did you get me on that horse?"

She took a sudden interest in the brass buttons on her waistcoat. After all, there was a great deal of detail hammered into the six small circles. "Ah...I required your help. Of course, a man of my stature cannot dream of lifting a man of yours."

Leaning his head back, he snorted. "You slapped me across the face."

"Oh dear, you remember that?"

His Grace rubbed his cheek, the same one she'd accosted. "Aye...and one more thing, Smallwood."

Julia shrank. Good Lord, she'd struck a duke. She'd be dismissed or worse. "Yes, Your Grace?"

"You must work on that hideous shriek of yours. God's blood, you'll never attract a wife screaming like a bloody hyena."

Cringing, she rubbed her finger over one of the button's pattern of a sailor surrounded by frothy sea. "I say, have you ever heard a hyena?"

"I've read enough to have a good sense of what the beasts sound like. Regardless, you must practice restraint."

"Very well sir." She dropped the dratted button on a sigh. God save Dunscaby ever attempt to play matchmaker. What would she do then?

"Go on—get some rest." He flicked his fingers her way. "You look like a bloodhound who hasna slept in a sennight."

"But someone ought—"

"Did you not hear me?" His Grace seemed to grow increasingly irritated. "I am perfectly well. Go find your bed before you force me to lead you to it."

AFTER SMALLWOOD TOOK HIS LEAVE, Martin threw back the bedclothes, lumbered to the washstand, and proceeded to pour the entire contents of the ewer over his aching skull.

Damnation, had he completely lost his mind when he'd smacked his pate? The blasted steward had transfixed him with his ridiculous cosseting. It wasn't until Martin sat up that he'd begun to regain his wits.

The more he thought about it, the more irritated he became.

This entire hunting expedition had turned into a disaster. Smallwood was a bloody impish steward who needed to keep his nose in the ledgers and out of Martin's affairs. Aye, he was an affable enough sort, but Martin obviously had been spending too much time in the man's company—first noticing Smallwood's slender neck last eve, then languishing in his gentle touch this night.

He dabbed his face with a cloth. Then, wrapping it around his neck, he marched to the sideboard and poured himself another dram. Bless it all, he ought to dismiss the man.

No. I need to distance myself from him. I'm Dunscaby, dammit. I told Smallwood to stop shrieking like a wee lassie, and I'll nay allow the man to tend my sickbed again. The next time, I'll ring for a buxom alehouse wench afore I allow a man to fondle my bloody hair when I'm unconscious.

Martin threw back his whisky, wiped his mouth with the back of his wrist, and poured another as his head throbbed and the room spun.

He staggered toward the hearth and plopped into the wingback chair. Perhaps he needed to rethink his plans for the remainder of the Season.

After his father had passed away, he'd been immersed in grief. He'd naturally taken the family to Newhailes for a time of mourning—everyone except Gibb. The navy commander had only been given enough leave to attend the funeral. And, not long after, his younger brothers had returned to their studies while Martin had decided to winter at the *wee cottage* with his mother and sisters. Though on second thought, perhaps he should have returned to London.

Parliament was still in session—would be until summer. And he'd heard from more than one peer that his vote was sorely missed in the House of Lords.

Martin sipped. *And* London was the trading center of Great Britain. There he'd be able to make enquiries into the viability of milling cotton—discover if the whole idea was truly as lucrative as Smallwood had let on, Irish sharecroppers and all.

Of course, Mother would be elated to return to Town. Except the Duchess would meddle—endlessly needle him about finding a bloody suitable wife.

God's stones, the idea of marriage to some simpering maiden made him shudder. Even after three years in London Martin had not met a single well-bred lady who'd caught his fancy. In truth, he hadn't exactly tried when doing his damnedest to enjoy bachelorhood. If only he were residing in his bachelor's town house now, enjoying cards with his friends at Whites. Such was the life—no cares, no distracting stewards, and no meddling mothers—at least not in his house.

Without a doubt, being a marquess with a courtesy title had been much more enjoyable than being a duke.

Martin slammed his glass onto the table. *I aim to change this state of affairs at once. After all, what good is a dukedom unless said duke makes his own rules?*

9

A few days later, seated at the head of the table in the Newhailes dining hall, Martin buttered his toast while glancing pointedly at his mother. "It is time for you to begin half-mourning."

Mama paused, holding her porridge spoon in midair. "Has it been six months already?"

"Yes, it has," said Grace, flanked by her two sisters across from their mother. "Which means I can wear any color I wish."

"Me as well?" asked Modesty.

After finishing her bite of porridge, Mama rested her spoon at the side of her plate. "By custom, Grace is correct, however, as head of the family, the decision is Martin's."

He held up his arm revealing the absence of his mourning band. Though there were no hard and fast rules, it was proper for children to mourn their parents for six months and, after three, Martin had allowed his sisters to dress in half-mourning. Of course, as the widow, his mother was expected to mourn for an entire year. "I do believe it is time for the girls to be done with half-mourning. It has been spring for five days even though the weather isna cooperating. None-theless, I ken Papa would have preferred to see his daughters clad in happier colors." He covered his mother's hand and gave a gentle squeeze. "And I do hope I will see you in lavender from time to time, since it is allowed."

While Mama gave a solemn nod, Grace squirmed in her seat and clapped her hands as if it were Christmas morn. "If only I were out, I'd be able to attend balls."

"But you are not out," Martin said, matter-of-factly. "And you will not be out for years to come."

The lass gave an enormous eye-roll. Of the three sisters, Grace had perfected the irritating gesture. "Humph."

Mama raised her glass of apple juice. "Lord save us all when she does come of age."

"Excuse me?" Grace objected, her mouth forming a delicate O. "How can you say such a thing? I am more proficient on the pianoforte than Charity, more graceful than she, and every bit as bonny."

A fiery blush spread across Charity's face as she cast her gaze to her hands. "Thank you for pointing out my flaws, sister. I'm surprised you didn't claim being *bonnier*, I've overheard you report as much to Georgette."

"Enough." Mama held up a disciplinary finger. "All three of my daughters are unique beauties with unique talents, and I'll not have you pitting yourselves against each other. MacGalloways always stand together." She leveled her gaze at Grace, who was in the midst of those awful early teens. "And, Miss Snooty Petticoats, you will do well to remember a boastful young lady is the most unseemly of them all."

Sitting very straight, Modesty moved to the edge of her chair and tilted up her nose. "A young lady shall embody wholesomeness, neatness, and cheerfulness."

Charity's shoulders shook as she stifled a giggle before clearing her throat. "She shall be humble, un-pretentious, kind, mannerly, and affable."

"Are you saying I don't embody those things?" Grace demanded, now the one growing red in the face.

"Not at all." Charity picked up her knife and gouged the butter. "I'm simply repeating what we hear every morn from Miss Hay."

Before the conversation grew further out of hand, Martin intervened, "Ladies, if you will allow me to continue, I must inform you that I have decided we shall be returning to London for the remainder of the Season."

"London?" asked Mama looking a bit dazed while Modesty took the news as if it were merely a report on the weather and bit into her toast. Grace clapped with a brilliant smile, and Charity turned a tad green, her knife clattering to the floor which was immediately replaced by a footman.

Martin dabbed the corners of his mouth with his serviette and tossed it onto the table. "Aye. My vote is needed in Parliament and I've a number of business dealings to which I must attend." He scooted his chair back. "We will leave in a fortnight."

To the chatter of four females speaking at once, Martin made his escape. But no sooner had he taken his seat in the library when Giles appeared, carrying a silver tray in his palm. Evidently, the butler had made a quick exit from the dining hall as well. "The Morning Gazette, Your Grace."

"Verra good." Martin grabbed the paper and sank

into his chair.

Giles rocked back on his heels. "I will inform Mrs. Lamont of the morning's announcement. Rest assured all will be ready for the family's departure for London."

Martin took note of the headlines before looking up. "I can always count on you."

"Thank you, sir. Is there anything else you will be needing this morn?"

"I think I've just piled enough on your shoulders for the time being."

The butler chuckled. "Indeed, sir."

Martin managed to skim the front page before the rear door opened.

"Would you have a moment, Your Grace?" asked Mr. Smallwood.

"Ah, I suppose you've already heard the news. It always amazes me how efficient the rumor mill is among the servants."

"I'm afraid I have been shut in my rooms this morning." The little man pattered across the floor. "How are you feeling, may I ask?"

"Fine. Never better."

"Are you certain? You did suffer an exceptionally nasty blow to the head."

"I'm sitting up reading the paper, am I not?"

"You are sir, but—"

"Smallwood, you're acting like a mother hen. I am fine. Fully recovered."

"My word, are you out of mourning, sir?"

"You never miss a detail, do you?" Martin folded the Gazette and set is aside. "What is it you wanted to discuss?"

"I should like to take a journey up to Stack Castle. With the fortress being your greatest holding, it is past time I took inventory there as well as meet with the crofters and audit the ledgers at the distillery in Wick."

"No, no, that willna do."

"No, sir?"

"Perhaps you ought to have a word with Giles about your inclusion in the rumor mill." Martin crossed his legs. He needed the steward in Town and would entertain no argument otherwise. "We'll be leaving for London in a fortnight. You'll have to re-arrange your inventory schedule and focus on the town house first. Besides, once we're in the city we will start looking into the viability of your cotton idea."

"Oh." Jules stood, appearing a bit dazed. "I see."

Since returning from the Lodge, Martin's ire had cooled, having been given time to develop an under-standing of the steward's lack of worldliness. After consideration, he had decided to take on the responsi-bility to educate Smallwood in the more manly pur-suits—activities Jules obviously missed upon the demise of his da. "I say, 'tis past time someone took you under their wing. You have been sheltered with your nose in your ledgers for far too long."

"I happen to like my work, sir."

"Which is fortuitous...for the most part." Martin flicked his hand toward the rear door. "That will be all."

THOUGH HER VALISE was already packed and stowed on one of the five carriages heading for London, Julia took one last turn about her rooms, mentally ticking off the items on her list. After Dunscaby completely upended her plans and insisted she accompany the family to London, one of the first things she'd done was to send money to Willaby and let him know her new address, as well as to express her concern for Papa's heath. Still, the butler hadn't written in a month and she had grown a tad concerned.

She'd also sent another payment to Mr. Skinner, Papa's insidious moneylender, and was very careful *not* to include a return address of any sort. Ever since Julia had started working for Dunscaby, she'd been fastidious about making the agreed upon installments at a ludicrous rate of one fifth. Papa must have well and truly been out of his mind to accept four times the fixed bank rate of five percent. But then Skinner was a snake who preyed upon men who were desperate.

After spotting her tooth powder pushed back on the washstand shelf, she put it into her satchel and headed for the courtyard. For amusement inside the carriage, she was taking along three novels and, for rest periods, her journal, ink, and quill.

Outside, all five carriages were queued in single file in front of the house. The family and servants who were traveling were all standing below the entry steps. Martin faced them all. "I'll ride with Mama in the first carriage, the girls in number two and, Giles, see to it the other three have equal numbers to disburse the weight evenly. Let us climb aboard, everyone. I'd like to depart at once."

Julia headed toward the butler when Lady Modesty latched onto her arm. "There you are, Mr. Smallwood," chirped the lass, her red pigtails bobbing as she hopped in place.

"Are you excited for the journey?" Julia asked.

The child skipped toward the carriage, tugging Julia with her. "Always. It is ever so fun to throw open my trunks and realize I've outgrown half my wardrobe."

"Truly?"

"Aye. It means a trip to the modiste when we arrive in Town and all new dresses."

Julia gave the mischief-maker a wink. "Now that you're out of half-mourning, what colors do you fancy?"

Modesty stopped skipping, grasped both of Julia's hands and all but dragged her toward the second carriage. "Mama says rose pink goes quite well with my complexion, though I quite like spring green and azure."

"You'll look like a leprechaun in green," said Grace.

Charity took Tearlach's hand and, before allowing the footman to hand her into the carriage, she regarded the middle sister over her shoulder. "You've seen many leprechauns have you?"

"I've seen enough renderings of them to know that red hair, freckles, and green would make Modesty appear positively impish and pixie-like."

"I think green would suit her nicely," said Julia, twisting her arm away from the youngest's grip. "As would azure, which would match your eyes."

"You're very opinionated for a man, are you not?" asked Grace, reaching for the footman's hand and following her sister into the carriage.

"He's merely observant," said Modesty, clamping onto Julia's fingers, obviously not planning to release her grip until they reached the coach steps. "I want you to ride with us."

With a circular motion, Julia managed to wrench her hand away. "Oh no, I'd best ride with Giles in the next carriage."

Charity popped her head out the doorway. "We'd love to have you, Mr. Smallwood. Being shut in such a small space all day with these two young ladies is enough to drive a sensible woman mad. I'm certain your presence will be a welcome diversion."

"Well, I say riding with you is *unbearably* dull," said Grace from inside.

Modesty circled around to Julia's back and shoved. "'Tis settled, then. You're riding with us."

As she reached for Tearlach's hand, the aghast expression on the footman's face reminded her that a steward did not need assistance boarding a coach and she quickly snapped her fingers away. "Very well," she said, planting her foot on the step and placing her palm on the side of the carriage for balance. "I'll join you until we make our first stop."

Julia settled beside Modesty facing backward, as was the typical conundrum for the last in. Thank heavens Charity sat directly across. Nothing against Grace, but she was fourteen and as with many adolescent young ladies, the girl was a tad surly and filled with self-importance. Julia remembered being fourteen. It was akin to being on a ship in unpredictable seas—one moment inexplicably happy and the next weepy or angry or withdrawn—all behaviors she'd seen the lass exhibit in the time she'd been at Newhailes.

With the crack of a whip, the carriage creaked and swayed into motion.

"Here we go!" said Modesty, clapping her hands and wriggling in her seat.

Julia couldn't help but smile at the girl's enthusiasm. "Off on a great adventure."

Charity sighed and pressed her head against the backrest. "If only we were going anywhere but London."

"We cannot arrive fast enough if you ask me."

Grace fluffed a pillow. "I intend to sleep for as much of this dreary journey as possible."

Upon that announcement, Julia could have joined the youngest in her clapping and wriggling. Rather, she eyed Charity with genuine concern for the eldest MacGalloway girl. "What is it about Town that you find off-putting?"

Tugging up her gloves, Charity groaned. "Aside from everything?"

Modesty kicked out her feet, barely missing Grace's knee. "I like that we can walk to the shops and to Hyde Park. There's always something to do. And the weather's warmer there than in Musselburgh."

Julia patted the child's shoulder. "Those are all very good points, but I would like to hear your sister's take on the matter."

"The air is rather stifling with every chimney belching black smoke," Charity said, though that alone could not be her reason for her abhorrence of the most bustling city in Britain.

"I daresay, every town of any size I've ever been to has that problem." Julia leaned forward. "Tell me more. Are you not out? And the sister of a duke, no less. Do you not enjoy balls and soirees, the theater, recitals, and—"

"All the shopping," Modesty added.

"Och." Charity pulled aside the curtain and cast her gaze outside. "I may be the sister of a duke, but I'm a Scottish lass. Whenever I walk into a ballroom all eyes shift my way, heads move together, and I'm certain the gossips are chattering about how awkward I appear and how unsuitable I am especially because of my *unseemly* burr."

"Nonsense. I happen to think your little accent is delightful." Julia found herself wanting to snap open a fan and cool her face. Instead, she crossed her arms. "I may be from the southwest of England but I have attended a London ball or two and I'd be more disposed to believe the gossips titter about how lovely you look, how they wish they were you, and that they think you'll be the first to receive a proposal."

As steward, Julia was also well aware that all three young ladies had sizeable dowries. The only thing they needed to worry about in the marriage mart were fortune hunters.

"That is very kind of you to say, but I find the Season and all that comes with it, especially parading young maids in front of eligible bachelors, mortifying. 'Tis like being trussed like a swan for a grand dinner only to find the meat is tough and bitter."

"Quite a vivid analogy, though I daresay if I were to see a lady such as yourself at a ball, I would be the first in line to sign your dance card."

A blush spread up Grace's cheeks. "You are too kind, sir."

"Even though you're an awful dancer?" asked Modesty.

"Oh, please." Julia laughed—if they only knew how much she truly adored dancing. "I am improving."

"Thanks to Miss Hay," said Grace, opening an eye.

"Speaking of your governess, why is she not riding in your carriage?" asked Julia.

Grace fluffed her pillow and nestled against it. "No, thank you. We endure enough of her as it is. Miss Hay watches our every move, corrects our every word. If she were riding with us, I'd be completely mad by the time we reached London."

"I daresay she can be a tad overwhelming," Charity agreed.

"She also likes to flirt with Tommy," Modesty added, definitely in need of some coaching in her namesake.

Julia looked to the eldest. "The footman?"

Charity nodded. "We haven't any real proof."

Grace opened an eye. "When we stop, I'll wager she'll be riding in the same coach as Tommy."

"But the footmen don't even ride *inside* the carriage," said Julia.

"Aye, though they do help the ladies embark and disembark," said Charity. She held out a gloved hand as if offering it to a gentleman for a kiss. "Oh, the lasting tingle of a lover's mere touch. I, for one, would ride in a carriage if I fancied the footman tending the door."

"You'd better hope a footman never takes your fancy, else there'll be a reckoning with Mama," said Grace, tossing the pillow aside. Either the conversation was too diverting or the lass wasn't yet sleepy enough to ignore the chatter.

Charity heaved a sigh while she pulled her embroidery out of her basket. It seemed the lass had been doing a great deal of sighing of late. Though Julia was well aware some of the darlings of the *ton* could be catty and vicious, in her experience there were far more young ladies who were affable. The eldest of the MacGalloway sisters had a bit of a Scottish lilt but her accent was endearing. And the girl was quite fetching with loads of rich, dark cinnamon hair. Her face was oval with a slender nose, eyes the color of a stormy sea, and a petite mouth complemented her delicate chin. In truth, she had absolutely nothing to fret about. Unless...

"Did you have an unpleasant experience when you came out?" Julia asked, genuinely perplexed.

The poor girl turned scarlet. "I'll say."

"Would I be prying if—"

"Aaaaack!" Grace squealed in an explosion of cloaks, skirts, and petticoats.

Julia shot to the edge of her seat. "Whatever is the matter?"

"A-a-a-a mouse!" she shrieked.

Modesty and Charity squealed incomprehensibly while the youngest drew her feet up onto the seat and wrapped her arms around her knees. If Julia would have blinked, she would have missed the tiny brown rodent dart across the floor and beneath Charity's skirts, the tip of its tail not quite concealed.

Julia looked her in the eyes. "Do not move."

"Me...where is it?" the lass squeaked.

"Not even a twitch," Julia warned, slowing bending downward to the whimpers of all three MacGalloway girls. "Nearly there."

Sucking in an enormous breath, she pounced, grabbing the vermin's tail and holding it up. "I have him!"

The poor little fellow thrashed, thrusting out its tiny little paws, frantic to escape while all three girls screamed as if they were being attacked by a crazed headsman. "Stop the carriage," Julia shouted, stomping her feet to notify the driver.

As the words left her lips, Tearlach threw open the door, his face twisted in a frightening scowl as if he were ready to fight Julia to the death to defend the girls' honor.

Recoiling away from the footman, Julia held up the mouse. "It seems a stowaway has the ladies in a bit of a dither."

"Och, ye've had a wee bit of excitement have you?" asked the footman standing back and gesturing to a clump of gorse just off the road. He then cupped his hands around his mouth and shouted, "'Tis merely a mouse."

Though she surely could have used a hand to step down, Julia managed to alight from the carriage without dropping the rodent. As soon as her boots hit the road, applause came from the drivers and footmen in the procession.

Dunscaby marched toward them. "Good God, Smallwood. When I heard the bloodcurdling screams, I feared the worst."

"No harm done, Your Grace. Aside from a few frayed nerves." Including Julia's. She hastened to the clump of gorse and let the mouse go. As she straightened, she kept her back turned while a shudder coursed through her entire body. Truly, she didn't mind mice when they were out and about in the countryside, it was just they were ever so out of place in a carriage, or in one's home for that matter.

Thank goodness, she hadn't joined the ranks of the ladies and screamed bloody murder, no matter how much she'd wanted to.

Brushing off her hands, she gathered her wits and faced the duke with her soberest expression. "It always amazes me how such a tiny creature can invoke terror in the hearts of women."

"I daresay you are the hero of the hour. I've no idea what the lassies would have done if they'd been attacked by the little fellow had you not been present."

"Aye, thank you," said Charity, smiling from the doorway, adoration filling her eyes. "We are in your debt, sir."

Julia bowed. "It certainly made for an exciting start to our journey, my lady."

"Very good, Smallwood." Dunscaby clapped Julia

on the back so hard, she lurched forward. He seemed not to notice as he continued, "Everyone back to your carriages. We will not be stopping until we reach Middleton and that willna be for a few hours yet."

10

"Mama already has my days filled with dress fittings and luncheons. She, or should I say *you*, have received invitations to all manner of recitals, balls, and soirees. Heaven's stars, it is enough to make anyone's head swim." Sitting on the settee across from Martin, Charity flicked open her fan and cooled her face though in truth a bit of a chill hung in the air of the town house's library. "Did you know our mother sent letters ahead as soon as you announced we would be returning to London?"

Martin opened his gold pocket watch and checked the time. "Why should that surprise me? After all, it is her duty as your mother to see you well-placed."

"Aye, but once we returned to Scotland, I was sure I'd have another year before I had to face the vultures again. Goodness, Marty, why did you have to go and decide to return so soon?"

With nowhere else to be at the moment, he slid the watch back into his pocket and gave it a pat. It was no secret that Charity preferred a quiet country setting to that of the city, but Newhailes or any of his other residences was no place for her to find a husband. She needed to be in London whether she liked Town or not. "First of all, I hate to shatter your illusions, but there were reasons for my return that had nothing to do with your marriage prospects."

"Such as?"

"Your brothers. Gibb may have been on the winning side in his past few sea battles, but make no bones about it, I would prefer to see him out of the navy and at the helm as captain of his own merchant ship. Then there are the twins who will be graduating from St. Andrews at the end of this term. Smallwood and I have a business venture to investigate, and the hub of commerce in Britain is in this very city. Not to mention, my vote is needed in the House of Lords."

The journey from Newhailes to London had been long and arduous just as always. Aside from the incident with the mouse on the first day, they'd managed to make the trip without anyone falling ill or breaking a bone, though they'd nearly left Charity and Grace's lady's maid, Georgette, behind when she'd overslept. No one had bothered to wake her even though the lass was sharing a room in the inn with three other servants.

Upon their arrival yesterday, Martin had left Mama to her unpacking and had taken a long ride through Hyde Park for some much-needed time to himself. But as soon as he'd left the breakfast table this morning, Charity followed him into the town house's library—merely one third the size of the grand library at Newhailes, but it was where the Duke of Dunscaby conducted his affairs when in residence.

The lass pushed to her feet and paced while swinging her fan in a circle. "Och, I ken ye are trying to do your best for the lads. I only wish I could have stayed at Newhailes—or gone up to Stack Castle with Mr. Smallwood. Your steward mentioned that he is planning to visit the castle soon." She stopped and regarded Martin over her shoulder. "Perhaps I ought to marry Mr. Smallwood. He's affable enough."

Martin leaned his head against the high-backed chair and cast his gaze to the ornate plaster relief on the ceiling above. At one of her first balls, Charity had been devastated when she'd overheard a gaggle of girls gossiping about her in the ladies withdrawing room. "Now that is a laughable notion if I've ever heard one. Your time of mourning aside, you've been out for all of what, a month? Two? I'll tell you here and now, you are not marrying my steward."

The corners of Chairity's lips tightened as she glanced to the window. "Why not? Why would I not be happy with a man like Jules Smallwood? Besides, I'd be able to live out my days at any one of the MacGalloway estates."

"I beg your pardon, but you are the eldest daughter of a duke, born and bred to marry into nobility or royalty. I'll not have you hiding because you overheard some jealous chit make an unseemly comment about Scottish lassies being provincial. You are not settling for a steward, no matter how affable he may be."

"But I like the little fellow. He seems to understand me. And when he rescued us from the mouse he was adorably heroic."

"Enough." Martin moved to his writing table and rifled through the stack of invitations until he found the one he wanted. Shaking it open, he scanned the scrawling print, noting the date. "The Marquess of Northampton is to host a private masquerade ball in a fortnight. I will escort you there myself. And, sister, I dunna want to hear another word about marrying my bloody steward."

Charity smacked the fan into her palm. "You're so unimaginative. Have you forgotten Mr. Smallwood is the son of a knight?"

Martin shook the invitation under her nose. "Not another word. I task you with finding appropriate masquerade costumes for the both of us forthwith."

A knock came at the door and the little steward popped in his head. "Oh, do excuse me, Your Grace."

Charity beamed and batted her damned eyelashes. "Good morn, Mr. Smallwood."

Stepping into the library, the fellow bowed. "It is a very good morning indeed, Lady Charity."

Martin glared at his sister. "You may go but pay heed to what I said." He waited for Charity to slip out and close the door before he leveled his gaze on Smallwood. "What the blazes did you do to the lass?"

"I beg your pardon, sir?"

"Stay away from her. She's young and impressionable and..."

"Of course she is, sir. In my observation, Lady Charity is ever so concerned about how she appraises in polite society. She feels the other young ladies hold her in low esteem because of her Scottish lilt. But let me tell you here and now, she is like a pure white rose among the brambles. And I find her accent nothing short of delightful."

Martin clenched his fist and pounded on his writing table. "Well, you can take your opinions and keep them to yourself."

Smallwood opened his mouth while a crease formed between his eyebrows. "Forgive me, sir. I-I most definitely did not intend to pry."

"Evidently you made quite an impression on the lass whilst you were catching mice in the carriage."

"It was only one very measly, underfed mouse, might I say."

"Aye, well, Charity thinks you would be a fine suitor. *You* of all people."

"Oh dear." Smallwood rubbed a hand along the jaw of his smooth-skinned face. "Though I hold Lady Charity in the highest esteem, I'm afraid we are not well suited."

Releasing a long breath, Martin sank into his chair. "Exactly what I tried to tell her."

Smallwood blubbered with a flabbergasted snort. "She's destined to marry into nobility for certain, not a doddering steward."

Though relieved to hear it, Martin was taken aback to hear the man refer to himself as doddering since he was neither old nor shaky. "Aye," he said, deciding an agreement was in order. "'Tis good to hear you do understand, though I am the first to admit you are of sound character, I would prefer it if you did not encourage her...ah...affections."

"Of course I will not. You can count on me where the lass is concerned."

"Verra well." Though relieved on one count, Martin gripped his chair's armrests while a flame spread like wildfire through his chest. "Tell me, exactly what is it you do not like about my sister?"

Smallwood's expression grew utterly bamboozled, turning apple red while his eyes grew as round as guineas. "N-nothing. Lady Charity ought to be the darling of the *ton*. In fact, I wouldn't be surprised if she had a dozen proposals within the next fortnight."

Martin sat back and rubbed the sudden throbbing pain attacking his temples. "Yes...Lord save us."

"Do you not wish for Her Ladyship to entertain proposals?"

"Of course I do. But we are talking about my sister. The wee lass I carried into the house when she scraped her knee. I taught her how to swim and climb trees." Closing his eyes, he pressed his fingers firmly, willing the headache away. "I'm not so certain I'm ready to see her wed. And I most definitely will not agree to any marriage unless it is to a man with an *impeccable* reputation. By God, no rake will place a hand on her, else I'll be forced to shoot a hole through his miserable heart."

"I'm sure with you at Lady Charity's side, all the rakes and fortune hunters in Town wouldn't dare request an introduction."

"Quite."

Smallwood pulled a slip of paper from inside his waistcoat. "After we received verification that the Irish sharecroppers are anxious to be our supplier in America, I made a few discrete enquiries and found Barry and Coates Shipbuilders have offices at the Pool of London and they've listed a number of seaworthy vessels for sale—half the price of building new."

Martin snatched the list and scanned the contents. "Why so steeply discounted? Are the vessels full of rot?"

"We'd definitely need complete inspections before seriously considering any purchase."

"I wonder when Gibb will next be in port." Martin pushed the list across the table and sat back. "I'll have a word with the admiral. If I'm going to buy my brother a ship, I want it to be one in which he wholeheartedly approves—be it new or be it a refitted, nearly new vessel."

"Hear, hear, sir." Smallwood turned the paper over. "On the reverse side, I've noted twenty acres on the River Tay near Kinclaven in Scotland. It is presently the site of an empty warehouse and might be an ideal location upon which to situate a cotton mill, what with being on the river that flows into the Firth of Tay and whatnot. I could make arrangements to travel to the property and conduct an inspection."

Martin leaned forward and noted the price. "On the Tay, did you say?" He not only liked the idea of being on a river to make use of the power of water wheels, he also preferred to have his brothers in Scotland and, with twenty acres, he could not only turn the warehouse into a factory, he could build matching manor homes for each of the twins.

"Yes," said Smallwood. "It is partially cleared, has road access, and wherries can ferry supplies from Dundee and Perth."

"Then buy it before someone else takes the parcel out from under us. I'll write to the twins and have them take a weekend jaunt to visit the site—that will whet their appetites for certain. And mind you, twenty acres on the Tay is a sound investment, regardless."

"Very well, I'll advise Mr. MacCutcheon that we wish to move forward."

❖

AFTER COMPLETING the transaction to purchase the land in Kinclaven, Julia returned to the town house by way of the mews. Now that she'd been in London the better part of a week, she was quickly growing accustomed to the freedom her disguise afforded. Though Newhailes was only an hour's carriage ride from Edinburgh, it was considered a country estate and, aside from her hunting expedition to the Highlands and her jaunt to the cobbler for new boots, she'd rarely left the grounds. However, in London, shopping and businesses were within walking distance, making it far easier for her to conduct business transactions and the like. And as was customary, she had a carriage and driver at her disposal whenever necessary.

Though her rooms were more spacious in Newhailes, she had a very cozy chamber in what was one of the largest town houses in the city. Located between the family's main residence and the mews, the steward's apartment was long and narrow with a door leading to the courtyard and another into a corridor on the first floor, directly above the kitchens. She had a writing table situated in front of a substantial hearth with bookshelves on either side. Across the chamber were her sleeping quarters, separated by a silk screen, painted with a lovely pastoral scene.

Another boon was the library was on the second floor which made her less accessible to Dunscaby. After her arrival, they'd quickly developed a pattern of discussing matters after the duke breakfasted, then Julia was usually on her own for the rest of the day which was exactly how she envisioned the role of steward to be.

As she opened the door to her chamber, two footmen came into the courtyard toting a trunk. "This arrived for you, sir," said Tearlach.

"For me?" she asked, holding the door while the men brought it in. "Who is it from?"

"It came via the post. Doesn't appear to have a return address." said Tommy, setting the crate down just inside.

"Thank you." Julia moved to shut the door, but the footmen hadn't brought the trunk in far enough. She tugged one end, but it jammed on the carpet. "Heavens, it is heavy."

After releasing the buckles on either side, she unfastened the hasp and opened the lid. On one side were neatly folded shirts and neckcloths, but as soon as she spotted her copper bed warmer with a J engraved on the top, she knew the package was from Willaby. She found the wooden handle and screwed it into the warmer, then held it up. "I could have used this in Scotland."

Beneath it was the enormous, scratched, and dented brass inkwell and quill holder that adorned the steward's desk at Huntly Manor. "Why did you bother to send this old relic?" she asked with grunt as she hefted it out of the trunk and set it atop her writing table.

Aha! The ugly inkwell had concealed a letter from Willaby. "Oh dear," she said with a bit of dread in her tone, her skin growing clammy as she pulled it out and slid her finger beneath the wax seal. Her father's butler had addressed the letter to Mr. Smallwood, wording it in a way that was more businesslike than familial, bless his heart. He knew how precarious her situation was and, if anyone aside from Julia happened upon the letter, no one would realize she was related to the earl, let alone his only child who happened to be female. But as she read, not only did she break out in a cold sweat, her hands shook.

"*Mr. Skinner has sent several letters demanding an additional payment of twenty pounds sterling to make up for the two months of interest not paid. He has also threatened to force His Lordship into bankruptcy and evict him from Huntly Manor, though I do have it on good authority that Mr. Skinner would have a very difficult time indeed if he attempted to take a peer of the realm to debtor's court. He has made it clear, however, that he will not allow the earl's exalted position to stand in his way...*"

"Blast," Julia cursed under her breath. In addition

to the ten pounds per month she was sending Skinner for interest, she had added an additional pound, which was supposed to count against the twenty pounds in default until she paid it off. For the love of Moses, after she paid the moneylender and sent funds home, she had but one pound fifty pence to herself. Fortunately, aside from buying new boots, she'd saved most of it. But she certainly did not have twenty pounds.

She read on...

"I hate to ask this of you but I see no other option but to request that you visit Mr. Skinner on the earl's behalf and settle this dispute. Mrs. May and I have agreed to forgo our wages if we must. In four months, that ought cover the sum he's demanding.

"Aside from the business with the moneylender, the earl is a tad jaundiced of late. Unfortunately, the physician has agreed that there has been a decline in his health. I do wish I had better news to report.

"You will find all you need for a visit with Mr. Skinner in the compartment of this trunk..."

Julia looked through the shirts Willaby had sent. They were not only threadbare, they were men's. She pulled them out and examined the bottom of the trunk, finding an iron key, yet she saw no keyhole. Odd, even though the butler had added the awful inkpot and holder, it was heavy for the few items it had contained.

Unless...

Smoothing her fingers around the edge of the wooden base, she searched for a ribbon, or bit of leather and found nothing. She stood back and eyed the trunk, tapping the key against her chin. Willaby knew she could not approach Silas Skinner as Jules Smallwood. Not only was there the risk that the vile snake might recognize her, she must not let the man ever know she was in the employ of the Duke of Dunscaby.

She pulled the straps to the buckles all the way off. Lo and behold, beneath the strap on the right was a keyhole two thirds of the way down. Julia quickly slipped the key into the lock and turned. With a resounding click, a secret compartment popped open, along with the white lace of her favorite chemise.

"What have you there?" asked a childlike voice which must belong to none other than Lady Modesty MacGalloway.

Julia slammed the compartment shut. "Ah, my lady...I received a parcel from my last place of employment—my old bedwarmer and inkwell."

The child examined the shirts still sitting on the floor. "These are as good as rags."

"I suppose they are, though it was very kind of Willaby, the old butler to send them to me."

"Ah, Mr. Smallwood," said Charity, following Modesty through the doorway, her gaze immediately falling to the bit of lace poking out from the hidden compartment. "My, that is a large trunk—far larger than the valise with which you traveled to London."

"Indeed, it is, my lady." Julia tugged on the handle, again jamming the blasted thing on the carpet. Though the trunk was lighter, it was still awkward to move.

Charity grasped the other side. "Let us lift it together, shall we?"

"Thank you." Indeed, it was far easier to move the beastly thing with two people. "Against the wall, if you please."

"We're off to the bookshop," said Modesty, holding the door.

"That sounds diverting." Julia gave a bow, careful not to look Lady Charity in the eye and unintentionally giving her the wrong impression. "Do enjoy yourselves."

After the two MacGalloway sisters took their leave, Julia locked both doors, then opened the secret compartment. Indeed, everything she'd need was there; petticoats, gloves, slippers, a blue gown and a yellow (worn but functional), a set of stays, reticule, hats to go with each dress, and a woolen pelisse for warmth.

Julia regarded her things before quickly replacing them exactly as she'd found them. She locked the trunk and refastened the buckles. In no way could anyone ever discover women's garments in her chamber.

But that seemed the least of her problems. Not only must she gain an audience with a vile scoundrel, she must find a way to don a gown without anyone in the MacGalloway household seeing her.

11

M artin rapped the silver handle of his cane on the door to the steward's chamber. "Smallwood, are you ready?"

The man immediately opened it, his expression a tad thunderstruck. "Good morning Your Grace. You wouldn't mind if I begged off for today? I-I'm afraid have a fair bit of correspondence to attend."

Grasping the steward by the elbow, Martin tugged him into the courtyard. "You've had your head bent over that writing table for too long. A man needs to stretch his legs. Exercise is good for the soul."

On the way out, Smallwood plucked his hat from the peg. "I daresay I agree. Though boxing isn't my sport of choice."

"Nonsense." Martin headed through the mews at a brisk pace. "All men need to be able to spar a few rounds."

"Wonderful," Smallwood mumbled, donning his hat. He pointed to a sedan chair covered with a dusty tarpaulin. "I say, does anyone use that contraption?"

"Not since my grandmother passed, I suppose."

"Hmm. Have you considered selling it?"

"Nay. With three sisters growing up faster than I

can blink, I'll wager it will come into use sooner or later."

"Very good, sir."

Leading the way out the rear door, Martin glanced over his shoulder. "Do you ever think of anything aside from your work?"

"I..." Smallwood brushed a bit of lint off his lapel. "Yes, I think about a great many things."

"Such as?" Martin asked, turning onto Grosvenor's Square from the mews and heading for Jackson's Saloon on Bond Street.

"I read the papers. There's a war on...and at a time when King George is no longer in his right mind and the country is in the hands of his foppish son, forgive any impertinence."

"You're not being impertinent when you are telling the truth." Martin tipped his hat to a passing carriage before crossing the road, his cane tapping to the cadence of his footsteps. "But what of other activities and family?"

"I have no family nearby. And I've said before I like long walks. London has been particularly helpful in that respect because I've been able to walk almost everywhere."

Martin had never met a single man who didn't smoke cigars, enjoy a turn or two at cards, play billiards, enjoy shooting, horse racing, chasing the odd skirt. But Smallwood never spoke of any of the typical manly pursuits.

Reading and walking? The man may as well be a monk.

No wonder he appeared to be so effeminate. Well, Martin intended to help the wee fellow along. Though most servants didn't marry, it wasn't unusual for a steward to take a wife. After all, the steward to a duke made a handsome wage. Moreover, if Smallwood were to marry, Charity might start taking the marriage mart more seriously.

Martin pushed into Thirteen Bond Street and spread his arms, gesturing to the expansive space with three rings, and a strength-building section along one wall. "I've arranged for you to have a lesson with the champion himself, Gentleman John Jackson."

When there was no reply, he glanced over his shoulder, only to see the outline of Smallwood's form through the etched glass. Martin opened the door. "You are meant to step inside."

"Yes, sir."

Martin tugged the little fellow into the saloon and pointed to a sparring ring, surrounded by ropes where Jackson was ducking and weaving while giving instruction to a pimple-faced lordling. "Ye ken not just anyone can obtain a lesson from the great."

Smallwood blanched a bit as he gaped at the enormous boxer. When the bout ended, the wee fellow turned in place, taking in the weights, fencing equipment, and the walls festooned with paintings of men facing off in famous bouts. "Perhaps I'm not highly born enough to meet Mr. Jackson's clientele requirements."

"Balderdash. You are the guest of a duke, not to mention the son of a knight."

"Your Grace!" said Jackson, throwing out his hand and gripping Martin's with an iron fist. "It is good to see you back in Town. Please accept my condolences for the loss of your father."

"Thank you. Da will be sorely missed." Martin gestured toward his steward. "This is Mr. Jules Smallwood, a *friend*. As I mentioned in my correspondence, I do believe he could benefit from a few lessons."

"Is that so?" Jackson crossed his arms and looked the steward from head to toe. "What training have you had, sir?"

If it was possible, Smallwood seemed to shrink an inch or two. "Aside from being somewhat skilled in archery, I'm afraid I'm a far better poet."

Martin squeezed one of Jules' arms, surprised at how scrawny it seemed. "On that I can concur. The man's quill is over-exercised for certain."

Gentleman Jackson rubbed his meaty palms together. "Not to worry, we'll start with some basic moves, shall we?"

"Oh, yes, please. The more basic the better." Jules stepped away from the very large fighter and waved his hands in front of his face as if already conceding defeat. "Just look upon me as malleable as a lump of clay."

Giving the boxer a knowing nod, Martin had been right to bring the steward here. If anyone could help Smallwood find his vigor and manly prowess, it was this gentleman.

HOW IN THE name of human civility had Julia ended up in a boxing ring of all places? The only fight she'd ever seen was when she was about nine years of age after a pair of neighboring brothers came to blows. And the lads weren't much older than she at the time.

"That's it, dance in place," said Mr. Jackson, mirroring Julia as she hopped from one foot to the other, except this boxing champion had to be well over twice her size and built like the hind quarter of a work horse. Never in her life had she seen such a hulking fellow. Merely looking at his fists made her quake all the way to her toes.

"Now show me your best jab."

Jab?

She glanced to her fists.

Ah yes, he wants me to throw a punch.

"Like this?" she asked, making her voice as deep as possible, as she whipped a punch through the air.

"That's the idea." The man clapped his hands together and held up his left palm. "Plant your best jab right here."

Eying her target, Julia threw her fist with all her strength.

Mr. Jackson stopped dancing. "What the hell was that? A bloody flea?"

Julia dropped her hands to her sides. What did the brute expect? He already knew she had no experience. She glanced at Martin out of the corner of her eye.

The duke threw a couple of punches in front of his nose. "Sharp, deadly jabs, Smallwood. Don't lash out like you're batting away flies."

Wonderful. Her employer thought her a weakling —which she well and truly was. If only she could tell Dunscaby to climb into the ring with this behemoth and allow her to watch.

Can I return to my tranquil little chamber by the courtyard now? I happen to enjoy idling the days away in my chamber, not bopping anyone in the nose.

"Perhaps if you give me a demonstration, I'll understand better the type of jab you wish for me to issue." There. At least she sounded in control. She'd even managed to keep her voice from trembling.

"Very well." Mr. Jackson swept his gargantuan fists in front of his face, issuing a pair of speedy punches. "You'll need to parry away my strikes like this. Come, sir, you've dropped your guard. Hands up."

Julia complied, slapping her hands in front of her face, she parried just as he showed her.

"Now stay on your toes. A fighter who stands in one place is asking for a click to the muns."

Julia had no idea what the devil a click to the muns was, but she figured it was best not to ask. "I think I have the idea, sir."

Thwack!

Before she blinked, Jackson's fist flew between her hands and landed a blasted *click to the muns* on her jaw. With her grunt, her head snapped back as she struggled to keep her feet beneath her. But her efforts were to no avail. Wobbling backward, her arms whipped in circles while Dunscaby's voice sounded as if he were shouting in a tunnel. "Smallwooooooood!"

Julia swallowed her urge to scream as gravity took over and sent her crashing to the floor in an ignoble heap.

"Ow," she whimpered.

Mr. Jackson's brutish face hovered above her. "Why did you not parry? I gave you ample warning."

Julia moved her jaw from side to side. Thank heavens it still seemed to be attached at the hinges. "Gave me warning? Is that what you call brutally striking a man with the speed of an asp?"

Dunscaby's face came into view—clear blue eyes filled with concern and far too beautiful. Julia well and truly swooned if that were possible when one was flat on her back. The duke would never smack her in the face even if he did think her a man. "Well done, laddie. It's never easy to take a punch but we'll make a fighter out of you yet."

Perhaps she might have misjudged his good-naturedness a tad. In truth, no matter how much Julia adored the man, if she didn't want him to strike her, she must never step into a boxing ring with His Grace —especially while impersonating Jules Smallwood. "That was quite invigorating," she said, sitting up and rubbing her jaw. She'd be bruised in the morning for certain. And just when she needed to confront Mr. Skinner, blast it all.

Mr. Jackson took her by the arm and pulled her up with such force, she nearly toppled forward onto her face. "Good God, man, no wonder you were lambasted by my little jab. I reckon you weigh no more than a bushel of oats."

Julia squared her shoulders and stretched her neck, doing her best to appear as tall as possible. "No one has ever accused me of being too large, of that I can attest."

Keeping his hand on her upper arm, the boxer squeezed. "I'd best send a weight home with you with which to practice. You'll need to put on some muscle afore you step into my ring again."

Julia glanced to Dunscaby. "Do you engage in such exercise, Your Grace?"

"Aye, and driving a team helps to build my strength as well."

The boxer jammed his fists onto his hips. "As does hefting barrels and bushels, I'll say. I can turn a dock-yard laborer into a fighting man in no time."

Julia followed as Mr. Jackson stepped thorough the ropes and out of the ring. "I can move casks and the like in the kitchens every morning. Would that suffice?"

"It will help." The boxer picked up an iron rod with what looked like two cannonballs attached to each end. In fact, there was an entire row of the things in different sizes. "How's this dumbbell suit?"

As she grasped the bar, the blasted torture device was so heavy, she had to brace it with her other hand to keep from dropping it on her toes. "My, there's a fair bit of weight in it, is there not?" she said, her voice straining.

"Merely twenty pounds."

Perhaps twenty pounds was a trifle for a chap who spent his days boxing, but to Julia, twenty pounds was quite enough.

Mr. Jackson picked up a smaller dumbbell. "Let's go with ten. Bend your elbows and lift it from your waist to your shoulders twenty times on each side. And do the same from your shoulders over your head like so."

He demonstrated a half-dozen exercises that he expected her to accomplish twenty repetitions each.

I'll be lucky to manage half that.

They exchanged weights and Dunscaby clapped her on the back. "Perhaps we can add a bit of exercise in the mornings before you delve into your ledgers."

She gave him a weak smile. "I'm sure you have far more important things to do, Your Grace."

No matter how invigorating Julia might find it to watch the duke flex his muscles, if he realized exactly how pathetic her weightlifting abilities were, he'd peg her as a woman for certain. She'd not only be unemployed, Mr. Skinner would find a way to boot Papa out of Huntly Manor in a heartbeat.

His Grace wrapped his arm around her shoulder and gave a squeeze. Though she knew it was but a gesture of fellowship, Julia couldn't help but close her eyes and lean into him. Oh, how heavenly it was to melt into his warmth and brush her cheek along his coat's soft wool. Even though he thought her a man and his hand squeezed her shoulder so powerfully it caused a tad of discomfort, she would endure any amount of pain to have Martin MacGalloway surround her in his arms. Truly, if she were not a destitute young woman, she undoubtedly would allow herself a hearty sigh.

Alas, the moment of intimacy passed much too soon and Dunscaby headed for the door.

She didn't follow right away, but rather admired his bold stride, his broad shoulders, and the confident way he carried himself. He took his hat, gloves, and cane from a footman then eyed her over his shoulder. "Come, Smallwood. There's much to do."

12

W ith her garments tucked away in her valise,
Julia waited until the bustle of the morning
chores had ended before she tiptoed into the mews.
The carriages were housed beyond the horse stalls,
divided by a wall. Since the family was on an outing
with the carriage, she skirted past the stalls without
being spotted. Once in the carriage house, she headed
straight for the sedan chair since Dunscaby had mentioned it hadn't been used in years.

She'd awakened this morning with a gargantuan
bruise on her backside and, thankfully, a much
smaller one on her chin. Bless Georgette, the lady's
maid had given Julia some rice powder that she'd used
to cover up as best she could—increasing the maid's
wages had gained her an ally and, when a woman was
posing as a man, no matter how worthy her motives,
said woman needed as many allies as she could find.

Once Julia was confident she was alone, she
slipped beneath the tarpaulin and into the dusty old
sedan chair. Coughing, she used her kerchief to wipe
it clean, then set her valise on the seat, bumping her
bruised backside on the wall. Changing clothes in
such a confined space was not going to be easy.

Scrunching her shoulders together, she took off her jacket and shirt, but found bending over impossible until she sat, removed her boots, hose, trousers, and unbound her breasts.

She first donned a chemise for modesty, then set to the task of lacing her stays in the front as she'd done many times and could do with her eyes closed. On went her hose, slippers, and petticoat. After donning her blue day dress and tying it closed, she pinned up her clubbed hair, pulled her bonnet atop, and tied a neat bow at the side. At least she thought the ribbon felt neat. Without a looking glass, she couldn't be sure and she didn't want to dawdle in the sedan chair any longer than necessary. Her appearance, however she looked, would just have to suffice.

Julia neatly folded her men's garments and stowed them in her valise, then listened very carefully—the sounds of horses in their stalls with gentle blowing and nickers drifting on the air. A carriage with a squeaky wheel traveled through the close beyond the rear gate. Footsteps pattered downward, Julia clapped a hand over her heart and held her breath. A latched scraped in the direction of the horse stalls.

Please do not hitch up a carriage. Not now.

"Come now, Rosie. 'Tis time we picked your hooves."

A silent whistle whooshed through Julia's lips as she recognized the voice of one of the grooms. The fellow began to sing a ditty as he worked, his song muffled by the wall separating the horses from the carriage house.

Ever so slowly, Julia stepped out of the sedan chair and slipped from under the tarpaulin. On the tips of her toes, she made her way toward the outer man door, passing a barouche, the duke's phaeton, and a number of the shiny black coaches they'd used for traveling from Scotland. Resting her hand on the latch, she stopped behind the wheel of the last carriage and again listened. Only when she was confident of not being seen did she slip outside and quietly close the door behind her.

BY THE TIME Julia stepped onto the footpath of the busy street, she suddenly became very aware of being an unescorted woman. After two months of impersonating a man, she had taken for granted the ease in which she was able to move around society without drawing attention to herself. She kept her eyes lowered and walked with purpose, trying not to attract the notice of passersby.

The farther away she moved from the duke's town house, the narrower the houses and store fronts became. Shabbier as well. Regardless, she had no choice but to trek the distance from Grosvenor Square to the unsavory and notorious fringes of St. Giles where, after consulting with a map in the library when the family was at dinner, she'd located the address of Deuces, Mr. Skinner's gambling hell.

When, finally, she arrived at Three West Street, she stood in front of the door, red of all colors, with a border in gilt relief, depicting nude Roman athletes. Thirsty and tired, her gaze moved upward to an enormous placard, that read "*Deuces*." She was aware the man owned a gambling hell, and this was definitely his address, but by the ostentatiousness of the building's façade, she didn't imagine he lived here.

Does he?

She prayed he did because she wanted this business over with. Heaven forbid she needed to change in the sedan chair again and come back at some other time. A large, liveried footman stood outside the door, looking as if he might have been recruited from the docks and trained to box by Mr. Jackson. Gathering her nerve, Julia strode directly up to the chap and looked him in the eyes. "I've come to see Mr. Skinner."

The fellow smirked and arched a single eyebrow. "We're closed."

Oh, dear, that simply wouldn't do. "When, pray tell, do you open?"

"Seven o'clock, luv. But no women are allowed…" With his smirk firmly fixed in place his gaze dropped to her breasts and remained fixated upon them even though she was wearing a fichu for modesty. "That is unless ye're lookin' for a position wiff the ladies above stairs."

Crossing her arms, Julia took a step back. "I most definitely am not. I have an urgent financial matter to discuss with Mr. Skinner I must see him immediately. If he is not here, please advise where I can find him."

"A financial matter, aye? Ye don't look like one of the dandies 'e tends to conduct business wiff."

"The nature of my visit is none of your concern." She pulled Willaby's missive out of her reticule and waved it, not giving the man a chance to really look at the document before she shoved it back inside. "This is a letter from Mr. Skinner demanding payment from my infirm father. I am not in London for long and it is imperative that I speak to him straightaway."

"Your faver's the dandy, aye?" The footman threw a thumb over his shoulder. "Go round back. Give only one solid rap with the knocker, ye 'ear?"

"My thanks," she said, giving a curtsy and hastening to the rear of the building.

Taking a moment to catch her breath, she stared at the cold and uninviting black door with a brass knocker depicting a very angry-looking skull. Beneath was a placard and upon it was the name *"Skinner"*. The word alone made her shudder. Julia had met the man only once when he'd come to Huntly Manor with his threats. That awful altercation had been right before her father had collapsed and taken ill.

As directed, she gave one solid rap with the vulgar bottom jaw of the knocker and waited until the door was opened an elderly butler. After her conversation out front, she decided to explain the reason for her visit straightaway and allay any assumption that she might be a woman of easy virtue. After all, she was knocking on the door of a nefarious gambling establishment.

The man grunted and allowed her inside, gesturing to a wooden bench in a corridor painted red without a single work of art on the wall. There was one door at the end, just past the stairs. Her hands began to perspire as she waited while mentally rehearsing her plea. Curse it all, this was the last person she cared to beg for mercy.

How could Papa have stooped so low?

The hinges on the door screeched as it opened and Skinner stepped through, his smile more like a yellow-toothed sneer than a grin because his lips were misaligned by an unseemly scar. "Lady Julia St. Vincent. What a surprise to see ye 'ere. Did ye travel all the way from Brixham?" he asked, his East End accent nearly as thick as that of the footman out front.

Her knuckles turned white while she gripped her reticule and rose. The man was taller and gaunter than she remembered. "Good day, Mr. Skinner," she said, avoiding his question. "I've come to have a word about the recent demands you have made on my father."

"Truly?" He gestured with a bony hand. "I find it odd the earl would send 'is daughter in 'is stead."

Though the hairs on the nape of Julia's neck stood on end, she moved inside the chamber, the walls painted scarlet beneath hand-painted filagree in a much darker shade of claret. Though the work was flawless, the décor was as overdone as the front doors. The chamber wasn't terribly large, and filling it stood an ornately carved desk in mahogany with a chair padded in red velvet behind it and a straight-backed wooden chair across. No surprises, the moneylender preferred his guests to be uncomfortable. "Yes, well, as you are aware, Papa has been confined to his sickbed for the past several months."

"Still suffering from swilling too much brandy, eh?" Mr. Skinner asked, sliding into the seat behind the table. "Please do sit."

As she perched on the edge of the hard chair, Julia wasn't about to let the man bait her into saying more. Her father was ill and the cause of his illness was none of Skinner's concern. He already was aware that she handled Papa's affairs and that was enough.

She cleared her throat. "Your letter stated that you are anxious to receive twenty pounds in back interest even though I've been making payments over and above your terms with intention to clear that debt. Mind you, I've already repaid four pounds of the twenty you claimed."

"Yes, I've received your payments. But ye do not understand the terms of my loan. I must be compensated for the two months where I received nothing. I am not in the business of grantin' charity."

"I understand and I have not come without a plan.

I am prepared to give you two pounds now, which is ten percent of the amount you've demanded. Furthermore, the two remaining servants at Huntly Manor have agreed to a cut in wages and I'll be able to pay you four pounds fifty pence additional per month until the debt is paid in full."

The man snorted, his sneer returning. "Ah, but you 'aven't considered the *penalty* for missing payments."

"Penalty? But, sir, my father could not have anticipated his illness."

The moneylender snorted with a sardonic frown, making his gaunt features even more cadaverous. "My lady, must I repeat, I am not a benevolent man." He licked his thin lips, leaving a bit of spittle at one corner of his mouth while he ogled her breasts just as the footman had done. "'owever, there are *alternative* methods of payment."

Uneasy, Julia drew her hand to her chest and stood. "Other means?"

Also pushing to his feet, Mr. Skinner came around the writing table, stopping only a hand's breadth away from her. "Think on it. Ye're not only a 'ighborn lady, ye are quite fetching. Why, I believe by 'aving ye in my employ, your debt will be repaid in a few years' time."

There was absolutely no doubt in Julia's mind as to what this cur was asking. How dare he demean her with such an offer. As she backed away, the licentious glint in the scoundrel's eyes grew blacker and eviler, making a chill cut straight to her bones. But if this man thought for half a second that she would stoop to such indecency, he was *sorely* mistaken.

"Sir, I assure you I am doing everything in my power to settle my father's debt." She jolted as her back hit the wall. "I-I would rather die than work for the likes of you. I bid you please do not further insult me with your lewd proposals."

Placing his palms either side of her head, the man trapped her there. "Unfortunate ye are unwilling, though I could..." He drew in a deep breath, his gaze dropping to her lips. "Ye are aware I am in possession of the deed to Huntly Manor, are you not?"

"I am." He might have the deed in hand, but the property was worth far more than the debt. Furthermore, she mustn't allow this miscreant to intimidate her. "And you are aware my father is an esteemed a peer of the realm and therefore exempt from debtor's court. I have given you a reasonable solution to repay the outstanding sum, and I ask you once again to honor it."

He leaned forward until his mouth was even with her ear. "Terms from a woman I can no more count on than a bedridden earl."

Julia shuddered. "Please."

"I shall accept your terms of four months, but the sum is thirty pounds."

"Thirty?"

She tried to duck under his arm, but he caught her face in his grip and forced her to look at him. "And this—"

As she drew in a gasp, the varlet sealed his mouth over hers and stuck his tongue inside, sweeping it around her mouth as she recoiled, her head hitting the wall. With all her strength, Julia shoved against his chest and forced him away. "You vulgar man!" she cried, dashing for the door.

His sickly laugh resounded through the corridor as she ran past the butler and outside. Gasping for air, the world spinning, Julia didn't stop running until she suddenly realized she'd dashed into the middle of a busy thoroughfare and was now gaping at a team of horses as their driver pulled on the reins shouting for her to move.

Stunned, she froze in place watching as the high-stepping pair bore down on her, the whites of the beasts' eyes assessing her as the horses heads turned with the pressure from the bits pulling their mouths wide.

This was the end. Within her next heartbeat she'd be trampled in London and no one would have a clue who she was. Dunscaby would be puzzled when Smallwood didn't return to the town house. What would happen to Papa? To Willaby and Mrs. May?

I can't die.

As the thought popped into her head, the horses came to a stop inches from her nose. Allowing herself to breathe, Julia reached out and stroked her fingers down a white blaze.

"What the devil are you doing crossing the road without looking, ye daft wench?" hollered the driver.

Regaining her wits, she gave him a quick curtsy and sashayed toward the footpath. "Forgive me. Your team came so fast, I did not see you."

The door to the carriage opened. "Julia?"

Recognizing the voice, she squinted to better see inside. "Sophie?"

A smiling, warm, and welcome face appeared in the doorway. "Oh, my heavens, it is you. But whatever are you doing in this dreadful part of Town of all places and without an escort?"

For the love of Moses, traveling within the carriage was none other than Julia's dearest friend from finishing school—a friend whose face she'd never forget in a hundred years. At once, Julia's eyes filled with tears. She covered her mouth and try as she might, she was completely unable to stop the flow of sobs from assailing her.

"Eustace!" Sophie clapped her hands at the footman at the rear of the carriage. "Help Her Ladyship into the carriage straightaway."

Julia was in no state to argue, and she was already making quite a scene with carriages backed up and going around while their drivers shouted obscenities. Thank heavens luck had decided to take a turn for the better. Sophie had been a dear friend for years. She was the daughter of a prominent baron, and they'd attended finishing school together. In fact, Sophie was one of the few people outside her home who was aware that Julia's father struggled financially—though only the two remaining servants at Huntly Manor knew how desperately.

Accepting the footman's hand, Julia held her skirts and climbed into the lovely coach, falling into her friend's arms. Unable to speak, she wept like a baby while Sophie patted her back and rocked. "That's it, have a good cry, and then tell me all about it."

Julia lost herself, trying ever so hard to gain control, gasping and hiccupping while tears rolled down her cheeks. "I-I paid a visit to Papa's vile moneylender. And-and he tried to force himself upon me!"

"That vile creature. How dare he? I'll have a word with Northampton this very day and have the man dealt with."

Julia tried to catch her breath. What had Sophie said? "N-Northampton?"

"Yes, my sweeting. I married the marquess two months ago. Did you not receive your invitation?"

"I'm afraid I-I've been...*ah*...away."

"Not to worry, there were so many people in attendance I can scarcely recall a face." Sophie patted Julia's arm. "Now, tell me, I who is this uncouth vulture?"

"M-Mr. Skinner."

"Oh dear," her friend groaned. "Silas Skinner?"

Julia drew her kerchief from her sleeve and dabbed her eyes. "Yes, he's the one."

"Good heavens." Sophie crossed herself like she so often had done when they were attending finishing school. "That man is the one person my husband refuses to go near. He's reputed to be as wealthy as the crown, perhaps more so, and he has some sort of vendetta against polite society. No self-respecting member of the *ton* visits Deuces—that is unless they want to tempt the devil. You'd best not cross him."

"So I've gathered. I only asked that he allow more time for me to make up for the payments Papa missed after he fell ill."

"Oh...that is not good, not good at all."

"No, but I think I was successful in satisfying him. He granted new terms, at least."

"And then proceeded to make unwelcomed advances? And you without an escort?"

Julia again shuddered. "Please, I beg of you to keep my confidences."

"Of course, I will." Sophie gave her a little hug. "Good Lord, here you are after all these years, still looking after your father and continuing to suffer for it."

"Forgive me." Julia knew better than to tell her friend the worst of Papa's matters. Now that she'd calmed herself, she needed to change the subject. One did not speak of their financial woes, not even with a good friend who knew something of her background. "Heavens, here we are talking about my miserable state of affairs and you've just told me you have married a marquess and I haven't even been courteous enough to extend my felicitations."

"Thank you, my sweet, but given the circumstances, you were in no state to say anything." Sophie brushed a lock of hair away from her face. "I don't think I've ever seen you cry, and with so much abandon."

"I doubt I have ever fallen apart like that." But Julia felt surprisingly good for having done so. "Thank the stars it was your carriage that nearly ran me over and not that of some pompous fop."

"It must have been destiny." Sophie flicked the tassel of her fan with her gloved fingers. "Now tell me, how long will you be in Town?"

"Ah...I'm here for a few weeks, no more."

"Oh?" Her friend's eyebrows shot up. "Have you rooms? Did your father not divest his town house?"

"I'm a guest of..." What should she say? She couldn't mention the Duke of Dunscaby because if anyone asked him, it would mean the commencement of her undoing. "Well, honestly, I'm renting a small room. It is quite sufficient for my needs."

"Truly?"

"Yes. The landlady is ever so reasonable." Well, that contained a modicum of truth. Martin and his family were incredibly accommodating and kind.

"Well, then, we absolutely must have tea."

"We must," Julia said, biting her lip. Could she dig herself a deeper hole? She'd stolen into the mews and dressed in a dusty old sedan chair, which she hoped never to have to do again.

"Oh!" Sophie thrust her fan upward as if she'd just had a marvelous idea. "Northampton and I are hosting a ball, have you heard?"

"A ball? I'm afraid I've been a bit removed from the *ton* for such information to...*ah*...reach me."

"Six days hence on May Day, mind you. And, my dearest, you cannot come to London without attending my very first ball as Marchioness."

Julia sighed, her head spinning. *How can I weasel my way out of this?* "Imagine that, my friend, Lady Sophia, a marchioness."

"I still cannot believe it myself." Sophie looped her arm through Julia's elbow and squeezed. "You will be my guest of honor."

"Oh, no." Shaking her head, Julia drew her arm away. "No, no, no. I haven't a thing to wear."

Sophie tapped her fan to her chin, giving Julia a look that said she would entertain absolutely no argument. "And you most likely haven't a lady's maid have you?"

Julia mouth dropped open and closed twice before she conceded, "I'm afraid not."

"Then you shall come join me the morning of the ball. I happen to have a costume that will perfectly compliment your coloring. And if you come early, my lady's maid will have plenty of time to make alterations...and style your hair, of course."

The racing of Julia's heart slowed. "Costume, did you say?"

"Yes, the ball is a masquerade, silly—all guests will wear masks and proper costumes, even the orchestra will be in fancy dress. And you cannot refuse me. Not only did you miss my wedding, you love to dance more than anyone I know."

It was true, Julia did love to dance—the woman's part, of course.

"You might even meet your knight in shining armor—someone who can help you slip out from under the enormous yoke your father has hung around your neck, poor dear."

Julia wasn't so sure she'd ever find her shining knight, but perhaps she *could* slip out one more time. Oh, how wonderful to actually dress as a lady and attend a masked ball where no one would know her identity—to dance and make merry after all the worry and months of tireless work.

13

"I am so happy that we have returned to London," said Mama, dressed in a lacy domino costume, completely covered in black including a veiled mask draped over her eyes. "Word is Northampton's ball shall be the sensation of the Season."

Martin peered closer at his mother, trying to look her in the eye through the black netting but failing miserably. "I'm certain it will be, but the question is how can you possibly see in that thing?"

"'Tis only fine tulle across the eyes. I can see just fine."

"Well, you look as if you've returned to full mourning."

Mama fluffed her skirts. "Be it half or full, my heart is still mourning your father and that is what truly matters."

Martin gave her shoulders a squeeze. "Forgive me. You look lovely as always." Feeling a bit silly dressed as Mark Antony, he glanced to his bare knees. Charity had done her duty and found him a costume but hadn't taken into account that he was far taller than most men. Even the Roman leather armor was a bit snug across his chest.

Mama pointed her fan at his sandals, complete with leather straps laced all the way up to his knees. "I hope your toes don't freeze." Her gaze shifting upward, she rapped his shoulder with the blasted thing. "Where is your mask?"

He pulled the black slip of cloth from inside his armor. "Not to worry, I'll put it on before we arrive—canna have anyone knowing Mark Antony is really a duke, now can we?"

"I don't know. I would recognize you regardless, and I imagine more than half the mothers in attendance will have your identity figured out by the end of the evening. Keep your eyes open. You may find your match."

"I will *not* find my match. I accepted the invitation to this masquerade to provide an escort for Charity so that she may find *her* match," he said as his sister started down the stairs, dressed as Cleopatra with a radiant smile beaming below a golden mask. However, her shimmering golden gown clung to her form a bit too tightly for Martin's liking. At least with an Egyptian collar encrusted with turquoise, the bodice wasn't cut too low as was the fashion in ballrooms of late. The black wig she wore had a sharp-angled cut, offset by the serpent crown perched upon her head.

"My heavens, sister, you are incredibly bonny this eve. I'm certain Cleopatra possessed nowhere near your beauty." Martin met her on the stairs and offered his hand. "'Tis a good thing I have a Roman sword in my scabbard. I can see it now—I'll be fighting off all the rakes and knaves worshiping at your feet."

The lass gave him a nudge. "You wouldna dare!"

He gave her a wink. "When it comes to your honor, you'd be surprised at what I would dare."

In a whirlwind of red curls, Modesty bounded

down the stairs and charged ahead of them. "Do you not think Charity looks like a real Egyptian queen?"

"I dunna like the wig," said Grace, appearing on the landing. "It is far too severe for her features."

"But the cut is the Egyptian style to match her costume," said Mama, taking Charity's arm. "That's the purpose of a masked ball is to have one's identity veiled, after all."

"Agreed." Martin looked to Giles standing with his cloak, hat, and cane, all of which would be out of place with his costume. "We'd best be off," he said, passing the butler and opening the door himself. After all, he did have a red cape attached to his shoulders. Heaven forbid he cover up such a flag of masculinity with a coat.

"Since it is a masquerade, why can I not go along?" asked Grace, her voice hopeful. "It would take but a moment for me to change. I could wear one of my old frocks with pantaloons and go as Little Bo Peep."

"No," Martin said simultaneously with his mother.

"Goodness you are incorrigible," Mama added.

"I thought I was the incorrigible one," said Modesty.

Charity tugged on the youngest sister's red curl and made it bounce. "It seems you've been replaced."

Together they headed for the waiting carriage and the short ride to the Marquess of Northampton's stately home. After they were introduced and moved inside, there was no doubt that His Lordship's new marchioness had not spared a farthing on the decorations. Enormous vases filled with house flowers adorned every surface. Brilliant chandeliers lit by thousands of candles made the ballroom glow. Even the servants were clad in an array of costumes.

"I wish etiquette allowed young ladies to dance

with their brothers," Charity whispered behind her lotus fan. "Goodness, Marty, we're all wearing masks, mayhap no one will notice."

"Mama will notice, and that's reason enough not to try it. Just be happy we've missed the grand march where we would have suffered strutting around the room like preening peacocks." As Martin spoke, he scanned the room. They'd arrived fashionably late as one would expect from a ducal party. A sizeable crowd filled the hall with nearly as many men as women. He reckoned his sister ought to have her dance card filled in no time. "I aim to see you dancing most of the night and I'll wager by the time the orchestra plays their last set you'll forget I'm the one who escorted you here."

"My dear." Mama looped her arm through Charity's elbow and gestured to a somewhat undersized King Richard. "It is my esteemed pleasure to introduce the Earl of Bixby."

The man bowed deeply. "My lady…"

Martin moved away, though he was a bit flummoxed. Before they'd left the town house, Mama had held forth about hiding one's identity at masked balls, and yet she was already making introductions. Though Bixby was entirely too old for his sister, at least the chap was signing her dance card and that ought to provide the lass with some encouragement. With Mama's enthusiasm, Martin didn't doubt Charity would be fully occupied this eve—giving him an opportunity to observe.

A dais spanned the far end of the ballroom with the orchestra situated on one side. On the other, King Arthur and Guinevere held court—obviously the Marquess and Marchioness of Northampton. They were seated upon gilt thrones, but the couple were not what drew Martin's attention. To Her Ladyship's left, a woman sat in a small, unpretentious chair. She was dressed as a Greek goddess and wore a canary yellow gown with a matching mask. A flicker of awareness sparked at the back of Martin's mind. Did he know the bonny lass?

Deep in his soul, he was absolutely certain he had met this woman before.

But where?

From across the ballroom, he stared. Though yellow had never been his favorite color, for some reason, it was now. The lady wore it so well from the daring neckline edged with crossed gold cord accentuating her breasts—incredibly well-formed breasts—not terribly large, but pert and round and ever so unignorable. Her chestnut hair was piled atop her head in a riot of curls framing her oval face. Her coiffeur was held in place by a sparkling circlet with a white swan nestled in a splay of myrtle, its symbolism indicating the beauty was costumed as Aphrodite.

Martin sighed as she turned her head, allowing him to regard her profile, revealing a small nose peeking from beneath her mask.

The woman opened her fan and inclined her head toward the marchioness, whispering something that made Her Ladyship smile.

Martin, leaned forward as if doing so would help him eavesdrop, even though he could not possibly hear across the expansive floor or above the orchestra. He skirted around the hall, watching her—a long, graceful neck, delicate shoulders that looked smoother than ivory satin. God save him, he was certain he'd seen those shoulders before. At the very least, he'd dreamed about them. Overcome with an uncanny sense of familiarity, he could not shake the idea that he knew this woman from another place and time, as if their destinies were somehow entwined.

But how?

As Martin approached the dais, a court jester stepped into his line of sight. The man bowed to the goddess and escorted her into the center of the floor.

Clenching his fists, Martin looked on with a scowl, swearing he'd never be seen anywhere dressed as a damned court jester. If the cur made one single ungentlemanly move, he would personally thrash the buffoon within an inch of his life.

"I say, Dunscaby, I haven't seen you in London for some time. Please accept my condolences for your loss."

"Thank you." Martin glanced at Northampton and regarded the marquess' medieval robes before returning his gaze to the dancers as a minuet began. "It appears my disguise is ineffective, even though I've been away from Town for nearly seven months."

"You're a difficult man to miss, given your size—and only a Scot would have the aplomb to step out in a tunic that short." The marquess bowed with an exaggerated flourish. "But forgive my impertinence. One does not ignore a duke when he accepts one's invitation."

Martin rocked back on his sandals which strained the leathers around his shins. "You and your bride are to be commended. The hall is stunning."

"'Tis all Her Ladyship's doing."

"Hmm," he mused, not really listening as the sable-haired beauty lightly touched her fingers to her partner's hand and seemed to float across the floor like a feather carried on a gentle breeze. "Astonishingly graceful."

"Yes, there is something about a minuet that is purely balletic."

If Northampton didn't go weak at the knees from watching the Greek goddess in the yellow gown, he obviously was still on his honeymoon. Rumors were his was a love match. "The lass who was seated beside your wife—I feel as if I know her."

"Aphrodite?"

"Come, come. I'll wager Her Ladyship has been whispering everyone's identity to you as they've been announced. Surely you ken the name of a woman who occupied such an esteemed place upon the dais."

The marquess scratched his temple, making his crown tilt sideways. "You didn't hear it from me, but she's Lady Julia, one of Sophie's dear friends."

Julia...

Martin wracked his brain, but he was dashed if he didn't know a Julia. The name was common enough. He *ought* to know a Julia. But he'd be eating crow if he owned to being clueless to Northampton. Perhaps his mother knew the woman. After all, if she was *Lady* Julia, she was the daughter of an earl or higher. There weren't all that many earls, marquesses and dukes in Britain. "Might I have an introduction?" he blurted before he thought better of it.

One of Northampton's eyebrows arched above his black mask. "On the marriage mart are you?"

"Hardly." Martin stood taller and rested his hand on the pommel of his sword. "I'm here for my sister. However, I may as well make the best of it and have a wee dance with the bonniest woman present."

Northampton snorted. "I beg to differ, Your Grace. No one holds a candle to my Sophie."

Martin didn't bother glancing toward the marchioness. After all, he'd seen the two women sitting together. And though the mysterious Lady Julia was in the smaller seat, she was like a shining beacon compared to the lovely, yet somewhat pallid, other woman.

The minuet ended on a harmonious chord while Aphrodite sank into a courtly curtsy. Martin immediately started moving toward her when Northampton grasped him by the arm. "My, it has been a long time since you graced a ballroom. Come this way. Her Ladyship's partner will escort her back to the dais."

Julia.

Name flowed like a Highland burn, babbling through Martin's mind with an accent on the L.

"My lady," said Northampton as she approached. "Please allow me to introduce the du...*ah*...Mark Antony."

As her lovely chocolatey brown eyes widened beneath the shroud of her mask, the icon of grace tripped on her hem. Though his heart jolted, Martin pretended not to notice while she quickly regained her composure. Perhaps the floor was a bit uneven. Had she recognized him? Or had the Marchioness pointed him out when he'd arrived? The steward had announced his party as "Mark Antony, Cleopatra, and the widow" which had made Mama a wee bit piqued.

Martin slid his foot forward and bowed, noting the lass was ever so petite in stature. "It is a pleasure, m'lady." As he straightened, her gaze lingered a tad too long on his legs and then trailed upward until she looked him in the eyes. Had a celestial bell just sounded? Was the delicate tinkling responsible for the sudden bout of bubbles levitating from the pit of his stomach?

He had no clue, but by the saints, he liked the unabashed way she looked at him.

After a moment's hesitation, she dropped her gaze

to the floor and curtsied deeply. "I am honored to make the acquaintance of Caesar's high-ranking general."

Had she drawn in a wee gasp? He hoped so. "Aye, but dunna play down the importance of a goddess." Martin gestured from wall to wall. "I see no other celestial beings in the hall."

"You flatter me, sir. Though I find it indubitably interesting that a preeminent officer of your rank is blessed with a Scottish brogue."

"Not all Scots are peasants," said Northampton.

"Forgive me if I was mistakenly construed as impertinent. The implication was certainly not my intention." Dashed if her gaze didn't slip to Martin's legs yet again. "It was intended as a simple observation."

"As is your impeccable English accent." Martin extended his hand. "Would you do me the honor of the next dance?"

The lady nodded to their host. "I do believe King Arthur signed my card for the next."

Northampton bowed and took a step away. "Do not let me dissuade you. I shall naturally forfeit my place for my esteemed guest."

Martin gave the man an appreciative nod and led Lady Julia to the floor while the orchestra played the introduction to a slow French waltz. With the music, the image of Smallwood clomping about the drawing room with Modesty came to mind.

"Are you fond of waltzing?" asked Her Ladyship placing her hand upon his waist as he mirrored her. Mayhap he couldn't have given a rat's arse about the new dance sweeping through Britain's ballrooms, but in this moment with this woman's hand touching him so intimately and allowing him to hold her in kind, it was his favorite dance in all of Christendom. Perhaps waltzing had become his favored pastime.

"Quite fond." Arching his hand over his head, he grasped her fingers and stared into those round, trusting, doe-like eyes. "I've recently had the opportunity to watch my sisters' dancing lessons."

As he began to move, Lady Julia effortlessly flowed with him, lighter on her feet than any woman with whom he'd ever had the pleasure of waltzing. "By the smile playing on your lips, I'm guessing they must have been enjoying themselves."

"I'm certain they were."

"Pray tell, if your sisters were dancing, why were you watching and not stepping in as a partner?"

"Their lesson had already begun when I arrived and the footmen were getting along nicely—except for my steward."

"Your steward was dancing?" she asked her voice a wee bit higher while those shaded eyes watched him, anticipating his every step, his every nuance. All Martin needed to do was apply the slightest of pressure and she responded as if she'd danced with him a hundred times before.

"The fellow was making an attempt at dancing. Unfortunately, the man isn't gifted with grace as are you."

Lady Julia laughed—a very audacious laugh and quite improper for a ballroom. But the happiness she imparted made his heart flutter. A warmth surged through him akin to the thousands of mirrored candles making the hall as bright as a sunlit day.

While they twirled, waltzing across the floor, his sense of familiarness grew as if he'd known this woman all his life. But if they had met, he definitely would have remembered.

The dance ended all too soon followed by the announcement that the orchestra was taking an intermission. Martin bowed and offered his elbow, the touch of her fingers on his arm nothing short of staggering. Together they strode toward the dais while he tried to convince himself of all the reasons he should not ask the woman for another dance when the musicians returned, the first being it was somewhat improper. Doubtless, the gossips were watching and if Northumberland knew Dunscaby's true identity, then so did they.

"Marty..." Charity stepped out from the crowd, covering her mouth with her fingers. "Ahem, I meant to say Mark Antony."

He stopped and looked for Mama who was chatting with a matron near the wall. "Cleopatra, please allow me to introduce Aphrodite, goddess and esteemed guest of King Arthur and Queen Guinevere."

Lady Julia curtsied simultaneously with his sister. "I am pleased to make your acquaintance."

"As am I." Charity hesitated for a moment, leaning toward Her Ladyship with an odd twist to her lips before she straightened and gestured to Mama. "The domino and I are heading to the lady's withdrawing room while the orchestra takes their intermission. Would you care to join us?"

"Oh no." Aphrodite shook her head, nearly losing the swan in her coiffeur. As Charity's smile waned, Lady Julia took his sister's hand in her palm. "Forgive me. I'm afraid I haven't been out in society for some time. Though I would very much like to go with you, I must return to Queen Guinevere. She is expecting me to...ah...return."

With that, Her Ladyship curtsied and hastened away.

"Do ye ken who she is?" his sister asked.

"I've no idea, but she seems familiar."

"I felt the same. She's a darling wee lass and her costume lights up the entire hall."

Martin posed no argument as he watched the mysterious Lady Julia head for the dais, where the marchioness was nowhere in sight.

14

When Sophie was nowhere to be seen, beads of perspiration broke out on Julia's forehead. Not only did she feel the heat of His Grace's eyes focused on her back as if he were homing in on a prized stag, she'd excused herself under the pretense of meeting the marchioness who was nowhere near the dais, nor was she in the ballroom.

Gah!

What had Julia been thinking? She had just danced with the Duke of Dunscaby and by doing so, she had risked everything. Yes, she ought to have realized Lady Charity would be here with her mother but she'd been given no clue that His Grace would be in attendance and most days he apprised her of his plans.

You complete and utter dolt!

Why hadn't Dunscaby said anything about dressing as Mark Antony and wearing a tunic that hardly covered his thighs? Regardless if he was wearing a mask, Julia knew the man as soon as he'd been introduced. She would have known him if he'd dressed as Marie Antoinette. Perhaps she might not have recognized the duke if he had been completely covered and dressed as a furry bear. When they'd first met she'd been flummoxed by his kilt and hairy knees. Good glory, the man's legs alone made a statement of raw masculinity. Not only that, his arms were scandalously bare. If in the first century Mark Antony looked as virile as Martin MacGalloway, Cleopatra would never have stood a chance!

Turning full circle, Julia's gaze darted across the groups of guests as she frantically searched for Sophie's blue gown. Had her friend slipped away to the withdrawing room as well? Holy macaroons, with three MacGalloways milling about, she absolutely must not go searching for the hostess. Julia had almost melted into a puddle when Dunscaby had introduced his sister. And there had been a spark of recognition in Charity's eyes. A trip to the withdrawing room would have ruined Julia's ruse for good. If she didn't escape this instant she'd be sacked before the night's end.

Worse, she'd all but swooned when she was dancing in the duke's arms. And the way his eyes focused only on her face stole the breath from her very breast. Her waist still tingled where he'd placed his hand for the waltz. But what had rendered her utterly spellbound was the hunger in his crystal blue eyes. Heaven help her, the expression on his face was one she'd dreamed of seeing every night for the past two months.

And he absolutely must never gaze upon me in such a way again!

Beyond the dais, Julia spotted a set of French doors leading to the rear garden. Without a backward glance, she hastened through them. She must take her leave immediately before she was recognized. First thing on the morrow she'd return Sophie's costume along with a letter of apology, claiming a sudden and violent illness.

Julia dashed past a few couples as she headed for...

Drat! The accursed courtyard was surrounded by a balustrade. Completely trapped, she spun on her heel and scurried toward the other side, finding, thank the stars, a set of stairs leading downward. She grasped her skirts, raised them just above her ankles, and pattered downward.

"M'lady Aphrodite!"

Freezing on the landing, every muscle in Julia's body tensed as her employer's deep voice commanded her to stop. Thank the Father Almighty he hadn't called her Smallwood.

While she regarded him over her shoulder, Mark Antony descended toward her. The light radiating from the hall above, accentuated his powerful frame, his red cape flapping behind him as if he were indeed the most influential general in the civilized world. "Are you in need of assistance?"

"I...ah..." Oh, holy help, how she wanted to reply with a yes. "I am looking for Lady Northampton...I mean Guinevere."

Martin stopped beside her. Now that he had moved lower than the beams of light, his crystal blue eyes appeared dark and mysterious behind his mask. He gestured upward to the patio. "I dunna think she is out here, unless..."

"Hmm?"

He peered into the darkness beyond. "Unless she has ventured down into the gardens."

Julia shot a longing look at the remaining steps. She'd nearly managed her escape. "Perhaps I ought to have a quick peek just to be sure."

"I do not advise it—not without an escort."

"Oh, no. You are ever so right. I-I wasn't thinking." She drew her palm to her dizzied forehead, her heart racing. If anyone had a clue she was alone, partway to an unlit garden with Martin MacGalloway, she would be ruined. But then, by posing as his steward Julia had already taken the steps to ensure she'd be ruined for the rest of her days. Nonetheless, if she could not escape this debacle and he realized she was his steward, she never again would be able to show her face.

"Wherever the marchioness is, I'm certain she'll return anon. After all, she is the hostess. Perhaps we ought to return to the hall." He slid his fingers around her elbow, brushing the bare skin just above the edge of her glove. She drew in a sharp gasp while frissons of awareness skittered from her arm to the back of her neck. "Have you a chill?" he asked.

The absolute last thing on Julia's mind was the temperature. "N-no, sir."

He took a step closer, the heat from his body warming her, luring her. Before Julia knew what she was doing, she, too, took a step toward him. Her hand grew a mind of its own and she stroked her fingers along his jaw as she had wanted, craved, desired to do so many times. A hint of stubble bristled beneath the thin doeskin as she imagined it did in the afternoons when he'd oft leaned down and consulted with her on matters of the estate. Oh, dear God, how much she'd longed to touch him every time he was near. And how she trembled as she commanded his attention, those eyes focused so intently upon her.

With her gesture, the duke drew in a sharp breath. "Please tell me, how do I know you, m'lady?" he whispered, deep and low, sending a thrill through her body.

"Know?" she asked, her voice shooting up and her heart hammering even faster than before. *Oh, help, here it comes.*

"Have we not met before this night?" he asked.

"I assure you, I have been away from Town for years and years—tucked away in a remote little village far away from Scotland, mind you."

He swept a lock of hair away from her face as his gaze lowered to her mouth. "But you are closely acquainted with the marchioness are you not?"

Julia tipped her chin higher. "Old friends," came her breathless reply. "From childhood."

"Childhood," he mused softly, his lips moving closer and closer, captivating her, mesmerizing her, making her powerless to flee. With a slight tilt of his head, he slid a hand behind her neck and kissed her. Oh, yes, yes, yes, at long last Julia kissed the man who had consumed her every other waking thought since the day she walked into the Newhailes library.

His tongue stroked her lips, slowly, not forcefully, but with command as if he knew exactly what he wanted. Indeed, as if he knew exactly what *she* wanted. Timidly, she opened for him and within a heartbeat her ability to reason melted away. He tasted of spice laced with a hint of whisky, sweet, yet potently hypnotic. A lush, decadent pleasure filled her and thrummed throughout her entire body, pooling between her legs in the unmentionable place that endlessly ached for him.

Oh, yes, how she ached for him.

As the kiss drew to an end, Julia's eyes fluttered open, and she gazed into Martin's masked face.

He cupped her cheek. "Och, lass, forgive me for taking liberties. But you have me bewitched—"

"Marty?" Charity called from the top of the stairs. "What are you doing down there?"

Julia's heart flew to her throat. "Please go. Now. And do not follow me!"

Before he replied, she raced down the remaining steps and darted into the darkness.

What in God's name am I doing?

"MARTY? WHO WAS THAT?"

Before he answered his sister, Martin stared after Lady Julia's retreating form, her yellow gown disappearing into the darkness in a flurry of billowing silk as if the woman were a ghost.

"...do not follow me."

Why? What was she afraid of?

He swiped a hand over his lips still tingling from their stolen kiss. Oh, by the rood, he'd been too forward. He'd caught her scent and tracked her like a predator, most likely frightening the lass half out of her wits. Why was he such a damned rake? Blast it all, after one dance with the woman, he'd lost his bloody mind.

I never should have kissed the lass.

Even if she hadn't told him to follow, he mustn't. Martin had escorted Charity and Mama to this masquerade. Not only would it be very bad form for the Duke of Dunscaby to leave his mother and sister behind to chase after a mysterious woman, the scandal would be the headline of every London paper on the morrow, which would do nothing to further his sister's prospects.

Clenching his fists, he climbed the stairs.

"You didn't answer me," Charity persisted. "Who was that?"

"I intend to find out," Martin said, offering his elbow as Mama stepped out the French doors.

"Charity, dear, why did you not wait for me?" asked the duchess, her fan oscillating wildly. "You must have a care for your reputation."

"But my brother is out here for heaven's sake."

Martin arched an eyebrow at his sister. It was very unlikely she had seen him go outside. "Ladies, I believe the orchestra is playing one more set before dinner, shall we return to the ballroom?"

"Indeed." Mama took his other elbow and they proceeded inside. "These masquerades are so confounding. I say, half the guests are dallying about as if the rules of etiquette do not exist at all. My dearest, do not let yourself fall into the ne'er-do-well half, heaven forbid."

At his first opportunity, Martin left his mother chatting with another woman in a domino costume while his sister danced with a pirate, who he first warned to be on his best behavior. Once free to pursue his own matters at hand, he found Lady Northampton by the refreshment table.

"Excuse me, Queen Guinevere," he said, bowing with a flourish. "May I say what a marvelous extravaganza you have organized this evening. I am certain this masquerade will be the highlight of the Season."

The marchioness curtsied deeply as she would do for a duke. "Ah, Mark Antony, how every kind of you to say so. And might I add I was pleasantly surprised to receive your acceptance. Are you fond of masquerades?"

He loathed them. In truth, he loathed balls in general. "I am. And it has been ever so diverting to accompany my mother and sister this evening."

"Ah, yes. Lady Charity...I mean Cleopatra looks particularly lovely this evening."

"Thank you, I thought so as well." Having engaged in about enough preamble as Martin could bear, he opted to broach the subject as to why he'd embarked on this conversation. "Earlier, you may have noticed I was dancing with Aphrodite, a woman your husband referred to as Lady Julia."

"Indeed, a dear friend from finishing school."

"She'd mentioned as much. Forgive me, but I canna place a Julia. I must know the lady's family name."

"Did she not tell you herself?" Her Ladyship scanned the crowd. "Wherever has she gone?"

Martin puzzled. Lady Julia had said she was looking for the marchioness. "Her ladyship didna find you?"

"No, I haven't seen her since the two of you enjoyed your waltz."

"I see." In truth Martin didn't see at all. The more he enquired about Lady Julia, the more mysterious the woman became. "I must know how to find her. My mother would like to invite Her Ladyship to tea."

Guinevere raised her finger with a flourish of her voluminous, medieval sleeve. "But this is a masquerade, Mark Antony. Tonight no one is who they seem."

No, he wasn't about to allow a marchioness to fob him off so easily. He leaned in, leveling his gaze and lowering his voice. "If you please, I'll have the lady's family name, and I'll have it now. Thank you."

The woman's face grew red as she gave a wee shake of her shoulders. "Very well if you must, it is St. Vincent."

Martin nearly jolted at the news. "Brixham's daughter?"

"The one in the same. And mind you, she is the kindest, sweetest, most pleasant woman I know."

Martin didn't doubt Lady Northampton's words, but why had Lady Julia been so emphatic that he not follow her? Then again, he most likely startled the lass half out of her wits. He'd kissed an unmarried gentle-woman in a public place. At least the landing of the portico was partially public. Anyone could have caught them—Charity practically had. Lady Julia must have been mortified.

"Did the Earl of Brixham not divest his London town house?" he asked, fishing for more.

"He did, indeed," she replied, flicking open her fan and cooling her face.

"Is Her Ladyship residing with you, then?"

"No."

"Where might she be staying? With a relative by chance?" Martin asked, doing his best to sound non-chalant, but failing miserably.

"She is renting a room...ah...nearby."

"Just nearby?"

"Yes." The marchioness curtsied. "If you'll please excuse me the steward is about to announce dinner."

Martin bowed. "M'lady."

Fancy that, Lady Julia was the Earl of Brixham's daughter and that meant only one fortuitous thing— Jules Smallwood must know the lass. Had they corre-sponded? Doubtless, his steward knew where to find her.

15

J ulia sat at her writing table holding a quill, dripping blobs of ink on the paper while she rested her chin in her hand and stared out the window. For the first time in her life, she was utterly unable to focus on her work. How could she have been so naive as to accept Sophia's invitation? Attending any ball was a disaster in the making. She'd broken her own hard and fast rule...had she not?

Yes, you dolt. I must never, ever let anyone know my true identity, and now my best friend, social butterfly, and new marchioness believes Julia St. Vincent is living in London not far from her house.

Though she had been vague about the location of the room she was supposedly renting, she'd admitted it was but a short walk from the Northampton abode, firstly so that Sophie wouldn't insist on ordering the driver to take her home after her debacle with Mr. Skinner. She hadn't stretched the truth either, because the duke's enormous town house was only two streets away.

Today as she sat completely distracted and unable to focus, no matter how much she admonished herself for her errant decision to attend the masquerade, Julia could not stop thinking about the fleeting moment she'd spent in Martin's arms. Yes, their waltz had been inexplicably erotic, his hand on her waist, and hers on his *very* solid, *very* masculine, *very* warm waist while they moved in tandem as if they'd partnered together for years. The dance had been akin to two swans in a balletic rendezvous upon a glassy pond.

All this time she'd been practicing opposite Modesty when little did she know the duke was undoubtedly the best dancer in the MacGalloway household. Obviously, he'd been enjoying himself at her expense, or Smallwood's expense as it were.

Last night, not only had they danced like two matched swans, he'd actually followed her outside as if he intended to pursue her. Of course, it was only one evening, and she'd been costumed as a goddess and wearing a mask, but he appeared to be, perhaps, a tad infatuated. Their entire encounter had been like a fairy story. Martin had been so gallant, so caring and, most especially, so awfully good at kissing.

"Lord save me," Julia groaned, her lips tingling at the mere thought of kissing him again. After setting her quill in the holder, she pushed to her feet and began to pace.

She absolutely must stop thinking about kissing the Duke of Dunscaby this instant. His Grace was her employer and her desperately needed source of income. There were people relying on her, for heaven's sake. Without her wages, not only would her father be in dire straits, Willaby and Mrs. May would be out on their ears.

"Attending the masquerade was a horrible mistake that can never happen again."

I must positively force myself to block the entire evening from my mind.

Julia bit down on her thumbnail. Exactly how did one forget the most erotic kiss of her life, especially when she was a spinster posing as a man and most likely would never again be kissed by the object of her affection, let alone anyone else?

"I had a severe lapse of judgment and, though I may have succumbed to a moment of enjoyment, I must lock the incident away in my heart and pretend it never happened."

Except it had.

"Even if I admit the evening at the ball did come to pass, I must promise myself never, ever to again take such a risk."

Satisfied, Julia thrust her fists onto her hips and took a deep breath. It had been a miracle that Martin hadn't recognized her, and Lady Charity as well. She may have been wearing a mask, but other than looking positively female, she and Jules Smallwood were identical.

Julia stamped her foot. "And I will stop calling the duke Martin this instant!"

"Smallwood!" Dunscaby boomed, bursting through the door. "You will never believe who I met last eve."

Oh, dear God in heaven, please let it be someone other than me. She clasped her hands together and tried to smile affably. "Who, Your Grace?"

"None other than Lady Julia St. Vincent."

She felt the color drain from her face while a bout of dizziness nearly sent her crashing to the floorboards.

"Surely you know the lass..." Martin looked her from head to toe. "Are you certain the two of you are not related, cousins perchance?"

What ought I say? I am one and the same with the daft little tart?

She was supposed to be the son of a knight, she couldn't be related to herself.

Julia squeezed her hands tighter while she stared at the man, her eyes wide, her mouth dry.

In truth it wouldn't be entirely inconceivable for the two mothers to be sisters...or cousins. Mayhap she ought to admit to such a thing...mayhap doing so might help to explain how she was able to come by the position with Papa at such a young age. "Distant cousins, which helped me secure the post of steward with the Earl of Brixham in the first place," she said, positive she was going to be struck dead within the next two minutes and catapulted directly to Hades.

"Och, what a boon!"

"Boon, sir?"

Martin rubbed his hands together. "Were you aware Her Ladyship was in Town?"

"In London? My word, I had no idea." Pressing the palms of her hands against her temples, Julia fought the spinning of her head. *How much deeper am I to dig my grave?*

"The Marchioness of Northampton said she was staying nearby. Och, as the estate's steward, I would naturally assume you would know where Lady Julia stays when in London?"

"I daresay, the last time I recall Her Ladyship visiting Town was years ago when she was introduced to society. If my memory serves, she resided in the city for one Season and then returned to Huntly Manor—and I do believe the earl still kept a town house in London at the time."

"Her Ladyship mentioned something about being

tucked away in a remote little village," Dunscaby mused.

"Yes, well, Brixham is not a large borough by any stretch of the imagination."

"Smallwood, we must find her." Dunscaby covered his eyes then quickly moved his hands apart, drawing her attention to the vivid crystal blue color. "Though Her Ladyship was wearing a mask, I tell you here and now, she is the bonniest creature I've ever had the pleasure of setting eyes upon."

Julia grew weak at the knees, her throat constricting so tightly, she was barely able to swallow. Martin thought her beautiful...well, bonny was the term he used, but everyone knew bonny to a Scot was beautiful to the rest of the world. Why, oh why could she not revert to being herself?

If only I didn't have Mr. Skinner in the wings demanding payment.

"I was thinking," Martin continued, "It might be less likely to make a stir if you were to write to her father and enquire as to her address, what with you both being in London."

"The earl?" Positive the archangel of death would truly descend upon her at any moment, Julia placed her hand on her writing table for support. How could she convince Dunscaby to abandon this idea? "Brixham is quite ill, you are aware. I am not certain I would receive a reply."

"Then write to a servant perchance? Does not Her Ladyship have a servant in whom she confides?"

"I believe the butler, Willaby, has always been her confidant."

Holy macaroons, why did I volunteer Willaby? Have I completely lost my sense of reason?

"Excellent." Dunscaby thrust his upturned palm

toward her quill and ink pot. "Send the man a missive immediately."

Julia gave a respectful bow. "Straightaway, sir."

"Oh, and regarding other matters at hand, I've ordered a carriage to be readied. In twenty minutes meet me in the hall. The admiral has notified me that Lord Gibb's ship is due to moor in the Pool of London this very afternoon."

Before she could congratulate him on his brother's return, the duke swept out the door as boldly as he'd made his entrance.

Julia sank into the chair at her desk, crumpled the spotty piece of paper into the smallest ball her fist could manage and threw it into the rubbish bin. She had best send Willaby something. Her opening line: "*I am an unmitigated fool and ought to be horsewhipped...*"

MARTIN TAPPED his toe on the carriage floor, feeling more like walking the four miles to the Pool of London rather than riding. If he weren't a duke, he might waltz the entire way, dancing with every lass he passed by, imagining each one to be Lady Julia. Never in his life had he felt such bubbling effervescence. He absolutely must seize an opportunity to meet with the lass as soon as possible. Had he been affected by the mystery of the masquerade, or was the woman truly as enchanting as she'd seemed? Martin had to know. He wasn't usually one to be driven by impulse, but he'd barely slept last night, reliving the fleeting moments he'd spent with the goddess. On top of it all, when he'd arisen this morning, his desire to find Her Ladyship had been nothing short of all-consuming.

Fortunately, Smallwood, who sat opposite in the

carriage, had been a steward in the woman's house and had already dispatched a missive to the earl's butler. "I would imagine as Brixham's steward you would have seen Lady Julia frequently. My sisters seem to enjoy chatting with you, I assume you were able to come to know her rather well."

"Um...yes, sir," Smallwood's voice shot up like a nervous finch. Truly, the man needed to expand his horizons. "She is quite pleasant."

"Pleasant? How can you be so dull? The woman is astounding. Not only is her figure perfectly proportioned, she dances as gracefully as a bird in flight. My God, you should have seen her at last eve's masquerade."

"Hmm?"

"She was dressed in the costume of Aphrodite—canary yellow, mind you, a Grecian gown with flowing skirts and a plunging neckline—oh, be still my heart, if you understand my gist."

"But, sir," Smallwood said as if female breasts didn't interest him in the slightest. "Is not the reason for a masquerade to conceal one's identity? How the devil did you uncover the lady's name? Did she tell you?"

Martin threw up his hands. Of all the questions Smallwood could have come up with, the man is worried about how he came by Lady Julia's name? "Of course not. I am a duke. When I ask for information it is bad form to refuse me."

"Ah yes, there are benefits to being near the top of the proverbial pecking order."

Placing his hands on the padded bench, Martin leaned forward. "Tell me, what is she like?"

The wee man gaped as if he'd been suddenly rendered dumb. "Lady Julia?"

"Aye, the woman whom we've been discussing since the carriage left Mayfair."

"Well..." The little man drummed his slender fingers on his thigh. "She likes to read a great deal, I'd say she's very skilled at embroidery, and is relatively accomplished on the pianoforte."

"Is she?" Martin suddenly could see himself standing beside an ornately painted instrument while the lassie's fingers magically danced across the keys. "I do hope she gives a recital whilst she is in London."

Smallwood's shoulders shook with his snort. "I doubt she will, sir."

"Why do you say that? Why would she not if she is a proficient?"

"Ah...I think...well, ah...Her Ladyship is bashful."

Martin deliberated for a moment. Was that why she'd seemed somewhat reticent? Not that she was standoffish, if he could judge by the way the woman had kissed him back. "I do believe it is a virtue to be a wee bit introverted."

"Yes, indeed, sir. Lady Julia always seemed to be content to remain at home in the country. She's quite fond of animals and...and she has a cat named Peaches."

"A Tabby?"

Jules shrugged. "I have no idea. Peaches is somewhat of a scruffy, spotty thing. She found him as a kitten abandoned on the side of the road, not far from Huntly Manor."

"Is that so?"

"Indeed."

Martin pulled the curtain aside and searched the faces of the passersby. "I wonder if she brought the cat to London."

"I wouldn't think so, sir, given cats are not fond of travel."

Damnation, not a single pedestrian resembled Her Ladyship in the slightest. "Well, you should see her waltz. I say, Smallwood, it is a shame you did not inherit her grace."

"Perhaps God saw fit to bestow grace upon my cousin rather than me because it is a far more important a virtue for a young woman who is bred to marry into the nobility."

Martin dropped the curtain. "I suppose you are right. I, for one, could watch Lady Julia dance for hours."

Smallwood cleared his throat and looked to his hands, seemingly uncomfortable.

"Do you think she would fancy a ride through Hyde Parke on my phaeton?"

The little man grinned for the first time that day. "What young lady wouldn't enjoy riding through a park and sitting beside a duke whilst he expertly manages a matched pair?"

Now the steward was talking.

"Do you really think she'd like it?" Martin asked, not giving a whit if he sounded like a wet-eared lad.

"I cannot see why she wouldn't, sir." Smallwood straightened his cravat. "Pardon me for being a tad insolent, sir, but you are not entertaining the idea of marriage are you?"

"Marriage? Me? Surely you jest!" Slapping the seat, Martin threw back his head and laughed. "Only a sheltered man such as yourself would ask such a question. Dammit all, I've only just met the lass. I'm still as staunch a bachelor as I was before the masquerade ball."

The carriage rolled to a stop. "The Pool of London, Your Grace," called the coachman.

And none too soon. Good God, the idea of death until we part made Martin shiver to his bones.

Almost as soon as they disembarked, Gibb marched down the gangway of the *HMS Cerberus*. Though a cocksure grin stretched across his lips, Martin was taken aback at how much his brother had aged in the time he'd been at war. Gibb was broader and leaner at the same time and, as he neared, lines etched by the sea furrowed at the corners of his eyes.

Martin thrust out his hand. "By the saints, I believe the Royal Navy has turned you into a man."

Gibb's grip was like a vice, though Martin could have sworn his brother's eyes misted. "Och, since we last met, you've turned into a bloody duke."

Martin pulled his hand away and splayed his fingers. The last time they'd been together was at Da's funeral. Not only were they all bereft, he'd not yet embraced the dukedom. And though he'd never admit it to anyone else, he still felt out of sorts at times as if he were only playing at dukedom rather than executing the role at a high level of efficiency.

He gestured to the wee man standing beside him. "Allow me to introduce Jules Smallwood, my steward."

Gibb shook the fellow's hand. "It is a pleasure, sir. I'm told you've been a fine addition."

"The pleasure is mine, my lord." Smallwood winced before glancing to Martin and back to Gibb. "My word, are all the MacGalloway men as dashing as you pair?"

"Good God, laddie, at times you come up with the most confounding drivel." Martin turned to his brother. "I hope you have a thirst, because I certainly do."

"Thirst?" Gibb swatted the steward on the back, making him lurch forward. "You never need to ask a sailor twice."

Martin nodded to the footman who opened the carriage door. "Then White's it is. Smallwood and I have something of import to discuss."

"White's?" Gibb asked, heading across the street. "Why drive all the way into Town when there's a perfectly good tavern right here? Unless being a duke has placed you above rubbing elbows with common tars."

16

W hat a stupid thing to have said when she was supposed to be impersonating a man. Heaven's stars, *"are all the MacGalloway men dashing?"*

Dashing!

Only a woman would use such a descriptor. Why hadn't she thought before spewing such nonsense? Lord Gibb might be nearly as attractive as his brother but he was a MacGalloway and that was reason enough to completely ignore his good looks or to notice anything remotely alluring about the chap.

Worse, as soon as Julia stepped into the bawdy, smoke-filled tavern, ice pulsed through her blood. Though the alehouse was filled with loud sailors, her gaze immediately snapped to none other than Silas Skinner. He turned from his place at the bar, his gaze narrowing and instantly homing on her.

As heat crept up her face, she quickly looked to her toes. Surely the moneylender hadn't recognized her in disguise. Even if there was an inkling of recognition, after neither Lady Charity nor His Grace had identified Julia at the ball, she was fairly certain that wearing her father's clothing, her hair clubbed combined with a beaver top hat upon her head, she looked nothing like the lady who'd visited Deuce's. Yes, there might be a resemblance, but what well-bred woman would take such an extraordinarily large risk to her reputation and pretend to be a man? It simply wasn't done, which is why Julia and Willaby had concocted the idea in the first place.

Careful not to again allow her eyes to stray to the ghoulish fiend, she followed as Dunscaby as he led the way to an empty table at the rear of the establishment, only to have a serving wench bump her arm, dousing her with a frothing beer. "Pardon me, luv."

Julia brushed the foam from her coat, chancing a glance at the moneylender. Dash it all, the fiend was still staring. "Are you certain you wouldn't prefer White's, Your Grace? It would be a great deal quieter, would it not?"

"If my brother prefers to satisfy his thirst here, then here it is." Martin stopped the wench before she returned to the bar. "Three brandies if you please."

"If you please, hmm? Aren't ye a fine dandy?" The woman fingered the lapel of his coat. "Would ye be needin' a bit o' company above stairs?"

Martin gently brushed her hand away. "Just the brandies, thank you."

"Schooners of ales all around as well," Gibb added.

Julia frowned against her urge to scowl. How dare the woman be so bold as to touch Martin...and then proposition him in front of everyone? Had the jezebel no shame? Though she'd never been to White's, by its reputation she was fairly certain the gentlemen's club was far more civilized. Besides, they allowed no women whatsoever and, she could wager, no salacious serving wenches.

While Dunscaby took a seat with his back to the

wall, Julia opted for a chair across from him where Silas Skinner wouldn't be able to see her face.

Martin caught His Lordship up on family news until three glasses of brandy were delivered. Julia turned hers between her fingertips, wishing it were lemonade and doing her best not to glance over her shoulder to see if Mr. Skinner was the person making her back feel as if it were afire. If only she could ask the duke or Lord Gibb to keep an eye on the seedy character at the bar.

In short order, Dunscaby turned the conversation to the navy. Though the casual exchange seemed to naturally flow, Julia knew the duke well enough to realize he was leading his younger brother down a well cultivated and plotted pathway. "Ye ken our mother was bereft when word came the *HMS Cerberus* had sustained heavy fire in the Battle of Lissa."

A dark shadow crossed Lord Gibb's ruggedly handsome features as he took a drink of ale. "It was like being in hell. We took the brunt of the musket fire —thirteen dead, four and forty wounded."

"My God," Dunscaby mumbled. "You know as well as I Mama would never be able to withstand losing a child. After all, she's still mourning Da."

"I'd be lying if I told you I hadn't thought about resigning my commission." Gibb gave a single nod. "A man tends to rearrange his priorities when staring death in the eye."

Julia shuddered. "I cannot imagine."

"No one can. 'Tis why young men eagerly march off to war."

Martin flicked a bit of lint from his expertly tailored black woolen coat. "Aye, but they all return hardened and scarred."

"If they come home at all," Gibb replied, his voice haunted.

"Which leads me to exactly what I want to discuss at the moment." Martin rapped his finger on the table. "I tasked Smallwood here with the conceiving of an enterprise—one that will sustain all of the MacGalloway sons, and I think our man is onto something."

"Oh?" asked Gibb, his tone guarded while he looked at Julia as if she'd suddenly become more interesting.

Taking a cue from the duke's nod, Julia squared her shoulders. "As I told His Grace, the cotton industry has grown by twelve hundred percent over the past few years and there simply aren't enough mills in England, let alone Europe, to meet the demand."

Gibb tossed back the remainder of his brandy, following it with a hearty drink of ale. Before he spoke, he wiped the froth from his upper lip. "I'm a sailor, life in a factory is not for me, nor is cotton for obvious reasons."

"Aye," Martin agreed. "That's why you'd be captaining your own merchant ship, delivering MacGalloway whisky and bringing harvests from the Americas, produced by Irish sharecroppers, mind you."

"Cotton picked by free men?"

"Aye, and sold exclusively to us."

"Irish sharecroppers," Lord Gibb said, looking into his empty glass as if cogitating on the notion. "I've never heard of such a thing."

Julia pushed her untouched brandy in front of the MacGalloway sailor. "I hadn't either until I responded to small advertisement they placed in the Gazette."

"Not to worry, brother," Martin added. "We have

verified their existence and they are eager to do business with us."

Lord Gibb gave Julia a nod and picked up her brandy. "My ship?"

"You are a commander, are you not?" Martin tapped his brother's glass in toast. "Dunna ye see yourself stepping into a captain's role?"

"I've considered the possibility." Gibb looked to the exposed beams overhead. "But then that would mean leaving my crew...turning my back on the war."

"I believe you have done quite enough for king and country. 'Tis time someone else filled your shoes." Martin pulled the list Julia had made regarding the available ships and pushed it toward his brother. "On the morrow, you and I will go to Barry and Coates shipyard where I fully intend for you to select the most seaworthy vessel in their fleet."

Gibb scanned the note. "Wait a moment, are you saying this will be *my* ship?"

"Consider it your birthright. And in exchange, I ask you to be our commander on the seas and support your brothers in this venture. As soon as Philip and Andrew have sat their exams, I'm sending them to take over a warehouse at Kinclaven on the River Tay and turn it into a mill. The property has already been purchased. Smallwood is in the process of ordering looms and equipment."

"Cotton grown by Irishmen in America?" Gibb said as if warming to the idea. "Andrew and Philip are amenable?"

"They are, indeed. I have received letters from both lads full of their ideas on the venture. Even Frederick has written me to ask if he can leave school and roll up his sleeves alongside them."

"I imagine Mama would have objected to the lad's request. How did you reply?" asked Gibb.

"Of course, I told him no. Frederick can join the twins and will be granted an equal share *after* he's earned his diploma."

Gibb snorted. "Freddy always did want to grow up faster than everyone else."

"Mayhap that's why he's earning top marks in his class—he's anxious to march through university and prove his worth to the world."

"Aren't we all?" Julia mused, more to herself than to the two gentlemen across the table.

Martin raised his tankard. "So, Captain, are you with us or will I need to search for some other commander for my ship?"

Gibb's blue eyes narrowed. "May I sleep on it?"

"Do you honestly need to? Or is it your conscience that is preventing you from making the most sensible decision?"

"I'm tempted, I'll tell you true, but if I decide to resign my commission, I need to ensure my replacement is onboard the *Cerberus* afore I go."

"That's only fair. It is good to see you shoulder your responsibility." Dunscaby reached for his hat. "I say, the MacGalloway lads all seem to be coming into their own."

Julia couldn't have agreed more. When she'd first walked into Newhailes, Martin didn't come across as duke-like. He'd also seemed a bit lost. It could have been due to the passing of his father, but over the past couple of months, he'd assumed his mantle responsibly, transforming before her eyes.

Dunscaby stood. "Drink up, Smallwood. I've a mother at home waiting to see her seafaring son."

Julia glanced to her brandy, still half full. "Forgive me but—"

"Smallwood, are you a man or kin of the mouse you escorted out of the lassie's carriage?"

On a sigh, she did her best not to wince as she gulped down the fiery liquid. *Bless it, brandy is even fouler tasting than whisky.*

Fortunately, Lord Gibb helped himself to her schooner, the man's Adam's apple bobbing as he guzzled it.

Julia swayed a bit when she stood, but finally allowed herself a peek at the bar. Thank the stars Mr. Skinner was gone. And though the crowd had grown, Julia had no problem winding her way out to the footpath, until she caught a look at the duke's carriage waiting at the curb.

Silas Skinner pushed away from where he'd been leaning against the wheel and gestured to the gold Dunscaby crest embellishing the shiny black door. "Good afternoon, Your Grace. Might I say what a surprise it is to see you in these parts. 'Tis a bit perilous to leave such an exquisite piece of craftmanship so near the Pool."

The duke took a bold step forward, towering over the gaunt man. "Skinner, is it? Why should I pay heed to a word you say?"

"I've no reason to lie. The truth is far too fascinating." Tipping his hat, the cur stepped past Dunscaby, his eely eyes cutting to Julia. "Is it not, sir?"

As he walked past her, he turned his lips toward her ear and lowered his voice to a whisper. "Or should I say, my lady? By the by, I shall require payment for my silence."

17

"Ah, Smallwood, it is good to see you taking John Jackson's training to heart," Martin said as he strode into the steward's quarters.

Red in the face, Jules blew out a breath as he worked the dumbbell up and down from his shoulder to his waist. "I've realized that you were right, Your Grace. I'm in need of toughening up—especially if we are to frequent taverns on the east end of Town."

"Excellent, excellent," Martin paced, pushing aside the reason for his visit. Instead, he took two pillows from a settee and held them up. "Show me your jabs."

Smallwood placed the dumbbell by the wall. "Fists up?"

"That's right." Martin held up the right pillow. "Give it your best shot."

The little man danced in place before he threw a punch, hitting the pillow square. "After the tavern and spending the past two nights at the tables in the East End with Lord Gibb, I've gained an appreciation for Mr. Jackson's advice."

"Agreed, no matter how highborn a man can be, he must gain proficiency in weapons as well as gaining a keen knowledge of how to defend himself. Now show me your left." Martin interchanged pillows while Jules repeatedly pummeled them, twisting his lower lip into a vicious scowl. "Och aye, you have been practicing."

"Thank you, sir." As he straightened, the little fellow's features relaxed until he once again looked like the mild-mannered steward Martin had come to know. "The exercise is invigorating."

"I'm glad of it. Perhaps we ought to return to the saloon for another bout with the champion?"

Smallwood brushed a sheen of perspiration from his forehead. "Perhaps, but I'm certain you are far better at sparring with Mr. Jackson than I can ever hope to be."

"I dunna ken about that. If you keep working, I'll wager you'll surprise yourself." Martin picked up the dumbbell and did a few curls with each arm, though the weight was far lighter than the one he practiced with in his chambers. "Giles informed me that you have received a missive from Huntly Manor."

"I did?" Jules squeaked, as he dropped his fists and turned toward his writing table. "I mean, yes, I did."

"And did the butler indicate where we might find Lady Julia?" he asked, pumping the dumbbells faster.

"Ah...he wasn't quite forthright about the...um... exact location. I...ah...Willaby said Lady Julia was somewhat embarrassed about her accommodations— a—an attic chamber is all...a-and—"

"Come now, I am not a snob. Though I do understand if she is uncomfortable with her boarding house. Perhaps we ought to extend an invitation to visit my mother or, say, Lady Charity?"

"That would be proper, though either Her Grace or Her Ladyship would need to author the invitation, if one of them would be willing."

"Of course, they would be willing, especially my mother." Martin placed the dumbbells along the wall. "On second thought, Mama might overreact and start sending out wedding invitations. I believe Charity would be the best option. Indeed. I'll have my sister invite Lady Julia for tea, and then I might happen past, at which time we could be properly introduced. After all, Aphrodite meeting Mark Antony at a masquerade will not suffice in the eyes of society."

"No." As Smallwood turned from the desk, his coloring appeared a tad green. "Willaby also mentioned that Her Ladyship is expected to return home soon. In fact, she mightn't be in London as we speak."

"Not here? Preposterous!" Every muscle in Martin's body tensed. She couldn't have left. Not now. He'd spent the past several nights without sleep, fixating on Aphrodite. He'd taken Jules and Gibb to not only the horse races but to every other gambling hell in town and had consumed copious amounts of spirits in his efforts to wait and put the woman out of his mind. But nothing had helped. He must see her simply to allay his curiosity.

Martin thrust his finger under Jules' nose. "You are her second cousin. Find out. God forbid we have to make a trip to Brixham when Gibb is in port and we are in the process of negotiating the purchase of a merchant ship."

Smallwood beamed, grasping his lapels. "*The Prosperity* is quite an impressive barque, I'll say. His Lordship certainly has a critical eye."

"Of course he does." Not happy with the change in subject, Martin grabbed the man's hat off the hook by the door and handed him. "Now go. Do whatever you must to find out if Lady Julia is in Town, then we shall have my sister write to her forthwith. I want you to hand-deliver the missive yourself. I fully expect Her Ladyship to arrive for tea on the morrow."

"The morrow, sir?" Jules squeaked as if he truly were a mouse.

"Aye, I must see her again before she leaves London. I need to determine for myself if those eyes actually do sparkle like polished mahogany—if her lips were painted or if her mouth indeed was shaped like Cupid's bow. The woman captivated my attention and it all seems so surreal, I canna decide if my imagination got the better of me."

Smallwood clapped a hand over his gob, using his pointer finger and thumb to pull down a dour frown. "I'll wager you were taken by the romance of the evening, Your Grace. After all, masquerades are fantastical events, are they not?"

"I've asked myself the same dozens of times. But it appears I'll have no rest until I know for certain. The lass truly was a vision—petite, exquisite, ethereal, extraordinary..." Martin strode to the door. "I'll leave you with it. And do *not* disappoint me on this, Smallwood."

HAT IN HAND, Julia stared at the door through which Dunscaby had just marched. What was she to do now? What if she *did* disappoint him? And what was it he'd said about traveling to Brixham?

Good glory, such a thing would be an unmitigated disaster.

His Grace was behaving as if meeting her was more important than purchasing a ship or the acquiring of the property on the Tay. Thus far, over the course of Julia's employment, he had never pointedly told Smallwood not to disappoint him when it came to matters that were actually part of the steward's scope of duties. She was quite certain finding a woman was nowhere in the contract she'd signed in Mr. MacCutcheon's offices before she'd traveled to Newhailes.

However, the clause containing the words "...*and carry out such duties as His Grace deems fit...*" certainly covered the locating of a reticent "faux" second cousin.

Julia's head swam as she added this conundrum to the mounting list of untenable predicaments she'd managed to get herself into since arriving in London. And she couldn't sit idle while Silas Skinner was out there threatening to expose her secret.

"*Or should I say, my lady? By the by, I shall require payment for my silence,*" he'd whispered.

She couldn't believe he'd had the gall to call her out and threaten her in front of the duke. Of all the lowlife scoundrels in London, he had to be the one of the foulest and most unpleasant.

And he needs to be silenced!

The time had come to be assertive. If he truly wanted Papa's debt to be repaid, he would heed her.

After opening the secret compartment of her trunk and pulling out her blue day dress and everything she'd need to change, Julia cracked her door open and peered into the courtyard. Against everything she had promised herself, she must slip into the mews and dress as a woman once again.

Fortunately, the coast was clear and she made her way to the sedan chair, managing to dress without being noticed. Afterward, she all but ran until she was a few streets away from Dunscaby's Mayfair town house. But that did nothing to allay the sickly churning in her stomach. Ever since Mr. Skinner had whispered in her ear, she hadn't been able to eat. She couldn't sleep. Goodness, breathing had become a chore.

And what was she to do with Martin's seemingly insatiable desire to find her? If only there was a way to both be Julia St. Vincent as well as Jules Smallwood. Why could their paths not have crossed during her one and only Season? Of course, at the time the heir to the dukedom was occupied with establishing the reputation of being a notorious rake. Nonetheless, the past was over and now she absolutely must find a way to dissuade him. If the Duke of Dunscaby ever realized that Jules and Julia were one in the same, she'd never again be able to show her face anywhere in all of Britain.

At a corner, a carriage cut the gutter too close and splashed muddy water down her skirts.

"Watch yourself!" Julia cried, doing her best to brush away the dirt, only managing to smear it into the wool. "Drat, drat, drat!" she cursed, plodding across the street. It was bad enough to have to meet the scoundrel, let alone face him with a mud-soaked hem.

After presenting herself at the rear entry to Deuce's, Julia didn't have long to wait. The money-lender greeted her with ice-cold fingers, applying an unwelcomed kiss to the back of her hand. "I'm surprised it took you this long to pay me a visit, my lady."

"This in no way is a social call." Julia pulled her hand away and rubbed it. "I have come to let you know that you will not receive another farthing from me unless you agree to keep my secret. You know as well as I that pursing my father in debtor's court will not only end in folly, Huntly Manor is worth far more than the amount of money he owes you. On top of that, you are charging extortionist terms, taking advantage of an earl and a peer of the realm when he is too ill to manage his own affairs. Such uncaring ruthlessness will undoubtedly be unfavorable for you, and I firmly believe your claim will be dismissed altogether."

Though she had done enough research to speak with a vague amount of authority, she prayed she sounded a great deal more self-assured than she felt. Julia had not had the convenience of discussing the matter with a solicitor. What with all the money she was paying this man, she couldn't afford to walk in a solicitor's door, and God forbid she should have to pay one if the matter actually were presented before a judge.

"Hmm." The lout raked his licentious gaze down her body as he'd done the last time she had stood in this spot. "You make some valid points, 'owever, you 'ave not thought everything through. I 'ave been lendin' money to wayward gentlemen for a very long time, and I have a number of 'igh-rankin' judges in me pocket."

He stepped nearer, far too near for Julia's comfort. "'ere me now, *my lady*," he spat as if the courtesy was an oath. "If I see fit to ruin you and your worthless father, I am quite certain doing so will not cause me an iota of inconvenience."

No matter how much Julia wanted to cower, she balled her fists and straightened to her full height. "Sir, you have my word that payments will continue to come in as long as my employment remains unchanged."

"Tsk, tsk," he said, tapping his finger to the scar on his face. "I'm afraid I am very bad at keeping secrets."

"Please. Everything has been working quite smoothly until—"

"Perhaps...we can come to an arrangement." Skinner's gaze flickered to her breasts once again as he ran his tongue across his lips. "Must I remind you 'ow valuable a woman of your stature would be in my employ?"

"N-no." Gulping, Julia slid a hand to her throat. She had put forth a very solid argument and he'd called her bluff, the cur. Regardless of her reasons, she had in fact lied and proffered herself as a man, accepting a post that she was qualified to perform. However, pretending to be Jules Smallwood was necessary. Julia wasn't a liar or a thief or an unprincipled villainess of any sort. She would not and would never become a woman of easy virtue or allow this vulture to lay a single finger upon her person. "I-I would rather jump off London Bridge than submit to...to...*that*."

A sardonic chuckle erupted from the man's throat. "Such a shame, luv. I could clothe you in better style and ye'd never step out with mud on your skirts again. But since you are not a willing bed partner, I do believe I could use a well-bred woman such as yourself to do my biddin' on occasion."

Lord, no. She couldn't very well slip into the sedan car and change her clothes every time Silas Skinner beckoned. "What sort of bidding?"

"Deliveries."

"A courier?"

"Precisely."

"What would I be delivering? Pray tell, nothing illegal..."

"Letters mostly—in places where I'd prefer not to be seen."

"Places like Mayfair?" she whispered, her mind

whirring. If she were to courier a letter or two, she could do so as Jules Smallwood and avoid the sedan chair.

"Yes." He took her hand and kissed it, but he didn't stop there. Pushing up her sleeve, he ran his lips from her wrist all the way to her elbow. "Ah, Lady Julia, so delectable. You have no idea what you are missing."

Leaning away from him, she tried to pull away. "Please stop."

"Very well." Mr. Skinner held her arm in a vice-like grip as he regarded her with an expression filled with malice. "But ye cannot deny me this request, my lady, else your secret will be exposed. Make no bones about it, if I am not satisfied, I will exercise all means to take Huntly Manor and leave the penniless earl to his disgraceful demise."

18

As Martin drove his phaeton with a matched pair of black thoroughbreds along the Serpentine in Hyde Park, he tipped his hat at everyone he passed. Though when in London he oft rode through the park, ever since the masquerade, he'd done so with more purpose, especially paying attention to petite women with chestnut locks curling from beneath their bonnets. To his chagrin, the gossip columns had caught wind of his excessive congeniality and now Mama was convinced he had begun seeking a wife in earnest.

He might be searching for a woman, but regardless of what his mother might think, he most certainly had no intention of finding a wife. He was merely curious, of course. Never in all his days had Martin been besotted. Presently, he might be a wee bit determined and perhaps a tad captivated, but he most decidedly wasn't fool enough to whisk Her Ladyship up to Gretna Green and pledge his undying love.

He just needed the answers to his questions.

Damn it all, if only he could find her. But this outing proved fruitless, just as all the rest had done in the past week.

Tugging on the reins, he pointed the team toward Grosvenor Square. With luck, Smallwood would present him with favorable news this afternoon. But, by the saints, where women were concerned, the steward was obviously unschooled and daft. If Martin didn't know better, he'd say the man was reluctant to find Lady Julia even though he'd admitted to knowing her well. Had they a rift, perchance? But wouldn't Smallwood have owned to any ill will between them?

No, a disagreement couldn't be the reason for Smallwood's disinclination. The chap had spoken fondly of Her Ladyship and knew of her pastimes.

Indeed, Julia St. Vincent was a musical proficient. Och aye, how Martin would love to spend an evening listening to the lass serenade him on the pianoforte.

He also chuckled at the idea of a spotty cat. How easy to imagine Lady Julia pounding the point of her parasol on the ceiling of her carriage, demanding the driver stop to enable her to rescue a skinny, wide-eyed stray.

Furthermore, she was bashful. No wonder she'd seemed so flustered in the garden, especially after he'd acted like a stag on the rut. By the gods, what red-blooded man wouldn't have acted on impulse given a moment with a goddess?

As he turned into the close and headed for the mews, his heart nearly catapulted out of his chest. A woman wearing a blue dress walked with her back to him, but by the hair standing up on his arms, his legs, his chest, the back of his bloody neck, it was she.

Martin knew he could count on Smallwood to find her. "M'lady!" he called, pulling the horses to a halt, and not giving a rat's arse if he'd just defied a dozen rules of propriety.

The woman stopped but didn't turn. Rather, her

shoulders tensed while she clutched her hands to her chest.

Martin tied the reins and hopped down. "Lady Julia?"

As she glanced over her shoulder, he read apprehension in luminous brown eyes before she bowed her head, making the brim of her hat hide her features while she dipped into a graceful curtsy. "Your Grace, how lovely to see you."

When she straightened and her eyes once again met his, he removed his hat and bowed. Good God, she was even more beautiful without a mask and, by the saints, the resemblance to Smallwood was uncanny. "How fortuitous to find you in this very close of all places."

The lady glanced toward the entrance to the mews. "Yes, well, Jules explained that he is in your employ as a steward."

"Aye, he is a fine man, I'll say." Martin tugged on his driving gloves. "You've met with him, then?"

"I did. In fact, I've just left his rooms."

Martin puzzled for a moment because if she'd just departed Smallwood's rooms, then she was walking in the wrong direction. Perhaps she might have been a tad confused, which mattered not in the slightest. "Please forgive my impropriety. I'd hoped to procure a proper introduction by having my sister invite you for tea."

A darling blush spread across the woman's cheeks. "I daresay, our brief interaction at Northampton's ball ought to have sufficed for the necessary preamble."

He chuckled at the use of the word. Indeed, he had misbehaved and must make amends before she dismissed him as an unabashed rogue. "I owe you an apology for my behavior that night."

"Oh?"

Martin resituated his hat and slid his fingertips around the brim. "I am not in the habit of sweeping well-bred women into my arms and kissing them."

Two delicate eyebrows arched with an expression of incredulity. "On the contrary, by your reputation, I understand you are quite adept at wooing women...*ah*...generally speaking, sir."

Cringing, Martin patted the near horse's shoulder. "Alas, my wayward youth has done me no favors. I assure you, madam, now that I have assumed my father's mantle my carefree days have passed," he said, wondering where such words had originated. He had no intention of giving up the pursuit of women. In fact, chasing women was one of his favorite pastimes. Which, come to think on it, he was presently doing exactly that, except this woman happened to be a lady.

She curtsied again as if intending to cut the conversation short. "Well, if you'll please excuse—"

"Would you do me the honor of accompanying me on a jaunt through the park?" He brushed his hand down the gelding's white blaze. "The lads still have plenty of verve."

"Oh, no, I couldn't."

"Unfortunate." Unable to help himself, Martin stepped a tad nearer. In the sunlight, her eyes were positively luminescent. And they weren't simply mahogany, they were flecked by amber and encircled with chocolatey rings. "'Tis a fine day and I would dearly love to chat with you a wee bit more. Where else do you need to be at the moment, if I may be so bold as to ask?"

Cringing, she gestured to her skirts. "I'm afraid I am not attired appropriately. Earlier a carriage splattered mud on my dress and I look a fright."

"How very impolite of the dastardly driver." Not about to accept her refusal, Martin offered his hand. "Though I reckon one would need a quizzing glass to discern stains as unassuming as those. I assure you, not a soul will see your skirts behind the footboard of the phaeton."

She glanced up at him through the fans of inordinately long eyelashes. "With an invitation such as Your Grace's, I am powerless to refuse."

Martin's heart skipped a beat, or several as he hastened to hand her up to the seat. Now that Her Ladyship had agreed to a wee jaunt, he wasn't about to give the woman a chance to change her mind.

"This is a fine carriage," she said as he picked up the reins and pointed the geldings back to the park, certain the scandal sheets would be having a heyday with his return. But let them quibble. He'd never given the gossips a care, why start now?

Wanting the journey around the ring to take as long as possible, Martin opted to keep the lads at an ambling walk rather than their usual trot. By the way they tossed their heads, they weren't happy about it at all.

"I say, your steeds want to run," said Julia, the sultry tenor of her voice making his insides buzz akin to the reverberation of a bass harp string.

"They're young and full of vigor. It'll do them well to amble for a time."

Out of the corner of his eye, he watched as Her Ladyship folded and unfolded her hands, then she brushed the dried mud on her skirts with quick flicks of her fingers. Honestly, once she'd drawn attention to it, she had been rather badly doused. The bloody careless driver. If Martin had been there, he would have given the man a firm talking to. "Smallwood tells me you're planning to return to Brixham soon."

"Indeed, I am. On the morrow to be exact."

The reins slipped in Martin's fingers. "The morrow? No, no, no, you canna leave so soon. Don Giovani is opening at the Theater Royal, and I have it on good authority it is not to be missed."

She smiled up at him and dash it if he didn't detect affection in those lovely browns. "Unfortunately, it will have to be missed by me. I'm afraid my father is in poor health and is reliant on my care."

"But surely Willaby can look after the earl for a few days more."

While the lassie's lashes lowered, the corners of Her Ladyship's mouth tightened, giving Martin a cue to change tack, though he wasn't about to completely give up and let her leave town on the morrow. It might take a few more turns around the park, but he'd figure a way for her to agree to stay another week or two—at least long enough for him to get to know her, to kiss her again, to hold her in his arms. But when an opportunity again presented itself, he wouldn't act on raw impulse, pull the woman into his arms and devour her. Clearly, she was every bit as shy as Smallwood had let on. Lady Julia needed to be handled with utmost care and respect.

The lass moved a bit nearer, or she leaned into him. Martin wasn't sure which. "I must be firm on this, I cannot attend the opera. I brought no theater attire with me."

A hundred solutions arrested at the tip of his tongue, the first being he'd take her to his mother's modiste straightaway and have an entire wardrobe made. Of course, it would be gauche to mention anything about her father's lack of funds. After all, the earl never would have parted with a man as shrewd as Jules Smallwood had he been able to afford him. "I'm curious," Martin ventured. "How was it you came by an Aphrodite costume, stunning as it was?"

"To be honest, I'm so removed from society I had no idea Lady Northampton was hosting a ball until our paths crossed not long before. The costume I wore was hers. She and the marquess offered to be my chaperones for the evening."

Good God, Martin had been so besotted, he hadn't considered enquiring who her companions might be. "And who might your chaperone be elsewise?"

"I'm quite embarrassed to admit that I'm traveling unescorted, but it couldn't be helped." Lady Julia gripped her hands together while her face turned apple red. "I'm afraid my father had affairs in London that required my urgent attention."

"What about Willaby?" Martin asked, truly concerned. When word spread that a lady traveled on her own it was only a matter of time before she was ruined. Perhaps it was fortunate Julia had faded from society's notice, though with her return to Town, the vultures would pick up her scent in no time. "Could the butler not have traveled in your stead?"

"Alas, no. My father needs the fellow more than he needs me. Willaby is far stronger and more able to assist with..." She glanced aside.

"Forgive me." Noticing far too many inquisitive heads turning their way, Martin turned down a less-traveled path. "I assume you wish not to be identified by the gossips."

"That would be preferable. Though it is difficult not to draw attention to oneself when riding alongside a duke atop his shiny black phaeton." Julia raised her palms in front of her face and opened them as if revealing a picture. "I can imagine the headlines on the morrow. The most eligible bachelor in London seen riding with a mystery woman."

He watched her out of the corner of his eye as he steered the team around a bend. "Surely there are people in London who'd recognize you."

The lady's bonnet jostled with her nod. "Sophie for one."

"Well, then, I will see to it that you have a proper escort for the duration of your stay."

"Considering that I'll be boarding the mail coach in the morning, my reputation ought to escape the notice of London's busybodies."

"That is *if* you leave on the morrow," Martin said, watching her eyes widen, her wee gasp was like a tinderbox spark, igniting a flame in his heart. He let the notion linger for a moment before he continued chatting as if he hadn't planted a seed, "I'm told you're quite accomplished on the pianoforte."

As she laughed, her shoulder brushed his, adding fuel to the flame. Aye she had the most adorable laugh that shook her body, not too high pitched, and it wasn't tittering like most of the young women in polite society. The sound was genuine, making him want to throw his head back and join her. She tapped her fingers to her lips. "Pardon my outburst."

"Not at all, I love to hear laughter. Especially your laughter." He maneuvered the team around a group of ladies out for a stroll with their parasols. "Now tell me, did my steward misspeak when he said you were a proficient?"

She again attempted to flick away the dried mud on her skirts. "I do play, however, I would never refer to myself as anything more than middling."

"Smallwood said you were a tad bashful, I'd venture to say you are a wee bit unpretentious as well."

"I'd say I am honest," she replied, primly folding her hands and sitting straighter. "To be a proficient, one needs to practice for hours every day. Since my father fell ill, I'm afraid I haven't been able to dedicate the necessary time to the craft."

Martin leaned just enough to brush her shoulder once more, the slight touch sending a thrill through him. "I'll wager you are far better than you let on."

"And I'll wager you are often accused of being an optimist."

"Accused?" Martin slowed the team as they approached a crossroad. "I see optimism as a virtue."

"Case in point, Your Grace." Lady Julia glanced up at him, her eyes hooded by those incredibly long lashes.

He arched a single brow. "What's wrong with being an optimist?"

"Absolutely nothing. As a general rule, I prefer to look at things positively, though I'd say I'm a realist. I like to take things at face value and not project my paradigms upon them, optimistic or nay."

"Hmm, then I suppose I'll require a demonstration so that I may form my own unbiased opinion."

Her Ladyship's mouth dropped open—then swiftly closed. "If I were going to remain in Town one might be arranged, however, unfortunately my talent or lack thereof will remain to be seen."

Oh, how he liked her banter. She was sharp, for certain. "If only my sister had invited you to tea this afternoon, I'd be listening to you play at this very moment."

Lady Julia gave her shoulders a little waggle the shift which, to Martin's delight, situated her arm flush against his. "I rather like being out. It is too fine a day to spend it inside listening to dreary scales."

His muscle flexed with his sideways glance. "You would play scales for a duke?"

She laughed again, such an infectious, happy sound. "I might be able to recall a recital piece from finishing school, though I make no promises."

As they came to the end of the pathway, a thunderous noise arose from the west. Out of the corner of his eye, Martin saw a carriage coming at breakneck speed with a wide-eyed youth cracking a whip, driving his team like a demon.

"Whoa!" he shouted, pulling on his reins.

Both of the phaeton's horses reared, jolting the seat as the carriage roared past. Gnashing his teeth, Martin fought to bring the pair under control. With all his strength, he pulled on the brake lever and forced his heels into the floorboards to keep from being flung to his death.

Beside him, a shrill scream turned his blood to ice. As he battled with the reins, Lady Julia was no longer beside him.

"God, no!"

After quickly tying the reins, Martin leapt to the ground. "My lady!" he shouted, sprinting toward a jumble of blue skirts and white, lacy petticoats.

But the lass didn't move.

"Lady Julia!" He dropped to his knees and pulled her into his arms. Her eyes fluttered open for a moment, then rolled back while a bead of blood ran from her temple. Brushing away the stream, he cradled her against his chest. "Please, please, please tell me you are unharmed!"

19

After galloping back to Mayfair at breakneck speed, Martin carried Lady Julia up the steps to the town house while Giles opened the door. "Send for a physician at once!" Dunscaby demanded, marching through the vestibule. "Is Her Grace still here? I need the Rose Bedchamber readied before I reach the top of the stairs!"

"Straightaway, Your Grace." Giles traipsed along in Martin's wake. "I'm afraid to report your mother has departed for Northbourne Seminary for Young Ladies with Lady Modesty and Lady Grace. However, as always, the Rose Bedchamber is prepared."

"Then why are you following me?" Martin barked over his shoulder. "Fetch the bloody doctor and send Lady Charity to me at once."

"Aye, sir."

Lady Julia pushed her palm against his chest, proving quite powerful for such a petite woman. "Forgive me, but I cannot remain here. I-I really must prepare for my journey to Brixham on the morrow."

"I doubt you'll be going anywhere, at least not until my physician pronounces it safe to do so." A maelstrom of conflicting emotions roiled inside him, making his chest tight. Damnation, a lady should never be expected to travel to London alone to dispatch her father's affairs. Aye, the Earl of Brixham may be ill, but how the devil could the man have gambled his livelihood away and forced this sweet, charming, witty woman to do his bidding? Had the earl no scruples whatsoever?

Her eyes rolled back but with her blink they regained focus. "Please, it was merely a fall."

"I beg your pardon?" Martin asked, doing his best to ignore the fact that his fingers were presently sinking into the softest, most feminine bottom he'd ever had the honor of touching. "You were thrown from a carriage. Have you any idea how many people die from carriage accidents every year? Just last week the Gazette posted a study done by Oxford University detailing the causes of carriage accidents, citing over fifteen hundred deaths per year and thrice as many serious injuries. Your fall, my lady, is nothing to be ignored."

The lass seemed to settle and, after they reached the third floor, he strode to the Rose Bedchamber and pushed open the door. "I'm sorry to say my mother and younger sisters are traveling to the Cotswolds to visit a finishing school. Lady Grace is emphatic about attending seminary in England."

"Is she?" Lady Julia mumbled, the inflection of her voice sounding as if the topic interested her. "I'm sure your mother will be delighted."

"Indeed. At least Her Grace will have one child educated in what she considers to be the more civilized southern half of Britain," said Martin rather absently while he strode to the bed and rested Her Ladyship atop the mattress. "You ought to be comfortable here.

I've sent for my sister who will oversee your care whilst you're here."

"Marty?" Charity asked from the doorway as if on cue. "Whatever has happened?"

Though he'd left the door ajar, Martin immediately straightened. Once the gossipmongers figured out who had been riding with him, Lady Julia absolutely must not be in a situation where her reputation might be besmirched. She was already suffering the misery of a precarious situation, and he was determined not to cause the woman any undue hardship. He gestured from one lass to the other. "Lady Julia St. Vincent, allow me to introduce Lady Charity MacGalloway."

He could have sworn Charity's eyes popped wider than he'd ever seen them. Had there been a hint of recognition? Lady Julia was a good deal older than his sister. Had their paths crossed? But then again, he'd never brought any woman home before and Charity had heard him declare his affinity for bachelorhood many, many times. It most likely came as a shock to see him doting over a lady now. Quickly schooling her features into a pleasant smile, his sister curtsied. "Pleased to make your acquaintance, m'lady."

"It is lovely to meet you as well, my lady," said Lady Julia, leaning forward as if she intended to stand, then thought the better of it and pressed a hand to her forehead. "However, I apologize for our introduction to be under such awkward circumstances."

"Not at all. It is an honor to have you here," Martin said, gently tapping Her Ladyship's shoulder with the tips of his fingers and urging her to recline against the pillows. He then addressed his sister who was gaping at their guest with the most peculiar expression. "Lady Julia and I were taking the lads out to stretch their legs in the park when a careless rogue drove his team so near, the cad spooked my horses, throwing Her Ladyship from the phaeton's seat."

"Och, nay." Charity rushed inside, clapping a hand over her heart. "And the bench of your sporty carriage is ever so far off the ground. Are you badly injured, m'lady?"

"Please, there is no need for such formality. And I am perfectly able to take my leave." Julia pushed up with one hand but her arm seemed to collapse with the pressure. And she grabbed it with a wince. "Ow... goodness, I fear I've injured my wrist."

"Allow me to have a look at that." Martin caught Julia's eye as he took her hand. "May I?"

Lowering her lashes as if she'd been caught gazing his way, she gave a bashful nod. He carefully pushed up her sleeve, revealing a swollen wrist the size of a cricket ball.

"Oh dear," said Charity, peering over his shoulder. "That does appear more than a wee bit awful."

Julia drew her hand away and cradled the wrist against her chest. "It isn't bad, really. I'm sure with a bit of rest I'll feel no pain whatsoever."

Martin didn't believe it for a minute. "The doctor shall be here anon and conduct his examination." He turned to his sister. "Her Ladyship also struck her head hard enough to lose consciousness."

"Only for a moment," Julia objected.

He understood her reluctance. Just this morning she had been planning to return home and now Lady Julia most likely felt as if she were imposing, which she definitely was not. Furthermore, he needed to convince her to stay and hoped the doctor would agree.

Moving to the washstand, he filled the bowl with

water and doused a cloth. "By the dried blood in your hair and across your forehead, I deign to disagree."

The lass gasped. "Goodness, I must look a fright." She clapped her hands to her head. "A-and I've lost my bonnet."

He glanced over his shoulder. "From what I saw, it ended up mangled beyond compare. Forgive me, but after a wind did away with it, I made a ducal decision and deemed it more important to see to your care. I give you my word, your bonnet will be aptly replaced."

Martin returned to the bedside but Charity took the cloth from his grasp. "Allow me, dear brother."

Though it was only right for his sister to tend to Julia, Martin watched intently while Charity used utmost care to cleanse away the blood. "Does it hurt?" he asked.

"A bit."

"Ahem." Giles cleared his throat from where he appeared in the corridor. "Dr. James, Your Grace."

MARTIN SAW the doctor out while Julia remained sitting up in bed, completely mortified as she stared down at her arm resting in a sling. How, for all her horrid luck, had she been so unfortunate as to have awakened this morning rather than succumbing to an ague, or consumption, or any manner of deathly ills? Not only had she endured a vile encounter with Mr. Skinner, Julia's worst fears had been realized when Dunscaby had caught her sneaking back into the mews. It was nothing short of a miracle that the duke hadn't recognized her. And she couldn't deny that riding alongside him atop his magnificent phaeton had been delightfully thrilling, their banter amusing...until the horses spooked, of course. For the love of Moses, she'd been thrown from the carriage.

And by the way her head ached, she must have landed atop it. Or perhaps it was her sprained wrist that had unfortunately spared her from certain death. Moreover, the dratted physician had insisted she keep her sprained arm a sling until the swelling went down.

How long will that take?

Worse, she wasn't to travel for at least a fortnight, a fact which she highly suspected Dr. James would relay to the duke.

Blast, drat, and curses!

Dunscaby would be seeking an audience with Jules Smallwood soon. Julia needed to flee from this bed and somehow slip into her rooms without being seen and without allowing anyone to notice her injury. Except Lady Charity had been ordered by His Grace to remain at Julia's side. Fortunately, Dunscaby had waited in the corridor while Dr. James conducted his examination, else Julia would have likely melted into a muddle of complete and utter humiliation.

Lady Charity remained as chaperone as was proper. But the eldest MacGalloway sister had been fidgeting all afternoon. For ages, Her Ladyship paced back and forth along the side of the bed. She was about to wear a hole in the lovely rose and ivory carpet when Julia could take no more. "I sense your unease, my lady."

"Charity," she said rather curtly, stopping and thrusting her fists onto her hips. "Did we not agree to dispense with formalities between us?"

"Yes we did." Julia looked to the door. "You must know, I am quite well, and ought to be going. There is no need for you to—"

"Going? Exactly where do you intend to go, Mr. Smallwood?"

The room spun.

Stunned, shocked, and mortified, Julia froze, completely unable to take a breath.

Holy.

Unbelievable.

Help.

This is the end of my life.

Her secret had been discovered and she was about to be cast out on her ear. Not only was her heart thundering out of rhythm, she would be ruined. She'd have to take a transport to Australia, and she barely had a farthing to her name. How could she leave the country without any money...and what about her father?

Is he well enough to travel?

Perhaps a captain would be so kind as to allow her some sort of employment on his ship while she and Papa sailed to purgatory.

"Oh," was all Julia managed before her throat closed.

"You've been trying to make excuses to take your leave ever since Martin brought you into this bedchamber." After moving forward, Charity brushed the back of her skirts and sat on the bed at Julia's side. "The first time I met you, I considered you to be a rather odd little chap. And I always wondered how you kept your face so free of whiskers. Even when we traveled to London your chin showed nary a shadow. Tell me without delay, why in heaven's name are you posing as the steward to a duke?"

Though Julia's chest felt as though she'd been skewered by a dagger, she forced herself to look the lass in the eyes. "Would you believe me if I told you I had no choice?"

Huffing an enormous sigh, Martin's sister wrung her hands. "Everyone has a choice."

"Not when facing debtor's court and watching an ailing father fall into demise..."

Charity covered Julia's hand and squeezed, her expression not one of anger, but reflected deep curiosity. "Explain your story, lass. I absolutely must hear every detail." Martin's sister tilted up her chin and raised a finger, looking quite a bit like her mother. "And not a false word. Mind you, I ken a tall tale when I hear it."

After closing her eyes and gathering her thoughts, Julia began. She shared it all—the work as a steward she'd done for her father which was the basis for her qualifications to apply for the position in the first place. Papa's fall into a sea of debt and subsequent illness. How she couldn't sit idly by and allow a scourge like Silas Skinner to evict her and Papa from the only home she'd ever known. How she traveled via mail coach to Newhailes with not much more than a few pennies in her father's great coat.

She mentioned the trunk Willaby had sent with the hidden compartment (which Charity had helped her move) and how she'd changed in the old sedan chair in the mews. Julia left nothing out, explaining about how Sophie had found her and insisted she attend the masquerade because Julia loved to dance. That fact earned a howling laugh from Her Ladyship because Smallwood was forever making missteps and foibles, not because he was a bad dancer, but due to the fact he had never practiced the man's part.

Of course, she omitted the kiss on the stairs leading to Northampton's gardens, then skipped to Dunscaby's seemingly insatiable urge to find her afterward.

As Julia revealed her story, the sharp pain in her

chest slowly eased, replaced by a floating sensation. True, she knew she was ruined beyond any reparation, but holding forth with the unabashed truth and admitting to all the humiliating details was incredibly liberating as if she'd been akin to a canary locked in a cage and suddenly set free.

Except now she was truly doomed.

"Dunscaby has been such a capital employer," she added at the end of her discourse. "Though I cannot believe His Grace didn't recognize my identity before you did."

Charity gave a knowing nod, while a sly grin spread across her lips. "That's because he is smitten."

"Oh, please, his interest is merely drawn to a woman who was dressed as the goddess of love at a masquerade. I'll wager when he escorts you to the next ball, His Grace will find someone else more enticing than me."

"No. Martin has never once brought a woman home." Charity soothed her fingers over the damask coverlet. "And when I first stepped into this chamber, I'd never seen him so afraid."

"Afraid?"

"He was clearly worried, even though you repeatedly said you were not badly injured. Did you not notice Marty hovering over you like a mother hen until Dr. James escorted him out of the chamber?"

"He did hover a tad, did he not?" Julia cringed. "But none of that matters now. My ruse is foiled and I will be booted out of this wonderful family and cast away in shame."

"I dunna ken. Martin is so blinded by your beauty, I reckon he merely thinks you and Mr. Smallwood resemble each other. You said yourself that you had concocted a ruse that you are second cousins. Obviously, my brother has assumed you look similar because you are kin."

"Yes, and I thought I was managing the situation fairly well." Julia leaned forward, covering her eyes with the uninjured hand. She did not want to cry in front of Her Ladyship. "I have no idea what I'm going to do."

"Not to fret, lass, because I might," Charity said, her eyes sparkling with a bit of Scottish mischief.

Splaying her fingers, Julia regarded the Her Ladyship through prison-bar-like gaps. "I beg your pardon?"

"Do you have any idea how marvelous it is to see Marty a wee bit smitten? Call me a hopeless romantic, but I think he deserves a chance to court you."

"Right. Did you not hear what I said? You do know His Grace has a reputation of being one of Britain's most notorious rakes. Only yesterday he staunchly admitted that he is not remotely ready to marry—and a courtship is...well...it is one step closer to the altar."

"All men say they cherish their bachelorhood and then something snaps and they fall madly in love."

Julia snorted. "Now I know you are a hopeless romantic. Highborn marriages are rarely the result from the basis of love."

"But they should, do you not agree?"

Cradling her injured hand, Julia hummed a sigh. "If only we lived in an ideal world."

"Aye, but never mind that. I've gone off on a tangent and must shift this little tête-à-tête back to the matter at hand." Grinning, Charity steepled her fingers and pressed them to her lips. "Though I thought you an odd little man, I came to like you, and it is not very often one finds amenable friends when one is the daughter of a duke. The same stands for Marty in a way. From my observations, he quite enjoys your company as Mr. Smallwood, which is why I believe you shall need some help if you intend to continue to perform your duties as steward by day and, perhaps, Lady Julia by night. Though I do think carriage rides in the middle of the day when you are supposed to be conducting your business as steward ought to be out of the question. From what you said about the money-lender, you canna forgo your wages."

Julia gaped, then, after what seemed to be an inordinately long pause, she blinked. Dare she hope? Yes, she loved Martin. She adored Martin. The greatest truth of all? Every waking hour in his presence, she had yearned to act as herself. At night her dreams tortured her with the unlikely circumstance of being courted by the dashing Scot. "Did you say I would need *help*?"

"Well aye. If you keep dressing in the sedan chair, sooner or later someone will find you. Besides, you mentioned that Willaby only sent two dresses and that blue frock you're wearing is all but ruined."

Julia couldn't seem to move past her shock. "Are you saying you will keep my secret?"

"Aye." Charity patted her chest in rapid succession. "Hopeless romantic, here. Besides, I believe helping you constitutes a good deed."

"But Mr. Smallwood cannot exactly traipse above stairs and slip into your bedchamber to transform into Lady Julia without the entire serving staff noticing."

"That's why I've decided to have Tearlach move a trunk of this and that to the attic."

"This and that?"

"You ken, last season's theater gown, a frilly pink ball gown, a promenade dress, all the matching accoutrements, and more. Mind you, the items to which I am referring have not gone out of fashion, nor have most of them been worn more than once." Charity drummed the tips of her fingers together as if plotting like a highwayman. "I've a pelisse that ought to fit you nicely, though everything will need a bit of hemming. And dunna fret, I'm quite skilled with a needle and thread."

Julia's mind raced. How was she to manage to slip from her rooms on the first floor all the way up to the attic on the fourth without being seen? Of course, there were the servant's stairs, which she could use when the majority of the staff was at dinner—aside from the lady's maids who were usually busy at that time of evening, especially if the family were going out, which happened nearly every night, given this was the height of the Season.

What if she agreed with Her Ladyship's hair-brained plan? At last, she'd be able to be with Martin as a woman. She was already in love with him. Of course, it was unlikely the duke would ever fall in love with her.

Nonetheless, a few nights out with Martin Mac-Galloway would provide the most splendid memories in her inordinately dull life. What she would give to be in his arms and kiss him once more.

"Perhaps..." she mused, considering the possibilities. "Lady Julia could request that all correspondence be dispatched through her second cousin because she would be bereft if His Grace saw her shameful living quarters."

Charity tapped her fingers together as if she were eminently enjoying their scheming. "Now you're onto something. I say, such a request is verra plausible."

"I cannot believe you have chosen not to expose me." If only Julia were as close to Charity as she was to

Sophie, she would hop out of the bed this instant and wrap her in an embrace.

"I can only imagine the hardship Mama and my sisters would have endured had my father left us penniless."

"And destitute," Julia added in a haunted whisper. Taking a deep breath, she gave the lass a grateful smile. "When you referred to me as Mr. Smallwood, I thought my life had ended. But I shouldn't have."

"Aye?" Charity asked, sitting on the edge of the bed.

"I knew when I first met you, had I still been myself, I would have cherished your friendship." Julia placed her hand on the woman's shoulder. "Thank you ever so much for your understanding and trust. I do believe I should like to experience being courted at least once in my life."

Charity threw her arms around Julia's shoulders and hugged her fiercely. "Och, we shall turn you into a woman my brother cannot resist."

"A woman he admires is quite enough."

Julia closed her eyes and prayed the debt for Mr. Skinner's silence would soon be repaid.

20

M artin balanced an invalid's tray in the palm of his hand while he knocked on the door of the Rose Bedchamber. "May I come in?"

Charity greeted him first smiling and then gaping at the ample selection of sandwiches, biscuits and fruit nestled around a teapot and three cups. "I say, brother, I do not believe I've ever seen you carry any service before, let alone a tea service."

"I thought our guest might care for a refreshment," he replied, sidling past his sister and looking to Lady Julia. "Since Mr. Smallwood mentioned your inclination to be a wee bit bashful, I thought it best to limit the number of servants traipsing in and out of your chamber."

"That's very kind of you," said the beauty atop the bed, looking radiant and nothing like a woman who'd been thrown from a carriage only hours prior.

"How are you feeling?" he asked.

"Quite well. In my opinion the doctor was being overly cautious when he ordered me to remain abed until the morrow."

Charity followed Martin as he strode to the bedside. "I disagree. Besides, since Mama is away with Modesty and Grace, it has been ever so diverting to chat with Julia."

The two women exchanged glances, looks Martin had oft seen shared between females as if they had some sort of unspoken code they conveyed with their eyes. He placed the tray with the posts on either side straddling Her Ladyship's lap. "It seems you two have been busy during my absence."

"We have, indeed," Charity agreed. "And I daresay we are two like-minded ladies."

Why was it he sensed the two of them had suddenly become fast allies in a very short time? To be honest, he was a tad piqued that his sister had wheedled her way into Her Ladyship's confidence while he still felt as if he was merely breaking the ice. "I take it both of you abhor the *ton* and prefer to idle your time at your families' country estates?"

"That would be it exactly," said Lady Julia gesturing to the teapot. "Shall I pour?"

As she spoke, the mantle clock chimed. "Heavens, look at the time." Charity pattered toward the door. "Georgette was emphatic about meeting me in my chamber at half five. She has a new hairstyle she wants to attempt before Almack's next ball. If you'll please excuse me, I must away."

Martin grinned.

Interestingly Julia did as well.

Of course, he'd summoned his sister to the Rose Bedchamber to ensure there would be no impropriety, but now that Lady Julia was here and the physician had come and gone, no one would utter a word if Charity stepped out for a few moments.

"Must you?" Julia asked as if an afterthought.

"Oh, I must. But not to worry, I'll return anon," Charity said as she swept out the door, closing it behind her.

Martin waited for a moment as he listened to her retreating footsteps, then he slid into a wooden chair beside the bed. "I hope you'll find something on the tray to your liking."

"It all looks delicious. I missed the midday meal and I've suddenly realized I'm famished. Now, as I was saying, please allow me to pour." Ignoring her sling, the lady wrapped her fingers around the handle of the teapot, but a bit of tea spilled out of the spout when she attempted to lift it. "Dear me, how clumsy."

Martin reached in, his fingers skimming hers with only the faintest of touches, but the contact created a thrill that shot through his blood, making every fine fiber of hair on his body stand at attention. "My dear lady," he said, filling a cup for her before seeing to his own. "I do believe when one is thrown from a carriage and suffers from a sprain as bad as the injury to your wrist, she canna be expected to wield a teapot like a well-trained earl's daughter."

"Apologies." She picked up her cup with her uninjured hand. "I suppose I'll need to use my left for a day or two."

He reached for his but watched while she sipped, pursing her lips and caressing the rim of the cup. "See, you've adjusted already."

"You overestimate my dexterity."

"I think not." After sampling the tea, Martin set the cup down and reached for a shortbread biscuit. "It seems my steward has stepped out for the moment, but I have taken the liberty of leaving him instructions to book a suite at Lady Blanche's Boarding House on the next street over."

"Oh?" Not meeting his gaze, Julia slowly lowered her cup. "I mustn't prevail upon your charity, sir."

"Balderdash." He waved a dismissive hand through the air. "It is the least I can do. After all, it was my carriage from which you were thrown. I have a responsibility to see to your recovery. And since Dr. James informed me it is not advisable for you to travel unless you are in a private coach, accompanied by a footman and a lady's maid, I felt Lady Blanche's was the best alternative."

The corners of her lips tightened. "I say, the doctor is overly cautious. I mentioned the same to Charity."

"Well, I for one, am glad he is erring on the side of caution. Besides, this will give us a chance to grow better acquainted. I'll appoint a maid to see to your needs—"

"I do not need a maid. Absolutely not." Julia sliced a sandwich through the air, making a bit of cucumber drop onto the tray. "I might be able to accept your generosity because it seems I've no choice in this delay, but I cannot take a maid away from her duties here."

"I assure you, it isna an imposition—"

"No," she said flatly, as if providing her with a maid crossed a forbidden line. "Though I thank you."

Her Ladyship smiled with her thanks, making Martin feel a tad better. She'd warmed to Charity so well, he might ask his sister to lend Julia a hand rather than appoint a maid. Besides, with Mama away for a few days, his eldest sister could use something with which to occupy her time.

Julia bit into her sandwich and her eyes lit up. "My, this is delicious."

"Ham?" he asked.

"No, it is some sort of mixture blended with a deli-

cious sauce." She held up the remaining morsel.
"Try it."

He opened his mouth and allowed her to feed him.
And though the taste was pleasing, Martin barely noticed while Julia leaned forward, her lips slightly
parted, watching him with keen anticipation.

"Well?" she asked, seemingly oblivious to the intimacy between them.

"Stunning," he whispered, moving toward her as if
drawn by forces beyond his control. "I meant to say it
is good, but when you look at me while the candle-
light reflects in those mahogany brown eyes, little else
matters."

With her finger, she wiped a bit of sauce from the
corner of his mouth, the friction of her touch, causing
him to emit a rumbling sigh. His cock might have
been already standing at attention, but when she slid
said finger into her mouth, her pink tongue licking off
the treat, he all but spilled. Martin gulped against the
thickening of his throat. "Forgive me, but I have an
overpowering urge to kiss you."

Julia's beguiling gaze slipped to his mouth as her
lips parted. Not uttering a word, she closed the distance and swept petal-soft lips across his. Martin
needed no more encouragement. He moved his fingers
to the nape of her neck and claimed her mouth,
showing her exactly the impact she'd had upon him.

Though the lass began a bit timidly, she soon
matched the languid sweeps of his tongue, placing a
firm hand on his upper arm and squeezing the taut
muscle there. She tasted of tea and sandwich and a
hint of sweetness. But it was her scent that stoked the
fire burning within. With his every inhalation, he was
reminded of an entire garden of lilacs, or lavender.

Damnation, her essence comprised so many fragrant blooms, the only thing on his mind was immersing himself in them all—all of her to be exact. As he surrounded her in his arms, it was as if he were diving into a pool of *Parfum de Julia*.

Martin traced the curve of her jaw with his lips, continuing to a lithe neck. With her shiver, a small voice at the back of his head chimed a warning. The last time he'd kissed this woman, she had fled into the darkness. And though she clearly harbored passion within her breast, he must not allow his hot Scottish blood to abscond with all reason, roll the woman onto her back, and take his plunder, no matter how much he wanted to do so.

Clenching his eyes shut, he forced himself to stop, though he couldn't help but stroke the fine hairs just below her chignon. "Forgive me. I should not have taken liberties."

"There is nothing to forgive," she said, sliding her warm palm from his arm to his chest. "Why do I feel as if I'm floating in a soap bubble whenever we are together?"

"A soap bubble, aye, I ken exactly what you mean." Martin took a ringlet curling beside her ear and lazily twirled it around his finger. "The feeling is disconcerting, yet I am unable to ignore it."

She nodded. "Mayhap 'tis a bit shameful."

"Never. I do not believe God gave us feelings for us to ignore that they exist." He kissed the silken hair wrapped about his knuckle. "And canna deny the incident in the park was fortuitous—excluding your injuries, of course. Lady Julia, I want to see you...ah...to *court* you."

Had he just uttered the word "court"?

Yes.

And it didn't seem to bother him in the slightest.

As she blushed, Her Ladyship looked to the hand resting over his heart and slowly drew it away. "I must be forthright in reminding you that my father relies on me for his care. I cannot be parted from him much longer."

"I understand and, believe me, as a man who lost his da far too soon, I ken the importance of family. But I will ask again—whilst you remain in London, will you do me the honor of allowing this somewhat re-formed rake to court you?"

Gradually, those long chestnut lashes rose until she met his gaze. Those lovely browns were filled with the same desire churning in his heart, a desire so intense he forgot to breathe. But then she shook her head. "I—"

Before she could utter a rebuttal, he grasped her hand and drew it over his heart, where it had been only moments ago. "Please, do me the honor of giving me a mere fortnight."

Her fingers pressed into him. "Only a fortnight?"

"Aye."

Ever so slowly, a smile as bonny as an angel's spread across her lips. "Yes, Duke. I would like that very much."

BEFORE DAWN and especially before the servants began to stir, Julia slipped into her rooms and changed into Mr. Smallwood's clothes, which was no easy feat considering her swollen wrist made her clumsy. As she stood in front of the looking glass tying her neckcloth, she spotted a parcel on her writing table. And by the clammy chill spreading over her skin, she knew who it was from.

Wiping her palms on her coat and tugging the cuff over her wrist to hide the swelling, she moved to the desk and stared at the brown sealed paper containing only one word. "Smallwood." She stood frozen for a moment as if breaking the seal would cause her to be smote by an act of God. Her every other thought might be of winning Dunscaby's affection but, far too often, she also wished she could have stayed in Scotland where things were far less complicated.

She broke the seal and pulled out the contents—a note addressed to her and another, smaller sealed parcel:

"Hand deliver this to Mr. Rodger Drummond at Messrs. Drummond and wait for a reply. To avoid scandal, the letter must be presented to Mr. R. Drummond directly. I expect a reply within a day..."

Julia dropped into her chair and groaned. Had Mr. Skinner no scruples whatsoever? Did he honestly think to swindle one of the wealthiest men in Britain —a man who managed the accounts of the royal family?

And when was she supposed to find a moment to carry out this task? Smallwood had to arrange for accommodation for Lady Julia before Jules was scheduled to visit the Pool of London with Lord Gibb and Dunscaby to take possession of *The Prosperity*.

Perhaps she shouldn't have agreed to allow the duke to court her. It was dangerous to be sure. On the other hand, Julia had enjoyed so very few dalliances of her own. For the first time in months, she could dress like a woman. For the first time in years, she would be

seen among polite society as Lady Julia, daughter of
the Earl of Brixham. Yes, she only had a fortnight, and
no, she didn't expect a proposal in that time, but was it
too much to ask to allow herself the comfort of Dunscaby's arms? To kiss him, to act on all the feelings that
she had suppressed since arriving at Newhailes?

However, there was no time to ponder upon it now.
The sun was about to rise and she must pay a visit to
Lady Blanche's and establish an inordinately expensive suite in one of the few of the luxurious boarding
houses provided exclusively for ladies of the *ton*. She
stowed the parcel from Mr. Skinner in her stationery
drawer and hastened out.

Unfortunately, Jules Smallwood was made to wait
in the boarding house entry for what seemed like ages
until the Lady Blanche met with her. Under the guise
of needing quiet and having an unnatural fear of
heights, she was able to secure a suite on the first floor
at the rear of the building where there was a window
looking out upon the gardens—Charity's idea, of
course.

By the time Julia returned, it was after the breakfast hour and she'd no sooner hung her hat on the peg
when Dunscaby burst through her door. "Where the
devil have you absconded to with your cousin?" he demanded with a deep furrow between his eyebrows.

Julia's heart nearly pounded out of her chest as her
mind warred with the urge to laugh aloud or the need
to grovel and apologize and tell him what a godawful
fool she truly had been.

If only she could reveal all and say Julia and Jules
were one in the same and that she was quite happy
with her accommodations near the mews. She was
also very satisfied with her employment, which absolutely must continue in order to satisfy Mr. Skinner.

But, alas, she merely turned from the peg holding her father's old hat in one hand and sliding her injured wrist behind her back. She affected a most businesslike expression, very careful to lower her voice as deeply as it would go. "Good morning, Your Grace. I have just returned from seeing to it Lady Julia is situated in a lovely suite at the boarding house."

"I see." The tension in Martin's shoulders eased. "Why did you not first have her venture to the dining hall for breakfast? Did she go hungry? Are you entirely insensitive to the needs of young ladies?"

"No, sir." To be honest, if anything, Julia was highly sensitive to the plight of women, especially when in such dire straits to force her to dress as a man in order to earn a respectable wage. "I indeed asked if she had eaten, and Her Ladyship explained that she'd filled up on the remaining biscuits and fruit which had been delivered to the Rose Bedchamber last evening."

Julia moved to her writing table and tapped the contract for the purchase of Lord Gibb's ship. There hadn't been much time to review the document, though it had been sent from Mr. MacCutcheon's offices with a note saying all was in order. "Her Ladyship also mentioned that she didn't want to pose any more of a burden to your household than she already had."

"Good Lord, I canna imagine that woman ever being an imposition." Dunscaby sat in the chair opposite Julia's writing table and propped his feet up, crossing his hessian boots at the ankles. "She is quite clever—witty I'd say, would you agree?"

"Ah...yes. I suppose she's a bit like Lady Charity in that respect," Julia mumbled, sliding into her seat.

Martin gave a knowing nod. "Aye, the two of them got on smashingly, for certain."

"How nice for them both."

A light knock came at the door.

"Enter," said Dunscaby as if these were his rooms, which in effect, they were.

"Oh, I didn't realize you were occupied," said Lady Charity, popping her head in. "I was wondering why we didna have the opportunity to enjoy Lady Julia's company in the dining hall this morn."

"She had already departed for the boarding house," Martin explained.

Charity stepped inside. "I hope she likes it there."

"She will," Julia said, "I am sure of it."

The lass twirled the tassel of the ribbons on her day dress. "I thought I'd ask Her Ladyship to accompany me to the modiste. She'd mentioned that she brought but a few items from Brixham and the dress she wore yesterday had been soiled with mud."

"Excellent idea," said Dunscaby while Julia gaped at his sister, ready to leap forward, grasp her shoulders and give the woman a good shake. What was she thinking? Julia didn't have money to spend on new gowns. Furthermore, Charity had offered to lend her a few things from last Season—they'd agreed.

Gah!

Yet another dratted knock came. "Gibb here."

Julia hopped up, opened the door, and beckoned him inside. "By all means, do come in, my lord. I have in my possession the contract for the purchase of your ship."

"Is all squared away with the admiral?" asked Martin, removing his feet from the table and perusing the document.

"Aye." Lord Gibb rubbed his hands together. "And as soon as the ink dries on that bit o' parchment, I'll set to recruiting my crew. I'll wager we'll sail for America within a month or two, returning in time to supply the lads' factory with a load of Irish sharecropper's cotton before the looms are ready to weave."

"I like the sound of that." Martin stood and clapped his brother on the back. "Mark me, the Mac-Galloway sons will establish a dominant presence in Britain and beyond."

"I do think it is a fabulous concept," Charity agreed. "If only there were something I was able to do to help."

Julia offered Her Ladyship a sympathetic smile before she collected the contract and slid it into her leather portfolio, trying not to wince with the pain the movement caused. "We must be going, sirs. The ship merchant at Barry and Coates is expecting us."

Martin seemed not to notice her discomfort and stepped in front of the looking glass to adjust his neckcloth. "Perhaps I'll accompany Charity and Lady Julia to the modiste."

"No," Charity blurted, earning a stern look from her eldest brother. "I-I mean, you ought to be there with Gibb whilst he takes possession of his very own ship."

"She's quite right, Your Grace." Julia said, trying not to sound hysterical as she grabbed her hat and shoved it onto her head. Good glory, this was only her first day of playing two roles at once, and things were already in a muddle. "You are needed at the wharf. *The Prosperity* may be Lord Gibb's barque, but as the Duke of Dunscaby, you must be there to christen her."

"Well, then, let us not delay." Martin strode to the writing table, pulled open the drawer—the same one with Mr. Skinner's parcel. Julia held her breath, ready to die while the duke gave it a cursory glance, pushed it aside, and took out a slip of stationery. "I'll send a note for Her Ladyship along with you, Charity. I shall invite her to attend the theater with us this evening—and I need you to see to it the lady agrees."

While the duke dipped the quill and set to addressing his letter. Julia quietly moved beside him and gently closed the blasted drawer.

21

"So, you're working for that bastard lowlife?" demanded Mr. Drummond, the most respected banker in all of Britain.

Julia had known walking into Messrs. Drummond was an enormous misstep but even entering the building as Mr. Smallwood and telling the secretary she must deliver the parcel herself caused an uproarious stir. As soon as Mr. Drummond peered at the contents, he turned so red in the face, Julia was afraid he'd blow steam out of his ears. "No, sir, I'm afraid to say that I owe a favor to the person to whom you are referring, and had I not hand-delivered those documents or whatever they are, I—"

"So, Skinner has blackmailed you as well, has he?"

"Yes, I'm afraid he has." Julia's face grew hot as she backed toward the door. She needed to make haste in order to have enough time to dress for the theater. "If you will provide the requested reply, I shall take my leave."

"How the devil does he do it?" the man demanded.

"What, exactly, sir?"

"We took the utmost care in hiding our client's identity, yet the maggot tracked him down like a bloodhound. How did he wheedle you into this? Debts? Cheating on your wife?"

"Debts." Julia placed her hand on the latch while her wrist throbbed. "Not my debts, but those of someone who is unable to pay." She didn't know why she was bothering to explain.

"Well, the man's ballocks have grown too large for his trousers." The banker pounded his fist on the writing table. "You tell him if he thinks he can swindle Messrs. Drummond, he will find himself swimming at the bottom of the Thames."

She shook her finger at the inkpot and quill resting beside the man's hand. "I beg your pardon, sir, but I rather think such a threat would not be anywhere near as effective coming from me as it would from you. After all, you are quite a fierce-looking chap."

The banker slapped the missive on his thigh as he gave her a glower from head to toe. "You are rather impish are you not?"

"Height challenged, I like to say."

Mr. Drummond jotted out a note, sealed it, and jammed the document into Smallwood's chest, grinding his knuckles to boot. "Just take this worthless rubbish and tell your henchman to find someone else to swindle. Unless he wants to spend the rest of his days in Newgate—and you along with him."

"Me?"

"Remove yourself from my presence! And if I ever see your face in my bank again, I'll personally have you arrested."

Julia turned and fled, doing her best to hold her head high and not dash out the doors in tears. This was an untenable state of affairs. There was every chance that she'd have to walk through those doors again when conducting Dunscaby business, and now the head of Messrs. Drummond had all but thrown her out on her ear. She needed to tell Mr. Skinner that she had a reputation to uphold and if he ruined it, his messenger would be useless to him.

Except the last time she'd tried to tell the man his tactics were unscrupulous, she'd ended up all the worse for it. She was better off staying as far away from that scoundrel as she possibly could.

Once she stepped onto the pavement, the clock tower struck the hour of four. Fortunately, it wasn't but a quarter of a mile to the town house—or ought she go to the boarding house?

Julia had her answer as soon as she stepped into her chamber off the Dunscaby courtyard.

"There you are!" Charity flew out of a chair. "Martin returned ages ago. And given the fact that you need to ready yourself for the theater, you haven't much time."

Julia took off her hat and hung it on the peg. "I do have my duty to perform. It isn't all parties and soirees for the working class, I'll have you know."

"Well, you are not of the working class, are you?" Charity pulled the dratted hat off the peg and handed back to Julia. "How is your wrist?"

Julia flexed it, doing her best not to wince. "Nearly healed." After all, the swelling had eased considerably since yesterday.

"Good, because we need to hasten to the boarding house. I had Tearlach deliver the trunk there this afternoon."

"Bless you, dearest. You truly are a diamond."

"I only wish a real gentleman would think so." She clasped her hands and batted her eyelashes. "It was ever so nice to chat with you when I thought you a man. I even told Marty I would marry you."

Putting her hat back atop her head, Julia chuckled. "Marry a steward who forever has his nose in his ledgers?"

"Is that so bad? I think I'd rather a man who works hard and prefers to spend his time reading rather than carousing like so many highborn dandies do."

"They all aren't rakes."

"No?" Charity threw out her hands. "Even Marty earned a carousing reputation."

"Aye, but he has reformed substantially of late. Perhaps you ought to set an age limit—say any prospective suitor under the age of five and twenty is too immature for your sensible nature." Julia gestured to the door. "You'd best slip out first. I wouldn't want one of the stable hands seeing us leave together. If you told your brother you might consider marrying Smallwood, the duke would be very difficult to dissuade if he caught wind of any impropriety between us."

"If he only knew the true nature of our impropriety, he would truly turn into a tempestuous ogre." Charity giggled as she headed for the door. "Do hasten along quickly. I've stacks of gowns and accoutrements to show you."

"Just make certain the window to the garden is unlatched and I'll meet you anon."

THE LIGHTS in the Theater Royal were not dimmed as low as Martin would have preferred, though the gaslights on the stage did much to illuminate the players in Mozart's Don Giovani. There were no more sconces lit in the theater than usual but Martin *felt* as if there were a torch the size of a brazier burning in the Dunscaby box. Prior to inheriting the dukedom, he hadn't frequented this particular box often. He preferred the one further along that he'd purchased when holding the courtesy title of the Marquess of Ross. The lights from the stage cast shadows across that particular box which made it secluded and private—an ideal place for the preamble to lovemaking.

The box reserved for the Duke of Dunscaby, however, was in the center of the theater and was bright enough to grow tomatoes. The only other box that made its occupants appear as if they were part of the opera was the one reserved for the royal family which, presently, remained unoccupied.

So, there he sat, his sister on one side and Lady Julia on the other, wanting nothing more than to brush his fingers across the back of Her Ladyship's gloved hand, which was not in a sling, since she professed to be completely and amazingly healed.

Unfortunately, the theater goers in the pit seemed more interested in who the new duke was entertaining than the soprano presently holding forth with an impressive aria.

Julia raised her fan, leaned in, and whispered, "She's fabulous."

Martin had spent much of the production watching Her Ladyship's fingers tap as if playing an imaginary keyboard. "Have you frequented the opera?" he asked, wishing they were alone and she serenading him with a private recital.

"I wouldn't say I've frequented much of anything in London."

Of course, he knew she had not. As far as the *ton* was concerned, Julia St. Vincent was a reclusive spinster. "By all the eyes looking your way, I'm afraid your secret has been brought to light."

Julia, gasped nearly as loud as Senora Catalani hitting a high B-flat. Her Ladyship clutched a hand over her heart, her face stricken as if she'd just received unfathomable news such as the death of a loved one, or the king, or the mass murder in an orphanage full of children. She opened her mouth, but only managed to form an O with those Cupid's bow-shaped lips.

Martin let his hand drop to his side and hooked her little finger with his pointer. "All the gossips in attendance will ken the Earl of Brixham's daughter has emerged after—what is it—four years of avoiding the London crowd?"

She tightened her finger around his while her expression softened into a shy smile. "I fear they'll be sorely disappointed when I leave before the Season is over."

"The gossips aren't the only ones who will be forlorn." He leaned nearer, turning his lips to her ear. "I want to kiss you."

She pressed the handle of her fan to her lips, a well-known lady's sign for telling a man she did indeed desire a kiss. A fluttering erupted in the pit of his stomach as if he were but an adolescent lad. Martin glanced to the door behind their velvet-padded chairs. If they slipped away now, on the morrow the papers would not only be holding forth about Lady Julia's presence in the Dunscaby box, but they'd incite a scandal vicious enough to ruin the lass.

He raised her hand to his lips and kissed it ever so gently and every bit as unobtrusively as possible. "Perhaps you can pretend to fall from the carriage and feign an injury so that you might again occupy the Rose Bedchamber."

She tapped her lips, obviously restraining a laugh. "Fortunately, the first incident avoided the papers. I wouldn't chance a second."

"You have an aversion for risk, do you?" he whispered, not giving a whit what was happening on the stage.

"I am most averse...though..."

Martin's eyebrow quirked. Her response was too tempting to ignore. "What were you going to say?"

"I don't know." Her shoulder ticked up. "It seems peril oft has a way of finding me."

"Such as?"

"Please, Your Grace. A woman cannot reveal every hazardous circumstance she faces. Besides, doing so might make me appear less worthy in your eyes."

As far as Martin knew, Julia was sheltered as much as if not more than any highborn female in the kingdom. "Facing risk or hazard, as you put it, only serves to make a person stronger. Perhaps more worldly."

A sultry chuckle was hidden behind the woman's fan, sounding far more like Aphrodite than a maid who hailed from a sleepy English village. "I say, your opinion mightn't be shared by three-quarters of the patrons presently in this theater."

Martin cast his gaze to the stage, but out of the corner of his eye he focused on Julia. How could this woman ever appear to be less worthy to him? She put her father's needs ahead of her own. She was spending the greater part of her marriageable years taking care of an infirm earl. If only Martin possessed half of her graciousness. If he'd been a more attentive son, he might have noticed his own father's decline. There was no question that Lady Julia was far closer to sainthood than he. No matter what secrets the lady might be harboring, they would pale in comparison to

Martin's former exploits including mistresses, gambling, drinking, not to mention a spell of week-long debauchery. Behavior which he oddly did not miss.

IT HAD NEARLY CUT Martin to the quick to escort Lady Julia to the door of her boarding house, kiss her hand and bid her goodnight. With Charity waiting in the carriage, he couldn't exactly ravish the woman before she ventured inside. And why the blazes had he come up with the idea to put her in a boarding house for women of all places? He should have asked her to stay on at the town house.

Except he doubted she would have accepted such an invitation while Mama was away even if it were extended by his sister. When he'd taken Julia for the ride in the park, the lass had every intention of returning to Brixham. Establishing rooms for her at Lady Blanche's was the best idea he could think of to keep her from boarding the mail coach for home. Aye, arranging respectable accommodation was the proper thing to do as well, even though, deep down, Martin didn't give a rat's arse about being proper.

After they entered the vestibule at the town house, Charity allowed Giles to remove her cloak. "Goodness, I'm weary. I think I'll head up to my chamber and crawl under the bedclothes with a good book."

"Perhaps a dram of whisky will help me," said Martin, giving Giles his great coat and cane.

"Did Julia tell you her rooms are on the first floor overlooking the garden?" asked Charity, looping her arm through the crook in Martin's elbow.

He escorted her to the foot of the stairs. "Are they?"

"Indeed—framed by trees as if that wee wing is tucked away in a forest."

"It sounds like the setting for a fairy story."

"I do believe it could be." Charity kissed Martin's cheek. "Sleep well, brother."

He watched her retreat upward until her skirts disappeared. *A secluded garden and rooms on the first floor?*

"Would you like your drink in the library, Your Grace?" asked Giles.

Martin retrieved his hat and coat. "I think not."

"Are you going out, sir?"

"I've a great deal on my mind—I believe a late-night stroll is in order."

Giles opened the door. "Very well, sir. Shall I wait up?"

"No, no. Go on to your bed."

Once outside, Martin pattered down the town house steps whistling a Celtic ditty. Perhaps his risk-taking days weren't entirely over.

22

Julia paced the floor of her boarding house bedchamber and wrung her hands, trying to decide where she ought to sleep. Of course, as an exclusive residence, this room was as opulent as any she'd seen in Dunscaby's residences. The furniture was in the latest Grecian style with burgundy velvet upholstery and gold-trimmed damask draperies on the four-poster bed as well as the windows. Even the ewer and bowl on the washstand were gilt-edged and hewn of the finest porcelain china. But then, this boarding house was quite dear and catered only to the elite—a class which she definitely did not feel a part, despite her birthright. Julia may have been born to an earl, but she had become one of the working class. Even when she resided in her father's house, she had taken on duties at which most well-born women would thumb their noses.

Fortunately, the arrangement at Lady Blanche's was only for a short time. The problem was whether or not Julia should don Mr. Smallwood's clothing and spirit into her rooms at the town house or sleep here and return in the morning. Because her bedroom window was hidden by thick foliage, there had been no difficulty slipping into the chamber as Jules and come morn, she could easily tell anyone who might happen to see her that she'd arisen early and had been out for a brisque walk.

That decided, she took a deep breath and reached back to untie the laces on her gown. Her fingers brushed the neckline but didn't touch the laces. Twisting her other hand up her back, she wrenched her arm, forcing her pointer finger as high up as possible, then traced down between the eyelets.

Where is the blasted end or the bow or a knot for the love of Moses?

Charity had played lady's maid and obviously had taken the role to heart. Her Ladyship certainly had done so when she'd cinched Julia's stays. It had been a long time since she was laced this tightly. As Aphrodite, Sophie had insisted the costume needed no stays—very scandalous of the Marchioness.

Just as Julia's fingertip found the bow tucked away in the middle of the bodice, a rap sounded on the window. Nearly jumping out of the gown including the breath-inhibiting laces, Julia gasped. There was no possible way Mr. Skinner would know where she was at the moment. The room hadn't even been let in her name. Furthermore, though the papers might mention she'd been present in the Dunscaby box at the Theater Royal, the news wouldn't be available until the morrow at the earliest.

As soon as the duke's name popped into her mind, Julia's gaze shot to her man clothes neatly folded and sitting on a chair. Was her clandestine visitor Martin? She hadn't told him about the garden window. But then again, Charity seemed most determined to see her brother in a courtship. Julia's stomach not only squeezed, an eruption of fluttering butterflies set to flight.

She quickly scooped the clothing into her arms and stuffed the bundle into Charity's trunk—the one containing all the lovely things the lass had managed to have Tearlach remove from the attic and shift to the boarding house for Julia to use during this charade.

The tap sounded again.

"A moment," she said as sweetly as possible, spotting her father's boots and hiding them away before she shut the trunk's lid and fastened the buckles, which proved more difficult than usual considering the stiffness in her wrist.

"Who is it?" she called, pattering to the window and kicking herself for not asking such an obvious question in the first place.

"'Tis me...ah...Martin. I hope I haven't frightened you," Dunscaby's hushed voice came through the heavy damask drapes.

Julia's heart took to flight as she reached for the curtain then stayed her hand.

I mustn't appear too eager. After all, it is very knavish to knock on a woman's window at this hour.

In fact, such a thing wasn't done during respectable hours, either. Except she was ever so happy to know he'd come, and even happier that she'd decided not to return to the town house this night.

Affecting an aghast expression, she pushed back the curtain and slid the window up. "What are you doing here?" she whispered rather hotly.

He grinned—not just a smile, but a turning up of the lips revealing his boyish crossed incisors that made any resolve she might have had melt into a mass of molten honey. Then the duke held up a red rose. "This was blooming in my garden and as soon as

I spotted it, I absolutely had to bring it to you directly."

He wasn't lying. There was a hedge of roses alongside the mews. "But how did you know this is my window?" Julia asked as if she hadn't a clue who might have told him. "Anyone could have been staying in this chamber."

"Perhaps my dear sister mentioned that your view is a wee bit like a forest within the midst of a bustling city." He held out the rose and she took it. "Please forgive my cavalier appearance, but as soon as I bid you farewell on the stoop, I felt empty as if I had not savored nearly enough of Lady Julia to satisfy my curiosity for the evening."

Unable to move, she stood dumbly while her heart hammered out of rhythm. He, Martin MacGalloway, the Duke of Dunscaby—the man Julia had pined for ever since watching him climb down from the library ladder with those hairy legs scandalously tempting her from beneath his kilt—had just said that he'd wanted to savor more of her.

She drew the rose to her nose and inhaled the heady, floral scent, which provided a dizzying effect. "I am not dreaming, am I?"

"No, lass. At least, you don't look as if you're sleepwalking. You're not even dressed for bed." He placed a hand on the ledge. "If I promise to keep my voice very low and behave like a gentleman will you allow me to come in?"

Julia, patted her thundering heart, doing her best to appear aghast. "And break Lady Blanche's cardinal rule of no men allowed?"

"I promise I won't tell her..." He winked—oh dear, how wonderfully delicious he was at winking. "Will you...please?"

Julia stepped aside and held the curtain. "I cannot very well deny the bearer of such a lovely bloom. But only for a moment, mind you."

Martin climbed inside, looking far more like a scoundrel than a duke, though once he straightened and brushed off his lapels, he once again transformed into the entirely irresistible man she'd come to admire. His blond hair was mussed as if blown by the wind. His neckcloth was no longer crisp and pristine but loosened and a tad askew.

Turning toward the table, Julia set the rose down, wishing she could wrap him in her arms and shower him with kisses, but terrified that he'd reject her if she appeared too forward. But then, hadn't she kissed him when they were alone in the Rose Bedchamber? Hadn't he just said he wanted to see more of her? Hadn't he said he wanted to kiss her at the opera? Hadn't he brazenly kissed her on the portico steps at the masquerade?

Why not take a chance?

This very well might be the only time in her life where she might enjoy a bit of passion. This was her fortnight. Once it was over, Julia would disappear and Jules Smallwood would return to his ordinary life, contentedly managing the Dunscaby estate.

Her mind decided, she faced him, fists clenched at her sides. "I want to kiss you."

Martin's eyes grew dark as he took a step toward her, one corner of his mouth ticking up. "Och, lass, I'm all too happy to oblige, if you promise not to run away."

She scraped her teeth over her lower lip. "Since I didn't run from the Rose Bedchamber, I'm assuming you're referring to the incident on the portico steps, are you not?"

"Yes, well, must apologize for that. I shouldna have been so forward. Mark Antony lost his head, so enraptured was he with the beauty of Aphrodite—"

Unable to wait a moment longer, Julia clasped his cheeks between her palms and kissed him. His guttural sigh rumbled through her as his body seemed to shed a mountain of tension. He cocked his head to the side and stroked her lips with his tongue. As before, Julia opened for him, allowing Dunscaby to take the lead and show her the nuances of kissing.

But this time, she didn't think of all the reasons she shouldn't be kissing the man for whom she worked. This time, she swirled her fingers across the prickly stubble on his face. She sighed when his hands grasped her shoulders and drew her closer before they slipped around her back.

Melting into his kiss, she explored further, sinking her fingers into the curls at the back of his nape, far softer than she would have imagined a man's hair to be.

She dropped her head back as Martin trailed his lips to her neck, making tingles thrum across her skin. Julia's mind swam with the ecstasy of his mouth plying her skin. Letting herself feel like a woman who was wanted by a man, she arched toward him, her hips shifting forward and connecting with his body.

Oh. Holy. God.

His manhood pressed into her stomach—far higher than she needed to feel him yet far more rigid than she'd ever imagined a man's tool would become in order to accomplish the act of copulation. Julia might be a virgin, but after once coming across a rather lewd book in her father's library, she had a fair idea of how the act was accomplished.

As his lips grazed the tops of her breasts, she

gripped his shoulders for dear life. If she died in this moment, she would pass thoroughly sated and content. "I cannot believe how heavenly you make me feel."

"You need no costume, you are a goddess, I swear to it," he growled, his hand slipping over her breast and kneading gently.

"I mustn't..."

"Hmm?"

"I cannot..."

His hand slid lower and rested on her hip. "I desire you, lass."

"But I—you—" Yes, she desired to lay with him more than life itself, but Julia knew full well the act of copulation planted a seed in a woman's womb. How could she explain to him what she wanted and the step she positively must not take?

Martin's hand paused on her hip while he straightened and looked into her eyes with the intensity of sunlit crystal. "Tell me what's troubling ye, lass."

Ever so bashfully, she allowed her gaze to flicker downward to the outline of his member, now straining against the falls of his trousers. Her mere glimpse making her mouth grow dry and the longing inside her ignite into an insatiable flame. "Earlier this evening I admitted to being risk-averse, and I cannot... ah...I absolutely must not...um..."

With the crook of his finger, he urged her chin upward, encouraging her to shift her gaze to his face, still so beautiful it arrested her breath. "Are you worried about what might happen nine months hence?"

Julia nodded, doing her best to stare into his eyes and not again brazenly glance down to the prominent outline of his tool.

He cupped her cheek in the palm of his hand. "I would never expect you to—"

"Even if you wanted to?"

"Och, lass, I most definitely *want* to," he said, moving his hand to her back. "But there are many things we can do without risking...well, you ken."

"Such as?"

"Kissing," he said, his voice but a low growl.

"I like kissing."

Julia shivered at the sensation of his finger sliding between the eyelets of her gown—the very spot where she'd been searching for the bow.

"Everywhere," he said in a deeper tone, his lips almost touching her ear.

"Forgive me?" she breathlessly asked. "Were we not just kissing *everywhere*?"

He easily tugged the ribbon as if he were most adept at blindly removing women's garments. "I want to kiss every inch of your body." The silk of her bodice eased as he nuzzled into her neck. "Will you allow me to worship you, oh, goddess of mine?"

Martin MacGalloway wanted to worship *her*? Could this night become more fantastical? The first time she'd set eyes on him, she'd nearly swooned. And then at the hunting lodge when she'd had to remove his wet clothing, it was all she could do not to stare. He'd trusted her, he'd befriended her, he'd become such an enormous part of her life, Julia could scarcely remember her life before they met. "I beg to differ. You, sir, are to be worshipped. Everything about you makes my blood thrum with molten desire."

His lips wickedly danced across her flesh as those deft fingers released her stays. In a blink, Julia's clothes dropped to the floor, leaving her wearing nothing but a shift and her stockings. "It seems we are of like minds."

Drawing in her first deep breath of the evening, her head cleared. She had admired this man from afar for so long, it was surreal to have his hands on her, his lips on her. "You have rendered me powerless to resist you."

"Then do not," he purred, as he tugged open the bow on her shift and bared her breasts. Heaven help her, she ought to be mortified, but from the hunger in his eyes, she felt not a thread of embarrassment. "You are nothing short of divine."

He backed her to the bed, his mouth trailing to a taut nipple. Julia whimpered as he eased her to the mattress and climbed beside her. "I cannot believe this is happening."

"Trust me," he whispered, focusing those light blue eyes upon her face.

She stared back, wishing she could tell him everything, but knowing she must not. "Yes. I trust you more than you know."

He chuckled, swirling a finger around the peak of her nipple. "You speak as if you've known me for years though you must ken my reputation has not been stellar."

"That is because the shallow people who spread gossip have never taken the time to come to understand you."

"But we've only just met, have we not?"

"True, but my heart knows you. My heart has a very good sense about these things."

"Does it now?" he asked, his mouth on her, kissing with wildly wicked strokes of his tongue.

Needing to see more of him, Julia tugged his neck-cloth away and let it fall. Her trembling fingers moved to his waistcoat and released the buttons. Frantically, she tugged open his shirt and slipped her hand inside, savoring the downy soft hair on his chest and finding an erect nipple. "I want to kiss you here."

"Later," he said, moving lower, allowing her to push the shirt from his shoulders. "I will see to your pleasure first."

Rendered speechless, she nodded her consent. Martin placed his palm on her thigh and slid it downward until he grasped the hem of her shift. "When you were dressed as Aphrodite, I caught a glimpse of the most alluring ankles in all of Britain."

"Scandalous," she tittered while his fingers encircled an offending ankle.

"But I want to see so much more," he purred, inching her shift up to her knees. "May I?"

Dare she allow more? What was it he'd said about the things they could do while avoiding pregnancy? "Yes," she uttered, her body responding, her mind elsewhere. "I trust you."

Moving higher, he toyed with the ribbon of her garter.

Julia gasped. "Oh my."

"Och aye, lassie." His fingers slid in between her thighs, sending a new wave of insatiable desire shooting through her. "You are exquisite."

Trembling, Julia gripped his shoulder, dappled with freckles and sculpted by the muscle beneath.

"But this is where I want to be," he said, brushing the tips of his fingers along her, parting the place where she quivered for him.

Oh merciful mercy!

He stroked again. "Does this feel good?"

Unable to utter a word, she nodded.

"You are so ready, so very lovely, so ripe." He

seemed to know exactly what she needed as his fingers worked magic in the most intimate place on her body. "Imagine me here...sliding inside you."

Julia gasped when he slipped a finger inside her core.

"I want to be here. My cock sliding in and out just like this," he said as he stroked back and forth, in and out.

"Yes," she whispered, closing her eyes, overcome with the image of his manhood replacing his finger, craving it, yet fearing it. Heaven help her she'd never felt like this before, never even imagined she could feel like this...then he licked her.

"Ah," she cried out. Stars crossed her vision. "Oh my."

"I said I wanted to kiss you everywhere," he whispered, sealing his mouth over her while his finger performed wickedly wonderful things inside.

"I-I don't know how much more I can withstand."

He paused and glanced to her eyes, his face devilish and cocksure. "I intend to take you to the stars. Ease back and allow me to worship you."

Julia dropped her head onto the pillow while Martin turned into a magician, his tongue licking and sucking, gradually increasing the tempo in tandem with the overwhelming increase of her need. Incomprehensible pleasure wracked her mind, body, and soul as she clutched his hair and rocked her hips, falling further and further under his spell.

"You are the duke of sin, the duke of temptation, the duke of... *Oh Goodness!*"

The rumble from his roguish chuckle vibrated through her. She was going to die on this bed, succumb to an overabundance of gripping, driving passion...until every sinew in her body tightened as if she were on the precipice of bursting. A gasp caught in the back of her throat as she shattered into a pulsating maelstrom of euphoria.

Martin eased his torture while Julia gradually regained her senses. "Wicked," she mumbled. "I must add duke of wickedness to the litany of your qualities."

He grinned—enchanting teeth, hypnotic eyes. Indeed, this man was no stranger to sin. "Mayhap every name is true but I will only own to them if my lady is utterly and completely satisfied."

"I say, my satisfaction is well underway, but is this interlude not yet complete?" As his smile faded, she urged him up beside her. "You said there are many things we can do. Surely, such satisfaction as that which you just delivered can also be imparted from a woman to a man? Please show me how to pleasure you, sir."

23

M artin's cock was so hard, when she'd asked him to show her how a woman could pleasure a man, a bit of seed dribbled into his smalls. "I would never ask a lady to stoop so low," he croaked, laying on his side and facing her. Yes, he'd enjoyed many a bed partner, but never a highborn woman. He was charting new waters and though Lady Julia had proved quite eager, he absolutely must respect her station.

Her tongue tapped her upper lip while her gaze meandered down his body, stopping at the obvious swell straining against the front of his falls. "I may be unschooled in the process by which a woman may satisfy a man, but I do believe there must be something I can do to...ah...relieve such...ah...seemingly *uncomfortable* tension."

A rumbling chuckle thrummed in his chest. Lady Julia most definitely earned high marks for an adventurous spirit as well as a healthy capacity for compassion, bless her. He slid a hand to the back of the woman's slender neck and kissed her. "My satisfaction comes from watching you come undone, lass."

A thrill pulsed through his blood as she swirled

her fingers through the hair on his chest until her fingers timidly brushed his nipple. "You said I could kiss you here."

Merciful God, the mere friction of her touch was enough to make him spill. Before he could stop her, she pushed him to his back and completely spread his shirt wide. With his next heartbeat, her warm tongue teased the taut bud, making him thrust his hips forward. He'd never wanted to be inside a woman as much as he wanted, needed, craved to bury himself inside Julia St. Vincent. And she gave no respite. After the thoroughly ravishing his chest, she trailed kisses downward until she suckled his naval.

"Holy be the saints," Martin grunted, his balls spun so tightly, he was cocked and more than ready to fire.

She looked up, her grin as sinful as Aphrodite's, a true likeness of the goddess of love. "May I... um...touch it?"

Knowing he should dissuade her yet utterly unable to do so, Martin gave a single nod.

Julia first traced the outline of his member, then her gaze held his with a sly smile while she released his falls with quick flicks of her fingers. As she ever so slowly pulled the flap downward, a wee gasp slipped through those bow-shaped lips. "Oh, my."

"Do not let the trouser snake frighten ye, lass."

She slid her hand under his cock and palmed it as if it were as fragile as a baby chick. "Does it hurt to be engorged like this?"

"Bloody oath it does." As her smile was replaced with a grimace and she snapped her hand away, Martin grasped her fingers and urged her to wrap them around his shaft. "But it is a heavenly sort of pain."

"What does it feel like?"

"Well, I suppose it is like craving something so much it drives a man to the brink of madness until..."

"Yes?"

"Until he finds release."

"Is that similar to the release I felt when you kissed me...um...in such a very private, unspeakable place?"

"Aye," he managed.

She tightened her grip ever so subtly. "So, may I kiss you here?"

Good God, he was already bare and exposed, there was no use continuing to try to be a gentleman. "Please."

The first lick produced another bead of moisture. "I'll not last long," he said while she took him into her mouth, then ran her tongue up and down the shaft. He wrapped his fingers around her hand and showed her how to stroke him. In no time she was sucking the tip of his cock while keeping a steady rhythm with her hand. "That's it, love."

Martin's eyes rolled to the back of his head. His hips thrashed. Losing control like never before, he sank his fingers into her glorious locks of chestnut. His entire body tensed as he pumped and strained until, with an explosion as violent as the fireworks at Vauxhall, he tumbled into the abyss of pleasure.

Julia wiped her mouth, glancing up with her eyes wide. "That was purely fascinating."

He pulled her beside him and wrapped her in his arms. What was it about this woman that made him feel so differently? In the past whenever he'd made love to a woman, afterward there was nothing left to do but don his clothes and head for home. But presently, he felt closer to Lady Julia than he had when he'd climbed in her window. Martin didn't actually

want to go. Though, given the fact that he was entwined in her arms in a ladies' boarding house, staying
until dawn was out of the question. He squeezed his
eyes shut and pressed his lips to her temple. "*You* are
fascinating."

"THE POST HAS ARRIVED, SIR," said Giles, delivering a
small stack of letters on a silver tray.

Julia quickly shut her journal where she'd been
careful to detail her dealings with Papa's moneylender.
She'd also been careful to lock the book away from
any prying eyes. "Good morning," she said trying to
sound as if she hadn't been awake all night in the arms
of her employer and, furthermore, was not being
swindled by a scoundrel.

Nonetheless, in the past week, she had grown to
fear Giles' silver tray. Evidently, Mr. Skinner had no
concept of the meaning of the word occasional. Since
the incident at the bank, the man had sent her out for
two more vile deliveries. She tapped the corner of her
writing table. "Thank you, just leave it here, please."

The butler did as asked, then cleared his throat,
gripping the tray between his weathered fingers. "I
thought you might like to know the servants are
casting lots regarding His Grace's latest dalliance."

Her stomach squelched so violently, Julia nearly
fell out of her chair. "I beg your pardon? What are
they saying?"

"Half believe he'll be married before the family
returns to Scotland. The rest of us believe it is another
of his passing fancies."

Dear God, marriage? Martin had repeatedly told
her—or Jules—he wasn't on the marriage mart. And

Julia's dalliance, as Giles had put it, had never been intended to pressure the duke into making a proposal. She ought to chastise the servants for being so brash, but then again, it wasn't uncommon for them to gossip below stairs, not to mention reprimanding them might make her more suspicious than she already was. "Put me down for passing fancy," she said, flicking a dismissive hand toward the door.

"At what odds?"

"Truly?" Julia coughed out a guffaw as she rolled her wrist, happy to feel no pain whatsoever. "You are taking odds? Moreover, are all the servants placing wagers?"

"My oath, they are." Giles rocked back on his heels as if he were very content with himself. "The thing that has us all baffled, however, is His Grace has never trifled with a lady before."

"I believe the correct term is courted."

"Is it?"

Julia gave the butler a stern frown. "I give you no odds. The only thing I know, as you are well aware, is that my cousin must return to the country. She only agreed to stay in London for a fortnight, a week of which has already passed. And I do know something of her circumstances. Even *if* Lady Julia wanted to stay longer, she is duty-bound to her father."

"So say you."

"Yes, say I. And which side are you taking? First you said, 'the rest of us' which indicates you're siding with the 'passing fancy' lot, are you not?"

"I am, though I might be a wee bit on the fence. I do find His Grace's zeal in this situation far greater than I've ever seen it before...at least where females are concerned."

Julia gripped the seat of her chair to prevent herself from jumping up and dancing. "Well, I say, you ought to pay more attention to your duties and to those of your underlings than placing wagers on any infatuation the duke may or may not have. It is not for us to judge, notice, or otherwise stick our noses into His Grace's private affairs."

"Then you would decidedly be with the passing fancy lot?"

"Yes, most decidedly and again, I'm not offering any odds." Julia thrust her finger toward the door. "And you'd best readjust the curiosity of the serving staff, lest they all end up sacked."

"Very well, sir. But might I say your sense of humor is greatly lacking."

Julia shook her finger. "That is because a sense of humor is not a prerequisite for the post of steward."

She snatched the mail as the butler took his leave. Good heavens, the staff was taking lots? Of course, all of them knew Martin had escorted Julia to a soiree, a ball, and a recital since the first night when they'd attended the theater. A few servants most likely were also well aware of his late-night jaunts. Giles was one, of course.

She glanced down to the letter on the top and, rather than squelch, a lead ball sank to the pit of her stomach. To her chagrin, she'd now recognize Mr. Skinner's jagged scrawl from across the room. The dark black ink applied with too much pressure made his writing look as foreboding and as cold as the man.

Her fingers perspired as she broke the seal, the parchment trembling in her hands. He had said he needed her for an occasional delivery. Every sane person in Britain knew occasional meant every so often, not frequent, and definitely not daily.

She fumed as she read the demand:

You must come to Deuce's forthwith. I have specific and confidential instructions for you. Please do not delay.

"Argh!" she cursed. The man was well aware she was not at liberty to flit about London doing his bidding at the drop of a hat. First and foremost, Julia had a duty to perform for His Grace, the Duke of Dunscaby. If only they had remained in Scotland, none of this would have happened. Mr. Skinner wouldn't have seen through her ruse, she wouldn't have been put in a position of bearing his despicable correspondence, and she wouldn't be summoned to the demon's gambling hell upon his untimely whim.

"Did I just hear a groan of frustration, Smallwood?" asked the duke as he pushed through the door.

Julia casually tossed an unopened letter atop the moneylender's, trying to appear as if nothing were amiss. "Not at all, Your Grace. Is all well?"

Martin sauntered inside and sat in the chair opposite her writing table. "I believe it will be."

"Hmm? It sounds as if you're plotting, sir."

"Indeed I am." His Grace crossed his ankles and clasped his hands over his immaculate waistcoat. "My uncle—"

"The one in charge of the distillery?"

"Aye, that's the one. He's staging a benefit for the foundling home in Wick—a village where many of the workers reside with their families as you're aware."

"I say, that's very enterprising of him. It ought to go a long way to bolster worker morale and whatnot."

"I agree." Martin lowered his feet and leaned forward. "Though I'm not in a position to travel so far north at the moment."

"Of course not." Julia reached for her quill. "I

would imagine we can send a note with a substantial donation."

"I have a better idea."

"And that is?"

"You'll go in my stead."

Julia felt the color drain from her face as she replaced the quill. "Me, sir?"

"Why not? Havena you been champing at the bit to visit Stack Castle as well as the distillery?"

"Yes," she coughed as the word caught in the back of her throat. "Ah...w-when do you envisage my departure?"

"The benefit is a month hence and I reckon you should prepare to leave in the next few days or so—as soon as you feel you are able to leave your affairs for a time." Martin checked his pocket watch. "I ken there hasna been much time for your education of late, but there will be plenty of time upon your return. Once Lady Julia returns to Brixham, we'll head back to Jackson's for his sound tutelage, and I promise we'll have the most diverting time at an exclusive hell I used to frequent."

"I shall anticipate darkening hell's doors with bated breath." Julia's mind raced. He wanted her to leave London? Now? "Ah...um...er...speaking of my cousin, how are things progressing with Her Ladyship?"

A sated grin spread across the duke's lips, one she'd seen a great deal of late, especially after an evening spent in his arms. "She is nothing shy of remarkable."

"I'm glad you think so." Julia drummed her fingers on an exposed corner of Mr. Skinner's letter while an idea began to form.

A rather brilliant idea, indeed.

If Jules Smallwood were to be out of town, the steward surely could not attend to the cur's bidding. "What would you think if I were to leave on the morrow? Doing so would allow me some time to make a stop at Newhailes and mayhap even the lodge."

"Verra well, I'll leave the planning in your capable hands. But as soon as the benefit is over, I'll need you to return. Perhaps you can sail from Wick. This time of year, a voyage ought to be faster for certain." Martin gave a nod as he pushed to his feet. "I'd best be off. I'm taking Her Ladyship to Vauxhall to see a play."

"Ah, yes, she ought to enjoy that." Julia drummed her fingers. He hadn't mentioned Vauxhall yesterday. "When did you say you are meeting her?"

"I did not, but if you must know, I plan to surprise her as soon as I leave these rooms."

"But…"

"What is it, man?" the duke asked, his tone growing annoyed. "You dunna usually have trouble forming complete sentences."

"Forgive me. I've been a tad preoccupied with my duties. However, I have it on good authority that Lady Julia is presently not at the boarding house."

"How do you ken?"

"Ah…er…"

Planting his feet wide, Martin thrust his fists onto his hips. "God's stones, out with it."

"Earlier your sister mentioned something about the library. Or was it the haberdashery?" Julia raised her palms and shook her head as if women posed too much of a quandary. "I'm not sure which, but I am quite certain my cousin is not presently at the boarding house."

"Good God, the woman is busier than a honeybee in a field of lavender." With a sigh the duke glanced out the window. "Well, then, I suppose my horse needs to stretch his legs."

As His Grace swept out the door, Julia took a slip of stationery, picked up her quill, and carefully composed a letter:

Dear Mr. Skinner,

Regrettably, I am unable to attend you forthwith as per your request. I am urgently needed in Scotland on the duke's business and will be away from London for the next three fortnights or more...

24

Martin rode his horse past the haberdashers and the library in hopes of happening upon Lady Julia, but luck wasn't with him. It was late afternoon before he exchanged his mount for his phaeton and headed to Lady Blanche's where he was promptly asked to wait in the parlor. Evidently, the lass had planned to be out all day, which he found oddly vexing. Before he'd established rooms for her at the boarding house, she'd been bent on returning home. But it certainly seemed as if the woman was unduly busy for someone who wasn't planning to be in Town. Just yesterday when he'd suggested they pay a visit to the art gallery, she'd been unable to accompany him because of an appointment with a milliner.

With hat in hand, he sat where he could see the door. And it wasn't long before any irritation he may have felt completely vanished. Her Ladyship entered, her cheeks flushed as if she'd been running, or at least walking very fast. She immediately saw him and smiled radiantly.

"Lady Julia," he said as he stood.

She moved toward him as if she were floating.

"Your Grace? What a surprise to see you here this early."

Martin reached for her hand and kissed the back of her glove. Though he preferred it when she called him familiar, it was proper for her to refer to him formally here where nosy eavesdroppers may be lurking. "You have no package, no books in tow?"

"No. Why do you ask?"

"Mr. Smallwood indicated you might be at the library or the haberdashers," he said, deciding to leave out the part of riding past to see if he might find her.

"Ah, yes. I was at the library where I sat and read for hours."

"Entertaining reading, I hope?"

"Quite." Julia ran one of the ribbons through her fingers and looked toward the settee. "Would you care for a refreshment? Lady Blanche allows us to pour tea for gentlemen callers in the parlor."

"Actually, I was hoping you'd accompany me to Vauxhall. I'm told there is an orchestra from the continent that's quite good. I've hired a supper box in the rotunda where we can have a bite of dinner whilst enjoying the concert."

"Oh, that does sound diverting—and you've reserved a box? I hear they seat eight or more. Will your mother and sisters be joining us?"

"Gratefully, no. To be honest, since Grace returned from Northbourne Seminary for Young Ladies, the lass has spoken about the school ad nauseum. It seems she's taken Mama's advice to heart and has employed a tutor to help her affect an English accent so she willna be out of place when she starts boarding in the fall."

"Oh dear. I suppose there is a great deal of pressure on young girls to conform, is there not?"

"Perhaps, but if you ask me, I'm rather fond of my Scottish brogue."

"As am I. In fact, I do like Charity's lilt as well. It makes her all the more endearing." Julia glanced toward the corridor. "Well, if we will be going to Vauxhall, I'd best hurry and change."

He caught her hand as she turned. "Have you need of assistance, m'lady?" he whispered.

A pair of lassies giggled as they headed toward the door while Julia's face turned scarlet. "You are awful," she replied, though her eyes danced with mischief.

"Awful is it?" He dipped his chin low enough to graze her ear. "I'll wager I willna be so dastardly in the wee hours."

She snapped her hand away and held up her finger. "Not another word."

Martin chuckled as she turned away with a swish of saucy skirts. The pink pelisse she wore over her day dress looked oddly familiar. He watched her disappear though the corridor. He didn't pay a great deal of attention to his sister's clothing, but he could swear Charity owned a pelisse that was an exact match.

MARTIN SAT BACK while the Vauxhall waiter filled his glass with arrack punch, a particularly potent brew, the recipe fiercely guarded by the proprietor.

"There aren't as many people here as I thought there'd be," said Julia, taking a sip of her drink.

"I'm not. 'Tis Wednesday and most of the members of polite society are attending the ball at Almack's."

"Oh." The lady licked her lips, making them moist

and undeniably kissable. "Is that where Charity and your mother are off to this evening?"

He leaned in, considering what sort of scandalous reports he might start if he actually acted on his urges. "Aye."

"I'm surprised you didn't go."

"I'm not. Besides, my sister is in good hands and I happened to have somewhere else to be." Deciding to save the kissing for later, Martin lightly brushed the back of her hand with his fingertips. "Did you enjoy the music?"

"Ever so much. I think it would be incredibly diverting to be a musician."

"Oh? I dunna believe I've ever seen a woman in an orchestra before."

"True, and whyever not?" She swirled the pink punch in her crystal glass. "Women, or should I say ladies, are every bit as skilled at all manner of musical instruments as men, yet they must relegate their talent to private recitals and the like."

"Hmm, I canna say I've given it much thought aside from the impropriety of the notion. Though I'd have to act the ugly elder brother if one of my sisters wanted to join an orchestra."

"Why, pray tell?" she demanded setting the glass down and making a bit of liquid slosh over the side.

Martin puzzled for a moment. The lass seemed vexed and passionate about the subject, yet the implication that a sister of a duke might join a musical troupe was entirely absurd. "First of all, it simply isn't done. Such a societal misstep would ruin not just the offending sister, but all of them."

"Ah, yes. Ruination." Julia sucked in her cheeks appearing as one does when they've just taken a bite of lemon. "That vile concept which keeps young ladies in check at all times."

He sensed something more underlying her words. What in her past had made her so entirely fervent? "Have you not feared ruination?" he asked almost in a whisper.

Her Ladyship's eyes darkened as if a tempest were brewing behind them. "Of course, I've feared it. No woman would ever willfully bring such shame upon her family. But—"

"Hmm?"

She clapped her hands and gave her head a wee shake. "Oh, don't mind me, I'm full of vinegar when it comes to the disparity that exists between males and females."

"Nay, I sense you are quite impassioned when it comes to the subject." He rolled his hand through the air to encourage her to say more. "Please, humor me."

Hesitating, Her Ladyship stared at him, her lips parted giving him the sense she had a great deal to say yet was terrified to utter it. "I don't know," she finally admitted. "Sometimes a young lady has no choice but to do whatever must be done in order to survive."

Martin considered her words for a moment. "But is that not exactly why men are put on this earth to care for women? It is our duty to honor and protect them."

"Yes, that is the way of things most of the time, is it not?" she asked, with an arch of a delicate eyebrow.

"Aye," he said, though the whole thing didn't sit well with him. Earlier this evening he'd noticed how well Lady Julia dressed given her father was reputed to be on the verge of bankruptcy. But in no way could he broach the subject with her. Enquiring as to one's finances was yet another taboo. "What say you we take a stroll through the gardens? I'll wager we'll find your favorite flower."

"I'd like that."

Martin let an exhalation whoosh through his lips, ever so happy for the change in subject. "What *is* your favorite flower?"

"Goodness, it is difficult to pick one. Hmm... Perhaps it is peonies."

"What color?"

"Violet," she said, gesturing to the color of her gown.

Martin stood and offered his hand. "I should have guessed. Lady Charity is fond of violet as well."

If he hadn't been watching Julia's face, he would have missed the twitch of her lips. Perhaps his sister had helped enhance the lady's wardrobe. "She has incredibly good taste," she said.

"I'll be sure to let her ken you mentioned as much." He escorted Her Ladyship down the stairs of the rotunda. "Mama oft chides my sister for being a tad eccentric and far too Scottish. Knowing she has earned your favor will make her very happy."

"Charity of all people deserves to be happy. I do believe her namesake is fitting."

Martin smiled to himself. Aye, he should have known Charity had helped Her Ladyship from the beginning, bless her.

As they walked through the ring where only a few moments ago the orchestra had been playing a Bach minuet, Julia's fingers tinkled a few notes on the pianoforte. Martin stopped abruptly. "Had societal norms been different, you might have joined an orchestra, aye? As I recall, Mr. Smallwood raved about your talent on this instrument. I do believe it is high time you played for me."

"Here?" she blubbered out an unladylike snort, reminding him of the little steward. "I couldn't possibly."

"But did you not just hold forth with all the reasons women ought to be allowed to perform publicly? I say, you canna leave me in suspense now, lass."

She brushed her fingers over the top of the instrument, the gesture one of reverence and appreciation. "I may have imparted a whimsical notion, but that does not mean I want to launch into a solo performance in the middle of one of the most fashionable venues in London."

Martin threw out his arms, gesturing to the empty rotunda above and the handful of couples heading for the gardens. "Did we not also comment about how small the crowd is this evening since over three-quarters of polite society are attending a ball at Almack's?"

"I do not believe three-quarters was mentioned."

"Enough." Martin thrust his upturned palm to the padded bench. "As the Duke of Dunscaby, I command a private performance and will entertain no more argument."

The lady's jaw dropped simultaneously with the widening of her luminous chocolate eyes. After a moment of hesitation, she groaned and slid onto the stool. "Very well, but if I am ruined because of this public display, you will be to blame."

Martin turned full circle. "I do believe all the gossips have absconded to Almack's as well."

Julia splayed her fingers above the ivory keys like a painter addressing a canvas and trying to decide where her muse might lead her this evening. "Mozart, Sonata Number Eleven," she announced.

His jaw dropped while he gaped. Though he played little, he was musically educated enough to know she had selected a piece with a high level of difficulty. Aye, the sonata began simply enough, quietly with an unassuming tune, but in true Mozart style, after a few bars, Julia's fingers began to fly. Her expression grew more intense, her teeth biting down on her lower lip as she conquered the difficult rhythms for which the master was famous. Furiously she played, picking up the tempo when the music demanded, while easing back in the seat and allowing a moment of respite while the instrument resounded with higher, more delicate notes.

With her final chord, silence slowly penetrated the air, replacing the fading beauty that had mesmerized him.

"I'm speechless," he uttered, clapping his hands together.

Her Ladyship smiled ever so shyly. "Rendering a duke speechless? Perhaps I'm not so badly out of practice that I've lost my touch."

"Out of practice? You were stupendous. Dare I say better than the pianist who just regaled us with Bach?"

Closing the lid on the keyboard, Her Ladyship kept her gaze downcast. "You flatter me."

"I am nothing but honest. I dunna believe you missed a note in the whole piece."

"I'm afraid I missed more than one." A lovely rose blush sprang in Julia's cheeks. "It isn't easy to sit down and play after months without touching the keys."

"Months has it been?" he asked, offering his hand.

"Yes." She placed her lithe fingers in his palm and stood. "I believe you were planning to find me a peony, though now dusk has fallen."

"Not to worry, the pathways are lit with torches, and you definitely must have your flower, my dearest."

As they started through the gardens, Julia stopped at a row of pink roses. "These are divine."

"Do you prefer pink, red, yellow, or white roses?"

"All of them." Bending forward, she gently cupped a pink bloom in her palms. "To me roses are miraculous."

He pinched the silk ribbon at the back of her gown and let it slide through his fingertips. "But not your favorite?"

She took his elbow and together they continued along the path. "I think they're most everyone's favorite which is why I chose peonies."

"A staunch non-conformist are you?"

"I'd agree with that."

"Here we are," Martin said, stopping at a bush filled with several of the desired blooms. He snapped one off and held it up. "A violet peony for a woman who herself is miraculous."

"Oh, please, I'm merely a maid who happens to enjoy playing the pianoforte." She took the flower and though the light was dim, he could tell she was blushing, a fact which made his heart dance with glee. What man didn't revel in the knowledge he was able to give the object of his affection a compliment and make her blush? "Is it not against the rules to pick the blooms?"

"I beg your pardon? What self-respecting gardener is going to hop out from the shrubbery to chide a duke?"

"Just because of your exalted position does not make it right."

"Consider it payment."

"For?"

"Your performance, of course. Now I know why

you've entertained notions about joining an orchestra."

Julia held the flower to her nose and started off. "Alas, I was born a blessed female."

Martin caught her elbow and tugged her just enough to encourage her to face him. "I, for one, am overjoyed that you are of the fairer sex."

"Thank—"

He didn't wait for her to finish. He sealed his lips over hers and drew her into his arms, ever so glad that they were alone on this pathway. He thrust his hips forward and pressed his erection into her softness as their tongues danced. With a wee moan, Julia melted against him, slipping her hands round his waist.

"You are brazen, Your Grace," she said, her voice breathless.

"I am beguiled." He slid a hand up and down her back while his heart squeezed. He'd spent every moment possible with this woman, knowing full-well half of their time together had already passed. The problem was he didn't want it to end. Good God, he almost wanted to marry her.

Almost.

Though he wasn't yet ready for marriage.

Am I?

Perhaps if they had more time, he might be. Perhaps he could convince her to come to London next Season. She might even stay at the town house as Charity's guest.

"I've been thinking about the future," he heard himself say, completely without forethought.

Julia immediately tensed in his arms. "Oh?"

"Aye, well, once our fortnight has come to an end, I would like to see you again and was thinking—"

"No."

The intensity of that one word uttered took him aback. "No?"

"I cannot." She scooted away. "You must understand."

He didn't understand at all. "Yes, I understand that your father needs you home, but you are here now, and he seems to be coping, is he not?"

Not meeting his gaze, she gulped. "It's not exactly about his ability to cope when I'm away."

"No? Then what is it?"

"I." Turning, she hid her face in her hands. "I cannot say."

He reached out, wanting to place his hand on her shoulder, yet stopping himself. From the night he'd met Julia at the masquerade, he'd sensed her inner turmoil, some unspoken anguish that seemed to be tearing her insides apart. "I ken it is uncouth to ask, but please tell me, is it the money?"

"Yes and... Oh my word, it is too awful to utter." Without a backward glance, she ran.

Martin hastened after her. "Lady Julia, I dinna mean to upset you."

Stopping, she grabbed his upper arm with a very firm grip, her eyes filled with torment. "If you care anything for me, you will not attempt to discuss this again. All I have is one more week. Please, do not spoil it."

25

Julia paced the floor at the boarding house, wringing her hands. The day before, as Mr. Smallwood, she had left word with Giles that she was leaving for Scotland at first light, and hence, this was the first morning she hadn't risen before dawn, dressed as the steward, and hastened out the window of her chamber at the rear of the town house.

But now she walked back and forth in front of the hearth, biting on her thumbnail, and wondering if she ought to pack her things and head to Brixham to see Papa forthwith. After she had so heatedly told Martin not to speak of anything beyond this week together, he had grown quiet and withdrawn. He'd handed her into the carriage without a word. Of course, he'd sat with the driver on the way home from Vauxhall, for propriety's sake, but after he'd left her at the boarding house, she'd felt empty and alone with an uneasy sense of foreboding weighing heavily upon her shoulders.

And her trepidation had not been wrong. For the first time since she'd begun occupying the rooms at Lady Blanche's, Martin did not come to her window in the wee hours.

She stopped and stared are her reflection in the mirror above the mantel. How could she have smiled sweetly while he spoke of the future when there was no future to be had? Julia didn't want to give him false hope any more than she dared to dream. And he had admitted that he was not ready to take a wife. Goodness, a fortnight of masquerading as herself when she was supposed to be Jules Smallwood was difficult enough.

She strode to the window and tied open the curtain. It was so odd for it to be midmorning with nowhere to go, no ledgers to review, no correspondence to return, no errands to run for His Grace. She had acted as a steward for so long from her father's house to Dunscaby's, she couldn't remember ever enjoying a morning without something pressing that must be done. Not only that, she presently had no idea if she would set eyes upon the duke for the rest of the week. Was he upset with her?

Of course he is!

Julia knew Martin well enough to realize if he wanted to talk about the future, telling him not to speak of it again would not only be annoying, she had pointedly stifled a duke, a man she loved with all her heart and now he was most likely doubting this whole harebrained affair and wondering exactly what unspeakable secrets Julia harbored.

And he would be right, I have a godawfully unspeakable secret and I am a horrible, appalling person for acting on my desires and encouraging his affections.

"You've a missive, my lady," came a voice from the corridor followed by a knock that nearly made Julia's heart pound out of her chest.

In an instant, her spirits soared. Perhaps, all her worry was for naught?

She flung the door open and took the letter from the maid's fingertips. "Thank you ever so much."

Julia opened the note as the girl took her leave, only for her dratted spirits to take another dive to the pit of stomach. The handwriting was not Martin's bold script. By the fluid loops and letters, the hand that had written this prose could only be female. Indeed, Martin's mother had extended an invitation for tea this very afternoon.

Folding the missive, Julia clutched it to her chest. Alas, she would not be seeing His Grace this afternoon. Worse, she suspected she would not see him this evening either.

JULIA WALKED the short distance to the duke's town house but before she reached for the knocker, the door opened, not by Giles but by Lady Charity herself. "I reckoned you would be exactly on time."

"No one ignores an invitation from a duchess, no matter how precarious her circumstances may be." Julia shot a nervous glance beyond the girl. "Where is your butler?"

"I sent him to the kitchens to check on the tea service." Charity stepped back and ushered her inside. "I ken he saw you after the carriage incident, but no use tempting fate. Quickly, come with me, Mama is in the parlor."

"Do you think the duchess will recognize me?" Julia whispered out of the corner of her mouth.

"I rather doubt it. She is far too busy to give my brother's steward a second glance."

"Thank heavens for small mercies," Julia mumbled as they crossed the threshold into the parlor.

Charity all but danced into the room, waving her arms with an overly enthusiastic flourish. "Mama, look who arrived just as I was passing through the vestibule!"

Julia bowed her head and dipped into a deep curtsy. "Your Grace, it is my pleasure to make your acquaintance."

"My lady, how lovely to see you." The duchess offered a warm smile, her gaze assessing and perhaps a tad gleeful. "I apologize for sending such a hasty invitation, but I only discovered this morning that my son's attentions have decidedly turned toward you."

"Oh?"

Charity tapped the folded newspaper atop the marble-topped tall table. "Compliments of the society pages."

Julia cringed, drawing a hand to her chest. "Dear me, I hope the news wasn't too terribly disparaging."

"Not in the least. I may be a tad annoyed with my son since he waited until I learned of this from the gossip columns rather than from his own lips. But I am delighted, nonetheless." Her Grace gestured toward the settee. "Please do have a seat."

While a maid entered with the tea service, Julia kept her head lowered, ensuring the brim of her bonnet concealed her face until the servant left. "Did you speak to His Grace about the article?"

"I did. I also told him that I didn't care to learn that he reportedly had been spotted in society with you on his arm no fewer than half a dozen times." The duchess picked up the teapot. "Moreover, my eldest daughter has evidently known about the whole affair for days."

Julia licked her lips as Her Grace poured. "I'm sure Dunscaby might have informed you had we not simply been friends. He was kind enough to offer me a ride on his phaeton. Unfortunately, my wrist was injured and he arranged for his physician to treat me. That said, I'm afraid London's gossips will be sorely disappointed because I must return to Brixham shortly."

"Shortly? And your arm, were you badly injured?"

"No, it was only a sprain." Julia rubbed her wrist, thanking the stars the swelling had abated quicky and presently only writing caused her a modicum of pain.

"I told Mama about your father's health, the poor dear," Charity added, taking a cup and saucer, and adding a shortbread biscuit beside it.

The duchess tsked her tongue as she replaced the teapot. "It is a shame to hear you will not be able stay in Town through the duration of the Season."

Julia picked up her cup. "I feel the same, regardless, some things cannot be helped."

"And..." Charity continued, dabbing the corners of her mouth, "at breakfast Martin mentioned how astounding you are on the pianoforte."

Julia released a long breath. Thank goodness her friend had the wherewithal to shift the direction of the conversation away from Julia's lack of time. In no way did she want to utter anything that might give the duchess the idea her son was remotely considering a proposal. In this household, it was no secret as to how anxious Martin's mother was for him to marry. And there were too many reasons for him not to marry, the first being the duke had professed that he was not on the marriage mart on a number of occasions, including such an admission last evening.

He Grace daintily sipped her tea. "Oh, Martin's face did light up when he spoke of your talent, dear. I would be ever so honored if you would allow me to host your recital."

"Indeed, I would love to if only I had more time." The handle of Julia's cup slipped between her fingers, making the cup clank against the saucer. "I'm afraid to admit that I'm rather out of practice and a recital requires a repertoire, and I could not possibly come up with one in less than a week."

On a sigh, the duchess reached for a biscuit. "Unfortunate. Perhaps another time."

Charity scooted to the edge of the settee. "I think that is a splendid idea. Perhaps next Season?"

Julia gave the lass a flabbergasted stare. When, exactly, was Mr. Smallwood going to find the time to practice the pianoforte?

"Let us count on it, shall we?" asked Her Grace.

"Should I be in Town, I would be honored." What else could Julia say? The daughter of an earl didn't ever refuse a duchess.

"My second daughter, Grace, has decided to attend Northbourne Seminary for Young Ladies, where my eldest chose to remain at home with her governess. Tell me, Lady Julia, did you attend finishing school?"

"I did," Julia said, wondering what hole she might dig by giving a reply, especially since it seemed everything she said caused her consternation. "Talcott's in Chippenham. I was fortunate to room with the Marchioness of Northampton during my two years there. Of course, before that, I had a governess."

"Which did you prefer?" asked Charity.

"Though I did enjoy Talcott's, I'm afraid the years of my tenure there were rather sad times in my life."

Her Grace set her empty cup and saucer on the low table. "Why, may I ask?"

"After my mother passed away, my father sent me

to Talcott's..." Julia looked to the tea service and sighed. There was no use explaining the rest. But the air suddenly changed and tingles made the fine hairs on her arms stand on end. Yes, she sensed Martin's presence but when the duke moved into the doorway, her breath caught all the same.

"Lady Julia," he said, bowing. "When my mother mentioned she intended to invite you to tea, I didn't realize it would be today."

Her Grace clasped her hands together. "Of course, it had to be today after your sister told me that Her Ladyship must return to Brixham so soon."

"Well, I'm glad you did," Martin said, sauntering inside, his light eyes reflecting the sunlight as beams streamed in through the window. "I have just purchased a new horse. Would you care to accompany me to the mews? The groom is brushing the laddie as we speak."

As he offered his hand, Julia took it. "I'd love to. Is it a colt?"

"A gelding. Geldings are so much better behaved when part of a team." Martin bowed to his mother and then to his sister. "If you ladies will please excuse us."

Julia kept her eyes lowered while her pulse thrummed. He was leading her though the town house as if they hadn't had a disagreement. In truth, he didn't have to stop by the parlor and greet her. Martin could have spent the entire day in the mews with his new horse. Perhaps he wasn't as angry with her as she thought?

Together they crossed into the courtyard, but when they came to Mr. Smallwood's chamber, His Grace stopped and rested his hand on the latch.

"Does Jules want to see the horse as well?" she

asked, wondering why the devil she hadn't kept her mouth shut and just allowed him to take charge.

Martin glanced from side to side before he winked, his tongue tapping the corner of his mouth. "I've sent your cousin to Scotland to take care of some affairs up there."

"Oh—"

As she uttered the exclamation, Martin opened the door, pulled her inside and promptly closed it. "Och, lass. I couldna walk all the way to the mews without a wee kiss."

Julia didn't know which one moved first or who closed the distance. With his single statement, all the trepidation she had dwelled upon earlier in the day shed from her shoulders as easily as the dropping of a shroud.

His warm hands tilted her face to his and he wasted no time plying her lips with a kiss demanding she meet his fervor. To think, she may have ruined everything last eve by pushing him away and attempting to run. But being in his arms, surrounded by his strength, his heat, his size, his unmistakable scent was exactly what she needed at this exact moment.

Julia offered him everything she had as he stoked, suckled, and loved her mouth with a dizzying and relentless kiss.

When, finally, he pulled back and met her dazed eyes, she drew in a breath, needing to apologize. "I'm ever so sorry for my reaction last eve. This morning when I thought I mightn't see you again, I realized how silly I had behaved."

"Nay, nay." He kissed her cheek. "You were right. I needed a reminder to rein in my enthusiasm."

"Because you are not ready to wed." She phrased her words as a statement rather than a question.

"Ah…" He glanced away. "Quite right."

Julia's gaze trailed to the narrow bed where she slept and, oh, so often dreamed of holding this man in her arms. "Have we not a horse to inspect?"

Martin stole another intoxicating kiss before he gave her an answer. "I've seen the wee beasty, but unless you want to pay a visit to the mews, may I tempt you elsewise?"

"Yes," she whispered ever so softly, reaching behind and turning the lock on the door. "Please."

In one fell swoop, the duke lifted her into his arms and carried her to the bed where he sat and settled her atop his lap, tugging her bonnet's ribbon and tossing it aside. "A woman with hair like yours should never have to pin it up."

Before she was able to respond, he sealed his lips on hers while he deliberately scattered hairpins and ran his fingers through her tresses. "You oughtn't to have cut it."

"I will never do so again," she said breathlessly, thankful he hadn't seen the mop when Willaby had first sheared over a foot off.

She tilted her head back, leaning into Dunscaby's caresses as he bared her neck. Emitting a low growl, he settled his lips on her skin, the soft strokes of his tongue sending rivulets of pleasure winding through her. With the wicked scrape of his teeth upon her sensitive lobe, she grasped and wrapped herself around him, eager for more of him.

A deep, guttural moan rumbled from him as he allowed her lips to wander across his eyes, his cheeks, his gloriously soft mouth.

"So bonny," he whispered, tilting up her chin and watching her with an intense desire in his eyes, an expression that sent a gush of feminine pleasure low and

deep in her body. She shifted her knees slightly apart
—so very wanton of her, but she needed him too
much to care. "Touch me."

With her words, she was on her back, sinking into
the soft folds of the bed she'd occupied alone during
so many wakeful nights. After one more searing kiss,
he nestled between her legs and then slid downward.
He moved quickly, raising her skirts, his hands roving
from her ankles, to her knees, to her thighs until she
gasped with the erotic sensation of his fingers grazing
the nest of curls at her core.

"Is this where you need me?"

"Yes," she said her legs trembling with want. Time
and time again, he had shown her what it was like to
be a woman pleasured, and his touch was quickly
turning into a compulsion she could not go without.

"You're soft, so wet, so ready..." He stroked against
her pulsing flesh, fulfilling her insatiable need,

"You are my elixir."

As he slid one finger inside, she swirled her hips
with the stroke of the pad of his thumb and his wicked
finger.

"More!"

With her demand, a second finger joined the first
inside her, thrusting deep in tandem with the rocking
of her hips, to her need to keep going, to her craving
desire to quicken the pace. And he knew exactly how
to pleasure her as the movement of his thumb came
faster and firmer as she pressed and writhed against
him.

"Let it go, my bonny lass."

A cry caught in the back of Julia's throat and her
eyes flashed open, catching the desire written on his
face as she shattered for him. There gazes remained
connected as she pulsed over and over again until he

eased the pressure and her breath slowly returned to an easy cadence. Martin gently rearranged her skirts before again pulling her onto his lap and pressing his lips to her temple. "Mayhap we ought to re-pin your hair and go have a wee gander at the horse."

Julia's shoulder's shook with the notion. "Agreed. After all, we wouldn't want a certain mother to find out we never did manage to make it all the way out to the mews."

26

After enjoying a breakfast at the boarding house, Julia opened the door to Charity's smiling face. "As you asked, I've brought your mail. Giles left it on the corner of Mr. Smallwood's writing table just like you said he'd do."

Julia took the correspondence and stood aside while her friend entered. "You're such a dear, thank you."

"Since you're supposed to be on your journey up north, I dunna ken why you're bothering with it."

"I don't want to miss a letter from Willaby." Of course that was true, but Julia wasn't about to tell Her Ladyship how badly she was being swindled by Silas Skinner and wanted to ensure none of the lout's correspondence sat where His Grace might intercept it. She sifted through the missives. "And here is one from the dear old butler."

Charity slid onto the settee with a whoosh of ivory muslin beneath a skirt of lace. "Do you miss the manor house?"

Siding her finger under the wax seal, Julia reflected for a moment. It hadn't been all that long ago when Huntly Manor was the center of her world—the one property owned by her father that she'd fiercely guarded, determined to keep it from the debt collectors. Well, she was still determined to keep it from the likes of Mr. Skinner but oddly, the preservation of the seat of the Earl of Brixham no longer preoccupied her thoughts. "I suppose not as much now as I did when I first arrived at Newhailes."

The lass chuckled. "You did make a rather odd little steward."

"Mind you I am still an odd little steward who is supposed to be on his way up to Scotland."

"Aye, but you're delayed. Travelers are delayed all the time for anything from inclement weather to a broken axle on their carriage." Charity threw her head back and laughed. "Or a carriage infested with mice."

"There was only one mouse," Julia said as she shook open Willaby's letter.

"Perhaps, but you proved your manhood to me when you caught the wee vermin."

"Indeed, and I'll have your know your brother told me—or Mr. Smallwood—not to encourage your affections."

The lass toyed with the pearl pendant on her necklace. "Did he now? And here I thought a match with my brother's steward would solve everything."

Julia read the salutation. "Everything?"

"Well, I might be taller than you, but as a man you're affable and easy to talk to. Moreover, if I married Mr. Smallwood I would have been able to live at Newhailes or Stack Castle. I love both, of course and cannot imagine living anywhere else."

"When you find the right husband, you will become the lady of a vast estate and—" Julia abruptly stopped as she read:

The earl has taken a turn for the worse, I'm afraid. He

has asked for you and I agree it might be helpful if you were to arrange a time to visit within a month or so. Whenever His Grace can see fit to grant you a bit of time of course...

"Is all well?" Charity asked, rising and stepping beside Julia's elbow. "You've turned as white as bed linens."

Julia tilted the letter so Her Ladyship could see the contents. "My father..."

"Oh dear, and you only have a few days left." The lass took the missive and paced. "Look at this, Willaby suggests a month right here."

"Yes, but Papa wasn't exactly well when I left to take the position as your brother's steward. In fact, it was because of my father's health that I was faced with no choice but to do so."

Her Ladyship turned as she refolded the letter. "Goodness, I'm certain you must be worried something awful."

"Of course I am. And I'm supposed to be on my way up to Scotland which—"

"—means you won't have received this letter until your return, which will not be for six weeks or more."

Julia clapped her hands to her head and huffed. "True, but I *have* received it."

Charity shrugged. "I suppose there's that."

Biting down on her thumbnail, Julia looked to the valise she'd packed with Mr. Smallwood's effects in preparation for his journey. "I ought to apprise Martin of this and leave in the morning."

"But your time in London is nearly at its end. Surely by the tenor of Willaby's note, you can wait a few more days." Charity wrapped her arm around Julia's shoulders and gave a thoughtful squeeze. "Then you can head for Huntly Manor as Julia St. Vincent planned and once you've been there a sennight or so, write to Marty as Mr. Smallwood and tell him you received word of the Earl's ill health and that His Lordship requested an audience with his old steward."

Julia leaned into her dear friend, wanting desperately to agree with her. "I'm not sure His Grace would understand the audience part. After all, the earl ought to be more interested in seeing his daughter than his steward."

"But isna Mr. Smallwood a relation?"

"A second cousin on his wife's side. Mind you, it would have been very convoluted if Jules had been a blood relative, especially since there is no heir in line to succeed."

"Quite." Charity led Julia to the settee and urged her to sit. "Nonetheless, I truly think you should adhere to my advice. Return to Brixham as you planned, then Jules can write and make his excuses."

"But what about the benefit in Wick?"

"Family is more important than a benefit, and no one kens that better than Marty. Heaven's stars, he was one of the most rakish men in London before Papa passed, but when the family needed him, he stepped in without a word of complaint and took up the reins." Charity squeezed Julia's hands and offered a warm smile. "Do what you must. My brother will forgive you. He thinks Jules Smallwood is astute and brilliant, and he believes Julia St. Vincent is Aphrodite incarnate."

Julia scraped her teeth over her bottom lip. "You truly believe I ought to stay until the end of the fortnight?"

Charity moved her fingers to Julia's her upper arms, giving a pointed stare. "What would your father say if he were in my place?"

Gulping, Julia tapped praying fingers to her lips. What would Papa say if he were himself again? If he were the man he was when Mama was still alive? It had been such a long time since she had felt his love. But at one time her father would have wanted nothing more than his daughter's happiness. And he would have been very proud to know Julia was being courted by a duke.

"Very well." She held up a finger to make a point. "I will remain here for the three days as planned, and that is *only* because Willaby suggested I return sometime within a month."

A knock sounded at the door. "I beg your pardon, m'lady," said the maid, popping her head inside. "The Duke of Dunscaby has come to call."

❧

"MUST WE KEEP THE CURTAIN CLOSED?" Asked Charity, toying with the tassel that usually tied back the velvet drape presently covering the carriage window. "The day is far too beautiful to ride inside this dreary coach without enjoying the scenery."

Martin gave his sister a dour frown, though he doubted she'd see his expression given the dim light. "That would spoil my surprise, would it not?" He hadn't yet told Lady Julia about his plans to build a cotton empire for his brothers and the first sailing of Gibb's ship was an excellent opportunity to do so. The summons he'd received from his brother was brimming with excitement, so much so, Martin, himself wanted to throw back the curtain and look to the Thames for his first glimpse at *The Prosperity's* unfurled sails.

"Shall we venture to guess?" asked Lady Julia. "I'm

thinking a jaunt across the river to Southwark. Just yesterday I overheard some ladies talk about an astounding show of acrobatics with a man who claims to be the strongest in all of Britain."

"I'm surprised they're not claiming Christendom," Martin mumbled.

"So, is it Southwark?" asked Charity.

He glanced down to Julia's hand flush against the seat between them. Unable to help himself, he shifted, placed his hand atop hers, and crossed his legs. Giving the lady a wry wink, he pretended as if the touch had been unintentional—for Charity's benefit, of course, since Her Ladyship was acting as Julia's escort. "Nay, we're not heading to Southwark."

"Hyde Park?" asked his sister. "After all, you're wearing your kilt so you must not be taking us to see the queen."

"No, no. The park is far too mundane for secrets. Everyone goes there." Julia's little finger brushed his outer thigh, the touch very light, yet extremely arousing. To add fuel to the fire, she returned his wink. "I'll wager His Grace has something far more amusing in store for us."

Good God, if only they didn't need a bloody chaperone, he'd pull the vixen onto his lap this instant. But they were traveling in an enclosed coach and time and time again he'd vowed not to take a chance and ruin her reputation.

"Och, I ken," said Charity, sitting across the carriage and tapping the tips of her fingers together as if she were scheming. "You're taking us to a boxing match. I've been dying to see one ever since Mr. Smallwood told me you took him to Jackson's Saloon for a wee lesson with the champion himself. Did you ken now he's practicing with a dumbbell every morn?"

Lady Julia coughed and patted her chest. "I do suppose Jules could use some toughening up."

"I could not agree more," said Martin. "When the man came to Newhailes he was far too sheltered—a veritable steward, mind you, but I've never met anyone so engrossed in his work. Not even Giles."

Charity opened her fan and giggled behind it. "A man more dedicated than Giles? Unfathomable."

Martin eyed his sister. "It seems you chat with the chap a great deal. I hope you're not being an annoyance to Mr. Smallwood."

"How can I annoy him when he's not even in London?"

Julia coughed again.

"Are you feeling ill?" Martin asked.

"I've never been better." Her Ladyship fanned her face, then sniffed. "We aren't nearing the Pool of London are we? I smell fish."

Martin thumbed the curtain. "We...might be."

"Gibb's ship!" Charity blurted scooting to the edge of the bench and looking out. "He said he'd be sailing soon. Is today his maiden voyage?"

Leave it to his sister to spoil the surprise.

"Perhaps I am feeling a tad under the weather," Julia said as she sank against the seat just when the carriage rolled to a stop.

"Hogwash," Charity said without a lick of concern. "You just said you've never felt better and, if you ask me, it is a beautiful day and curmudgeons never go out when the weather is fine."

"Curmudgeons?" Martin asked, looking between the two.

"Och, dunna mind me." Charity took the footman's hand as he opened the door. "We all ken Julia to be the antithesis of a curmudgeon. Come, m'lady, we cannot miss *The Prosperity's* gallant voyage out to the Channel."

Martin caught Julia by the elbow before she disembarked. "Are you truly unwell?"

Before answering, she popped her head out the door and panned her gaze across the bustling pier. "Forgive me, I coughed a few times but the tickle is gone now."

"Thank heavens." The new venture was coming together and it astounded him how excited he'd become. Most men of his ilk would never lower themselves enough dabble in trade, but the idea of establishing a dynasty with his brothers truly excited him. "My closest brother, Lord Gibb, has acquired a new ship for a textile operation Mr. Smallwood and I have established for the benefit of my brothers and the MacGalloway name." He grazed his teeth over his lip. For some reason he couldn't put his finger on, he desperately wanted Julia to see the ship. He wanted her approval. He wanted her to see he wasn't just a duke who owned vast estates, but he was working to the lay the foundations for his family and the future of the MacGalloway clan.

"How enterprising of you," she said, taking the footman's hand and disembarking.

Once Martin stepped onto the footpath, Charity grasped one of his elbows while he offered Julia the other. "Why did you not bring Mama and the lasses?" asked his sister.

"In truth, this is only a test run. Gibb is taking her out—assessing his new crew and seeing what the ship will do when she reaches the open waters." Martin led the ladies toward the river's edge. "He's merely sailing out to the Channel to make a few maneuvers then will return to the Pool for any necessary repairs. If all goes well, *The Prosperity* will sail for America in a week—her true maiden voyage."

"Oh look, are those her sails I see?" asked Charity.

Martin hastened his pace a bit, his heart taking to flight. Goodness, he was proud of his brother and all that had come together to make this dream a reality. "Aye. Look there, by the way she's listing to and fro, the ship has weighed anchor."

"How marvelous!" Julia said, her feet shuffling with his fast pace, her face alight with as much excitement as he felt. "Look there, she has fifteen including the fore and aft. Standard barques have thirteen sails, but this one is a cut above, is she not?"

Martin ought to have known a lass who hailed from a wee seaside village in the south of England would know her ships and rigging. But at the moment, his little brother was standing at the helm of his very own ship, looking as noble and dignified as any captain Martin had ever seen, as if Lord Gibb MacGalloway was born to command the waters. He raised his hand to bid his brother farewell. "Aye, *The Prosperity* is a cut above."

"I'm so proud of him." Charity leaned on the rail and craned her neck while the barque began to pick up speed. "And of you, Marty. Papa would have been astounded with all you are doing for our brothers."

Julia turned her face up and smiled at him, her eyes shining as if he were the only person on the pier whom she cared to see. "I agree. Your dedication to your family is not only admirable, it is an example for all."

"I dunna believe the firstborn should be the only one who benefits from a—"

"Did ye 'onestly believe you could thwart me?" demanded a gaunt character, grabbing Her Ladyship by the wrist. "I warned ye not to cross me."

"Mr. Skinner!" Before Martin could step in, Julia wrenched her arm away, her face suddenly apple red. "I-I have not thwarted you in the slightest. I-I will be departing London three days hence and on top of everything else, I have given you every spare farthing to my name."

"What the devil is the meaning of this?" Martin stepped between them, thrusting out his chest as he wondered, *what did she mean "everything else"?* "You, sir, must show proper courtesy when speaking to a lady."

"Oh, aye? She might be the daughter of a fallen, ruined earl, but she 'as been lyin' to ye for months." The vile creature thrust a gnarled finger at the lass. "And now she's playing the 'igh and mighty lady, putting on airs in 'opes of trappin' a duke in an unlikely marriage."

Julia thrust her fists at her side. "I am not trying to trap him!"

Trap?

A stone the size of a cannonball lodged in Martin's chest. He knew of this Mr. Skinner and the only reason any member of the *ton* ever dealt with him was if they were in such financial difficulties they had nowhere else to turn. But was there truth in what the moneylender had said?

Julia is trying to trap me?

The cannonball burst into flames throughout his chest as Martin shoved the cur in the shoulder. "I suggest you remove your person from my sight before I lodge my boot up your backside."

Skinner didn't budge. "Ye still don't know, do ye?"

"What are you blathering about?" Martin demanded, sauntering forward and towering over the scoundrel.

Julia pushed herself between them. "Please don't."

Martin scarcely blinked as his body went numb. "Why would you plead with the likes of him?" he asked, but neither of them glanced his way.

"I said I would ruin ye if ye dared cross me." Mr. Skinner sneered as his snake-like eyes finally shifted to Martin. "Ye are damned fool if you 'aven't realized by now that this wench is not only Lady Julia St. Vincent, she is your bloody steward!"

"You despicable bastard!" Julia fumed, her eyes filling with tears.

"She's right!" Charity grasped Her Ladyship by the elbow and pulled her toward the carriage. "There is not a kinder, more giving lass in all of Christendom, and you see fit to ruin her in the eyes of polite society?"

Skinner sauntered after them. "She owes me."

"Her *father* owes you," Charity countered.

Martin grabbed the cur by the collar and yanked him back. "I've never darkened the halls of your miserable gambling hell because you take pride in ruining any gentleman with a title." He raised his fist while Skinner recoiled. "If you ever approach me again or if you ever dare to insult a lady whether it be in private or in public, I will see to it you will rue your actions."

Gnashing his teeth, Martin shoved the blackguard to the cobbled footpath. "Scurry back to the gutter where you belong!"

His blood pulsed with hellfire as he watched the maggot hasten to his feet and dart across the busy road. Only after Skinner disappeared into the crowd, did the fire in Martin's blood turn to ice. People bustled around him on the busy pier, but he stood rooted to the spot while his breath arrested in his chest.

Dear God, I've been a damned, blind fool.

"I'll clean out my rooms and be gone before dark," said Lady Julia, or whoever the hell the imposter actually was.

"Nay. You canna go now!" Charity insisted.

The pier began to spin Martin's mind rifled through the past few weeks. Damnation, he'd been deceived and blinded by a charlatan.

And then I played directly into her trap like an imbecile.

Clenching his teeth, he grasped his sister's elbow. "You and I are going home." Before he climbed into the carriage, he leered at the traitor. "And you, *Smallwood*, I hope to never set eyes upon you again."

27

Julia endured three days in an overcrowded coach which then left her in the square of the little seaside village of Brixham in the midst of a squall. Rain stung her face as she trudged the two miles to Huntly Manor. By the time she reached the entry to the drive, she was soaked to the bone, water sloshed through her slippers, and her fingers felt as if they'd been rubbed raw by the handle on her valise.

Tears streamed onto her cheeks, mixing with the rain and sliding into the corners of her mouth. Once the house was in sight, she leaned into the wind and hastened her pace as best she could. The place looked haunted with overgrown flowerbeds and weeds sprouting in the drive. Even the wisteria trellis had broken in half and lay in a heap beneath the library's window.

The door opened as she approached the stoop. "My lady?" asked Willaby, hastening outside and grasping her elbow. "What the devil has happened?"

Merely hearing the old butler's voice made an enormous sob wrack her body, bringing her utterly undone. "I-I-I have ruined *everything*."

"There, there, come inside where it is warm." Julia

futilely wiped her eyes and allowed Willaby to lead her into the entrance hall. "Why didn't you hire Mr. Brown and his hackney in town? I cannot believe you walked all this way in the rain, you could catch your death."

Julia's teeth chattered as she removed her sodden pelisse while trying to stop the flow of tears. "I can ill afford a hackney, not when I must pay for transport for the lot of us to sail to Australia—that is if you are willing."

"Australia?" Willaby asked, taking her coat. "Of course I would never allow you to go on a voyage alone, but what is this talk of ruination? Tell me what has happened at once, my lady."

Julia removed her dripping bonnet and gave it to the butler. "S-S-Silas Skinner confronted me at the Pool of London and told His Grace that I have been masquerading as his steward for months." Julia buried her face in her palms. "Y-y-ou should have seen the look of horror in Dunscaby's eyes. And there was nothing I could do but resign at once. I-I am so asha-a-a-med!"

"Dear Lord, when I watched you set off for Newhailes in the mail coach I feared something like this would happen."

Julia bit down on her lip as she tried to bring her weeping under control. She wasn't about to tell Willaby all of it—not coming across Sophie and meeting Martin at the ball dressed as Aphrodite. She wouldn't admit that she had pretended to leave for Scotland so that she might enjoy her few remaining days in Martin's arms without being saddled with her duties as steward, even though she had every inten-tion of going to Scotland once her two weeks had come to an end. She wouldn't even bother mentioning that Lady Charity had been incredibly helpful, making it easier to manage the ruse.

Willaby draped the sodden pelisse over his arm, his expression bereft. "The lot of us are well and truly ruined."

He didn't know the half of it. "And I can never again show my face in polite society." Peaches, her cat came strutted into the entry, swishing his tail and rubbing against Julia's leg. At least something, if not someone, thought her worthwhile. "Not only that, 'tis a matter of time before Mr. Skinner finds a way to evict us."

"And you think Australia is the answer? Truly?"

She picked up the cat and ran her fingers through his soft fur, finding little solace as Peaches began to purr. "As soon as Papa is well enough to travel we shall board a transport and leave this place forever."

The way Willaby's bushy eyebrows drew together made Julia's stomach churn. She'd been so wrapped up in her own remorse, she hadn't noticed how weathered the elderly butler looked. His shoulders stooped a bit more than they did the last time she'd seen him. The lines around his mouth were drawn and his complexion sallow.

"Oh, heavens, forgive me. How is Papa?"

Willaby rubbed his fingers from his neckcloth, down the front of a once crisp white shirt. "I hate to be the bearer of more bad news, but just this morning the physician told me to send for you at once."

Julia clapped a hand over her mouth while her breath stopped in her chest. "At once? Is he...?" She couldn't say it.

"I'm afraid it won't be long, now." As the walls closed in around her, Willaby placed a comforting hand on Julia's shoulder. "Why don't you don some dry clothes? I was about to take His Lordship his afternoon tincture. Give me a moment to set him to rights. I know it will raise his spirits to see you—especially once you've had a chance to freshen up."

Peaches hopped from her arms as Julia glanced down to the mud splattered on the dress she'd been wearing for three days now. She didn't need a mirror to know she looked a fright. "But I must see him straightaway."

"A quarter of an hour will make no difference. Besides, if His Lordship sees you looking like a drowned kitten, he'll know something is amiss. He's far too frail to withstand more worry."

"Of course. We shan't burden him with my misfortune."

Willaby gave an indecisive nod as he headed for the kitchens. Without a moment to lose, Julia took in a deep breath and made her way to her bedchamber. She'd spent the past three days in utter misery on her journey home from shame. She did derive some comfort from being back home, though it seemed oddly unfamiliar as well. So much had changed since she'd left. She had changed most of all.

And now, everything in her life was crumbling about her feet all because she was too selfish to deny herself a bit of romance. Yes, Mr. Skinner was a vile miscreant, but she was solely to blame for her deception.

JULIA QUICKLY CHANGED into a dry muslin dress—albeit worn and frayed at the seams. She'd forgotten how tattered most of her clothing truly was. Willaby was already inside her father's bedchamber where they were speaking softly. She knocked on the door jamb and popped her head inside. "Papa?"

Sitting up with a few pillows tucked behind his back, his gaze immediately shifted her way. "Julia?" He held out a jaundiced hand. "Have you been away?"

She moved inside and grasped his chilly fingers. "Yes. Yes I have been."

By the saints, he looked like a shell of the man he'd once been—hollowed cheekbones, yellow complexion, even his eyes were rheumy and yellow. The sleeve of his nightshirt slid up his arm to reveal a dark, purple bruise. "Have you taken a fall?" she asked.

A vacant expression filled his eyes as his smile faded. "I...ah...do not think so."

She turned to Willaby, widening her eyes with a questioning expression.

"He bruises with a mere touch."

And he was obviously experiencing some confusion, but she didn't want to discuss it with the butler now or speak about anything Papa might find upsetting.

She pulled over a chair and sat at the edge of his bed. "I've been in London for the Season."

"Have you? I didn't even realize that you've been away."

A new bout of tears stung the rims of her eyes. "I wasn't gone for long, but I did attend a ball and danced with a duke."

Papa's eyes widened with his faint smile. "A duke? Did he propose?"

Julia batted her hand through the air. "Hardly after one dance."

"If I were a young nobleman, be it duke or earl, I wouldn't allow a lass as fetching as you slip away."

"That's very kind of you to say, Papa." She traced

her finger over the paper-thin skin on the back of his hand. "I've missed you."

"You have? Have you been away?"

"Yes," she repeated without providing anything further. A tear dribbled down her cheek as she looked him in the eyes, shattered by the lack of spark in his eyes. "'Tis raining something awful today. The drive is full of puddles."

A semblance of a smile played upon his lips. "I quite enjoy the rain."

"You do, indeed. I remember when I was a little girl and together we stomped through the puddles. We laughed and laughed while thunder clapped overhead, which made the chiding Mama gave us ever so worthwhile."

"Mama..." He mused. "Is she here?"

"No." Julia's throat thickened as she looked to Willaby. She ought to be truthful. She'd had enough of covering up the truth for the rest of her days. "Your countess is in heaven."

Papa released a heavy sigh as he sank into the pillows. "Then I shall see her soon."

28

Martin slouched in his chair and threw back the dregs from his glass of whisky. The library swam with the volumes of leatherbound books seeming to float in uneven waves on the shelves, yet he had no intention of slowing down. "Giles," he shouted, "bring me another bottle."

The door opened as if the butler had been standing at the ready. However, it wasn't the doting servant who stepped inside. His sister, Lady Julia's bloody accomplice, pattered inside and sat in the chair across from him.

He gave her the soberest stare he could manage. "I am to be left alone."

"Aye, I ken your ridiculous orders. Heaven's stars, you've been wallowing in here like a drunkard for the better part of a week—six days for heaven's sake."

"I command you to leave me be!" he bellowed, not caring for the slur of his words or how despicable he sounded.

The vixen pursed her damned lips and folded her arms as if she were planning to stage an insurrection. "I'd like nothing better, but Mama sent me in here and she told me not to remove my person until I've had my say."

"Och aye? Our mother has sent my devious, scheming sister in for a chat. Tell me, what cunning plan does our mother have up her sleeve to thwart me?"

"I beg your pardon? You are referring to the woman who bore us, our father's wife who does now and always has wished the best for her children."

Since Giles had not yet responded to Martin's request for more whisky, he stood and stumbled to his writing table. "After what transpired at the Pool of London, I am thoroughly convinced that all women are devious." He pulled a bottle out of the drawer and turned it upside down only to discover it empty. "Giles!"

Charity stamped her foot. "Would you please do me the kindness of resuming your seat so that I may have my say and leave you to your self-destructive, unseemly inebriation?"

Martin stubbed his toe on the rug and stumbled back toward his chair while thrusting an accusing finger at his sister. "You helped that woman and do not deny it. The two of you were colluding together."

Charity placed a palm on the table and leaned forward. "Only because you didna recognize Mr. Smallwood for who she was from the outset."

"I am not accustomed to being deceived by stewards who have been vetted by my solicitor of all people." Martin plopped into the seat, trying to look Charity in the eye, but blast it if she weren't weaving all over the library. "I thought you were being kind when I realized you'd given Lady Julia some of last Season's clothing."

"I was merely helping her."

"But you kent she was Mr. Smallwood all along, yet you did not reveal her deceit to me. You most likely watched and laughed while the Duke of Dunscaby made a damned fool of himself."

Charity pounded her fist hard enough to make his inkwell rattle. "I did no such thing."

"Aye." Martin belched. "I'll believe that when I see a chubby swine sprout wings and fly past this window."

"Stop it. You are doing nothing but feeling sorry for yourself like a pathetic fool." Charity shook a stack of missives and a small black book at him. Had she come in with those in hand? "Goodness, Marty, you liked Lady Julia—you truly liked her. I've never seen you so enamored with a woman. Not ever."

He shoved a damned lock of riotous hair out of his eye. "It seems I have very poor taste in the opposite sex."

"Wheesht your gob, whilst I finish what I came in here to say."

Martin's jaw dropped. Had he just been shushed by his sister? And why the devil had he not yet booted her out of his library?

"I'll have you know that I admire that woman for her courage."

He snorted. It took cast-iron balls to carry on as Jules had done. Except he-she had no testicles, which Martin should have realized when he caught sight of her damned silken shoulder on the eve he'd walked in on Smallwood taking a bath at the hunting lodge.

Charity threw back her shoulders, as if she were ready to do battle. "Lady Julia's father ran his estate into the ground. He drank himself half to death exactly like you are doing now. The poor woman was in dire straits at no fault of her own. She had no choice but to don men's clothing and take a position that would pay enough money to keep that horrid money-lender from stealing her home—Huntly Manor, the seat of the Earl of Brixham."

Martin glowered. "No one takes an earl to debtor's court."

"I disagree. Mr. Skinner is too well connected in London to be ignored. He threatened and cajoled and took every farthing until there was no more money left to give. Julia was not only paying her father's debts, she was paying for the earl's physicians and the only two servants remaining at the manor, who, mind you, she kept on to care for her undeserving father." Charity clapped her chest and took in a sharp breath. "Forgive me, undeserving is *my* word, not Julia's."

He drummed his fingers on his empty glass, wishing the copious amounts of alcohol he'd consumed had done something to ease the stabbing pain in his heart. "But she should have been honest with me."

"And risk your ire? Risk losing the only thing keeping her and her father from utter ruination?" Slapping her materials on the table, Charity leaned forward like a prized fighter about to go on the offensive. "I might understand your anger if she had been a bad steward, or if she had stolen funds, but I say she was the best steward you could have had. Look at what she's done for our brothers! She works tirelessly and—"

"She is not a man."

"Who gives a fig that she doesna have a penis between her legs?"

Snapping his eyes wide, Martin gulped. Had his sister just uttered such a vulgar word?

"Dunna look so shocked. I ken the difference between lads and lassies. If you'll recall our nursemaid oft bathed me and Freddie together when we were wee ones."

He raked his fingers through his mop of tangled hair. "God save us."

"Can you not get it into your thick head that Julia only wanted a chance to be courted for once in her life. Moreover, she was resigned to only allow herself a fortnight of happiness. Lady Julia had absolutely no intention of trapping you—she was leaving, remember? But that vile swindler had to step in and ruin everything."

"Skinner," Martin mumbled, then name making his skin crawl. Only the most desperate of gentlemen borrowed money from that snake. And the lout had conjured the nerve to call him a damned fool.

Not that he was wrong. I am an unmitigated fool.

"I found these in a hidden compartment in Julia—er—Mr. Smallwood's trunk. Silas Skinner was not only extorting money from Julia, and thus from her father at the exorbitant rate of a fifth, he was blackmailing her into doing his bidding."

Martin leaned forward. "Blackmailing?"

"Aye, she made a note in her journal of every meeting she had with Mr. Skinner and those letters from the lout substantiate every word she wrote." Charity leafed through the little black book rife with the handwriting Martin had come to know well. "Here it is. She clearly writes that Silas Skinner offered to wipe the slate clean if she would take a position as a woman of easy virtue at Deuce's. But because she refused, he not only demanded back payment on installments missed by the earl, he demanded that she do his bidding."

Sitting back, Martin crossed his legs as well as his arms. "What kind of bidding?"

"Deliveries of some sort." Charity leafed through the journal's pages. "It seems her first was to a bank manager at Messrs. Drummond where she feared for her life when the man berated her for merely delivering a message."

Martin reached across the table and leafed through the journal. It wasn't one of those diaries young ladies oft like to record their secrets in. It chronicled the earl's debt and every payment she'd made to Skinner, every meeting, every letter. He stopped at an entry that made ice pulse through his blood.

He backed me against the wall and forced his tongue into my mouth. I would rather be sent to Australia for ten years transportation than allow that fiend to ever again place his hands upon me.

Sobering markedly, Martin shifted his gaze to his sister, his icy blood turning to fire. "I'll thrash the bastard to within an inch of his life."

"LUNCHEON IS SERVED, my lady, my lord" said Willaby, popping his head into Papa's bedchamber.

Her father didn't wake as Julia glanced up. "I'm afraid I'm not hungry."

The old butler shuffled inside, carrying a tray with a bowl of cabbage soup which he spoon-fed the earl twice daily. "How about I bring you a spot of soup and some of those egg sandwiches you like so well?"

"Perhaps later." She collected a book from the bedside table. "Mayhap I'll read aloud whilst Papa eats."

Willaby set the invalid tray across the earl's lap and pulled over a chair. "I'm worried about you."

"Don't be."

"If you continued to miss meals," the butler continued whether she wished for him to do so or not, "you'll end up ill and then I'll have two St. Vincents to care for."

Julia smoothed her hand over the leather volume. "I wish I could eat. Perhaps in a day or two my appetite will return."

"The sooner the better." The butler picked up a spoon. "Open wide, your lordship."

It seemed her father wasn't hungry either because he didn't budge. In fact, he'd drifted off to sleep an hour or so ago and Julia had sat there rambling about her adventures over the past few months—more for her sake than anything.

She opened the book. "The Scottish Chiefs by Jane Porter." Emitting a blubbering snort, she rolled her eyes to the scarlet bedcurtains. She hadn't noticed the title when she reached for the book which had been the third in a stack, the first two, she'd already read over the past few days. Why couldn't she have opened a chronicling of Africa's flora, or something about the construction of British canals, or the Roman occupation of Britain, or anything that had nothing to do with Scotland.

She cleared her throat and turned to Chapter One. *"It was the summer of 1296. The war which had desolated Scotland was at an end..."*

"My lord?" said Willaby, his tone hollow and eerie.

Julia's gaze shot to her father's face. His eyes were no longer closed, but half-cast and vacant. His color, though it had been papery and pale moments ago, had now turned nearly translucent. His blue lips parted slightly.

Blue.

As tears stung her eyes, Julia clutched at her heart. "Papa?"

Willaby set the spoon aside and placed his fingers at the side of Father's throat. "My Lord Brixham, please respond."

The book dropped from Julia's fingers and clattered to the floor. Standing, she grasped the earl's icy hand and rapidly patted it. "Papa!" When her action gathered no response, she patted his cheek. "Please! You cannot be gone!"

"My lady," said Willaby sounding as if he were in a tunnel.

But Julia paid him no mind. She flung her arms around her father's shoulders and wailed. "Please. Not now. I cannot lose you along with everything else."

Crying, she babbled about all the things she'd planned for them to do. About Australia and how they might start anew. At some stage, Willaby came around and tried to tug her away but Julia shrugged him off.

Why must her life be in such a shambles? Why could her father not recover and revert to the man she knew as a child? She wept and wept until moonlight flooded the chamber while crickets sang their high-pitched farewell.

Dear God, what am I to do now?

THERE WAS a reason Martin preferred to stay away from the halls of Deuce's Gaming Club. First and foremost, his father had warned him to stay away from the establishment. Normally, after such a warning from

Da, he might have done the opposite, but his father put it in rather sobering words. At Deuce's, the house didn't lose. No one had been able to prove Silas Skinner to be a cheat, but the man was as underhanded as Satan himself. He had a reputation as the king of temptation, his club touting the best whores, the cheapest liquor, and the most generous of terms. Except the generosity was not for the benefit of the patrons. Oh, no. The only person Skinner was generous with was himself. On the one occasion when Martin had stumbled into the club with a mob of dandies out for a good time, he'd witnessed Skinner gloat over a gentleman who had gambled his last farthing.

After he'd watched the moneylender in action, enjoying issuing his torment and the resulting public humiliation of the sorry chap, Martin made up his mind that Deuce's was decidedly deuced. Furthermore, because of the incident involving Lady Julia and her father, in the future, he intended to take steps to ensure every member of polite society agreed with him.

It was already past ten in the evening and at this time of night, the lout was sure to be standing on the mezzanine of his hell, gloating out over the hapless frowns of the fools he intended to swindle. On top of Charity's chastising, Giles had found a very small mention of the Earl of Brixham's passing in the Gazette which the butler had failed to mention for nearly two days. Martin sobered quickly, sent a messenger for his solicitor, and hastened for the East End. He absolutely must confront the moneylender before the cur had a chance to take steps to evict Julia from Huntly Manor.

Martin cued his horse to a stop outside the club and tossed his reins at a groom along with a silver guinea. "Tend my horse if you please. I dunna intend to be long."

"Ta, my lord."

"Your Grace," Martin seethed under his breath as he mounted the stairs.

The doors opened to a smiling attendant dressed in immaculate livery, his smile too broad, his eyes too wide and filled with greed. "Welcome to Deuce's, Your Grace. It is our greatest pleasure to receive ye." He stepped too near. "May I take your coat?"

"No." Martin cast his gaze to the mezzanine, but Skinner wasn't there. He started for the stairs. "I need a word with the swindling owner of this establishment forthwith."

"B-but Mr. Skinner is not 'ere."

"I find that difficult to believe," he said, marching upward.

"That may very well be so, but he ordered his coach ready and left town this morn. I saw 'im myself."

At the top of the steps, there wasn't a bloody person in sight. Martin rounded on the attendant, grabbing his lapels. "Where. Is. He?"

"I-I've no idea." The man blanched. "I am merely a servant. I—. Please don't 'urt me."

Martin gave the man a shake. "Who in this contemptable hellhole can tell me where I can find the bastard?"

"J-just 'ave a seat in the saloon, a-and I'll fetch someone straightaway, sir."

Releasing his hands, he gave the fellow a push. "I'm not waiting a second longer than necessary. Lead on."

Evidently, Martin's presence had already run through the building because a door screeched open and an elderly butler walked through. "Your Grace,

Mr. Skinner has left London to claim some property that has come to him. I'm afraid he won't return for at least a week. Perhaps a fortnight."

"Over my dead body," he growled. Martin didn't need to probe further to find out where the scoundrel had gone. He only hoped he wouldn't be too late. "The Earl of Brixham is indebted to your employer and it is of utmost urgency that I understand to what extent."

"That information is highly confidential, sir."

"Wrong answer." Martin grasped the butler's arm, twisted it just enough, and walked him out the same door he'd just come through. "Either you find the information I need now, or I'll have this place shut down and so tied up in the courts that you'll be begging for alms on the curb before Skinner will be able to crawl out of the hole."

29

The funeral was a small affair as one might imagine for an impoverished earl. Afterward, Julia wandered the halls of Huntly Manor wearing a black mourning gown that had once been her mother's. She'd told Willaby she wanted to take an inventory of the items they would put up for auction but in truth, blindfolded she could point to every piece of furniture, every vase, picture, and item of silver remaining in the house.

After living in the opulence of the Dunscaby residences, everything appeared a bit shabbier and worn than it had done before she departed. But with no money to make repairs, it was little wonder the draperies were faded, the velvet on the settee in the parlor worn, and a leak in the roof had left telltale streaks down the wallpaper in one of the unused bedchambers.

On the following day, she dragged herself out of bed and, while she dressed, she leaned toward the looking glass and examined the dark circles that had taken up residence beneath her eyes. "Willaby is right," she said to her reflection. "I need to eat and take care of myself. Then I'll take a pot of tea into the library, sit at my old desk, and prepare a list for the auctioneer. There's no use putting it off any longer."

The sooner the household effects could be sold, the sooner she and the old butler could purchase tickets to sail for Australia and escape her mortifying shame. The housekeeper, Mrs. May had already given notice and had moved to a new position in Cheltenham.

Though wracked by melancholy and a sense of loss, Julia had no reason to stay, and ought to be looking forward to the new adventure. There were so many opportunities in Australia.

Are there not?

Unfortunately, she couldn't think of one positive thing awaiting her in the new country. Reports were the place was full of convicts and poisonous snakes. Life was hard, even for the wealthy. Julia had no hope of ever making her fortune, or marrying anyone regardless of his post, be it a swine farmer or a vicar. Worse, the voyage could take anywhere from three to eight months, depending on the weather and the wind. And though Britain had done much to battle piracy, there were all sorts of horrible things that could happen at sea...like the ship capsizing on rocks and splintering into bits, sending all those aboard to a watery grave.

"Stop," she chastised herself after she'd eaten a bowl of porridge and was heading for the library. Inside, she strode straight to the old globe and slowly turned it until she found the island continent. She placed her finger on the dot that marked Sydney and traced a line to Portsmouth where she and Willaby planned to board a ship. "See? Though it might be halfway around the world, Australia doesn't seem all that far when looking at it this way. There is absolutely nothing for me to worry about."

In truth, it wasn't the journey that had her tied in knots as much as the awful, humiliating way she'd left the MacGalloway household. Never in all her days would Julia be able to erase Martin's bereft expression from her mind—the horror in his eyes when he realized she had been deceiving him all that time.

If only she could explain that she had indeed worked as Papa's steward and had executed her duties with utmost care and proficiency. Julia always prided herself in a job well done no matter what she was doing, no matter how much or *if* she was being paid. Of course, she hadn't been paid by her father, but nonetheless, she had performed her work as if she had actually attended university and earned top marks.

She gave the globe a pat before pulling out the last slip of unused paper from the writing desk and embarked on the task of listing the inventory. With luck, the sale ought to not only pay for passage to Australia, but there might to be enough money left for her and Willaby to eke out some sort of existence while they searched for work. Perhaps she'd find a position as a governess or seamstress. Furthermore, as the former butler to the Earl of Brixham, Willaby ought to find a new post in no time. It had surprised her when he'd agreed to accompany her to Australia, but the old man was faithful to the family and had insisted he would never allow her to travel abroad unaccompanied.

When Willaby came in and cleared his throat, the sound more like a groan than a polite interjection, Julia had already compiled a list consisting of four columns and had turned the paper over. "I'm *afraid* to say that you have a visitor. I cannot believe that vile scoundrel has pounced this quickly."

Placing the quill in the holder, she tried to keep her hand from trembling, though the feather still twitched as she drew her fingers away. There was only one scoundrel to whom the butler could be referring. Julia, too, didn't expect Silas Skinner to stake his claim only a day after the funeral. "Afraid?" she asked with a nervous chuckle, praying she sounded far more self-assured than she felt. "That sounds rather ominous."

"I wish he had waited—had shown a modicum of respect for his betters, but I fear the blackguard must have raced for Brixham as soon as the papers reported the earl's passing."

One of her shoulders ticked up as she tried to feign indifference. "I, for one, am not surprised. Everyone knows that without an heir, Papa's title will be rendered extinct. Mr. Skinner no longer has the peerage to dissuade him from taking his claim to debtor's court. That is if we were planning to fight him."

"Which we won't." Glowering, Willaby tugged on his cuffs. "We haven't a rat's chance in hell of winning."

A rock as heavy as lead sank to the pit of Julia's stomach. "No."

"Shall I show him in?"

She managed a hapless smile. "Is there any other option?"

It seemed as if Julia hardly had time to move in front of the writing table and compose her person when the moneylender was introduced and the door closed behind him. Licking his lips like a licentious cur, Mr. Skinner moved forward, gripping what could only be the deed to Huntly Manor in his fist.

She stood very still, clasping her hands in front of her midriff, her knuckles white. "Have you come to tell me you've had a change of heart and are dropping your claim to my home?"

His lips disappeared into a craggy line, making the ugly scar on his face more prominent. "Hardly. I've been waiting for this day to come for far too long to throw away the spoils on an ungrateful wretch."

A hundred retorts played on the tip of Julia's tongue. She hadn't thwarted him, not really. The duke had sent Smallwood to Scotland where she fully intended to go after she fulfilled her promise to stay in London as herself for merely a few more days. If Martin had not taken her to the shipyard, Mr. Skinner most likely wouldn't have found out about her delay. But all of that was in the past and not a whit of it mattered to this man.

She gestured to her list. "Now that we have laid Papa to rest, I'll sell the last of the estate's furnishings. Once that is done, I'll not stand in your way."

"You are already in my way."

Julia pursed her lips. The man should have greeted her first and offered due courtesy. But, no, he was too bent on claiming the manor for himself. Heaven's stars, she'd heard enough about Deuce's to know it was gauchely opulent with not a penny spared from the enormous crystal chandeliers to the red velvet fainting couches above stairs where the women of easy virtue were reputed to flaunt their wares.

"I assure you, within a month, I will have all traces of the St. Vincents removed from Huntly and the manor will be yours. As my father's only heir, there will be no need to pursue me in debtor's court."

"Unfortunate. I would 'ave rather enjoyed watching ye fall further into ruin." He smirked. "But I am not willing to wait a month. I'm not willing to wait another day." He moved his hand inside his coat and pulled out a shiny flintlock pistol. Julia shrank, as he stroked his fingers along the barrel, her gaze darting to the door behind him. Should she run?

"Since ye 'ave refused my generous offer for a position at Deuce's, I've decided to take possession now. Today."

When Peaches jumped down from the settee, Mr. Skinner swung the barrel toward the cat who swiftly disappeared behind a curtain. Julia dashed for the door, but before she reached the latch, the cur grabbed her arm and jerked her against the wall, making the back of her head hit the plaster. "You, you vile snake," she seethed, ignoring her inner voice, demanding that she cower like a simpering waif. "You are reprehensible. Surely you do not plan to shoot me? You may have connections in high places but murderers in the town of Brixham are tried and convicted rather swiftly. There's even a gnarly old oak ready and waiting with a hangman's noose."

He sneered, stale breath skimming her face, while he brushed her cheek with the tip of his pistol. "I'm merely a man defendin' me due and I am prepared to use as much force as necessary, luv. That is unless ye want to reconsider my offer." He licked his lips and raked his gaze down her body. "Think about it, luv. Ye'll never feel the knives of 'unger stabbin' your belly, unable to sleep for the pain. Ye'll never know what it's like to live in the gutter in midwinter, shiverin' until your chatterin' teeth feel as if they will rattle out of your 'ead."

Julia recoiled from the cold iron muzzle as he carelessly waved it too near her head. As she moved, Mr. Skinner jutted his knee against the wall, pinning her in place. He might sound as though he'd been raised in the gutter of London's streets, but no one disputed the fact that the moneylender was a self-made man with wealth beyond compare. Why was he driven by some demonic desire to first ruin her father as well as her, no matter the cost?

With trembling breath, she stared at the deadly weapon. "W-why are you so intent on acquiring Huntly? Residing a two-day ride from London makes no sense at all, given your involvement in Deuce's."

His nostrils flared. "I don't recall sayin' I intended to live 'ere."

That would be right. He'd force her out and let the manor stand empty while he searched for new tenants. Her mind raced as she glanced from the pistol to his knee. "You seem delighted with a base, sick satisfaction because you were the catalyst of my ruination. And now, only one day after I buried my father, you refuse to grant me the slightest amount of time to grieve, let alone set the estate's affairs in order."

"Why should I care?"

"Because it is the humane thing to do."

"Is that so, luv?" Mr. Skinner leaned into her, making it all the more impossible for her to flee. "I'll 'ave you know your father did not see fit to show *me* a modicum of 'umanity. And I was just a lad of ten, dressed in rags, and fendin' for meself."

Sliding her foot to the side, she pressed her leg against his offending knee. "My father? You had an altercation with Papa when you were a child?"

He slapped his hand onto the wall beside her head, stopping her progress. "Let us just say your dear old sire is the reason I made it my life's goal to ruin those 'ighbrow snobs who comprise the stench of their so-called polite society."

Though frightened out of her wits, Julia couldn't believe what she was hearing. Yes, her father had fallen to vice, but only after her mother passed away. Mr. Skinner definitely appeared to be no more than ten years younger than Papa. Capturing her bottom lip with her teeth, she tried to knit the puzzle together. "If you were ten years of age, my father would have been how old? Twenty?"

"Old enough to be a foolish earl."

Well, twenty had to be a good guess. Her father had inherited the earldom at the age of eighteen—and he hadn't married Mama until he was five and twenty. "I find it difficult to believe Papa would have crossed paths with you let alone do something so abhorrent you've held a grudge all these years. Please, help me understand," she said, hoping to buy enough time for the man to err, for his attention to be drawn away. "What awful misdeed did my father commit?"

"Allow me to paint a picture for ye. I did 'ave a mother, though it seems all my father was good for was a bit o' seed. It turns out gin was Ma's only true love. I was a mere five years of age when she sold me to a tyrant—a man who'd use any excuse to crack a whip across me back. At least he provided a roof over me 'ead until the bastard was gutted in his own bath, leaving me without so much as a pallet to sleep upon or a farthing to me name. I'd spent the better part of a year on the streets when a shiny black carriage with a crest etched in gold on the door rolled to a stop in front of the wooden crate I called 'ome."

Julia's heart sank. "The Earl of Brixham's crest?"

"How did ye guess?" Mr. Skinner mocked, his breath decidedly foul. "After ye refused my generous offer and then thwarted me, I figured ye for an imbecile."

Julia caught the glint of the flintlock's muzzle pointing away as Skinner spoke. She rubbed her fingertips, inching away ever so slightly. "Did you ask the earl for help?"

"I asked 'im for a penny—the measly price of a loaf of bread." Mr. Skinner again trapped her, jutting his face to within an inch of hers, tapping his gun barrel against the hideous scar slashing through his lips. "'e rewarded me with a strike with the silver 'orse 'ead on his bleedin' cane. And I'll wager ye'll never guess what your dear papa said."

Julia gradually moved her fingers toward the weapon, but the fiend quickly pointed the barrel at her chin. Dear God in heaven, would she pay in blood for her father's sins? She could only imagine how the privileged young earl might have replied. She'd seen her papa's ugly side but found it difficult to believe that he was truly tarnished before he'd met Mama. Perhaps it was her mother who had turned him into the good man who filled Julia's childhood memories?

"'e told me to crawl back into the gutter and pray for a swift death 'cause the outlook for my life was misery at best, though most likely more 'ellacious than 'ades."

Julia's stomach turned over as she closed her eyes and drew in a shaky breath. She had no cause to doubt the man, she'd heard her father use the term "more hellacious than Hades" a time or two. How could he have been so careless with a human being? A child, no less. "I'm so very sorry," she whispered, desperate to explain that the earl hadn't always been a rogue. At some point he'd become a responsible husband and father. But then he'd fallen again—and this twisted man standing before her was so filled with hate. She feared nothing she said or did could make up for the damage done.

The expression on Mr. Skinner's face grew hideous

as he snarled. "Your apology is empty, oh 'igh and mighty lady."

Julia pushed her fists against his chest but the fiend was immovable. Her gaze met his merciless grey eyes and a chill thrummed through her blood—a chill she absolutely must not allow to paralyze her. "P-please allow me a mere fortnight and Huntly will be yours!"

"I think not." Within the blink of an eye, he clamped his icy fingers onto her chin and squeezed. "I'm throwin' ye out. I know ye are destitute and penniless. I want ye to pay for your father's cruelty. I want ye to know what it is like to be so 'ungry, you'd eat an uncooked rat. To be so cold, you'd give your cherished virginity to warm your 'ands by a fire."

"I would never stoop so low."

His eyes blazed as his fingers dug into the sensitive flesh on her face. "You 'ave no idea the vile deeds to which you would stoop, ye despicable wench."

Sneering as if sickened by the sight of her, he shoved her to the floorboards. Shrieking, Julia threw out her hands to stop her fall. Out of the corner of her eye, Mr. Skinner drew his foot back clearly intending to deliver a kick. Scrambling to scoot her feet beneath her, she lurched away just as his boot smacked into the wall.

He spun the pistol her way. "Dammit, you bitch. I'll make ye suffer for that!"

"Willaby! Help!" she screamed, darting for the door. As her fingers brushed the latch, the miscreant grabbed her chignon and yanked her against his chest. Needling pricks of pain shot through her scalp while he slid an arm around her throat.

The vile blackguard pressed the length of his body

against her back. "I ought to take ye now. Show ye what it feels like to be swived by a real man."

"Unhand me!" Julia croaked against his strangling hold as she smacked her head against his chest, making a hollow thud. She clenched her fists, ready to deliver a jab—just as soon as she could twist enough to break free.

The door swung open, blinding her with a flood of light from the window across the hall. Through the glare, a tall, dark figure barreled inside. "Release her now or meet your end."

The pressure against her voice box tightened while Skinner dragged her deeper into the room. "Martin!" she croaked, her voice but a garble.

The cold, steel barrel of the pistol pressed against her temple. "Take one more step, and I'll shower the walls with 'er Ladyship's blood."

A click echoed through the chamber as Martin pointed a flintlock pistol just over Julia's shoulder. "And I'll see to it you hang from Newgate's gallows with a placard bearing the word thief draped around your neck."

The sound of her own breath rushed in her ears while silence swelled through the air like a boiling kettle about to burst its top. Each man glared at the other, waiting for someone to be the first to move.

As she tightened and balled her fists, a realization dawned. During this entire time, she had not heard Mr. Skinner cock his weapon.

Can I take a chance?

If she didn't, Martin might very well lose his life and that she could never bear.

Drawing in and enormous breath, Julia thrust herself against the blackguard's chest, stepped to the side, and ducked beneath the barrel of pistol while slamming her fist backward against his loins with all her might.

With his shriek of pain, the fiend buckled forward.

Martin lunged in, throwing and uppercut, his fist striking Skinner's jaw so hard, the man's head snapped back before he crashed to the floor. Without hesitation, the duke pounced on the dastard's chest, pressing his pistol against Mr. Skinner's forehead and pinning the man's gun-wielding wrist with his knee. "Lady Julia St. Vincent now owns Huntly Manor and you are trespassing."

After Martin produced the note hastily drawn up by his solicitor not only proving all debt was settled but that he had transferred the title of Huntly Manor into Julia's name, he took great satisfaction in booting the scoundrel's arse out the door. He slammed it closed and brushed off his hands, turning to find Julia standing in the archway of the entry with the note in her grasp.

But she didn't rush into his arms as he'd imagined she'd do during Martin's hours upon hours of thunderous riding. The paper in Her Ladyship's hands trembled, the expression on her face stunned, unsure, and filled with worry. "You did this for me?" she asked with a shaky voice. Though she was wearing black, there was no question that Julia was thinner, her face a tad drawn with dark smudges beneath her eyes.

He'd behaved like such a cad, first admiring the woman for her unselfish and dutiful care of her father, then casting her aside as if she were vermin because she had done the unthinkable to safeguard her family's estate. "I did."

She dropped her hands to her sides. "But I thought you never wanted to see me again."

"Forgive me." In two strides, Martin crossed the vestibule and collected her hand between his much larger palms. "There is no excuse for my behavior at the pier—"

"But you were caught unawares. And I did defy convention, don men's clothes, and accept a position only reserved for a man for the sole purpose of—"

"Paying your father's debts. I ken, lass. And after you left, my sister helped me see exactly how extraordinary you are. I know not a single woman who would have risked everything to pay her father's debts and keep his estate afloat. I didn't properly listen when you explained the disparity between the fairer sex opposed to their unfeeling male counterparts. Yes, a man's role is to protect his own, but when a lass has lost that protection, she canna be thrown to the wolves."

Julia's eyebrows slanted outward while she clutched a fist beneath her chin. "Then you agree she ought to be allowed to join an orchestra?"

"Aye, or become a steward." He drew her hand to his lips and kissed it, hoping he imparted a modicum of the strength of the love in his heart. "Och, ye were the best steward I've ever known. My word, you single-handedly pulled me from an icy loch and saved my life."

Julia said nothing while a single tear slid onto her cheek.

What could he say to make her realize how much she'd come to mean to him? As a steward he'd come to know her in ways he never would have imagined. She was not only brilliant, she was funny, fiercely loyal, and fearless. He took her palm and flattened it over his heart. "I owe you not only an apology, but a debt of gratitude."

"No," she said, splaying her fingers across his chest. "It is I who must make amends. It is I who was wrong."

"Never. You are a shining beacon among thorns. You are a wondrously astounding and talented woman, and I do not wish to spend another day away from you."

"You would have me return as your steward?"

"If being a steward will fulfill all your dreams, I would employ no one else, but you can do so much more as the Duchess of Dunscaby." Martin dropped to one knee and gazed into a pair of the most beautiful mahogany eyes flecked with amber he'd ever beheld. The eyes that had transfixed him and claimed his heart. "Lady Julia St. Vincent, it would make this duke the happiest man alive if you would agree to be my wife."

Those glorious brown eyes flecked with amber widened with her wee gasp. "Wife?"

"Aye. Please say you will marry me." He took the palm of her hand and pressed it against his cheek. "I love you more than life itself and promise to spend the rest of my days making amends for my deplorable behavior."

A tear dribbled from the corner of her eye as Julia's head bobbed. "Yes. Yes, I will marry you. I fear I have loved you since the day you climbed down from the library ladder and served me with your own hand." She pulled him to his feet. "I cannot believe you are here."

He didn't care if they were in the vestibule or in a crowded hall or if it were the middle of the day. Martin tugged her into his arms and kissed her. "Believe it lass. I am here now and shall remain by your side always. I give you my solemn vow you will never want for anything."

"With you, I know I could face any hardship." An adorable chuckle rumbled through her nose as Martin took his kerchief and wiped her tears. "How did you come to arrive so quickly?"

"There are some benefits to being a wealthy duke. Mr. MacCutcheon secured Huntly Manor shortly after I paid a visit to Deuce's. When I discovered Skinner had already left town, I rode day and night, only stopping to change horses."

"My word, you must be exhausted."

"Never when you are in my arms." Unable to drink his fill of her loveliness, he tilted her chin up with the crook of his finger. "You should have told me how deeply indebted your father had become and that you were shouldering his burden."

"I could never have burdened you with my problems."

"Nay." He brushed his lips across her forehead. "Instead you bravely ventured out and stepped into a man's role."

"I was capable, if not the right gender."

"You were and are and I am ever so glad you came into my life."

She ran her finger across his lips making them tingle with the need to kiss her. "As Mr. Smallwood?"

Martin grasped one of her wayward fingers and licked it. "Mr. Smallwood was quite efficient, and very accommodating, it turns out. Though after watching him box, I reckon he never would have amounted to much of a man."

"I beg your pardon?"

"Och, what I meant to say is the woman surpasses the man tenfold." Before he dug his hole any deeper,

Martin captured Julia's bow-shaped lips with his own and kissed her. When their lips fused together, he fully intended to start slow, but by the way the fire in his heart inflamed, he clutched her flush with his body and showed her exactly how much she meant to him. His hands roved up her back and down the soft curves of her bottom.

Julia sighed when she pulled away. "Did you not say you were hungry?

"Ravenous."

She took his hand and tugged him into a drawing room. "I do believe we have some fresh bread and jam."

He stopped abruptly and inclined his head toward the stairs. "It isna food I covet, lass."

SURREAL ANTICIPATION SWIRLED around them as Julia kept ahold of Martin's hand, leading him through the house until she pushed into a bedchamber in pinks and lavenders. It smelled of roses and lilacs, but most of all, the scent of Julia floated through the air. The lace bedcurtains on the fourposter presented the lair of a fair maiden, making Martin's mouth grow dry. "What do you want?" he asked while she tugged him inside, the door softly closing behind them.

She met his gaze, brown and serious. "You." She fingered his neckcloth and tugged, releasing the knot. "All of you."

"Are you certain, lass?"

She released the buttons on his topcoat. "Did you not just ride day and night to save me from a vile miscreant? Did you not just propose marriage?"

"Aye," he croaked, removing his coat, waistcoat,

and shirt within three ticks of the mantel clock. "It might hurt."

"I care not." Her eyes raked up and down his torso before she stepped nearer and smoothed her hands over his chest. "You are perfect. Like a marble statue but real, hot-blooded, and virile."

If a man ever wanted to beat his chest and roar, Martin did in this moment. Rather, they came together in a frenzy of caresses, kisses, bodies connecting and rubbing while clothes fell to the carpet. Completely naked and fused together, they tumbled to the bed.

In a tangle of legs and arms, Martin rolled her on top of him, allowing Julia to take control while, in broad daylight, they explored each other—every inch of skin, finding every sensitive crevice as they delighted in each other's pleasure.

Martin removed the pins from her hair, pulling handfuls of silken waves to his face and inhaled. "This is heaven."

"You are heaven. Nothing could feel better than this." Straddling him, she pushed up and looked into his eyes with wonder. "Does it feel as good for you as it does for me?"

"Aye. Better, I'd reckon."

"And this?" she asked, kissing his nipple and swirling her tongue around the sensitive peak. "How does it make you feel?"

"Ravenous," he growled.

Chuckling, she moved downward until she placed her lips upon his cock, licking tentatively before she sealed her lips around him and suckled, interchanging with light scrapes of her teeth while her hand worked magic along his shaft. God, the woman had taken to pleasure like a swan to a loch.

Martin gasped, plunging his fingers into her mane of chestnut locks and whispering her name. And when he could bear no more, he gently urged her chin upward.

"Is something amiss?" she asked.

He laughed and pulled her beside him. "God, no. It feels too good. Did you not say you wanted..."

"It all? Yes." She rolled onto her back, looking like Aphrodite incarnate as she opened her legs for him. "Show me."

Kneeling between her silky thighs, he placed his palm on her nest of curls. "Are you certain, *mo leannan*?" he asked, uttering a Gaelic endearment that seemed so entirely right in this moment.

"I've never been so certain of anything. I want to join with you."

He slid the pad of his thumb over her sensitive button, making Julia arch her back and buck. Martin chuckled, sliding a finger into her slick core, ever so wet. "You are ready for me."

"Now, please."

Unable to wait a moment longer, he settled himself over her, shifting until he barely pushed inside her, allowing her body time to adjust. "Does it hurt?"

"Only a little." Her lithe fingers grasped his buttocks and she tugged him further, causing a wee gasp. "It feels... Oh my, it is indescribable."

"Then dunna try to put it into words, just be."

Martin pushed a bit more, clenching his muscles to keep himself from thrusting, trying not to hurt her.

"More!"

"More?" he asked, moving deeper and earning another gasp. "Does it hurt?" he asked again.

Her fingers clenched with urgency as she arched

her back and tugged him deeper still. "This is what I want, Martin!"

"I love hearing the sound of my name on your lips," he whispered into her ear, reveling in being buried to his hilt. He reached down between them and stroked her. "You are in control, my love. Show me what you want with your hands and your body."

"This," she said rocking and tugging, arching, and writhing.

Teetering on the edge of the abyss, Martin matched her fervor, thrusting and obeying the demands of her fingers. "You'll bring me undone, lass."

"Yes!" She tossed her head from side to side, convulsing around him. "Yes, yes, yes!"

And he was lost, sailing over the precipice of no return, Martin lost his mind as with three more deep thrusts, glorious release took him to the stars and back.

His breath came in fast pants as he collapsed atop her, the only sound in the chamber, their gasps for air as together they gradually sailed back to this time and this place.

Martin rolled to the side, urging her to face him and they lay there for a moment, saying nothing, staring into each other's eyes. No words existed to express the depth of the love he held for this woman, but he wanted, needed to tell her, to reassure her. "I love you."

The joyous smile spreading across her lips was enough to make him happy for the rest of his days. "I love you more than you'll ever know."

"I have a lifetime for you to show me, *mo leannan*." He kissed her, then pulled away just a tad. "Now that Huntly Manor is yours, what do you intend to do with it?"

"Well..." She swirled her finger through the curls on his chest, making him hard again. "If only there were a way to open it up to ladies who've lost their means of support as I did with Papa."

"Now why dinna I think of that? What a fabulous idea."

She tapped his chest. "We'll have to find a woman to run it—someone who's kind and considerate, yet efficient."

He licked her finger. "I'm certain with the right enquiries the ideal candidate will soon be upon our doorstep."

She grinned again, curling against him. "How can I be so happy?"

"Because you deserve to be the happiest woman in all of Christendom," he said, kissing her temple. "You selflessly gave up your dreams to care for your father. You're brilliant and enterprising and, now that this house is yours, you have decided to help others with it. I have never met anyone with a heart the size of yours."

Julia wriggled. "Believe it or not, your heart is every bit as large as mine."

"Nay."

"I beg to differ. What would have happened if you had not arrived when you did and confronted Mr. Skinner."

Martin pressed his lips together. He didn't want to argue, nor did he ever again want to hear that vile miscreant's name.

Julia balled her fist with a triumphant glint in her eyes. "Mr. Jackson's lesson did come in handy."

"Aye, your aim was astounding." Throwing his head back, Martin laughed and laughed. "I canna believe you actually stepped into the ring with a goliath like Gentleman Jackson."

"Mind you, I tried to beg off, but you were ever so insistent on enhancing Smallwood's masculinity."

He closed his eyes, recalling how intent he was to give the little steward an education. "I still canna believe you fooled me all that time."

"I hope I performed my duties to your satisfaction."

"Och, I'm verra satisfied lass." He wrapped his arms around her and held her close. "And so verra, verra happy."

31

After his frantic dash to Huntly Manor, finding Julia being accosted by that ill-begotten scoundrel, fighting for her, followed by a night of the most passionate lovemaking he'd ever experienced, Martin opened his eyes after a long, much needed sleep. When he slid his hand across the linens, he wasn't surprised to find Julia's side of the bed cold to the touch, but it was a shock to see the hour hand on the mantle clock pointed at one in the afternoon.

With a grunt, he flung the bedclothes aside and made quick work of washing at the basin and dressing. When Martin stepped into the corridor, he scarcely remembered ascending the two flights of stairs that Julia had led him up with lust-filled eyes. Before he headed downward, he opened doors and peeked into a few chambers, finding the furniture within covered with dust cloths. One room had dozens of streaks ruining the wallpaper where the roof had sprung a leak.

Martin continued on, looking into rooms as he passed them and gaining an appreciation for the size of the manor. Though it was in sore need of updating, it was clearly once a grand house befitting the station of earl. Eventually along his circuitous journey, he ended up in the library where he found his fiancée at a writing table. She looked a tad like Jules Smallwood stooped over a ledger, aside from the curls framing the side of her face, and the black mourning gown, its bodice hugging the shapely breasts he would never tire of worshiping. Goodness, Julia must have had a dickens of a time wrapping those lovelies every morn.

Stilling her quill, she glanced up from her work and gave him a coy smile. "Good afternoon, Your Grace."

He rubbed the back of his neck. "It is rather late, is it not?"

"Yes, but I thought you might sleep the day though, given how long you went without rest."

"Never."

"Are you hungry?"

"Famished."

She gestured to a table with a teapot and a loaf of bread on a cutting board. "I'm afraid we haven't much aside from bread and eggs. Fortunately, the hens are still laying. The eggs are quite good poached, shall I prepare a couple for you?"

"You?"

"I'm quite skilled in the kitchen, I'll have you know. Besides, Mrs. May has moved on."

Martin sliced himself a bit of bread and slathered it with butter. "This will do for now."

Julia picked up her quill. "Very well."

"What are you working on?" he asked, pouring himself a cup of tea. If the lass truly intended to turn the manor into a home for desolate ladies, she needed a great many servants, starting with a cook and an overseer able to bring in a host of laborers to repair the roof, paint, hang wallpaper, tend to the overgrown garden, and Lord knew what else.

She held up the slip of paper, which looked as if there might be a letter on the reverse side. "I'm compiling a list of repairs for Huntly in order of importance."

He craned his neck and read the salutation on the letter side. "It looks as if you're working on a piece of correspondence."

"I am in a way. I used the last sheet of blank paper to list the household effects for the auctioneer, and now all there is left to use is the back side of old letters."

After washing a bite of bread down with a sip of tea, Martin moved to Julia's side, bent down, and whispered in her ear. "Perhaps we ought to appoint a caretaker at once, someone who can oversee the improvements whilst I abscond with you to Scotland."

As he nibbled her long, slender neck, her shoulders shook with a playful giggle. "Scotland?"

"Unless you'd prefer I send for a special license this verra day. But I thought Stack Castle might be—"

"I beg your pardon, my lady, Your Grace," said Willaby, stepping into the library and bowing. "The Dowager Duchess of Dunscaby, Lady Charity, Lady Grace, and Lady Modesty are in the vestibule. Might I add their carriage was followed by two more containing a multitudinous number of servants. Truth be told, it reminds me of the old days when the earl and countess were in residence."

"Bless Mama." Martin straightened as the butler's words hit a chord. "*Dowager* did you say?"

"Yes, sir. Your mother was quite emphatic that I place a great deal of emphasis on the title."

"Well do not delay," said Julia, standing and

brushing out the skirts of the same mourning dress she'd worn the day before, the sleeves worn and almost sheer at the elbows. "Show them in at once."

"And send a wagon into town for food." Martin shoved the rest of his breakfast into his mouth. "We canna feed a family let alone two carriages full of servants on bread and eggs."

Willaby bowed. "Straightaway, Your Grace."

The rustle of skirts and the tapping of heels echoed through the corridor before Mama waltzed through the doorway wearing lavender and smiling from ear to ear. "Oh, my dear son, as soon as Charity told me the story of how the daughter of the Earl of Brixham had won your heart, I knew we could not delay."

"No?" Martin asked, gesturing to a settee an eyeing his eldest sister while Mama led the lassies like a goose leading her goslings.

"Of course not." Mama grasped Julia's hands and kissed each cheek while Grace and Modesty sat. "I say, you are far more fetching as a woman, my dear."

"Thank you?" Julia posed her reply as a question, looking most uncertain.

But uncertainty had never dissuaded Martin's mother. "And please do accept our sincerest condolences for your loss."

Julia offered a somber nod, glancing down to her dated mourning dress.

"My daughter explained the deplorable circumstances you have been facing. And now that we have arrived, I truly commiserate with how difficult things must have been for you, my dear."

Cringing, Julia looked to Martin. "We were just discussing some of the more urgent repairs needed."

"Repairs?" Asked Mama moving to the settee with

a flourish of silk skirts. "When you have a wedding to plan?"

Julia followed, standing across. "Forgive me for being forward, but I am surprised to learn that you approve."

"Well, to be honest I'll admit to suffering more than a few moments of shock, but there has been no mention of the incident at the Pool of London in the papers, and everyone in Town is already raving about what a fine match you two make. Of course, I'm ever so delighted that my son has at last found a woman to marry." Mama flicked open her fan and cooled her face. "Though I daresay Martin will need to appoint a new steward forthwith."

Martin eyed his mother, imagining she had suffered far more than a few moments of shock. "Aye, we've agreed on that count, though there are other things that must take precedence."

"When is the wedding?" asked Grace.

Martin held a chair for his fiancée. "I beg your pardon, but how do the lot of you ken I've asked Lady Julia to marry me?"

"Because you'd be an unmitigated mutton head if you havena," said Charity, sending a pithy glance his way and taking a seat beside his betrothed.

Martin's sister had proven to be wise beyond her years. She was right, of course, and there was no reason to pretend otherwise. "To be honest, we were also discussing—"

Mama slid her fan into her sleeve. "I've already sent word to Stack Castle."

"You did what?" Martin asked, grasping the post at the back of Julia's chair. "Prior to this very moment, you couldna have known Her Ladyship agreed to my proposal."

Affecting an innocent expression, Mama gave a wee shrug. "Come, now son. Time is of the essence is it not? Her Ladyship's reputation may not yet be ruined, but given everything that has transpired, it is imperative to move quickly and quash any ugly rumors that may arise."

"And it is tradition for the Duke of Dunscaby or his heir to marry at the castle," Grace added with her accustomed air of hauteur. "After all every duke has taken his vows there since the first tower was erected after the Norman conquest."

Julia drew a hand to her chest. "Is that so?"

Charity held up her palms, her gaze shifting across the book-lined walls of the library. "You mentioned you were making a list of necessary repairs. Does that mean you're planning to keep the manor?"

"Yes," Julia and Martin said simultaneously.

He bowed to the brown-eyed lassie. "May I?"

His bride-to-be clasped her hands. "By all means."

"I purchased the house for my future duchess, and she has decided that Huntly Manor should become a home for ladies who, like her before we were betrothed, have no responsible party to support them."

"Oh, what a wonderful idea," said Charity, clasping her hands over her heart. "I would love to help."

"When do you have time for such a venture?" asked Mama.

Charity leaned forward. "I have nothing but time."

"I beg your pardon," the Dowager Duchess scoffed. "You must prepare for the next Season."

"But couldn't Charity prepare here?" Julia asked. "I think overseeing the affairs of Huntly Manor for a time would give her invaluable experience in running a household and prepare her to be the lady of any manor in Britain."

"Do you really think so?" Charity's face lit up as if a ray of sunshine had just landed upon her shoulders.

"I do." Julia grasped the eldest sister's hand and squeezed. "I have it on good authority that I will be far too busy as Martin's wife to take care of Huntly."

"That is ever so true," Her Grace agreed.

"I think it is a splendid idea," Martin added. "After the wedding, with Julia's tutelage, Charity can return to Huntly and command the household as she sees fit."

"Absolutely not," said Mama.

"I beg to differ. I have made my decision and I wholeheartedly agree with Lady Julia." Martin moved his fists onto his hips and met his mother's gaze. "It isna as if we'll abandon the lass here. She will have a host of servants and, since Grace will be attending Northbourne, why not add Modesty and Miss Hay to the mix to keep Charity company? Och, spending time putting this house in order ought to provide your eldest daughter with a great deal of satisfaction not to mention give her an excellent education in the running of a household."

"And I can help as well," added Modesty. "I'll even give the new cook our secret chocolate recipe."

"Of course, it is your decision." With a blink, Mama shifted her gaze away and huffed. "But I'll agree to it only until the Season resumes."

Martin dropped his hands to his sides, releasing a silent breath. His mother might be an assertive duchess, but she also wanted him to succeed as duke and the final decision on family matters rested upon his shoulders. "Agreed, until the Season resumes."

"After which, who will run Huntly Manor?" asked Charity.

Julia patted the lassie's forearm. "Perhaps we ought to task the new steward with appointing someone who is not only capable of running a country estate, but a woman who is sensitive to the plight of ladies who have nowhere else to turn."

Charity ran her fingers over the worn velvet armrest on her chair. "I rather like it here. The manor has such a homey feel to it."

"A shabby feel is more apt," said Grace.

"I beg your pardon, young lady," Mama clipped. "Never belittle another's domicile especially when you are a guest. Apologize to Lady Julia at once."

Grace rolled her eyes to the chipped paint on the ceiling. "Forgive me. I missspoke."

"Not to worry." Julia smiled up at Martin, giving a wink. "We all know the place needs a great deal of work before it is fitting for a duke or an earl, for that matter."

※

"The existence of Huntly Manor should be by word of mouth," Julia said, pacing her bedchamber while Charity sat embroidering in the window embrasure with the curtains opened to a cloudless day.

"But how will anyone ever find it?" asked the lass, her brow furrowing.

"Believe me, a whisper in the right parlor will travel for miles."

Charity stabbed her needle into the Holland cloth held taut by a round hoop. "Who's parlor would you suggest?"

Julia joined her future sister-in-law on the embrasure bench and glanced out the window to find Martin heading across the back lawn. "Well, I've put some thought into it, and have already sent a letter to my dear friend, the Marchioness of Northampton."

"And you reckon it will work, aye?"

Julia craned her neck to admire his bold stride, the pleats of his kilt slapping the backs of his legs in a steady cadence. Where was he off to? "If I know Sophie, you'll have boarders just as soon as you return from Scotland."

Charity pulled her thread up and made a French knot. "I hope so."

Now that Martin had moved out of sight, Julia sighed, wishing she were with him. Things had been so hectic the past few days as they worked to address Huntly's most urgent needs. So far they'd hired a cook, a groundskeeper, a roofer, but had yet to find a replacement for Mrs. May. All the while, the Dunscaby serving staff had cleaned every chamber from hearth to ceiling to removing the carpets and beating them with brooms. "And I'd like to venture that it wouldn't be all that bad to have a sennight or two to yourself."

"Modesty will be here, mind you."

"Perhaps, but she's no trouble, is she?" Julia picked up a skein of pink embroidery thread and shook it under her friend's nose. "I say, being the lady of the house without Lady Grace and Her Grace's influence ought to be liberating for you." In truth, after living with the family for several months, Julia had observed that Grace and Her Grace both could be overbearing and Charity often withheld her opinions.

"I beg your pardon, my lady," said Georgette, tapping on the door as she entered. "You have a missive."

"Thank you," she said, a tad puzzled since the post had already been delivered. As soon as she saw the handwriting on the address, a swarm of fairies started dancing in her stomach.

"Who is it from?" asked Charity, leaning in.

Julia moved the missive aside while she ran her finger under the duke's wax seal applied with his signet ring. "Who do you think?"

"Does he want a secret rendezvous?" asked Martin's sister with a saucy shake of her shoulders.

Julia read, making the fairies dance faster. "You are awful."

"I ken my brother."

"I'd best answer his summons."

"You'd best hasten to the altar."

"Believe me, nothing will stop me from saying 'I do'," Julia replied as she pattered out the door and through the overgrown back garden. When the woodshed came into sight, she stopped for a moment and slid her hands over her head.

"Och, m'lady, in your haste I do believe you've forgotten a piece of your costume."

She grinned as Martin peered around the corner of the rickety old shed. "Shame on me, I'll be all splotchy for the wedding."

"Never." He tugged her behind the woodshed and into his arms, his lips sealing over hers, imparting a kiss that was both familiar and filled with passion. "I've missed you, lass."

"Since this morning in the coal cellar?" she asked, smiling at their stolen interlude, nearly interrupted by a scullery maid. Since his mother and sisters had arrived they'd agreed to abstain and wait until the wedding, which was proving to be nearly impossible as well as imposing a myriad of chance meetings in the most unlikely places. "At least black coal matches the color of mourning."

He flicked the ribbon on her bodice. "I want to see you in bright colors, especially yellow."

"You'll be pleased to know your mother has agreed that I should be allowed to go into half-mourning after we arrive at Stack Castle. At least I'll be able to wear lavender for the wedding."

"I'd marry you even if you were wearing sackcloth."

Julia rose up on her toes, adoring how Martin's long lashes fanned his cheeks as their lips met. She ran her hands up and down the sinewy muscles in his back, losing herself in his languid kiss...

"Oh my goodness! Grace was right. You are kissing behind the woodshed!" exclaimed Modesty, standing not but three feet away with her mouth agape.

Julia leapt from Martin's embrace. The very reason they had agreed to abstain was because there were innocent ladies in the house and now the most innocent of innocents had just caught them intwined in each other's arms.

In true ducal form, Martin sternly stared down at his sister, tapping a finger to his lips. "Grace put you up to this?"

"Aye, she saw you head for the woodshed and not long after, Julia followed."

"That may verra well be, but Grace of all people should be well aware it is poor form to interrupt a couple who are engaged to be married when they are stealing a wee kiss."

The lass twisted one of the red curls from her pigtails around her finger. "But Grace dared me."

"That doesna make it right. I bid you apologize to Her Ladyship forthwith."

"I'm sorry, m'lady." Modesty curtsied. "I think I

liked it better when you were Mr. Smallwood. Your dancing was improving, at least."

Julia gave a proper bow, one reminiscent of the steward addressing his partner. "Perhaps we can continue to practice, though you're growing so fast, I daresay you'll soon be taller than I am."

Martin clapped his hands. "Back to the house with you and tell your meddlesome sister to mind her own affairs."

The young lady's bottom lip jutted out as she gave her brother a woeful look and turned on her heel. "I'll never accept a dare from Grace again."

"That is sound reasoning," Martin replied looking after her.

Julia leaned against the woodshed wall and pressed a hand to her forehead. "Oh dear, that was rather embarrassing."

"I hope it was more so for the wee lassie. She's old enough to mind her manners."

"Even after given a challenge by her dragon-hearted middle sister?"

"Aye, though I'll be having a word with Grace, mark me." Martin plucked the bow on her bodice and slowly pulled open the tie. "Now, where were we?"

Julia's heart thrummed as the ugly black fabric fell open. "You are a naughty duke."

He nuzzled her neck. "I certainly hope so."

Sliding away from the wall, Julia took his hand and grinned. "Did you know there were ruins on this property?"

"Nay, I havena seen a crumbling old tower as of yet."

She started toward the path, hoping it was still there. "Perhaps that's because it is hidden by the bluff."

"Intriguing. How many others ken of these ruins?"

"Hmm, Willaby knows of them, but I doubt he's paid them a mind for a decade or more."

"I reckon I must see this old fortress without delay." Martin's eyes grew dark as he followed. "Ye ken it is driving me mad knowing you are sleeping one floor above whilst I lay awake in the lord's chamber."

"Whoever said I was sleeping?" She giggled as she tugged him along, quickening the pace. "You are not the only one lying abed, plotting our next rendezvous."

She led him through a copse of trees that opened out onto the bluff. With a gesture of her palm, she pointed to the tops of the tower's ruins below. "See, the old relic is completely hidden from the world."

Martin wrapped his arm around her shoulder and drew her close. "Och, why did you not tell me about this before?"

"Between wedding preparations, hiring roofers, a groundskeeper, a cook, and interviewing prospective housekeepers, there hasn't exactly been much time... aside from a few moments in the coal cellar."

"Or behind the stables."

"Or under the writing table in the library."

"Not to mention the china closet."

"How can I possibly forget the china closet?" She giggled. "It is amazing we didn't break a single dish."

Julia led the way down the steep, zigzagging pathway overgrown with vines, but otherwise still intact. "When I was a little girl, I used to hide from my governess and pretend I was a fairy princess."

"Do you mean to tell me you werena a perfectly behaved young lady?"

"Far from it, though I will admit to being a bit of a bookworm." She pulled him across a rickety-looking stone bridge that joined the mainland with the promontory upon which the old fortress had been built. "Here we are."

They crossed beneath an archway that opened to a blanket of grass, surrounded by four grey walls and a ceiling of blue skies.

Martin swept her into his arms and spun in a circle. "This is a fantastical place."

Throwing her head back, Julia laughed. "At it is all our own."

He kissed her, a long kiss imparting a thousand promises, and then he set her down. "What makes me think you're about to have your way with me, lass?"

Sliding her tongue to the corner of her mouth, she unfastened the brooch at his shoulder. "I've become somewhat of a proficient at seducing a duke with a rakish reputation."

A low chuckle rumbled in his throat as he released his belt and let his tartan drop. "Do no' tell a soul, but this rake has been completely reformed."

He spread his plaid on the ground and together they made love with a cool breeze caressing their skin. And though Martin took Julia to the stars, she was ever so happy the next phase of their journey would begin on the morrow, setting out for the northern tip of the mainland of Scotland where they would take their vows as husband and wife.

32

The dowager duchess did her part to ensure the wedding was well-attended. Not only was Sophie there with her Marquess, the ancient medieval nave of the church was so full, Julia imagined that a quarter of the *ton* was in attendance.

For the first time, she was introduced to Lords Andrew and Philip who had just graduated from St. Andrews University, as well as Lord Frederick who was about to start his first year. Martin's only immediate family member not in attendance was Lord Gibb, who was duly excused since he had embarked on his first voyage with a hull full of MacGalloway whisky bound for America and would be returning with cotton ready for the mill for which Andrew and Philip had already purchased looms and equipment.

Stack Castle, an absolutely enormous fortress, its five hundred and twenty-one rooms surrounded by medieval curtain walls and acres upon acres of land sporting, vast stables, a fishing loch, and hunting grounds. On one side were sheer cliffs to the sea with the Stacks of Dunscaby standing like proud monoliths just beyond the shore.

The reception held in the enormous great hall was

an extravagant affair with thousands of candles above and innumerable glasses of champagne served by footmen dressed in scarlet livery complete with powdered wigs. As was customary, the bride danced with every man in attendance, until her feet could take no more. At last, when the final waltz was played, Julia was reunited with her husband and the crowd seemed to fade into oblivion as they stared into each other's eyes. Their dance was even more intimate, more ethereal, and more transportive than their first waltz at the masquerade had been. And after, Martin swept her into his arms and headed for the stairs. Julia hardly noticed as the crowd followed them into the entrance hall, bidding the bride and groom a good eve. She curled into her husband, savoring his warmth and the strength of the powerful arms cradling her.

"Are you happy, wife?" he asked, stepping into the corridor while the muffled voices of the guests grew fainter.

Julia placed her palm over his heart. "I do not recall ever being this happy in all my days."

He grinned with the same alluring smile that had attracted her months ago—one incisor slightly crossed over the other reminding her he wasn't perfect—at least not quite. "Then we are of like minds."

"One spirit with two bodies?"

"Two bodies soon to be joined." Tapping open the door with his toe, Martin carried her across the threshold and into the ducal bedchamber. "Ye ken, I intend to make love to you in every room, beginning with this one."

She fingered the clan tartan he wore pinned at his shoulder. "All five hundred and twenty-one?"

"Aye," he said placing her on her feet and sliding his hands to her waist and kissing her.

"Even the servants' quarters?" She asked breathlessly while his lips plied the sensitive skin beneath her ear. "What about the kitchens and the laundry?"

"The servants' quarters might pose a wee conundrum, we'll have to enlist Giles' services to conduct a series of inspections outdoors, but I reckon I'll have ample opportunities to raise your skirts in the laundry and especially the kitchens in the wee hours."

Julia arched her back as his lips caressed the tops of her breasts. "So, the famous rakish behavior continues?"

"Aye, lass." Martin straightened and met her gaze. "But only with you."

"I'm glad." Julia held out her hand and admired her wedding ring with an enormous sapphire. "Hmm, five hundred twenty-one rooms with, say, three rendezvous a day...we ought to have the task accomplished in a half year."

"Who said only three per day?"

"I love you."

"I love you more, Smallwood."

AUTHOR'S NOTE

Thank you for joining me for A Duke, by Scot. Being an author of both Scottish historical romance and Regency romance, I have embarked on this series to combine the two genres in a witty and fun series about the children of a dukedom. The MacGalloways and the Dunscaby empire are fictitious, though in all my books I do try to create a world with as much historical accuracy as possible.

In 2019 I visited Newhailes, a manor house in Musselborough, Scotland. At the time it was undergoing renovations. Fortunately, I was able to secure a private tour from Mr. MacLean of the National Trust for Scotland, which now holds the property. Newhailes was the home of the powerful Dalrymple family, and the trust has embarked on an innovative conservation strategy in an effort to maintain the original character of the estate and change as little as possible. I was amazed with the banisters on the opposing staircases leading to the front door. The old iron work looked as if it were crumbling, but Mr. MacLean explained that the trust had dismantled and sent out the pieces for preservation so they would not further deteriorate, thus ideally preserving the original work.

When writing this story, I battled a bit with introducing the cotton industry as the foundation of the family dynasty because of the American South's history. In truth, the cotton industry had grown by more than 1200% and it made sense for Martin to establish a mill for his brothers, but only if he could obtain cotton grown by free people. At this time in history the Irish did flock to the Americas (including one of my own ancestors) and even more so after the 1845 potato famine. They were generally poor and hardworking folk. Also, after the Civil War, African Americans and Irish Americans engaged in cotton sharecropping. Because of the importance of the present-day movement for equality, I took literary license and created the Irish sharecroppers who will be mentioned in future books.

In 2017 I visited John o'Groats as well as the Stacks of Dunscaby on the northern tip of Scotland and was very surprised not to see a castle overlooking the sea and the astounding monoliths dominating the water just beyond the shore. Though there is a lighthouse where whales, seals, and puffins are often spotted (most frequently by multitudinous flocks of sheep), I saw no castle remains, which really surprised me. A very prominent family ought to have held that point for king and clan and may have at one time. As I stood there marveling at the beauty of the site I asked myself, why not create a powerful family and make a series out of it?

If you haven't already guessed, the next story in The MacGalloways series is about dear Charity and how she meets a very unconventional earl.

ALSO BY AMY JARECKI

The MacGalloways

A Duke by Scot

Her Unconventional Earl

The Captain's Heiress

The King's Outlaws

Highland Warlord

Highland Raider

Highland Beast

Highland Defender

The Valiant Highlander

The Fearless Highlander

The Highlander's Iron Will

Highland Force:

Captured by the Pirate Laird

The Highland Henchman

Beauty and the Barbarian

Return of the Highland Laird

Guardian of Scotland

Rise of a Legend

In the Kingdom's Name

The Time Traveler's Destiny

Highland Dynasty

Boy Man Chief
Time Warriors

ABOUT THE AUTHOR

Known for her action-packed, passionate historical romances, Amy Jarecki has received reader and critical praise throughout her writing career. She won the prestigious 2018 RT Reviewers' Choice award for *The Highland Duke* and the 2016 RONE award from InD'tale Magazine for Best Time Travel for her novel *Rise of a Legend*. In addition, she hit Amazon's Top 100 Bestseller List, the Apple, Barnes & Noble, and Bookscan Bestseller lists, in addition to earning the designation as an Amazon All Star Author. Readers also chose her Scottish historical romance, *A Highland Knight's Desire,* as the winning title through Amazon's Kindle Scout Program. Amy holds an MBA from Heriot-Watt University in Edinburgh, Scotland and now resides in Southwest Utah with her husband where she writes immersive historical romances. Learn more on Amy's website. Or sign up to receive Amy's newsletter.

CPSIA information can be obtained
at www.ICGtesting.com
Printed in the USA
LVHW051546131221
706054LV00010B/1144